Books by
Stan Nicholls

THE RIGHTEOUS BLADE
THE COVENANT RISING

BOOK ONE OF THE DREAMTIME

THE COVENANT RISING

STAN NICHOLLS

An Imprint of HarperCollinsPublishers

This is a work of fiction. Names, characters, places, and incidents are products of the author's imagination or are used fictitiously and are not to be construed as real. Any resemblance to actual events, locales, organizations, or persons, living or dead, is entirely coincidental.

EOS
An Imprint of HarperCollins*Publishers*
10 East 53rd Street
New York, New York 10022-5299

This book was originally pusblished in Great Britain under the title *Quicksilver Rising* in 2003 by Voyager, an imprint of HarperCollins Publishers.

Copyright © 2003 by S.J. Nicholls
Excerpt from *The Righteous Blade* copyright © 2004 by S.J. Nicholls.
Preiously published in the UK as *Quicksilver Zenith*.
ISBN-13: 978-0-06-073890-7
ISBN-10: 0-06-073890-1
www.eosbooks.com

First Eos paperback printing: December 2005
First Eos trade paperback printing: January 2005

HarperCollins® and Eos® are registered trademarks of HarperCollins Publishers Inc.

Printed in the U.S.A.

10 9 8 7 6 5 4 3 2 1

For making a stranger feel a little less alien in a strange land, *The Covenant Rising* is dedicated to the Brum Balti Boyz – Mike Chinn, Peter Coleborn, John Howard, Joel Lane, David Sutton; and to the Gurlz – Jan Edwards, Sue Edwards, Sandra Sutton.
And, of course, to my
wife, Anne.

1

It was a place of cheap magic.

A swarm of tiny sphinxes gathered, fluttering just above her head. Snapping jaws, whipping wings, curling tails. They weren't convincing. Their colours were wrong, and up close they were semi-transparent.

Serrah swatted irritably, her hand passing through them as if they were dawn mist. They disintegrated into countless infinitesimal specks, like glowing rust. The tips of their spread wings were the last to go, popping out of existence in little burnished puffs.

'We going to skulk here all night, Ardacris?' Phosian hissed.

He hid next to her, but the alley was too dark to make out his features. His garb, like hers, was uniformly black, with a silk mask covering nose and mouth. Where flesh showed, it had been smeared with ash. The sheen of their blades was dimmed by grease and soot.

Serrah inwardly bridled at his familiarity and the disregard of her rank. But in deference to his connections she whispered only, *'Patience.'*

Phosian sighed. Serrah needed no light to picture the conceited expression on his callow face.

Nothing much stirred. The street was a midden lined with hovels, all gloom and demented angles. Its glistening cobbles were silvered by a half moon. Flies teemed, the air stank. Now and again a low-priced glamour walked, crawled, flew or drifted by, waning, and was ignored.

The house they watched was grander than the others and set apart. Two guards were visible at its front. There were more at the sides and rear. Again Serrah wondered if her modest forces would be enough.

'Think our strength's up to it?' Phosian asked, hinting criticism of her.

She was struck by the idea that he might have read her mind. But she knew such magic was likely mythical. And if it did exist it was so rare even *his* relatives probably couldn't afford it. 'Numbers aren't everything,' she said. 'I'd take one seasoned fighter over a regiment of conscripts any day.'

'And what would you call those inside, seasoned or green?' Sarcasm dripped.

'Ruthless bastards,' Serrah replied, still seething at having him foisted on her. 'But I've a team I can trust.' With one exception, she thought, adding, steely-toned, 'It's taken weeks to get to tonight. Nothing's going to jeopardise it.'

His silent contempt was almost tangible.

By knowing where to look, and straining to see, several others in her group could be faintly made out, grey against the blackness. They were in position.

'It's time,' she decided. 'You know what to do. Stay close.'

He gave an indolent grunt.

She had a short piece of twine, and worried its end with thumb and forefinger, as though flipping a coin. Suddenly the tip glowed cherry red. Less conspicuous than a naked flame and generating no heat, it was a very basic glamour; just an ember, but enough for those alert to it. Serrah quickly signalled, then pinched it out.

They waited.

The nearest guard, a shaven-headed colossus, stood gazing at the night sky. His broadsword was thrust into the ground at his feet, his palm absently caressing the hilt. Further back, a leaner companion prowled with meagre enthusiasm.

A sound cut the air. High, smooth, and abruptly stilled by a soft impact.

An arrow quivered in the big man's chest. He looked down at it dumbly. The sound repeated and his comrade dropped. A second bolt winged into the giant. Arms outstretched, he fell heavily.

'*Move!*' Serrah barked.

Dashing out of the shadows, limbs pumping, she ran for the house. Phosian chased her, his scrawny form contrasting with her athletic build. As they arrived at the entrance, two more of her crew slipped from the darkness to join them. Like Phosian, they hefted axes.

The double doors were oak with iron bracings. At her sign, the battering commenced. Almost immediately the rest of her team began pounding at the back of the house.

Serrah scanned the street, feeling vulnerable. Imperial agents weren't exactly popular in this quarter and she half expected to see locals rushing in to take issue.

But she was more worried by what might be waiting inside.

The doors gave.

A dimly lit passageway stretched ahead of them. There was another door at its end. A corridor was set in the right-hand wall. Serrah motioned for one of the party to keep watch, then she, Phosian and the fourth group-member carefully advanced, weapons drawn.

Something came out of the side passage. They froze.

It slinked, ebony fur bristling, a mass of fangs, claws and ill temper. Its hard, tawny eyes regarded them haughtily. It let out a wheezing snarl.

The barbcat was waist-high to Serrah. Had it stood upright it could have laid its forepaws on her shoulders while it tore her throat out.

Absolutely still, they watched as a second cat padded into the hall. It was just as big, just as irate. Its ears pricked tensely, its ample pink tongue lolled.

Serrah couldn't be sure about the creatures. She took a chance and edged forward.

'Chief . . .' one of her team cautioned.

She paid no attention and moved in on the nearest cat.

It leapt.

Her response was instant. She fell into a half crouch, simultaneously swinging her sword up, two-handed, teeth gritted with effort, carving an arc. It crossed paths with the slavering animal, slicing cleanly through its body. But not as though it were flesh.

The bloodless halves of the cat hung in the air for a second, then dissolved into golden shards and nothingness.

Rising, Serrah expelled a breath. 'Sentinel glamours,' she declared, unnecessarily. And well made, she judged. Costly magic.

The other barbcat turned and loped back to its alcove den. They ignored it and readied themselves.

'Let's *move*,' Phosian urged testily.

Serrah glared at him. She swung her boot at the door. It flew open.

At first sight, the chamber was unoccupied. Large, with a high ceiling, its windows were covered. Candles and brands gave light, and several tall braziers were scattered about. There were stacks of chests and barrels. Threadbare cushions and shabby sticks of furniture had been randomly dispersed. Chicken bones, shattered wine flasks, scraps of stale bread and general detritus littered the floor.

A crooked line of benches ran along one wall. They were

laden with stone bottles, funnels, vials, jars, mortars and pestles. There were hessian bags, slit open and disgorging dried plant matter, and two or three cauldrons with rising wisps of milky vapour.

On a table at the end of the line was something Serrah knew too well; mounds of faintly crystalline, yellowish-white powder. The sight of it rippled her insides like ice.

As they took in the scene she was aware of Phosian straining at the bit. 'Easy,' she chided.

'More loitering,' he grumbled. 'What are we, petitioners?'

'We have to be sure.'

He spat scorn at her. 'To hell with that.' Then he elbowed past and bounded into the room.

'Phosian!' she called, dumbfounded.

He took no notice. In the centre of the chamber, brandishing his axe, he began to yell. 'Come out, you scum! Face us!'

'*Idiot!*' Serrah mouthed. 'Stay!' she snapped at her comrades, and went after him.

'Filthy, low-life trash!' Phosian raged, puffed-up with gauche bravado. '*Cowards!* Show yourselves!'

'*Phosian!*' She approached warily, though her anger was barely restrained. 'What the *fuck* are you doing?' She glanced around nervously. 'When I give an order, you obey!'

'My people give the orders, Ardacris. You mind that.'

'I don't care a damn about your kin! When it comes to my command, you're just –'

An object soared past her, end over end, wicked edges glinting.

The hatchet struck Phosian square to the heart. He cried out and staggered back. His axe slipped from his fingers and clattered on the flagstones. Blood streaming from his wound, eyes rolling to white, he hit the floor.

Serrah gaped.

Then too much happened at once.

Figures emerged from behind barrels and boxes, and from a blind corner. A sharp grating noise rang out to the rear. She spun around. A second, inner door, heavy and metal banded, dropped like a portcullis and met the ground with a weighty reverberation, cutting off her companions on the other side. They started hammering.

She swung to face the advancing gang.

There were five of them. Wiry, tattooed, granite-miened. Scarred and broken-toothed, with eyes of flint. Men well versed in the profession of violence.

They flowed into a horseshoe pattern, aiming to take her head-on and from the flanks. But the room's clutter meant the shoe's nails were unevenly spread. She had two bandits on her right, with a third crowding them. A fourth was at her left. The last, directly ahead, couldn't have been anything but their leader. He was brawnier and meaner looking than the others, and his smirking menace was even more palpable.

For a beat, nobody moved or spoke. It seemed as though the leader studied her.

At last he rumbled, 'Butterfly'.

Whatever she had expected, it wasn't that. She was lost for a response.

'*Shining* butterfly,' he added, staring glazedly at her. 'Black silk butterfly.'

Serrah understood then. They'd been sampling their own wares. They were crazed, unpredictable. Ramped.

Her gaze went to the heap of white powder, and for a second she was at the void again. 'Ramp's forbidden. You know that.'

He was deadpan. 'Just making a living.'

She eyed Phosian in his spreading crimson pool. 'Some living.'

The pounding from outside increased, and now there were

sounds of fighting elsewhere in the building. Enough of a distraction for Serrah to slide her free hand into the folds of her shirt unnoticed.

'I know you,' the leader said, resuming his scrutiny. 'Even with the mask. You're known to my kind.' He wasn't making a benevolent link.

'Good,' she replied dryly. Jabbing her sword at the table, she repeated, 'The ramp's illegal. By the authority vested in me by the government of Gath Tampoor –'

They burst into scornful laughter.

'Save your breath for dying,' the leader grated.

'Right,' she agreed, favouring them with a smile. 'Let's get this over with.'

They moved. She was quicker.

Wrenching her hand free, she flung its load at the knot of bandits on her right. A score of barbed throwing stars soared in their direction.

Three were real. The charm was so good, she didn't know which ones.

Nor did her targets. They were in a confusion of dodging, blundering, shielding themselves as the stars flashed in. Most burst harmlessly on impact, vanishing silver blooms against their bodies and the surrounding jumble.

Razor-sharp reality was another thing.

A genuine star cleaved the throat of the middle bandit, spraying blood and felling him. His cohort to the right, batting at illusions, caught a star in the cheek. The third man, shoving from the left, was drizzled by plaster as the last genuine star struck the wall above. A gory scrum ensued.

That was the end of her spells. Now blades would settle the issue.

The leader was roaring orders, and the man on Serrah's left was closing in. She swiftly drew a knife to augment her sword.

The bandit came at her with a whipping scimitar and she
blocked it with a cross from her knife that jolted them both.
At the same time she wielded her sword in a low, curving
slash, aiming for his vitals. He deflected it, just, and sent out
his own pass. Serrah parried, retreating a step.

There was no time and the odds were too long. She
powered in again.

Working her blades in unison, she rapped aside his scimitar. Her follow-through employed the knife, laying open his
sword arm. Howling and swearing, he pulled back, wound
gushing. Serrah charged him. Still clutching his sword, he
tried to fend her off. She swept away his guard and buried
her blade in his chest. Pitching, he jammed the path of the
hollering leader.

Vaulting a shabby couch, an outlaw landed six paces away.
She saw it was the man her star had narrowly missed, covered
in plaster dust. Serrah took a swipe at his head. He ducked
and kept coming. She beat at his defences, eager to down
him before anybody else got to her. Stasis ruled for a moment,
neither giving. Then, more by luck than by design, the tip
of her blade scoured his jaw. Stumbling, hand to face, he
crashed into the table and sent the ramp flying. Powder
dispersed, a swirling white blizzard, and Serrah pressed the
back of a hand to her mouth and stilled her breath. The
leader screamed his wrath.

She had a glimpse of the bandit she'd wounded in the
cheek, the star still embedded in the side of his face. He
scrabbled in a corner, throwing crates aside. The racket from
her men outside grew louder.

Her respite was brief. The thug with the copiously bleeding
jaw disentangled himself. He and the leader attacked
together. Checking the latter with a lashing cross, she focused
on Wounded Jaw. He swiped wildly at her. She turned aside
the blow, knocking his blade high and wide, then her darting

sword took the opening and found his belly. He fell, a dead weight.

Blazing with ramp-quickened fervour, the leader piled into her. Serrah backed off, footing unsure on the debris. A breath later, she rallied. They churned metal, toe to toe, hacking and chopping. Breaching his guard, she dealt his stomach a hefty kick. He doubled over, mouth springing open. But he had the presence to keep his blade in play, impeding her follow-on. Serrah withdrew.

She saw that Gashed Cheek had almost cleared the crates, revealing the outline of a trapdoor. Now she knew why they could afford to linger. That split second of wandered concentration nearly cost her dear.

Raving incoherently, the chief snatched up a clay vessel and tossed its contents at her. She leapt aside, narrowly avoiding the shower of liquid. It splashed on boxes, fabrics and litter, seething and smouldering, billowing acrid smoke. A few spots of the vitriol peppered her hand and side, stinging like fiery needles. She clenched her teeth against the pain and kept moving. He stalked her, hurling obstructions from his path.

Her flight took her close to the bandit by the crates. Blood dribbled from the protruding star. He was on his knees, tugging at a rusting metal ring, and had the trapdoor raised about an arm's span.

Serrah seized her chance and hewed his neck. Man and trap went down.

She was panting. Her muscles ached and sweat prickled her spine. But there was no lull.

The maddened chief caught up and unleashed a battering storm. They fenced hard, brows furrowed, hands blistering. Wrong-footed, Serrah had to vault when he tried hamstringing her. Her return blow missed, struck one of the tall braziers and toppled it. Burning coals bounced in all directions.

Strewn rags and tattered furniture ignited. A dozen small fires broke out.

They battled on. Serrah stumbled against the prone Phosian and nearly fell. A stroke intended to decapitate came close enough to rend her collar.

A mouldering couch started to burn. Fire caught the pitch on a barrel, quickly leaping up the rest of the pile. Flames took hold of a window drape and raced to the ceiling. A thick, black haze began to fill the chamber. Serrah was thankful for her mask, though it did nothing to stop her eyes smarting.

Now stamina and nerve were all that mattered, and the duel became a slogging match.

A series of detonations rocked the room as pots and jars exploded on the blazing benches. The combatants ducked from flying pottery shards. Then an axe-head penetrated the door.

The concatenation of events threw the bandit off his stroke. Serrah homed in. Leading with the knife, she evaded his careless defence and raked his chest. He wailed, clutched the pumping lesion and, recoiling, crashed into an upended chair. Sprawled on the floor, he tried to hold her off. She dashed the sword from his hand and it bounced away, steel on stone, chiming.

He focused on her through pained eyes, and recognised the pain in hers.

'Butterfly?' he whispered.

'This butterfly has a sting,' Serrah told him, and drove home her blade.

She straightened slowly, short of breath, blinking from the smoke. Fire had taken hold on all sides and the heat was crushing. The back of her throat was grievously sore.

An axe cleaved the door again, and another joined it. In a cacophony of splitting wood and rending metal, her group broke through. They spilled in with raised weapons and taut bows, then stopped to stare.

Serrah got a hold on herself. *'Report!'* she demanded huskily.

The foremost group-member tore his eyes from the carnage. 'Er, nest cleared, ma'am.' He looked at Phosian. 'No . . . other casualties.'

'Good. Now everybody out. *Fast.*'

He nodded Phosian's way. 'What about . . . ?'

'Bring him. *Hurry!*'

Arms across faces to shield themselves from the inferno, they ran to retrieve their comrade. Then Serrah shepherded them out, bringing up the rear. The passageway funnelled smoke, and they were all coughing and retching by the time they reached air.

Outside, the rest of her men were waiting. They set Phosian down and Serrah felt for a pulse. The band exchanged looks. At length she shook her head, though she had really known all along.

She took in the faces of her crew and knew what they were thinking. 'I don't like losing anyone,' she said, 'even a wilful dolt. But there are overheads in our work and this was one of them. There'll be no indiscipline about it. The mission's not done till we're home.'

'Of all the people to lose,' somebody muttered.

Serrah thought Phosian's loss was preferable to any of her seasoned crew. But it was going to cause a lot more trouble. She concentrated on priorities. 'This place will be crawling with citizens soon and they won't all be glad to see us. Eyes peeled. And if we run into opposition, no quarter.'

No one chose to debate the issue. She assigned a detail to carry Phosian's body and they started out. Behind them, flames were playing on the roof of the ramp den. Inky smoke and eddying sparks belched from the windows.

They moved through the streets warily, keeping to the shadows. As they went they rid themselves of their outer layers of clothing, balling masks and shirts and pitching them into bushes and ill-lit alleys. They wiped the ash from their faces.

Serrah discarded her mask and shook loose a tumble of barley hair. She spat on her hands and rubbed them together. The reaction was starting to set in; the pain of exertion and of the acid burns made itself felt. Above all, what had happened to Phosian. Taking deep, regular breaths, she willed herself to stop shaking.

They could hear noises behind them, a commotion of faint shouting. Serrah increased the band's pace, and thought about splitting them up. But they reached the piece of waste ground without incident, seeing nothing save an occasional errant glamour. In the curtain of trees they rejoined their horses. Two men wrapped Phosian in a cloak and draped the body over his saddle.

Reaching the road, they saw a group of horsemen approaching, but not from the direction of the raid. They were too close and too numerous to outrun. Serrah and her crew steadied their horses and fingered their swords.

As the riders came nearer there was just enough light for their distinctive red tunics to be made out.

'That's all we need,' one of Serrah's band grumbled.

Thirty or forty strong, the advancing company was three to four times bigger than Serrah's, though how many of them might have been chimeras was anybody's guess. The paladin clans had access to the finest magic.

They arrived in good order, their military bearing contrasting with her band's more casual demeanour. The paladin captain halted his column. A goatee-bearded, hard-faced individual, he wasted no time on niceties. 'Serrah Ardacris?'

She nodded.

'Escort party for Chand Phosian.'

Serrah said nothing, and nobody else dared speak.

'We're here for Chand Phosian,' the paladin restated deliberately, as though addressing a moronic child. 'Where is he?'

'We're fresh from a mission,' Serrah told him. 'There're likely to be repercussions any minute. Let's get out of here and –'

'Where's the Principal-Elect's son?' He read their expressions and added sharply, *What's happened?*

Reluctantly, she motioned for Phosian's horse to be brought from the rear. At the sight of the burden it carried, the captain's face darkened. He dismounted and went to the steed as the others watched in silence. Pulling aside the cloak, he bared Phosian's pallid features.

'Combat casualty,' Serrah explained.

The captain looked up at her. 'You've been very careless.'

'We take losses on missions, you know that.'

'Some losses are unacceptable.'

'Oh, come on! It was just –'

He swiped the air with his hand, cutting her off. 'Save it, Ardacris! You're coming with us.'

2

Before the empires, before history, there was the Dreamtime.

The earth's energies were known then, and mastered, and the Founders chose to mark out their channels of power. Scholars speculated that the whole world had been embellished in that golden age. They pictured an all-pervasive, varicoloured grid covering plains and valleys, forests and pastures, mapping the spirit of the land and its alliance with the heavens.

Since the Founders left the stage, epochs ago, the mesh had fallen into neglect, though it still animated the magic. But in some places, through respect or fear, the old ways were honoured, if not entirely understood.

One such was a remote hamlet not far from Bhealfa's inhospitable eastern coast. An indigo dye line, the width of a man's fist, ran arrow straight along its central street, marking the power's flow. Most people tried not to step on it. The stranger arriving on foot as the sun rose didn't seem to care about that.

His appearance, too, turned the heads of the few citizens up and about at that hour. Taller than average, and muscular, he walked with easy confidence. His weaponry included two swords, one conventionally sheathed, the other strapped across his back. Clean shaven when the norm was more often hirsute, his eyes matched the hue of his lengthy, jet-black ponytail. He had handsome features, in a chiselled, weather-beaten fashion, though the set of his face was melancholic. His clothing inclined to sombre black.

He moved through the village unfazed by the stares, appearing sure of his bearings.

The sun was climbing when he emerged from the settlement's northern end and the street became a curving track. He took a left-hand trail, rougher and weedy. The indigo line lanced off into the countryside and faded back to dereliction.

At last he came to a house, practically hidden by untended trees. It was rambling and dilapidated. He went to the door and rapped on it. A second, louder round of knocking was necessary before he got a response.

The door was half opened by a bleary youth yet to come to terms with either the new day or manhood. He blinked at the stranger, eyes red-rimmed. 'Yes?'

'I'm looking for Grentor Domex.' His voice was mild, but commanding all the same.

The youth stared at him. 'Who's asking?'

'No one who means you harm. I'm not an official or a spy, just somebody who wants to consult the enchanter.'

'I'm not Mage Domex,' the youth confessed.

The stranger looked him up and down, noting his spotty complexion and the flaxen bumfluff on his chin. His solemn expression softened into a thin smile. 'No offence, friend, but I think I'd already worked that out. This *is* the Mage's house?'

There was a hesitation before the youth replied, 'It is.'

'Can I see him?'

He thought about it, then nodded and stood aside.

The door led directly into a large, gloomy room, redolent with the aromas of the sorcerer's craft. As the stranger entered and his eyes adjusted he saw something looming ahead of him. He blinked and recognised it as a figure standing in the partial darkness. It moved forward into a bar of daylight and revealed itself.

A battle-hardened warrior, sword levelled, about to attack.

In one swift, fluid movement, the stranger's hand darted to the back of his collar, plucked out a snub-nosed knife and hurled it. The blade pierced the warrior's forehead. Then it travelled on, embedding itself in a wooden beam. The warrior melted into a honeyed fog that quickly vanished. A lingering smell of sulphur overlaid the other heady scents in the room.

The youth realised he was gaping and snapped shut his mouth. Falteringly, he said, 'Good thing you were right.'

'About what?' the stranger asked.

'About it being a glamour.'

'I didn't know.'

'But –'

'If he was real he would have meant a threat. As he was a glamour, it didn't matter. An even bet either way. Look, I said you have nothing to fear. There's no need for party tricks.'

'Oh, that had nothing to do with *me*. It was one of the Mage's protective measures.'

The stranger was at the beam, tugging his knife free. 'Was?'

'Yes.' The youth sighed glumly. A world of worry settled on his naive features. 'You'd better come.'

He took him to a much smaller side chamber. It contained little except a table, and on it a body, covered by a shabby blanket. The youth peeled it back with something like reverence, exposing the head and shoulders of an elderly, white-haired man.

'So much for protective measures,' the stranger remarked.

The youth looked pained at that, but held his tongue.

There were rope burns on the old man's neck. The stranger indicated them.

'Hanged,' the youth supplied. 'By paladins.'

The stranger's eyes hardened. 'Why?'

'The Mage was unlicensed. Apparently that's a capital offence now.'

'Always was. They just don't talk about it.' He inspected the corpse again. 'I don't see any likeness, so I'm assuming you're not his son.'

'No. Apprentice.'

'How are you known?'

'Kutch Pirathon.'

'Well met, Kutch, even if I've come at your time of trouble. I'm Reeth Caldason.'

Recognition dawned on the lad and he gawked at the stranger, saucer-eyed. '*The* Reeth Caldason?'

'Don't worry,' Caldason replied dryly, 'I'm not dangerous.'

'That's not what I've heard.'

'You shouldn't believe everything you hear.'

'Are you *really* Reeth Caldason?'

'Why would I lie?'

'Or dare if you weren't, true.' Kutch gazed at him with new interest. 'I've never met a Qalochian before. Don't think I've even seen one.'

'Few have these days,' Caldason returned, his manner turned frosty. He stirred and headed for the door. 'Well, I'm sorry for your loss, but –'

'Wait.' Kutch managed to appear bashful and eager at the same time. 'Perhaps I can help you.'

'How?'

'That depends on what you wanted to see my master about.'

'Well, it wasn't a love charm or poison for an enemy.'

'No, I suppose not. You could get those anywhere.'

'What I'm saying is that my needs might be beyond . . . an apprentice.'

'How will you know unless you tell me?'

Caldason shook his head. 'Thanks, but no.' He started to leave again.

In the larger room, Kutch dogged him. 'I have skills, you know. The Mage taught me many things. I've studied with him since I was a child.'

'Not very long then.'

Kutch ignored the gibe. 'What have you got to lose?'

'My time.'

'Would a few more minutes make that much difference?'

'And maybe my patience.' There was distinct menace in Caldason's tone for all its apparent mellowness. Like finding a piece of glass in a milky pudding.

They were at the front door now. 'At least let me show you,' Kutch stammered. 'Let me demonstrate what I can do. And we could break fast. I'm sure you could use food and drink.'

Caldason regarded the youth. 'You're persistent, I'll give you that.' He exhaled wearily. 'All right. I'll take bread with you, if you have it to spare.'

'Plenty. And there's fowl, cheese, some fish, I think, and –'

The Qalochian held up a hand to staunch Kutch's flow. 'But I won't be staying long. I've other enchanters to find.'

'Well, there you are; I can give you some names. Not that you'll want them once you've seen what *I* can –'

'All *right*!' Caldason snapped, adding more gently, 'All right.'

'Magic now?' Kutch inquired meekly.

'Let's eat first.'

Caldason's reference to bread was literal; it was all he took, along with some water. He sat cross-legged on the floor, spine ramrod-straight, swords laid beside him. Deftly, he dissected

the hunk of bread with a sharp knife, carrying small pieces
to his mouth on the side of the blade.

Apparently grief hadn't lessened Kutch's appetite, and his
repast was less frugal. He lounged opposite Caldason, back
against the wall, legs stretched out, a wooden bowl in his
lap.

Some of the shutters had been opened and dust motes
floated in the shafts of light. Caldason surveyed a room
stacked with books, floor-to-ceiling shelf-loads, many in
ancient bindings, some near crumbling. A plain, sturdy
bench, several chairs and a moth-ravaged hanging on the
only unshelved portion of wall comprised the furnishings.

Kutch put down his spoon and, swallowing, said, 'I've
heard many stories about you.'

'So have I.'

Silence descended.

At length, Kutch said, 'Well?'

'Well what?'

'Are they true?'

Caldason took a drink from his cup. 'How do you come
to be here?'

'You're changing the subject,' Kutch protested.

'No, I'm interested.'

The youth looked cheated, but complied. 'There's not
much to tell. My father got himself killed when I was a
toddler. My mother struggled to keep me and my older
brother. Eventually he went into the army. I was sold to
Master Domex. I haven't seen my mother or brother since.'

'Why did Domex choose you?'

'He always said he saw my potential from the first.' He
shrugged his lean shoulders. 'Sorcerers have their ways. But
he was a good master.'

'How did he meet his end?'

'An informer, I reckon. We don't see too many paladins

around here, or militia either, then suddenly the village was crawling with them. They knew exactly where to come.'

'But they did *you* no harm?'

Kutch reddened and bowed his head. 'I . . . I hid.'

After a pause, Caldason said, 'The paladins aren't to be gone against lightly.' His voice was unexpectedly gentle. 'There's no shame in it, Kutch, and you shouldn't feel guilt either.'

'I wish I could believe that. All I know is that I wasn't here for him.' Caldason thought he saw the boy's eyes misting.

'And what do you think you could have done? Fought them? You would have died too. Used your magic? They have better.'

'I feel a coward.'

'Retreat's a sign of intelligence, not cowardice. It means you live to fight another day. Why wasn't your master licensed?'

Kutch sniffed and ran a hand across his head, smoothing back his shock of blond hair. 'He didn't believe in it. The Mage was a nonconformist when it came to the system, and most other things. The bastards would never have accepted him anyway. He was too much of a free thinker.'

'That's seditious talk.'

'To you? I don't think so.'

Another rare, dilute smile came to Caldason's lips. 'What are you going to do now?'

'I don't know. I've always been with the Mage. Different places, but never apart. I can't stay here though. The paladins left, but what if they come back to finish the job?'

'It's probably wise for you to go. Any idea where?'

'Somewhere different. Somewhere *really* . . . free.'

Caldason gave a hollow laugh.

'You're mocking me.'

'No. It's we who are mocked.'

'You're saying nowhere's free?'

'I've seen most of Bhealfa, and something of Gath Tampoor and Rintarah, and a few of their protectorates, and I haven't found it. Not true freedom. Just the pretence. The silk glove hides an iron fist everywhere I've been.'

Kutch was impressed. His cheer resurfaced. 'You've visited all those places? The empires themselves? *Both* of them?'

'I've been travelling a long time.'

'Aren't you worried about being recognised?'

'I try not to take unnecessary risks.'

'You were out there hunting paladins, right?' It was said conspiratorially, lacking only a wink.

Caldason ignored that and lithely got to his feet. 'Time's passing. How about showing me your magic?'

Kutch rose too, feeling as though he'd been blocked again. 'Upstairs,' he explained, taking a lead candleholder to light their way.

The narrow staircase was creaky and winding, and low enough that Caldason had to stoop. It was lined with recessed shelves holding more books. The upper floor revealed another spacious chamber, the twin of the one below, and unmistakably an enchanter's workroom. All the paraphernalia of the sorcerer's trade was on display, along with yet more books and parchment scrolls. The smell of potions, unguents, solvents and incense was even stronger than downstairs.

One of the benches held four objects, each about the size of a lobster pot, covered by black felt cloths. Kutch went to them, and allowed himself a sense of the theatrical.

'For your delectation,' he proclaimed, 'a wonder of the arcane arts.' With a flourish he whipped away the first cloth.

What he unveiled was a large, bell-shaped glass jar with an immense cork in its neck. Caldason leaned forward to examine its contents. He saw scaled-down trees, bushes and rocks, and small slabs of granite piled up to make a little cave. Something had been slumbering inside. Now it woke, slanted yellow-green eyes snapping open.

A miniature dragon swaggered into the light. It arched its back and extended its wings. Head up, jaws wide, the creature's roar was smothered by the thick glass. Then it exhaled a spume of orange flame and black smoke.

Judging the time right to move the show on, Kutch pulled off the next cloth.

The second jar held a prairie scene, its sward running to the lip of a cunningly constructed timberland. In the foreground a pure white unicorn pawed the grass before rearing, its twisted horn jabbing skyward.

A harpy occupied the third jar, its habitat a jagged, dimly lit cavern. Hanging upside down like a bat, leathery wings flapping, angry red eyes ablaze, it couldn't have been longer than Caldason's thumb. The fourth jar was filled with water. It housed a pink coral palace. A fetching mermaid swam slowly around its turrets, silvery tail swishing, hair flowing free. Streams of tiny bubbles issued from the corners of her voluptuous lips.

Kutch beamed proudly. 'Admit it, you're impressed. Do you know how much homunculi of this quality would cost on the open market?'

'You made them?'

'Well . . . no. But I helped.'

'I grant they're well constructed. But, don't take this the wrong way, they're hardly original.'

'No,' Kutch allowed, smile freezing, 'I never said they were.' There was an air of slight annoyance in his response. 'It's not the homunculi themselves, it's what I'm going to do to . . .' He considered, then pointed at the dragon. '. . . *that* one.'

From a cluttered shelf he selected two flat, polished stones, reddish brown in colour and of a size to fit comfortably into his palms. The stones were decorated with runic patterns. 'You're going to witness a transformation. Using the Craft, I'll change this dragon into another form. It needs quite a bit of concentration, so please be quiet.'

Caldason raised an eyebrow. He leaned against the wall and folded his arms.

Kutch held the stones to the jar on opposite sides, facing each other. He closed his eyes for a moment. Then he began droning an incantation in what Caldason supposed was the elder tongue. The dragon watched.

Pinpricks of light appeared in the centres of the stones. They expanded, joined, spread and began pulsing. The dragon homunculus bared its fangs and lashed its forked tail. Kutch rambled on, mouthing incomprehensibly, face screwed with effort. A faint sheen of perspiration dampened his forehead.

The glowing stones emitted a stronger radiance.

There was a kind of eruption then. Both stones sent out miniature incandescent, slow-moving energy bolts that melded midway, forming a horizontal fiery tightrope. It flickered and crackled. The dragon snapped and postured.

A second later the fluctuating flow sent out a pair of tendrils. They probed the bottom of the bottle, searching out the scuttling dragon and finding it immediately. Twin sparkling currents latched on to the reluctant glamour. In turn they drew down the greater flux passing between the stones above. It bowed, U-shaped, and joined the dragon too. All the energy generated by the stones ran through the creature and bathed it.

'Here it comes!' Kutch cried out, lips trembling. 'The transformation!'

There was a muffled explosion. The jar shuddered violently. Its inner surface was instantly coated with a viscous green lather. There were bits of scale and bone mixed in.

'*Oow!*' Kutch yelped, dropping the stones. 'Hot!' Hopping, he blew furiously on his hands and flapped them about.

'You need to work on your craft,' Caldason suggested tactfully.

'I don't understand it.' He was still puffing on his hands and grimacing. 'I'll try another.'

'Don't bother. I'm not very enamoured of magic anyway.'

Kutch found that vaguely shocking. 'You aren't?' he said, discomfort forgotten. 'What about all its benefits?'

'Let's just say there were never many for me.'

'You mean you can't afford it,' Kutch concluded knowingly.

'You could put it that way.'

The youth's manner moved to serious. 'I really don't know what went wrong.' He glanced at the jars and appealed, 'Let me have another go.'

'Not on my account.'

'If you only give me the chance, I'm sure I could –'

'*No*. It's past my time to leave. I must get out of here.'

It seemed to Kutch that suddenly there was an almost desperate edge to Caldason's words, and he looked tenser and furtive. Kutch made to speak, but his guest was already deserting the study. He pounded the stairs after him.

'Look, I'm sorry it didn't work out quite the way I expected,' he apologised once they reached ground level. 'But there's no need –'

'It's nothing to do with that. I have to . . .' He swayed, as if about to fall.

Kutch was alarmed, but something about Caldason stopped him stretching out a hand. 'What's wrong?'

'Nothing.' Caldason collected himself and straightened. 'I'm all right.'

'Let me mix you a healing draught.'

'No.' His breathing was becoming laboured. He cradled his head in his hands.

'What ails you?'

'Just a dose of . . . reality.'

'I don't understand.'

Caldason didn't elaborate. All but staggering, he made his way to the swords he'd left on the floor. Looking close to passing out, he scooped them up. 'Do you have a secure place here?' he asked.

'Secure?'

'Somewhere under lock. Somewhere solid.'

'Why –'

'*Do you?*' Caldason barked.

The boy flinched. He strove to think. 'Well, nothing except . . .'

'What?'

'Only the old demon hole.'

'You have one? Here?'

'Yes. My master had need of it sometimes.'

'Take me. *Now.*'

Growing fearful, Kutch led the way to the cellar door. Still holding the swords, Caldason negotiated the dank steps uncertainly.

The demon hole was a small vault at the cellar's far end. It was constructed from robust stone, with a sturdy door into which a barred grille had been cut. Inside, stout iron rings were embedded in the floor, with chains and manacles attached.

Caldason lifted one of the swords.

'Please don't,' Kutch pleaded. 'There's no need to lock me in there. I won't tell about you.'

'Not you. Me.'

'What?'

He thrust the sheathed swords at Kutch. 'Take them! And these.' Several knives joined the haul. 'Hide them.' He stretched a hand to the youth's shoulder to steady himself and peeled off his boots. A buckled belt followed them. His movements were becoming erratic. He sweated, and breath didn't seem to come easily.

'What is it?' Kutch said. 'Is somebody coming? Do we have to hide?'

'We've got to trust each other. Now listen to me. Do not, under any circumstances, let me out of there until . . . well, you'll probably know when. But if you have any doubts just leave me be.'

'None of this makes sense.'

'Just do it. Please.'

Kutch gave him a dazed nod.

'Are those the keys for the fetters?' Caldason waved a hand at a bunch hanging from a hook on the cell's door frame.

'Yes.'

'Then chain me.'

'You want to be chained too?'

'We've no time. *Hurry.*'

With shaking hands, Kutch secured Caldason's ankles and wrists.

'Whatever I say or do,' Caldason restated, 'don't open that door. Not if you value your life. Now get out. And stay away.'

In a state of confusion, Kutch backed away from the cell. He closed the bulky door and turned its lock.

Then he stood by the grille and watched what happened next in amazement.

3

His people thought honour meant something. Until betrayal rode in on a thousand horses.

The raiders came under cover of a moonless night, with no aim but murder. They were welcomed by paltry fences and open gates. A sparse watch, taken off-guard. An alarm raised too late.

They set to slaughter, and savoured the task.

But his folk were warriors, first and last, and they met the traitors. There were inexhaustible numbers to unhorse and cut down, and still they made no impression on the tide. Victory was hopeless. Yet better to die with sword in hand.

He did his share of killing. In vain he tried to organise a defence in the face of chaos. Where he could, he protected the weak.

In the confusion of running, screaming, burning and dying he saw a woman and her child cowering before a raider. She pleaded as the youngster wept, balled fists to his eyes. He hacked his way to them and struck down their would-be assassin. The pair fled, the woman clutching the boy's hand. Then he watched, powerless, as another rider swooped in to spear and trample them.

Dead and wounded littered the ground, most of them his own people. He walked, stumbled, ran over them as he dodged and slashed. The wave of attackers seemed endless. He looked to the central lodge,

the communal hub of the camp and traditional sanctuary in times
of strife. Some of the more vulnerable, the young, the old and the
ailing, had been swiftly shepherded there. That might include his
closest kin. Now he wanted only to be with them for the end.

The great round house's thatch was already ablaze before he
battled his way to its door. His arrival, gore encrusted, panting,
found the building in full flame. Victims of the conflagration, staggering fireballs, groped shrieking from the burning lodge. Around
its entrance lay evidence of a particular massacre within the general
carnage. The corpses of family, comrades, and siblings by right of
blood oath. His despairing thought was to get away, perhaps then
to join with other survivors and strike back at their enemy.

A group of raiders lashed ropes to the camp's corral and brought
it crashing down. Scores of terrified horses galloped out to compound
the anarchy. The stampede acted as a diversion for his flight. He
sped to a cluster of huts, several of which were also on fire, and
weaved through them. His goal was the perimeter fence, the pasture
land beyond and then the forest.

He didn't make it.

A pack of the distinctively garbed attackers appeared and blocked
his path. More closed off his exit. He tore into them, fighting with
the frenzy of hopelessness. Two he downed at once, ribboning the
throat of one, skewering the heart of the next. Then he was at the
centre of a storm of blades. He took his own wounds, many of them,
but gave plenty in return. Another opponent fell, chest caved, and
another, stomach slashed.

His reckless fury brought a small miracle. All but a pair of his
opponents were dispatched, and one of them was injured. But
his hurts were too many and put paid to hopes of escape. Near
collapse from loss of blood, vision swimming, a blow across his shoulders brought him to his knees. His sword slipped from numbing
fingers.

He thought he saw, just fleetingly, the figure of an old man cloaked
in black smoke, standing at the door of a nearby hut.

His gaze went up to the face of his killer. An ocean of time flowed slowly between them.

Then he felt his ravaged body pierced by cold steel.

Cold water battered his face.

He came round in a spasm, fighting for breath, eyes wide. His arms and legs were held fast, and instinctively he jerked at the chains binding them.

'Easy.'

Caldason blinked at the figure kneeling alongside.

'I think it's over now,' Kutch told him.

Sitting up, painfully, Caldason took in his surroundings. They were in the cramped demon hole. The hard, irregular stone floor was uncomfortable and wet.

'How long?' he grated, wiping blood from his lips with the back of his hand.

Kutch put aside the bucket. 'All day. It's late evening now.'

'Did I do any harm?'

'Only to yourself.' He surveyed the Qalochian's bruised face and grazed arms, his dishevelled hair and the dark rings under his still slightly feral eyes. 'You look terrible.'

'Did I speak?'

'You did little else, though rave might be a better word. But not in any tongue I recognised. You've no need to fear you gave away any secrets.'

'I have few enough, but thank you for that, Kutch.'

'I've never seen anybody the way you were, Reeth. Unless they were ramped or possessed of demons.'

'Neither covers my situation.'

'No, that was something else. Is that why you wanted to consult my master?'

'Part of it.'

'*Part?* You nearly uprooted those restraining rings! You *frothed*, for the gods' sake! And you have *other* problems?'

'Let's say they are complicating factors.'

Kutch could see he wasn't going to get any more on that subject. 'I'd heard you were a savage fighter,' he said. 'Is that because of these . . . fits?' It was an inadequate word.

'Sometimes. You've seen I don't control it.'

'How did you –'

'Kutch. I ache. I'm soaked and I could use food and something to drink.' He thrust his manacled wrists at him. 'Get me out of these.'

Kutch looked wary.

'The seizure's passed, you're in no danger. I have some warning of an onset. If it's going to happen again I'll come back here.'

Still the boy hesitated.

'It's not as though I'm in a permanent state of derangement,' Caldason persisted. 'I'm no Melyobar.'

Despite his apprehension, Kutch had to smile as he reached for the keys.

The royal court of the sovereign state of Bhealfa hadn't stood still in almost twenty years.

When he gained leadership, though technically not the throne itself, Prince Melyobar was eighteen. Some said he was eccentric even then. Given the unusual constitutional situation he found himself in, with his father, the King, neither dead nor properly living, there were doubts about the Prince's legitimacy as a ruler. It took an interminable time to sort out the problem. Melyobar distracted himself by consulting seers and prophets, hoping to hear something of his coming, ersatz reign.

It was then that he learned the true nature of death.

Nobody knows which of the numerous mystics he received first put the idea into his head. But the result was that, for Melyobar, death became Death. An animate creature, walking the world as men do, dealing out oblivion. Worse, intent on stalking *him*.

Backed by the counsel of some of his more pliable sooth-sayers, the Prince reasoned that if Death walked like a man, he could be outrun. In eluding Death, death could be cheated.

At vast cost, Melyobar ordered the construction of a move-able dwelling, smaller than the present palace but as opulently furnished. It contained hundreds of apartments, including a ballroom and a chamber given over to meetings of his puppet Elders Council.

The new court resembled a ship without sails, its prow and stern squared off. Its motive power was fabulously expensive magic. Steered by hand-picked enchanters, it floated silently above the ground at about the height of a man with his arms raised. It travelled at the pace of a canter-ing horse, though this could be varied somewhat. The Prince had two lesser versions built to accompany him as escape vessels.

Dozens of courtiers spent fortunes on their own conveyances, vying with each other in size and ornamenta-tion. The Prince's personal guard, representatives of the sorcerer elite, scholars, lawmakers and servants occupied more land ships. Others carried victuals and provisions. For the lower orders and mere camp followers there was no magical impetus. Their wagons relied on teams of horses, hazardously changed on the move. Everything depended on a complex logistical system, and the administrators who ran it took up yet more vehicles.

As the vast cavalcade journeyed the length and breadth of Bhealfa its route was varied to confound Death. Sometimes that meant the flattening of harvest crops, the fording of swollen rivers, even the destruction of an occasional village if it couldn't be avoided. The priority was to keep moving at any cost.

This night, the flotilla crossed a relatively unpopulated region of the Princedom. It blazed with light from swaying lanterns and flickering brands. Nor was it quiet. The caravan brought with it the sounds of thundering hooves, squeaking wheels, music, and lookouts hailing each other when collisions threatened.

A carriage arrived at the periphery of the cortege and matched its speed. It was met by outriders who checked the visitor's credentials. Then they escorted it into the convoy, a chancy undertaking at the best of times. But they reached the gliding palace with a minimum of bumps.

The carriage door opened and an elegantly dressed passenger stepped across onto the rungs of a short ladder. Deck crew assisted him aboard and a uniformed welcoming party saluted.

He was taken to an antechamber and subjected to the indignity of a light search. Not for weapons, but to ascertain that he was who he appeared to be, rather than the entity so much was being done to evade. Familiar with the Prince's obsession, he suffered it without protest.

At last he was ushered into a lavishly appointed stateroom.

'The Imperial Envoy of Gath Tampoor,' a flunky announced before discreetly exiting.

The room's only occupant sat at an exquisite desk, studying a parchment held flat by a pair of silver candlesticks, seemingly unaware of his visitor's arrival. Containing his impatience, the emissary gave a polite cough.

Prince Melyobar straightened and regarded him. His manner seemed vague, if not actually confused, and recognition took a moment. 'Ah, Talgorian.'

'Your Highness.' The Envoy delivered a small head bow.

They were roughly the same age, but the Gath Tampoorian had worn much better. He was lean and fit, where the Prince was stout and pasty-faced. Talgorian had a neatly trimmed beard; Melyobar's rotund face was shaved, against the prevailing fashion, and his hair was prematurely white. The Envoy was possessed of diplomatic calm, at least outwardly; Melyobar's disposition was jumpy.

'To what do I owe . . .' The Prince trailed off, preoccupied.

'Our regular meeting, Highness,' Talgorian reminded him firmly, though remaining on the right side of protocol.

'Oh, yes.'

'And the matter of the provision of additional troops.' He enunciated this more slowly, in the way a peasant might address an obstinate cow. 'Bhealfan troops. For our new campaign against Rintarah, Highness, and their troublesome clients.'

The Prince didn't seem to comprehend. 'To what purpose?'

'As I previously explained, my Lord, to protect your sovereignty and the security of the empire.' He was having to work to keep his composure, as usual. 'It wouldn't do to let Rintarah get the upper hand, would it?'

'No, I suppose not.'

'We need your gracious assent to draw more soldiers from Bhealfa's ranks to support the cause.' He slipped a hand into his coat and brought out a rolled document tied with red ribbon. 'I will trouble you only for your signature, Highness. The details you can leave to me.'

'You want me to sign something?'

'It's all strictly in compliance with the accord that exists between your government and mine,' Talgorian explained reasonably. 'A trifling matter of legality.'

There was a hiatus, with the Prince wordless and self-absorbed. At length he said, 'You may approach.'

The Envoy stepped forward, unfurling the paper. He placed it on the desk and watched as Melyobar added his trembling signature. When the sand shaker had been applied, the Prince

dipped his seal ring in hot wax and clumsily impressed the
document with it.

When it was done, Talgorian all but snatched away the
edict. 'Thank you, your Highness,' he cooed smoothly. He
was relieved that the Prince hadn't been awkward about the
request. It would be tiresome to have to remind him again
where the real power lay.

'Rintarah, you say?' Melyobar made it sound as though
he'd never heard of the rival empire.

Talgorian bit back exasperation. 'Yes, sir,' he replied, carefully rolling the document. 'A great threat to us all. Your
troops will help keep it in check. Not to mention the warlords
in the north. We need defending from them too.' It was like
speaking to a baby.

'There are always warlords. They come and go. What
concern are the barbarous lands to us?'

It was almost an intelligent remark. Talgorian was
impressed. 'True, Highness. But there is some small disquiet
about this new one we've had reports of. Zerreiss.'

'Never heard of him.'

'Except when I last mentioned him to you,' the Envoy
muttered.

'What?'

'I said I must have forgotten to mention him to you.
Apologies.'

'What's so special about him?'

'Only that he seems to have accrued some impressive
conquests in rather a short time. It's always as well to keep
an eye on such things. We don't want Rintarah making
pacts with these savages and gaining undue influence in
that area.'

'They'll be doing better than Gath Tampoor if they do,'
Melyobar responded bluntly. 'What's known about this . . .'

'Zerreiss, Highness.'

'What do we know about him?'

'Very little at present. In fact he's a bit of a mystery.'

For the first time during the audience, a spark of anima-
tion came into the Prince's eyes. 'Perhaps it's . . . *him*,' he
whispered.

Talgorian was baffled. 'Highness?'

'Him. *Him!* The reaper. The gatherer of life essences.' His
voice dropped to an undertone. *'Death.'*

The Envoy should have guessed. 'Of course. Tricky
customer.' He knew that sounded feeble.

Melyobar didn't seem to notice the lack of empathy. He
was warming to the subject. 'It could be him. He's a shape
changer, you know.'

'Indeed.'

'And where better to snatch lives than in the barbarous
lands?'

'All the more reason to take precautions.' Talgorian tried
to steer the conversation into more placid waters. 'Which is
why your assignment of the troops will be so very useful in
respect of maintaining order and stability.'

The Prince ignored the platitudes. Nodding at the papers
on his desk, his tone became conspiratorial. 'Just between
ourselves?'

'Naturally,' the Envoy promised, wearing a look of hurt
effrontery at the very notion of indiscretion.

'These are a secret,' Melyobar confided, laying his hand
on the sheets of spidery scrawl. He leaned closer and hissed,
'They're part of my plan to kill Death.'

Unusually for a diplomat, Talgorian was lost for a coherent
response.

He was spared. A gust of chill wind, somehow penetrating
the quarters, rustled a drape. Several candles briefly guttered.
The Prince shivered and pulled his ermine cape closer. His
uneasy gaze darted about the chamber.

'Then best that the scheme be kept a secret,' Talgorian said, stroking Melyobar's paranoia.

'You're probably right.' The Prince hastily turned over the papers and anchored them with a regally engraved inkpot. Fresh anxiety etched his features.

'There is just one more matter I would like to discuss, Highness,' the Envoy continued. 'A topic of some importance.'

The Prince paid heed to Talgorian's graver countenance. 'What is it?'

'Your Royal Highness, have you ever heard of a man called Reeth Caldason?'

4

The city stood in a wide valley between low, black hills. A pewter river wormed through it. Towers and spires marked its heart, with villas, lodges and houses radiating from the core. Huts, shanties and lean-tos, many clinging to the slopes, formed a crusty halo. To the passing birds it demonstrated all that needed to be known about the seep of power. Not that everything flying above was a bird.

Merakasa, capital of Gath Tampoor and hub of its empire, was never entirely dark. The lights being kindled as night fell, of wax and oil, were rivalled by constant eruptions of magical energies, making for a continuous, shimmering glow. But this glow was uneven, with feeble emissions in the poor quarters, gleaming splendour around the mansions of the rich.

The streets teemed. Costers and tradesmen jostled artisans and itinerants. Merchants led mules weighed down with cloth bolts and sacks of spices. Laden carts vied with horse riders. Pavement sellers hawked fruit and bread from makeshift stalls as tattered, thieving boys eyed their wares. Wagons bobbed in the flow of humanity.

And non-humanity.

Falsities walked the streets too. Or padded, slithered or floated over them. Some were fantastical, mythic, grotesque, designed to entertain or threaten. Others were indistinguishable from the everyday, mimicking pets or trophy mistresses. Some were wholly credible, others less so, depending on their price.

Every so often a glamour vanished in silent pyrotechnics as it expired or was voided. New ones appeared with about the same frequency, disgorging from thin air in bursts of radiance. The supply was plentiful. Licensed magic vendors worked the crowds, dispensing spells and potions while their bodyguards kept watch.

The bustle washed against the walls of the palace Merakasa suckled; thick, high ramparts surrounding a city within a city, immense and rambling. By contrast to the streets, its grounds seemed deserted, and somehow the din from outside was muted.

Its innermost buildings were grand and had the magical lustre of conspicuous wealth. Outlying utilitarian structures were in a colder style. One particularly bleak example was set apart. It was squat and windowless. Its function had to do with state security and the maintenance of order, so naturally it was very large. But all it showed the world was a modest two storeys. Only someone luckless enough to be dragged inside would learn that it burrowed well below ground, through sub-levels, cellars and vaults.

Its deepest reaches contained the holding areas; a honeycomb of stone passageways, lined with featureless, barred doors. Behind one, at the far end of an especially remote corridor, was a cell much like all the rest. Its sole furnishings were a hard bed and a wooden bucket. Faint light was supplied by a paltry glamour.

A woman sat on the cot. She had been given nothing to eat or drink. Her boots, belt, anything that could do harm, had been taken from her and a drab ankle-length smock replaced her normal clothes. She had a distaste for confined spaces that bordered on dread, and that added to her anguish.

They had interrogated her incessantly. Her answers weren't what they wanted to hear, but they hadn't laid hands on her. She wondered how long that would last. Exhausted, confused, her anger at the way she was being treated, at the inequity of it, had abated to churning resentment.

She had been left alone for some hours now. Or so it seemed – her unvarying surroundings made it hard to judge. She thought it might be evening, but wouldn't swear to it. Already she had grown used to the silence.

Which made her start all the more when it was broken.

Distant doors slammed. There were voices and echoing footfalls. The sounds grew nearer. Some kind of procession turned into her corridor. She heard muffled conversation and boots scuffing on stone. They stopped at her cell.

After a second's quiet, the lock was turned, then the door creaked open. She tensed.

Someone was framed for a moment, outlined by the greater light outside; greater than the gloom of her cell, but still petty. The figure was tall, cadaverously thin, slightly hunched at the shoulders. It took a step towards her. She saw others in the passage, holding back.

Her visitor was completely bald and his features were angular, like a carrion bird's. His china blue eyes were quick, his mouth thin lipped. It was hard to tell his age, but he was probably around sixty. He wore the discreetly affluent garb of a high-ranking servant of the state.

She recognised him instantly. Perhaps her astonishment showed on her face.

He came in and closed the door, leaving his escort outside. He was the kind of man who always had an escort.

They had never met. In her position you didn't get to meet someone so illustrious unless you excelled or fouled up badly. But she had seen him from afar several times, as well as his likeness in paintings and the odd statue. She thought, absurdly, of standing and making a show of obeisance. Before she could move, he spoke.

'Captain Ardacris.' He was smiling.

She stared at him, and although it was a greeting, not a question, nodded.

'Do you know who I am?' he asked.

'Yes,' she replied distantly, then got a hold on herself. 'Yes, *sir*. Commissioner Laffon, Council for Internal Security, sir.'

'Good.' The smile remained fixed. He indicated the bed. 'May I?'

She nodded again and shifted for him. Laffon perched.

He regarded her, then said, 'Serrah, you need my help.'

'I do?'

'Wouldn't you say so? To get this business cleared up and put behind us?' His manner was kindly, avuncular.

'Well . . . yes, of course. But what more can I do than tell the truth?'

'Perhaps something more.'

His presence emphasised the seriousness of her situation, and she felt a little overawed. 'What would you have me do?'

'Explain what happened. About the Principal-Elect's son.'

'I've already told the story so many times, Commissioner. Why do I –'

'Indulge me. You can summarise.'

Serrah took a breath. 'My unit was on to a gang of ramp dealers. We watched their hideaway for nearly a month. Last night, we went in.' It felt a lot longer ago than just last night, she reflected, but went on, 'Phosian acted like a hothead. He stepped out of line and they killed him for it. I might add that it wasn't the first time he'd disobeyed orders, sir. He made a habit of it.'

Laffon considered her words, then stated, 'No, it didn't happen like that.'

She was dumbfounded. 'Sir?'

'That isn't an approved version.'

'*Approved?* I thought there was only one version of the truth.'

'Not for official purposes,' the Commissioner informed her softly.

'Perhaps you'd like to tell me how it *did* happen, sir.' Her fury was creeping back.

'Phosian died a hero.'

Ice fragments swirled in the pit of her stomach. All she could think to say was, 'Is that so?' It was meant bitingly, it sounded weak.

'It is, Captain. Moreover, it will be said that he bravely gave his life as the result of bad leadership.'

'With respect, sir, that isn't how it was.'

'The Council has appraised it otherwise.' He maintained the sympathetic air.

'My unit. They'll confirm what I've said. Ask them.'

'Ah, yes, a devoted band. Nothing but respect for you. I'm afraid they all said your behaviour fell below acceptable standards.'

She couldn't believe they had, willingly. 'This is wrong, Commissioner. Everything's been twisted, just because of Phosian's family connections.'

'I know this is difficult for you. But you can make things so much easier. Simply confess to what happened and –'

'To what *you* say happened, sir.'

'Confess to it and I promise I'll do my best to get you a lenient sentence.'

'You're asking me to *lie*. Not to mention condemning myself.'

'I'm asking you not to give succour to the empire's enemies.'

'You're *what*?'

'Rintarah, and their fellow travellers here, the insurgents. It would only strengthen their cause if it got out that the scion of one of our ruling houses was . . . less than perfect.'

Serrah gave a hollow laugh. 'That, sir, if you'll pardon the expression, is horse shit. Phosian was a spoilt, reckless brat. Any Rintarahian spy worth their salt would already know that. It took his fancy to play at being a militiaman, and because of who he was, that meant an elite unit, despite my objections. Now I'm supposed to pay for his stupidity.'

'You would do well to refrain from speaking that way about your betters, Captain.'

Did she detect a slip in his benevolent pose? A slight tension in that turkey neck?

'I've always been loyal,' she argued, playing what felt like her last card.

'You will best demonstrate your loyalty by doing as I ask.'

'Does it matter what I say? I can't stop you putting out any version you want, so why this charade? Sir.'

He ignored the mild insubordination. 'It's a question of credibility. It has to come from you. If you confess to your failings publicly there will be no doubts, no void to be filled with rumours by the dissidents and troublemakers. And as far as Phosian's family is concerned, honour will be satisfied.'

'Then I demand an open trial. Let my peers judge me.'

'That's out of the question.'

'As a citizen of Gath Tampoor I have rights.'

'You have only as many rights as we allow you.' Laffon's tone was distinctly flintier. 'When it comes to state security we don't wash our soiled linen in public, you know that.'

'If I agree to this ... declaration, what happens to me afterwards?'

'As I said, I'll use my influence to ensure your punishment is light.' He held her gaze. 'That's a pledge.'

Serrah couldn't help thinking how convenient it would be for them if she simply disappeared after her confession. No possibility of her reneging. No loose ends. She looked at Laffon and for the first time in her life doubted the word of a superior. It was a frightening, heady notion. 'And if I refuse?'

'I can make no promises in that eventuality.'

Heads or tails I lose, she thought. 'I don't deserve to be treated this way, Commissioner.'

'Nobody said the world was fair. We all have to make sacrifices for the greater good.'

Whose greater good? she wondered.

He pressed her. 'Will you do it? Confess?'

'I ... I can't.'

Laffon sighed. A moment passed in silence. Finally, he said, 'Consider this. Perhaps my truth *is* the truth.'

Serrah raised her bowed head. 'I don't understand.'

His eyes narrowed. 'Your daughter. Eithne, wasn't it?'

'What about her? What's she got to do with this?'

'I believe she was fifteen when it happened, isn't that so?'

'Why are you bringing this up?' His course rattled her. She didn't want to go there.

'Tragic,' he tutted, slowly shaking his head. 'Such a waste.'

'That has *nothing* to do –'

'Think about it, Serrah. Your daughter. The ramp. Isn't it possible ...'

'No.'

'... given the circumstances of Eithne's death, seeing the drug there, faced with the traffickers ...'

'*No.*'

'. . . that your judgement was clouded? That, understandably, you reacted emotionally and –'

'*No!* I'm a professional! I work on facts, not emotions!'

'Really? The way you're behaving now hardly bears that out.'

That struck home. With an effort of will she calmed herself. 'My daughter has nothing to do with any of this. Last night wasn't the first time I've been up against ramp dealers. I hate them, yes, but that's never affected the way I do my job. But this isn't about me, is it? It's about you needing a sacrifice.'

'You still don't understand the extent of this thing, do you, Ardacris?' There was no vestige of sympathy now. 'What you allowed to happen has repercussions, and they go all the way up to the Empress herself.'

'I'm flattered,' Serrah replied cynically.

'Enough,' Laffon decided. 'There's no more to be said on the subject.' He delved in his pocket and brought out a folded parchment. With an irritated flick, he shook it open. 'You can make a start at rehabilitating yourself by signing this.' He held out the confession to her.

Everything crystallised in Serrah's mind. She abandoned hope of justice. All that kept her alive was that scrap of paper remaining unsigned. The only choice was to be defiant.

'Well?' Laffon demanded.

'No,' she said.

'You're refusing?'

'I am.'

'Be absolutely sure about this. Because what happens next won't be to your liking.'

She shook her head.

Laffon could see her resolve. He stood. 'You'll regret taking the hard road. I'll leave you this for when you change your mind.' He dropped the document on the bed. Next to it he tossed a small, reddish, tubular object. A graphology glamour, useless for anything but. Probably strong enough for no more than her signature.

'I won't be needing it,' she told him.

He paused on the point of leaving. 'Remember, you've brought this on yourself.'

Three men entered as Laffon slipped out. It happened so quickly, Serrah was taken off-guard.

They were muscular, stern-faced individuals. Each held a short length of thick rope with one end knotted. She started to get up.

Without warning, the nearest man swung his rope cosh at her. It cracked hard across her shoulder. She cried out and fell back. He moved in and lashed again, striking her just below the throat. Scrambling away from him, she kicked wildly, catching his shin. He cursed and backed off, hindering the other two.

Serrah rolled from the cot, landing heavily, and snatched the bucket. Ignoring the pain, she rose quickly, swinging it. The bucket raked the second man's temple as he rushed in, knocking him senseless. But the first man had recovered. He landed a hefty punch to her stomach and she doubled over. The third man joined him and they rained blows on her. Serrah tried to ward them off with the pail, using it as both shield and weapon. A stinging rap across the knuckles broke her grip and sent it flying.

The man she had downed was on his feet again, adding his fury to the beating. She covered her head with her hands and retreated. But only a step or two took her to the tiny cell's limit. She was trapped in the narrow space between bed and wall. It cramped her attackers and they had to take turns to swing at her. But that didn't stop them delivering continuous punishment to her arms, legs and body.

Serrah half dived, half pitched sideways, onto the bed. That only made it easier for them. They set to with a will then, bent like men threshing corn, not speaking, dedicated to their work. She curled into a ball and suffered the storm.

When she was sure they would go on until they killed her, the beating stopped.

All she knew was pain. Every inch of her body was ablaze. The battering left her ears ringing and her vision blurred. She was bloodied, sweat-sheened, drifting on the rim of consciousness. Breathing hard, she flopped onto her back.

One of her tormentors loomed over her. He reached down and grasped the hem of her smock. With a violent jerk he yanked it up above her waist.

They laughed, jeered, made lecherous comments. Then they told her plainly and crudely what would happen if they had to come again. At the last, somebody threw the confession down on her.

They left, slamming the door.

Serrah coughed weakly, pain stabbing her ribs. Blood trickled from her nose and a corner of her mouth. It was agony to think, let alone move.

She passed an indefinite period of time immersed in an ocean of misery. Eventually nature took a hand and despite her injuries she fell into an exhausted slumber.

That gave the nightmares their chance to afflict her.

Leering faces and flaying bludgeons. The dungeon shrinking to crush her to pulp between its rigid walls. Her daughter sucked into a pitch black maelstrom, fingertips brushing Serrah's as she strained to reach her. Dreams of fire and suffering and loss.

She woke with a start.

Blood had crusted on her face and arms, and bruises were already rising. She ached horribly, fit to vomit.

It seemed to her that the cell was even more dimly lit than before. And the silence was oppressive. Then an indefinable but not unfamiliar feeling dawned; that sixth sense which let her know when someone quietly appeared at her back. The tickle up her spine that said she wasn't alone. Painfully, she struggled to a sitting position and blinked into the gloom.

Somebody else was in the cell. Standing by the door, quite still. Their features hard to make out.

'Who's there?' Serrah called, her voice cracked, hoarse.

There was no answer, and the stranger didn't move.

'Show yourself!'

Still nothing. Serrah had a dread that it was her torturers back to do worse. Toying with her first, to heighten her fear or their pleasure. But no assault came, so she began the agony of standing.

She narrowly won the battle to get to her feet. When she moved, she shuffled like an arthritic old woman. As she approached the figure she realised it had its back to her. It wore a dark, full-length cloak, tightly gathered. There was a hint of blonde hair above the upturned collar.

Serrah challenged the intruder again. 'Who are you?' This time it was nearly a whisper.

The figure turned.

Reality crumbled. Shocked disbelief hit Serrah like a tidal wave. Her pain was forgotten. She couldn't speak, she couldn't move. What she saw made her distrust her sanity.

The apparition stretched out a hand and lightly touched her arm. Its caress was warm, solid. Real. There was no threat in it. Serrah fought to say something. No words came. She took in the other's long, golden locks, hazel eyes, slightly plump, puppy-fat features. Her visitor smiled.

'Mother,' she said.

5

'*Eithne?*' Serrah whispered.

Her dead daughter's grin widened.

Serrah had never been the fainting type. Now she felt ready to drop. 'Eithne?' she repeated.

'Yes. Don't be afraid.'

'But . . . *how*? You're –'

'I'm more alive than I've ever been, Mother.' The sunken sockets, the pallor, the drawn features had all gone. She was as she had been, before her descent and the final days. Her eyes sparkled. 'I've come back to you.'

Serrah was aware that her arm was still being held. She felt the girl's fingers pressing into her flesh. How could this be a spectre, a deceiving glamour? 'Is it truly you?' she asked.

'It's me, Mummy.'

Serrah wanted to believe so badly. She moved to embrace her daughter.

'No,' Eithne said, letting go of Serrah and stepping back. 'It'd be painful at the moment, I'm too . . . delicate. I've only just . . .' The smile was unwavering. 'I'm feeling tender. Like you.'

Serrah remained with her arms outstretched, stunned at not being able to hold her child. For a moment, her grip on sanity seemed just as elusive. 'I don't understand any of this,' she said.

'All you have to understand is that I'm here. They brought me back.'

'Who? *How?*'

'The sorcerers of the imperial court, no less. You've no idea the kind of magic they command. Wonderful magic.'

'You said you were in pain.'

'Just some discomfort. It'll pass. The coming back . . . it was like waking up, that's all.'

Serrah had never heard of such a thing. 'But they can't –'

'They can. They *did*.'

'Why?'

'For you. Us.'

'Why would the highest-ranking concern themselves with us?'

'Because of this situation you've got yourself into. They're showing you a way out.'

'I must be blind not to see it.'

'Then look on me as a kind of reward.'

'For what?'

'For something you haven't done yet.'

Serrah was sure she knew what that was, but asked anyway. 'What do they expect from me?'

'You have to do as they say, Mother. You have to confess.'

'Eithne,' Serrah replied, still feeling strange at mouthing the name after so long, 'I have nothing to confess to. I didn't do anything wrong.'

'Does that matter?'

'Yes.'

'But does it matter if it means I can be reunited with you, that I can live out the life I lost?'

'There wouldn't be a life together if I confessed. I'd be locked away, or worse.'

'They promised me they'd be merciful.'

'You believe them?'

'The fact that I'm here proves they're serious about their side of the bargain.'

'And if I don't confess?'

Eithne's expression grew troubled. 'That would be bad for me.'

'What do you mean?'

'The spell they used to raise me is temporary. Unless they cast another that makes my state permanent, and soon . . .'

'How soon?'

'Hours.'

To have her back only to lose her again. Serrah felt her eyes filling. 'That's what they're offering in exchange for my confession?'

'Yes. They'll let me live again.'

'Doing it this way, it's . . . beyond cruel.'

'No, Mother! It's a miracle. Don't you see? They told me that at worst you'll spend a short time in prison or a re-education camp. Then we can be together again.'

A small part of Serrah's mind marvelled at how she had so readily accepted talking with the dead. Her dead. If this wasn't madness it would pass for it. 'Eithne, I – '

'I forgive you.'

'Forgive me?'

'For when I was . . . ill. When you weren't there for me.'

It was all the more wounding for being stated so matter-of-factly. Guilt knifed Serrah in the ribs. Her eyes were welling again. 'I'm . . . I'm so sorry. I did my best. I tried so very hard to –'

Eithne raised a hand to still her. 'I said I forgive you. But

I don't think I could again. Not if you don't do this. Sign that confession, Mother.'

Serrah was taken aback by the severe tone in her daughter's voice. It seemed out of character. Even in those terrible final weeks Eithne had been secretive rather than manipulative. Could her personality have been altered in some way? By the experience of death and rebirth? By some design on the Council's part? 'I need to gather myself, Eithne. I have to think about what you're saying.'

'What's there to *think* about? My time's running out, Mummy. You always did seesaw.'

'That's not true.'

'Just do it. Or do you want me to face death again?'

Something had been nagging Serrah, just beyond thought. It surfaced. 'If resurrection really is possible,' she said, 'why haven't they used it on Phosian? I mean, they couldn't have, could they? Otherwise I wouldn't be here.'

'I don't know anything about that,' Eithne replied after a pause. She sounded defensive. 'I think it might have something to do with the way a person died,' she added as an afterthought.

'A lethal wound, too much ramp; what's the difference? Dead's dead, isn't it?'

'I'm no expert on magic. I don't *care* how they did it.'

Serrah played her hunch. 'What do you think Rohan would have to say about this?'

'What?'

'Rohan. He'd have something to say, wouldn't he?'

Eithne was obviously perplexed but trying to hide it. 'I don't –'

'You do remember Rohan?'

'Of course! But what's he got to do with this?'

Serrah's heart was sinking. But she would see it

through. 'I think his opinion's important, don't you? Humour me.'

Her daughter sighed. 'I suppose . . . I suppose I'd expect him to say you were behaving foolishly by being so stubborn, and that you should do what's best for both of us.'

'And I'd expect you to say, "Don't be half-witted, Mother; real dogs can't talk. And Rohan's a *she*, not a he."' She glared at whatever was calling itself her child.

'You're confused.'

'I don't think so.'

'You're doubting me just because I couldn't remember the name of a *dog*?'

'An animal you were inseparable from all your childhood. Or rather, Eithne was. I don't know what you are, but you're not my daughter.'

'That's ridiculous. The beating's affected you. You're not seeing things straight.'

'You mean I'm not supposed to.'

'Look at me; I'm your daughter. How can you disown me, Mother?'

'Don't call me that. All I see is a fraud.'

'Sign the confession. Save us both.'

Serrah had ceased to believe in the illusion. 'I deny you,' she hissed.

The girl saw her expression. She began edging away. Serrah noticed that the door was slightly ajar.

They moved at the same time. Despite her aches, Serrah was faster. She caught the pretender by her arms. They struggled. Serrah loosed a hand, drew it back and delivered a hard slap across the girl's face. A tingling sensation suffused her hand, like transient pins and needles.

'You stupid *bitch*!' the impostor wailed. Her voice was changing, dropping to a lower pitch.

Transfixed by what was happening, Serrah let go of her.

It was as though a seething swarm of golden bees covered the girl's face. Then the myriad glimmering shards dispersed, flying out in all directions and dissolving.

A partial glamour, designed to enfold its host's face, and in this instance imitate a dead child. Advanced magic, worth a small fortune.

When the dazzle cleared, Serrah was facing a stranger. A plain woman, not a girl, and quite different to her daughter. Only her build matched. She looked frightened.

Serrah lunged at her. She met a blow to the abdomen. It knocked the wind out of her and rekindled the fire of her earlier thrashing. Gasping, she went to her knees.

The woman was through the door in a flash, slamming it behind her. Serrah scrambled to it and started hammering with her fists. She raged and cursed until her hands were bloody and her voice gave out.

At some point her passion spent itself. She had sunk to the floor, and remained there. The door was bloodstained from her pounding.

Now she hugged her knees to her chest and gently rocked. And due to her masters' deceit, grieved again. Physical brutality she might withstand. She didn't think she could take much more of their artifice.

For some while she had been staring at the top of the door frame. The cross-beam projected like a narrow shelf. If her smock was torn into strips and wound together, the makeshift rope could be looped over it. Then she just had to tie a noose, haul herself up, wriggle her head in and let go. There wasn't enough of a drop to snap her neck. It would be a slow choking. But even that seemed preferable to her present state.

Her trance was broken by noises outside the cell. They were coming for her again.

Serrah was halfway to standing when the door flew open.

It framed one of the men who had beaten and threatened her. His expression was unreadable. Serrah backed away, meeting the bed.

The man took two faltering steps in her direction. He stopped, swayed, then fell head-first. A dagger jutted between his shoulder-blades.

There were other people outside. Serrah blinked at them, bewildered, as they spilled in. Their faces appeared blank at first. She thought it must be more glamours to cheat her, then saw they wore fabric masks, quite crudely made.

'Who are you?' she challenged.

'Friends,' one of them responded crisply. 'Come on! We've no time!'

The thought that this might be her unit flashed through her mind. She soon realised it wasn't. 'Where are we –'

'Out of here.'

He took her arm. She winced as they bundled her into the corridor.

There were four of them. One went ahead, one took the rear; the other two stuck by her. They began moving down a long, low-ceilinged passageway. It was badly lit and the men at front and back activated soft illumination glamours.

She asked again, 'Who are you?'

'We've a way to go before we're out of here,' her escort told her, ignoring the question, 'and likely to meet opposition. Stay with us, keep moving.'

'Give me a blade,' she said.

'You're in no state.'

'If I have to defend myself I'll need it. You want me out of here, don't you?'

After a brief hesitation he passed her a long-bladed knife. Its cold, firm gravitas reassured her.

'Use it only if necessary,' he cautioned. '*We're* here to do the fighting.'

She shook loose their steadying hands and walked
unaided. They said nothing but stayed close to her. Hobbling
from her pains, Serrah had to work hard to keep pace.

They came to two bodies sprawled in their path; one a
warder, the other wearing a paladin's red tunic. That meant
real trouble. If it was possible to be in more.

Stepping over the corpses, they warily approached a
corner. Once round it they were in another passage, much
like the first but shorter. Three more masked rescuers lurked
at the end of it. Serrah's group hurried to them, and she
ached with the effort.

They were guarding the foot of a winding staircase. There
was a quick, whispered consultation. Then together they
started to ascend, weapons ready, with Serrah in the middle
of the pack.

Five or six turns brought them to another level. This
proved to be an axis of corridors, each following a point of
the compass. All looked empty. The party continued climbing.

The level above saw the end of the stairs and a single
passageway. It wasn't much more than a tunnel. With whispers and signals the one who seemed to be their leader
explained that the next stairwell was at its far end. By
drawing a finger across his throat he indicated that it was a
particularly dangerous stretch. As they began walking, she
saw why. Other corridors branched out from theirs, but at
oblique angles, meaning the mouths of several were blind
to them until they drew parallel. They crept past two such
without ambush.

As the stairs came into sight they found another body,
lying in a scarlet puddle. He was one of theirs, no doubt left
as a lookout. His mask had been pulled up to his hairline
and his body bore numerous wounds.

They all glanced around nervously. Serrah gripped the knife
tighter, her senses heightened. Twenty or thirty paces ahead

were two more side passages, one to their left, one to their right, almost facing each other. There was a flurry of hand-signalling among Serrah's party. Then they quietly spread out and began a slow advance. A pair of her unknown companions shadowed her, not touching but close enough to.

About halfway there, the pathfinder motioned a halt. He knelt and picked up a small piece of stone. This he pitched ahead of him. It landed mid-corridor, clattering.

The echo died. Nothing happened.

They decided on the simplest stratagem: a rush *en masse* for the stairs. The company readied themselves. Serrah's escorts looked ready to drag her if necessary. Their finger-tips brushed her arms, within grabbing distance.

The leader gave his sign and they started to run.

A dozen swift paces on, disaster struck.

Armed men poured from the tunnel mouths. Warders and militia mostly, with a smattering of paladins. Serrah reck-oned their number at above a dozen. At least half as many again as her side.

The rescuers' dash became an unplanned charge. They had no choice. The two groups' leading edges met. There were cries and clashes of steel.

Serrah allowed herself to be steered through the initial chaos. As the mob distilled into a series of separate fights, she shook free. Her escorts stayed close but their attention turned to the advancing melee. Whoever her mysterious allies were, they fought like maniacs.

The tide rolled in and Serrah found herself at the centre of the brawl. For a long moment, incredibly, it engaged everyone but her. She seemed to exist in a bubble, with duels raging on every side. Her abused body throbbed. She was sucked dry and disoriented. But all she felt was fury. Blistering resentment and hatred of her persecutors smothered any other thought.

She needed to kill something.

The battle had drawn her bodyguards away. As she moved, she heard one of them calling out to her. She ignored him and plunged into the scrum.

A blade scythed the air above her ducking head. Another cleared her ribs by a hairsbreadth. The twisting and dodging was excruciating. It didn't matter.

She picked a target. A stocky militiaman, fencing with a rescuer and getting the better of it. Serrah had no taste for honour or subtlety. She buried her knife in his back. As he went down she took his sword. Her victim's opponent turned away and piled into another foe.

One of the masked rescuers collapsed in front of her, his chest ribboned. She leapt over his corpse and into the path of a warder with a rapier in play. Deflecting a blow with the knife, she thrust her sword into his belly. Nearby, one of his comrades lost his footing on the dank flagstones and fell heavily. A masked rescuer impaled him, delivering his broadsword two-handed to the heart. Bathed in the catharsis of violence, Serrah looked for more trouble.

It found her. Moving with liquid agility, a paladin laid siege. He was a head taller than Serrah and powerfully built. Like her, he wielded sword and knife. Their legendary fighting skills and savagery made paladins opponents to be avoided at the best of times. But in the worst of times, and impelled by bloodlust, caution had no hold on Serrah.

Their swords collided. The strength behind the paladin's blow sent a spasm through Serrah's knotted arm muscles. She took a swipe at his face with the knife, forcing him back a pace. Swift as thought he retaliated, sending a downward slash that could have split her to the waist. She replied with a combination of jabs and swipes that briefly staved him off.

They joined again in a flurry of scathing passes and grating blades. It seemed his defence was impenetrable. Then with will and luck guiding her hand, Serrah battered through. He tried to block a side-swipe. Her momentum was too great and snapped his sword in two. The paladin brought up his knife. She evaded it and planted steel deep in his guts.

He slumped to his knees, mouth agape, eyes wide. Serrah drew back her sword and sliced into the side of his neck. Blood sprayed, the paladin toppled.

Breathing hard, she backed off and looked around. The frenzy was decreasing. Her allies had downed the last of the enemy and bodies littered the corridor. Two of them were rescuers. Several others had light injuries. Some of them were staring at her, but nobody said anything.

Healing salves were quickly pressed to wounds. One or two of the group broke small phials under their noses and inhaled restorative vapours. Then the signal went out to move on. This time, nobody offered to help her.

The depleted band reached the stairs and began to climb again. They ascended four more levels without incident, save for disturbing the odd rat. But they could hear sounds of pursuit from below and hurried their flight. The effort vexed Serrah's body. It felt like she had lava coursing through her veins.

Finally they arrived at a wide, high passageway marking ground level. The entrance was here, its robust doors standing open. A handful of masked men guarded it. Corpses of militia and paladins had been dragged to one side of the corridor. The guards eyed Serrah, but no questions were asked about their missing comrades.

'How does it look?' the leader of Serrah's group wanted to know.

'Our luck won't hold much longer,' one of the guards replied. 'We have to move now.'

The leader nodded and steered Serrah to the door. It was night outside and a fine rain was falling. He pointed to the massive wall opposite. Three thick ropes hung down it. 'Could you climb that?' he said.

'Yes.'

He held out a hand. 'Your weapons.'

Serrah tightened her hold on the blades and shook her head.

'How will you climb?'

Reluctantly, she gave him the sword and knife, and suddenly felt naked. He passed them back to his crew.

'Who are you?' she asked yet again.

'Now isn't the time. We'll explain when we're away from here.' He indicated one of his men. 'He'll go with you. The rest of us will be right behind. Just keep moving. Don't stop for anything.' He took her silence as assent and mustered the others.

'Go!' he barked.

Serrah and her attendant raced through the doors. The chill night air jolted her and she took an involuntary gulp. Rain lashed her face. Underfoot, the ground was spongy. She could hear the others thundering along behind.

Somebody shouted. She turned her head. A large party of armed men, including many paladins, was rushing at them from the corner of the building. They were yelling too.

'Keep moving!' the leader bellowed.

Serrah slammed into the wall and grasped a dangling rope. Her escort did the same. They began pulling themselves up, feet slipping for want of purchase on the wet walls.

An ear-shattering explosion rang out. There were flashes of light, brilliant as lightning. She looked down. Somebody was letting off magical munitions.

They detonated in great round clouds of green and red and gold, then spewed their deceptions. Grotesque beasts erupted, and dozens of chimera duplicates of the rescuers, designed to confuse.

'Look away!' her companion cried.

She understood and averted her eyes. A tremendously intense light bathed them, illuminating the wall brighter than full daylight before it flickered and died. An optical glamour. A light burst that blinded. She wondered which side had used it. Screams and other sounds of combat drifted up to them. They continued climbing.

The edifice seemed eternal. About two-thirds of the way up, Serrah's arms grew numb and her strength faltered. Her companion, keeping pace, urged her on. Something sliced the air and stilled his tongue. An arrow quivered in his back. Serrah reached out to him. He fell. A downward glance showed her his fate.

Mixed with phantasms and dazzlements, men were fighting in the grounds below. A couple of her rescuers had made it to the ropes and were hauling themselves up. She kept going, fearful of an arrow meant for her.

At length she arrived at a broad ledge topping the wall, fighting for breath as she dragged herself onto it. She crawled to the far side and looked down. Three more ropes hung on the outside of the wall, tied to a segment of crenellation on the ledge. In a side street directly below, a hay wagon had been parked, full of stuffed sacks. Two masked men looked up at her and gestured furiously.

A whoomp and crackle sounded to her rear. In the palace grounds a geyser of purplish smog billowed high. As she watched, it took on the form of a gigantic red dragon, tall as a temple tower, its green eyes ablaze, spiked tail lashing. A glamour, though the fire it breathed was real enough. She saw men engulfed in flame. But the ones on the ropes were still coming, despite arrows clacking all around.

Serrah crossed the ledge and began lowering herself to the street. All she could think about was getting away, and of her revulsion at being so completely at the mercy of others.

In that moment she vowed it would never happen again.
When she had scrambled about halfway down, she let go of
the rope and dropped.

She landed heavily but unharmed on the pile of sacks.
One of the waiting men moved to take her arm. She dodged
him and jumped from the wagon. Then she ran. They shouted
after her.

Serrah discounted her pains and ran faster still. Perhaps
they tried following, she never knew. Soon she was in a
maze of bustling lanes.

Barefoot, smock tattered and bloodstained, wet hair plastered to her forehead, she limped into streets where nobody
stared.

6

Rain lashed Bhealfa's eastern region all through the night. But dawn broke sunny and clement.

Kutch Pirathon sat by a swollen brook, idly lobbing pebbles into the rushing water. He was growing restive. For the hundredth time he glanced at the tumbledown stone cottage further up the barren hill. Its ill-fitting door remained resolutely closed.

He sighed and continued bombarding the stream. There was little else to do. The hillside had nothing to offer but dripping scrub, a few withered trees and a lot of rocks. His only company was a brace of circling crows.

In truth, he could have employed himself gainfully. He was obliged to, in fact. More than obliged; bound by an oath. He should be undertaking the mental exercises necessary to advance in the Craft. His time was supposed to be spent honing his will, recognising the vital currents and channelling them. But they were techniques taught to him by his master and he couldn't focus properly for thinking about the old man. There was no shaking off the feeling that he had let Domex down, that he might still be here if it hadn't been for his timidity. Neglect of duty

added to his guilt. Yet, for the moment, his heart wasn't
in it.

His melancholy would have deepened had the door of the
cottage not creaked open. He looked up to see Caldason
emerging. Flinging the last of the stones at the stream,
Kutch stood and dusted off his breeches. He watched as the
Qalochian addressed a few last words to the elderly hermit
he'd consulted. Then he waited as he made his way down
the crude path to him.

During their short acquaintance, Kutch had found that
Caldason wasn't one to volunteer information. Nor was he
easy to read. Now was no exception.

'What happened?' Kutch asked.

'Nothing.'

'Oh.'

'But you weren't to know he couldn't help. I'm grateful
for you bringing me here.'

They began their descent.

Kutch still didn't know what Caldason's problem was,
beyond the so-called fits. He tried fishing. 'Did he, er, say
anything at all about your . . . condition?'

'He didn't *say* anything. He wrote his questions on a slate.'

'Ah, yes. Of course.'

'Is he naturally dumb?'

'No. When he was a boy, his father cut his tongue out. To
stop him talking about the mysteries of the Craft. It was the
kind of thing they used to do in those days.'

'The world's just full of delights,' Caldason remarked cynically.

'His father would have had it done too, by *his* father. The
knowledge was passed down, generation to generation, and
that was the price. It was considered normal in some branches
of the Craft until not that long ago.'

'I thought magicians were constrained by secrecy anyway.'

'True. Though I'm not sure how reliable some of the licensed ones are.' Kutch jabbed a thumb at the hovel. 'But he can be trusted.'

'So why did they go in for mutilation?'

'It was extra insurance. Some of the older practitioners think it was a good thing and should be brought back. Maybe they've got a point. It seemed to work.'

'You wouldn't have minded your master doing it to you then?'

'Well . . .'

They continued in silence.

After a few minutes, Kutch ventured, 'You don't seem disappointed. About him not being able to help, I mean.'

'I've learnt not to be.'

'There are other seers I can recommend.'

'Maybe provincial sorcerers aren't up to what I need.'

'A lot of them are as good as any you'll find,' Kutch replied indignantly. 'They just prefer the solitude of the countryside. They're less likely to get harassed by the authorities too.'

'Like Domex? All right, low blow. Sorry. But the fact is there's more money and status in the cities, and that tends to attract the best talent. Perhaps that's where I'll find the right magician. If there are any left I haven't already tried.'

'Come on, Reeth, there must be *thousands* of them.'

'I've been searching longer than you know.'

Kutch didn't expect any expansion on that and was proved right. Silence descended again. They reached the foot of the hill and struck out for the house. A gentle wind ruffled the trees.

The quiet was broken only by distant birdsong.

At length, Caldason said, 'So, how far advanced in magic are you?'

After yesterday's display with the homunculi, Kutch reckoned his companion already knew the answer to that. It was

Caldason's way of changing the subject, or being polite. But he played along with it. 'Fourth level, going on fifth.'

'Sounds impressive. Out of how many?'

'Sixty-two.'

'Right.'

'Mind you,' Kutch quickly added, 'anything above twenty-three's considered pretty rarefied.'

'I think I must need the highest possible level.'

Caldason's expression was inscrutable. It was difficult to tell if he was serious or making an uncommon attempt at humour.

'I may have a way to go in my practical studies,' Kutch admitted, 'but I do understand something about occult philosophy. Whatever ails you should have a magical remedy. It's just a case of finding it.'

'I'm not so sure of that.'

'Let me tell you about one of the Craft's basic principles.'

'Careful, you don't want to lose your tongue.'

'It's not really giving anything away. We're taught that magic is energy, and energy can't be destroyed. It can only be converted into something else.'

'That much I've heard.'

'Then you'll know that spells vary in quality and durability.'

'Of course. That's what determines their price.'

'I'm not talking about their coin value. I'm referring to their strength. For example, there's no reason why a building couldn't be a glamour, and last forever. But creating and maintaining it would be incredibly expensive.' He pointed to a boulder at the side of the track. 'That rock could be a glamour. It would only take a simple spell. Except nobody would bother. What would be the point?'

'What are you getting at?'

'I'm guessing that what's wrong with you is magical in

origin.' Caldason gave no hint that Kutch was right. The youth carried on. 'If you are under some kind of enchantment, it should be possible to convert its energy from malignant positive to benign negative. In the same way that the rock could become non-rock or the building cease to be and rejoin the energy pool. At least, that's the theory.'

Caldason looked thoughtful. 'You put it better than most other magicians I've spoken to, Kutch. But why haven't any of them been able to do it?'

Kutch felt a glow at the compliment. He also took the Qalochian's words as tacit confirmation that his problem *was* magical. 'I don't know. Maybe the spell, if it *is* a spell we're talking about, is especially powerful. Or the result of some really esoteric branch of the Craft. There are many different disciplines, you know.'

'Something rare enough to be unknown to most sorcerers, you mean?'

'It might be. Or it could be a question of balance.'

'Balance?'

'Another cardinal law of magic. The Craft has rules just like the mundane world, as we call it. For instance, drop a stone and it falls to the ground. It's obeying a rule. A glamour looking like a stone might fall upwards, or fly, or mutate into something else. But it would still be following a rule; one dictated by the type of spell governing it.'

'I don't see where balance comes in.'

'My master would have said that a real stone falls because of the balance between our expectation and experience. We expect the stone to fall. Stones have always fallen. So the stone falls. In magic the balance is between reality and unreality. There has to be symmetry for the spell to work. The same way the military and magical balance between Rintarah and Gath Tampoor stops one empire overcoming the other.'

'I think I almost understand that,' Caldason said. 'But how does it apply to me?'

'Maybe you're caught too tightly between the real and the unreal. As if you were in a clamp.'

'Like Bhealfa.'

Kutch smiled. 'Yes. Or it could be that the balance is out of kilter, blocking rescue.'

'Neither seems a comforting thought.' If Caldason resented learning from someone so much younger, he had the grace not to show it. 'Ironic that it should take a humble fourth level . . .'

'Nearly a fifth.'

'. . . practically a fifth level apprentice to make it clear to me.'

'I've not told you anything you couldn't have found out for yourself. You look for a solution in magic, Reeth, but take little interest in its workings.'

'I see it as a malevolent force.'

'It's the foundation of our culture.'

'Yours, not mine. Not Qalochian. For you, magic is a needful, benevolent thing. To me it's deceiving and pernicious. It helps maintain injustice.'

To Kutch that seemed close to blasphemous. 'My master always said that magic has no morality, any more than the weather does. The people who command it decide if it's light or dark, as suits their purpose. Your argument should be with them.'

Caldason's severity mellowed a little. 'I grant there's wisdom in that. But if there was no magic the temptation wouldn't exist.'

'I intend using my skills only for good.'

'I don't doubt it. And when you speak on the subject you show more passion and insight than you do about anything else. You shed the half-child and talk more like a man.'

The youth's cheeks coloured, underlining the point.

'I can see magic's your calling,' Caldason added. 'But who can say what enticements the future might bring?'

Kutch tried steering back to the issue he thought more important. 'Tell me what's wrong. I'm not advanced enough to help, I know that, but I'd be better armed to find you somebody who could.'

'What I suffer from tends to . . . trouble people.'

'It wouldn't vex me. Together, we could –'

'*No*. I don't form attachments. I've no need of them. Anyway, I have to move on, you know that.'

Kutch was disappointed, but knew the futility of arguing with the man. 'You'll not go before my master's funeral?'

'I promised you I wouldn't. But let's make haste, I want to be out of these parts today.'

They pushed on, exchanging few further words.

Twenty minutes later they reached a wood. This they skirted, their journey taking them by the cultivated fields that served the village. A handful of farmers tended the fledgling crops. Though none of them acknowledged their passing, the duo had the distinct feeling of being watched. Beyond the meadows the hamlet itself came into sight, nestled prettily in the palm of a shallow valley. Even from this distance the indigo power line that slashed through the settlement could be plainly seen.

But the village wasn't their destination. When the path forked they took the coastal road. A short climb brought them to the cliff's edge. Beyond its rim and far below lay a vast expanse of calm, shimmering ocean.

On the grassy ribbon of land running to the lip of the cliff stood a funeral pyre and atop it lay the seer Domex, resplendent in the robes of his calling, hands crossed on his chest. Paraphernalia was heaped about his body – a grimoire, journals and scrolls, pouches of herbs and a sceptre were among the personal belongings that would accompany him to the next world.

The whole of the pyre was encased in a glistening, transparent half bubble, rainbow-hued like an oil and water mix.

Kutch's first act was to remove the protective barrier. He took a small, flat runestone from his belt pouch and approached the pyre. Mouthing a barely audible incantation, he placed the stone against the bubble. The magical shield soundlessly discharged itself into non-being.

He looked around. The cliff-top was deserted, as were the modest hills on either side. 'No mourners,' he said, his voice catching. 'I'd hoped somebody would turn up, given how much he did to help the people hereabouts.'

'I expect they were too afraid to come because of the circumstances of his death,' Caldason told him. 'Don't be too hard on them.'

Kutch nodded. He dug into his pouch again and brought out a sheet of parchment. His hands trembled slightly as he unfolded it. 'There are some words that need to be spoken,' he explained.

'Of course.'

Falteringly, and in a soft tone, the apprentice began reading his lament in the old tongue. When he stumbled over a particular phrase, eyes brimming, just a boy after all, Caldason laid a hand on his heaving shoulder. It seemed to strengthen Kutch and he carried on more or less evenly.

What was being said meant nothing to Caldason, though somehow its rhythm and feeling conveyed something of its poignancy to him. His gaze went to the horizon and he contemplated the scurrying clouds and distant sea-birds.

At last the dirge was over. Kutch screwed up the parchment and tossed it onto the pyre.

After what he thought was a decent interval, Caldason asked, 'How do we apply the flame?'

'I have to do it,' Kutch sniffed, 'and it has to be kindled using the Craft.' He gave the Qalochian a shy, lopsided grin. 'I've been a bit worried about that bit.'

'You'll be fine.'

'Right.' He cleared his throat noisily and straightened. Caldason took a step back to give him room.

Kutch started some kind of low-throated chant, attended with a series of increasingly complex hand gestures. He gazed at the pyre intently, brow creased. At first his utterances and movements were uncertain, then his confidence visibly grew and his voice rose.

All at once the wood stack and corpse were bathed in dazzling white light. Flames erupted, burning with unnatural, magic-fuelled intensity. The pyre blazed.

'Well done,' Caldason said.

They stood together for some time, watching the fire do its work.

Then Caldason gently tugged at Kutch's arm. The youth turned and looked to where Reeth was pointing.

On the top of an adjacent hill stood a lone figure, staring down at them. The distance was too great to make out much detail, but they could see he was an older, distinguished looking man. His tailored white robe was of a quality denoting rank. The wind ruffled his three-quarter length cape. His posture was straight and proud, his expression sombre.

'Any idea who that is?' Caldason wanted to know.

Kutch blinked at the stranger. 'No, I don't think I've seen him before. Perhaps he's someone who owed Domex a debt of gratitude.'

'It seems your master wasn't forgotten after all.'

They watched the figure for a while, then returned their attention to the blaze, its heat stinging their faces. When Caldason looked again a moment later, the stranger was gone.

The pyre roared and crackled, belching thick, inky smoke.

Mesmerised by the sight, Kutch fell into a reflective mood. 'You know, if my master had lived I really think he might have been able to help you.'

'Perhaps.'

'I'll never forgive myself for my cowardice, Reeth.'

'I thought we agreed you weren't to blame,' Caldason replied firmly. 'There's no way you could have stood against his killers, get that into your head.'

'I'm trying to. It isn't easy. I keep thinking that if only I'd –'

Caldason raised a hand to quiet him. 'That's enough. Don't sully the moment with regrets. They serve no purpose, believe me.'

'I still think he could have done something for you. He was a great man, Reeth.'

'I have a feeling I need the kind of help I'll never be able to find.'

'Who's being a doubter now?'

They both wrapped themselves in their own thoughts then.

The warmth sent ash and cinders billowing above the pyre. Orange sparks danced in the smoke.

'*Phoenix*,' Kutch whispered, half in reverie.

'What was that?'

'Phoenix,' he repeated, as though it were some kind of epiphany.

'I don't –'

'Why didn't I think of it before?'

'What the hell are you talking about, Kutch?'

'Covenant, of course. Don't you see? If anybody can help you, they can!'

'Covenant's a myth. A story mothers tell to frighten their sucklings.'

'My master didn't think so.'

'He was wrong. They don't exist.'

A succession of noisy pops and cracks issued from the pyre as it consumed wood and bone.

'They do, Reeth,' Kutch insisted, eyes shining, 'and I'm going to prove it to you.'

7

They saw a bird, flying low and fast, wings beating frantically. It had the shape and size of a raven, but was betrayed by its colour; a burnished silver that made their eyes ache. In an instant it was gone, lost to sight among trees and rolling hills in the direction of the hamlet.

Caldason and the boy dismissed it.

Kutch took up the thread as they tramped on. 'My master was adamant on the subject,' he persisted. 'He said Covenant was real and I believe him.'

'Real once,' Caldason allowed. 'But they were suppressed. A long time ago.'

'They tried to stamp them out, yes. Some escaped and Covenant grew again.'

'Well, I've never met a member.'

'That doesn't mean they don't exist!'

'I'm not trying to pick an argument with you, Kutch. If Domex told you they're still around, fine. But what makes you think a bunch of unlicensed sorcerers could help me?'

'Because they're much more than that. Some say their magic's a strain that goes back to the time of the Founders themselves.'

Caldason didn't reply. His silence could have been thoughtful, or it might have been disbelieving. Kutch couldn't tell.

Far behind them now, a column of whitish smoke rose lazily from the cliff-top pyre. Kutch glanced back at it. His shoulders sagged, and a host of cares pinched his features.

'What do you know about their leader?' Caldason asked, perhaps to distract him.

'Phoenix?' Kutch bucked up a little. 'Probably no more than you've heard yourself. You know; that he, or she, is somebody with great skill in the Craft, and can't be caught. Can't be killed either.'

'How can that be?' Caldason said, real interest in his eyes.

'What does it matter? The important thing is that Covenant could be your best chance of aid. They don't just have the magic, Reeth. They're patriots, and they oppose Gath Tampoor. Which means they're a thorn in the paladins' side. Makes you natural allies, I'd say.'

Caldason's expression hardened. 'You know what I think about allies. And I'm no patriot. Not as far as Bhealfa's concerned anyway.'

The ground began to level. They were in sight of the hamlet's outlying buildings.

'You should go and find them,' Kutch ventured.

'Where?'

'Valdarr.'

'Do you know where in Valdarr?'

'No . . . no, I don't. But it's the biggest city. It makes sense Covenant would be there, doesn't it? We could –'

'There's no *we*, and you're just guessing they can be found there. If I go looking for Covenant, I'll be doing it by myself.'

'Why can't I come with you?' the boy pleaded.

'I've *told* you. I travel alone.'

'I wouldn't get in your way, and I can shift for myself.'

'No. People around me tend to end up dying.'

'I know it'd be dangerous, with you an outlaw and all, *and* a Qalochian, but –'

'They don't just die the way you think. There's ways other than violently.'

Kutch didn't understand. But they'd reached the edge of his settlement, putting their conversation on hold. 'This is a quicker way to the house,' he announced morosely, leading Caldason into a side street.

The street became an alley, darkened by overhanging upper storeys of houses. It narrowed, twisted, intersected other byways, all deserted. Then they turned into a downward-sloping, cobbled lane, lined to the right by stables, to the left by mean cottages.

Twenty or thirty paces ahead, with his back to them, someone walked briskly in the same direction they were heading.

'It's him,' Kutch whispered. 'The man at the funeral.'

Caldason regarded the figure and nodded, adding, 'He takes risks.'

'How?'

'He's far from young, and by the cut of his clothes, moneyed. Yet no sign of bodyguards.'

'He has protection. There's a defensive shield around him. Good quality, too.'

'Damned if I can see it, Kutch.'

'You have to know how to look. Come on, let's talk to him.'

Reeth caught his arm. 'Why?'

'Aren't you curious to know who he is?'

'Not greatly. If a man looks like a threat, or like somebody who could help me, I'm curious. I doubt he's either.'

'He was the only one at my master's funeral apart from us.' Kutch shook loose his arm. 'I'd like to know why.'

Reeth shrugged. 'All right. But I'm not for lingering, remember.'

They quickened their pace.

Kutch was right. As they approached, Caldason spotted an indistinct sheath of agitated air, a finger's span deep, enveloping the stranger's body. It shimmered like a heat haze.

The man heard their footfalls, stopped and turned. The questioning look on his distinguished, grey-maned features mutated into apprehension.

Kutch stretched his hands placatingly, palms up. 'We mean you no harm!'

Tensely, the stranger retreated a step or two, staring at them but saying nothing.

Reeth glanced around. 'This isn't right.'

'What isn't?' Kutch asked. 'What's wrong?'

'You have to know how to look,' Caldason replied dryly.

Something fell into their field of vision, a blur of glistening silver.

The fraudulent bird they had glimpsed earlier descended with wings fluttering languorously. Time seemed to slow to a glacial pace as it came to rest on the stranger's outstretched arm. There was a flurry of radiant feathers. The creature's eyes, vivid crimson, fixed upon him.

'*Treachery!*' the bird screeched.

Then it raised its wings as though to take off. Instead it soundlessly imploded, crushing to a tiny ball of pulsing brilliance that immediately consumed itself.

Blinking, the stranger assumed the pair facing him were the object of the warning. He made to run.

'No!' Kutch shouted, still dazed. 'We don't want to hurt you!'

Caldason's attention hadn't been on the glamour or the stranger. He was scanning the doorways and stables. Face hard, gaze intense, he began drawing his sword.

Kutch noticed. He managed a puzzled, 'What –?' before he saw why.

Men were emerging from dingy stables and out of shadowed nooks. There were a good half-dozen of them, and if there was any doubt about their intent, the blades in their hands dispelled it.

All but one had a look Caldason had seen many times. The mark of predators. Street pirates. Men who killed for coin, or for the sport of it. The exception appeared to be unarmed and his garb was less martial. Unlike the others, he wore a cloak, and held a staff too short for a weapon, embellished in gold.

Fanning out, the brigands moved to surround the trio. The man Kutch and Reeth had been following seemed more self-possessed, but still suspicious of the pair's allegiance. He looked from them to the encircling ambushers, then back again, undecided.

Ever watchful, Caldason reached over his shoulder and slowly unsheathed his second blade.

As he freed it there was a flash of fierce white light.

It lasted no more than a second but dazzled them all. Fiery motes in his eyes, Caldason found its source. The unsuitably dressed brigand had his ornate staff in a raised hand. He was pointing it at the elderly stranger.

Kutch cried out something unintelligible. Reeth saw that the stranger now stood unprotected. His buffer of magic was gone, the radiant bubble had dispersed.

A negating glamour. Caldason hoped they didn't have anything worse.

One of the ambushers on the right began to move their way, sword raised. A bandit on the opposite side did the same. The rest stood their ground.

Caldason shoved Kutch hard, propelling him towards the stranger. The boy exclaimed, stumbled, almost collided with the old man.

'*Stay!*' Caldason snapped, as though commanding a dog. Then the pincer closed on him.

He remained perfectly still, immobile as a rock. Kutch, watching fear-flushed, unbelieving, saw that Caldason's eyes were shut, and that he looked incongruously serene. But that lasted only a second, before the waves struck.

A sword in each hand, he parried both incomers, side-on, blocking expertly to the right and left. Then he swung out and round to face the pair.

They engaged him again instantly. Four blades rent the air. Steel clamoured in earnest as the three of them enacted that lissome dance, old as malice, which could only end in death.

At first it seemed to Kutch that Reeth did no more than hold the attackers at bay. But he soon realised his error. Caldason was deploying a strategy. For although they attacked him with equal ferocity, his response was two-tiered. The man on his right he held off. The one to the left, he fought. As they jockeyed to challenge him, his blades flashed from one to the other; defensive to offensive, soft to hard.

When it happened, it was quick and brutal. From the storm's eye, Caldason lashed out at the man he'd worn down. To those looking on it was as though he quickly wiped his blade across the brigand's chest. But the gash was deep. It liberated a cataract of blood. The victim made a sound, part outcry, part groan of pain, and let slip his sword. He swayed, then fell, broken.

It was the only sound any of them had made. Kutch was struck by how strange that seemed; no words exchanged, no shouted challenges or muttered threats. Just silence, save grunts of effort and clashing steel. It seemed the assassins plied their trade gravely and had no need of discourse.

Now there was general movement. As Caldason took on his other opponent, a fresh brigand waded in to join the fight. And Kutch had his own troubles. Two bandits were coming towards him and the stranger. The last of the band, his magic-eating staff marking him out as a sorcerer rather than a combatant, held back.

Kutch and the stranger instinctively moved closer together. 'It's me they want,' the old man hissed.

It was the first thing he'd said and it made the boy start. But Kutch had no time to respond. Their assailants were a sword stretch away and closing the gap. The stranger tossed back his cloak and jerked a pair of daggers from his belt. But he didn't have the look of a fighting man, and their enemies had superior reach and numbers. The assassins smiled. Prickling with sweat, Kutch tried to clear his mind of all but the Craft.

Caldason was delivering a righteous blow when his third attacker lumbered in. The newcomer, full-bearded, beefy, swung a two-handed axe. Caldason avoided the stroke, flowing beneath it, and countered with a wide, cutting sweep. It would have ribboned the axe-man if he hadn't tottered backwards from its path. In retreat he nearly fell across the body of the accomplice Reeth had killed.

The Qalochian's other opponent was nimbler. He favoured a sabre, and came in swift and lean, swiping like a barbcat. Reeth dodged the pass and commenced trading blows. Then the axe-man rejoined the fray and it was back to hacking at both.

Kutch and the stranger eyed their circling foes and tensed for the onslaught. It came suddenly when one of the thugs lunged, targeting the old man. Showing unexpected agility, the stranger side-stepped the charge, and managed a curving slash of his knives in answer. That sent the brigand into retreat. But his crony, a scabrous, gangling individual, slid in to menace Kutch. The boy recoiled, all the while trying not to garble an incantation he was murmuring under his breath.

The stranger grasped Kutch's sleeve and pulled him closer. As one, they backed off, the stranger brandishing his daggers at the advancing bandits as though they really were a remedy against swords.

They took three paces before their backs met a rough brick wall. Pressed against it, the stranger held out his knives in an imperfect display of boldness. Next to him, Kutch continued his muttered chant, and began to make small movements with shaking hands. The bandits gloated.

Abruptly, a swarm of minute lights materialised, like luminous grains of sand. They swirled about Kutch and the stranger, then as quickly vanished, replaced by a misty luminescence that girdled man and boy. The bandits' murderous leers turned to frowns. Wary, they held back.

On the principle of downing the biggest adversary first, Caldason fended off the leaner of his two opponents and concentrated on defeating the burly axe-man, showering him with weighty blows.

Several were blocked, glancing off the axe's cutter or its sturdy wooden haft. Others whistled close to the thug's bobbing head. Then Caldason saw his chance.

The blow he got through was savage. It shattered the axe-man's skull, immediately felling him.

Even as the assassin went down, his companion darted in, bent on reprisal. Caldason swung round to meet him. There was a swift, frenetic exchange. It was broken by Caldason deftly catching the bandit's sword between his pair of blades. The assassin struggled to free it, teeth bared with effort, muscles knotted. Reeth's hold was like a clamp. Sharply, he twisted the hilts of his swords, turning the man's wrists painfully. Another jerk wrenched the blade from his grip. It flipped, pirouetted, went clattering on cobblestones.

The ambusher stood with empty hands, confounded, mouth slack. It was a transient state. Reeth's swords blurred.

Two strokes, right then left, carved his foe's chest. For a breath the man stood, perplexed, a scarlet cross growing on his grubby shirt front. As he went down, Caldason was turning from him.

Reeth saw Kutch and the elderly stranger wrapped in a glittery mantle that flickered and faltered. The two remaining bandits were crowding them, weapons levelled. But now their attention was divided between their prey and Caldason, and what he'd just done to their comrades.

He quickly cleared the separating distance. The bandits turned to meet him, their intended victims forgotten. Blades clashed, pealing, as Caldason braved the scything steel and matched them blow for blow, repaying in kind. For infinite seconds the flurry of swordplay saw neither side gaining. Then Caldason realised a flaw in one of their defences. Every time the man attacking from the right delivered a stroke, he let down his guard. Just for a heartbeat.

Swerving to avoid a pass, Reeth struck out at the man to his left, warding him off. A swift turn brought him back to the right and he rammed home his blade. It ploughed through ribs and viscera.

The sword point erupted from the thug's back. Blood flecked Kutch and the stranger huddled behind him, proving their protective shield useless. The old man ran the ball of a fist across his eyes to wipe away the gore. Shaken, Kutch felt embarrassment mingling with the fear; shame that his magical skill had turned out to be so ineffective. Concentration shot, he let his mental hold slip. The shield melted into filmy wisps and dissolved.

Caldason wrenched his blade free, letting the corpse drop. The last brigand charged at the Qalochian, bellowing, his sword carving a path. Reeth side-stepped, dodging the full force of the swing. But he didn't avoid it entirely. The rapier's tip gouged his left arm from wrist to crook. Reeth's sword was dashed from his hand. His tattered sleeve welled red.

Kutch's intake of breath was audible.

The wound didn't hinder Reeth. He barged the man side-on, striking his shoulder with enough force to knock his next blow off course. Then he set to with his remaining sword, battering unmercifully. The bandit's resistance grew shambolic. Reeth upset it terminally with a boot to the groin, and what was left of the assassin's guard crumbled.

Reeth took the gap and forced home his blade. Its trajectory saw it through flesh and into his mark's heart. Lifeless, the bandit fell.

Caldason turned from the carnage, looking to Kutch and the stranger. They were ashen.

Half a moment of numb silence held sway. It was Kutch who shattered it.

'Reeth!' he exclaimed, pointing in the direction of the stables.

They had forgotten the final ambusher, the one they assumed was a sorcerer. He stood further along the lane, in semi-shadow, but near enough for them to see his anxious expression. One end of the wand in his hand spewed a thick stream of tawny-coloured smoke. Instead of dispersing, the smoke was being drawn to the wand-bearer and wrapping itself about his body. Dense tendrils enfolded him from feet to waist and were rapidly spreading up his chest.

Caldason snatched one of the stranger's daggers. He spun and lobbed it the sorcerer's way. Even as it flew the yellow smoke had all but enveloped the knife's target. As the last wisp covered the crown of the sorcerer's head, the cloak of fog immediately solidified and turned translucent. The soaring blade struck the magical buffer and bounced off impotently.

At once the sorcerer turned and started to run. The stolen

shield made it seem as though a thin layer of lustrous, flexible ice encased him. Just as it had when its original owner wore it.

'Let him go,' the stranger urged.

For all the interest Caldason showed in giving chase, he needn't have bothered; and Kutch had still to conquer his trembling. They watched the survivor flee, arms pumping, cape billowing. Fifty paces on he rounded a corner and disappeared from sight.

The trio regarded each other.

'Your arm . . .' Kutch said.

Caldason glanced at his dripping limb. He pressed a wad of torn shirt over the wound, apparently unconcerned. 'It's nothing.'

The stranger spoke, his voice hoarse. 'Thank you. Thank you both.'

Kutch was dispirited. 'I did little enough,' he sighed. 'So much for my skill with the Craft.'

'You tried,' Caldason told him. 'That does you credit.'

The boy nodded, unconvinced, and addressed the stranger. 'Who *are* you? What were you doing at my master's funeral? Who were those –'

'There's no time for that now,' Caldason interrupted. 'If we loiter here we'll have the Watch to contend with.' He fixed his sights on the stranger. 'Which I imagine is something you'd rather avoid.'

'Your friend's right,' the old man confirmed softly, directing himself to Kutch. 'I'll explain everything. But it'd be best not to be found in these circumstances.'

Caldason bent to the nearest body and wiped his soiled blades on the man's jerkin. Then he rose and re-sheathed the weapons.

'Move,' he ordered, grasping the stranger's arm.

They hurried from the lane and its litter of corpses.

8

As far as they could tell, no one saw them arrive at Domex's run-down house.

Kutch fished a large iron key from the folds of his shirt and fumbled with it. Once the rusty lock was turned, Caldason unceremoniously kicked the door open. Bundling Kutch and the stranger inside, he shot the bolts.

'Windows!' he snapped.

Kutch went to draw the blinds. He was pale and unsteady. The stranger seemed calmer. He studied Reeth closely, tight-lipped, his gaze shrewd. But he held his peace. Caldason shoved him, not too gently, in the direction of the main room.

With daylight barred, save for tiny chinks in the tattered drapes, the chamber was gloomy and oppressive. Kutch lit a lamp. Cupping the taper with a trembling hand, he moved to the fireplace and applied the flame to the candles in a pair of bulky lead holders on the mantelpiece. Shadows played on the tattered spines of the books lining the walls.

'Now sit,' Caldason said.

'You're still treating me like a dog,' Kutch complained, but did as he was told.

The Qalochian looked to the old man. 'You, too.' He pushed against the small of his back again, driving him towards an overstuffed chair. The stranger plumped into it, sighing. Dust motes swirled in the candlelight.

Even up close his age was hard to guess. He was certainly of advanced years, but more autumn than winter. It was his careworn appearance that made him seem older. Worry lines crimped his beardless face. His silvered hair, grown perhaps a mite too long for his age, gave him a venerable appearance. He dressed affluently.

When he spoke, his tone was easier, almost dulcet. 'I owe my thanks to you both, and an explanation.'

'You owe me nothing,' Caldason replied brusquely. 'I don't much care who you are or what problems you might have.'

'Yet you risked your life for me.'

'I had no choice.'

The stranger scrutinised him. 'I think there was more to it than that,' he said gently.

'Think what you like. *My* thought is that you've involved me in your troubles, and likely there's more on the way. It'd be best to get out of here and not linger over it.'

'I agree leaving would be wise. But word of their failure will take a while to get back to their masters. I don't believe they'll send more against me at this point. In any event, it's not how they work.'

'They?'

'Our rulers.'

'The government?' Kutch piped up, wide-eyed.

The stranger nodded.

'Who *are* you?' the boy asked.

'My name is Dulian Karr.'

Kutch straightened. '*Patrician* Karr?'

'You're well informed.'

'Everyone's heard of *you*.'

'What's an Elders Council member doing in a place like this?' Caldason said. He was at a window, watching the path outside, curtain bunched in his fist. Now he let the drape fall back.

Once more, Karr studied him. 'You have the advantage of me. You know my name, but –'

'He's Reeth Caldason!' Kutch butted in, adding knowingly, 'The *outlaw*.'

If the patrician was jarred, he didn't show it.

It was Caldason who reacted. 'You're privy to my business only by chance, boy. I'll thank you to keep it to yourself.'

The words were like a bolt to Kutch's breast. Reddening under Caldason's frigid gaze, he began an apology that faltered and trailed off. A brittle silence took hold.

'And you must be Kutch Pirathon,' Dulian Karr interjected, taking pity.

They stared at him.

Kutch stumbled through, 'How did you know that?'

'Grentor Domex was one of my oldest friends. He often spoke of you. I had no idea when I came here that he was dead.'

'All right.' Caldason showed his palms like a man surrendering. 'I can see we're not going to escape your life story. Just keep it brief.'

The suddenly lighter tone, typical of Reeth's mercurial nature, Kutch was starting to think, made the apprentice feel a little better about the scolding. 'So, why did you come to see my master?'

'And why no bodyguards?' Caldason added.

'I had a phalanx of them when I set out. Good men, every one. My enemies thinned their ranks until I alone remained. That was why my would-be assassins were armed with no magic worse than a negating glamour.'

'Yet still you came.'

'As still you defended me. And for a similar reason, I suspect; I had to.'

Caldason said nothing. He leaned against the dusty table's edge, arms folded.

'As to why I came here . . . Many years ago, a group of like-minded individuals, Grentor and myself included, joined in a common cause. Our passion was to see true sovereignty restored to Bhealfa. To have genuine freedom, not the pretence of it, by getting our tormentors off our backs.'

'Fine words.' It was impossible to tell if Caldason meant that cynically.

Karr disregarded it. 'We were young and idealistic I suppose, but that made the object of our anger no less real. In due course we each took the path we thought best to achieve our aim. I chose politics and talking us to liberation.' He smiled thinly. 'Others favoured the military, a mercantile life, even banditry, and some fell along the way. Your master carried on being what he always was, Kutch: a maverick. What is it they say? A square shaft in a round hole. But I'm damned if I know which of us has been the more effective.' A fleeting reverie clouded his eyes. He gathered himself and went on, 'I came here with news of the progress of . . . a scheme. A plan Domex helped conceive and steer over the years.'

'You had to come personally?' Caldason said.

'Few others could be trusted with my report. And I wanted to see him; it had been too long.'

'What is this plan?'

'Forgive me. It's a confidence I can't share.'

'So why mention it at all?'

'You saved my life. That warrants some measure of trust.'

Caldason shrugged dismissively.

Kutch had fallen quiet during their exchange. Caldason noticed his crestfallen expression. 'What's the matter?'

'I'm hearing about a side of my master I never suspected. I mean, I knew he had no love for the state. Now it turns out he was involved in something big. Something *important*. But . . . I didn't know. He never told me about any of this.'

'It was for your own protection,' Karr replied, 'on the principle that what you didn't know couldn't endanger you. Domex was engaged in a selfless purpose. That's why they killed him, whatever pretext they may have used. Have no doubts about that. You've every reason to be proud of him, Kutch.'

The boy swallowed the lump in his throat and nodded. 'Is it because of this plan of yours that the government wants you dead?'

'Perhaps. I don't fool myself that they're entirely ignorant of it. There are informers and spies enough in the dissident ranks.'

'That messenger glamour in the likeness of a bird. It was sent to warn you of the attack?'

'Yes, by associates in Valdarr. I could have wished it had arrived earlier! There's treachery in my circle, and lately near to hand. But I think it more probable this latest attempt on my life was because I'm a general thorn in the authorities' side. My death at the hands of apparently common brigands would suit them well.'

'They've tried before?'

'Several times.' Karr sounded as though he took pride in it.

Caldason broke in with, 'Why should they bother killing one of their own?'

The patrician regarded him narrowly. 'What do you mean?'

'The way I see it you *are* the government, or near as damn. You play their game.'

Karr laughed, half cynically, half genuinely amused. 'You have a properly jaundiced view of authority. Politics has been my way of challenging the state. I don't claim to be very effectual, and at best my views are barely tolerated, but it's what I do.'

'How much bread does it put in hungry mouths? When does it ever favour the weak over the strong?'

'You're right, politics is a fraud. I know. I've been a practitioner of the black art all my life. It makes accommodations, turns a blind eye, appeases those who tyrannise us.'

'That's rare honesty from your kind. So why bother with it?'

'Because I believed governance was about the best interests of the citizenry; that the system could curb the excesses of our colonial rulers, maybe even help break their hold. They've branded me for that belief.'

'I've heard. They call you naive, militant, insurrectionist, radical –'

'And they call *you* pitiless.'

'Depends on who's doing the calling.'

'Exactly.'

Kutch said, 'If it means getting out from under those who grind people's faces, isn't radical a good thing to be?'

Karr smiled. 'Well put.'

'It was something my master used to say,' the boy admitted, a little shamefaced.

'Then it's to your credit that you honour him by repeating it.'

Caldason shifted, looked down at Karr. 'This great scheme of yours, it's some kind of political manoeuvre?'

'Politics . . . plays its part.'

'What are the other parts?'

'Protest takes more than one path.'

'That sounds like another way of saying it's something to do with the Resistance.'

Karr held his gaze. 'I'm with the Opposition. Others are the Resistance.'

'They've been known to shade together.'

'As I said, our rulers slander those who stand against them. They'd have people believe all their opponents are terrorists.'

'Does that mean you think the Resistance are terrorists?'

'Why, do you?'

'No.' He glanced Kutch's way and added caustically, 'But then I'm an outlaw, remember.'

'What's your point, Caldason?'

'Any plan meant to really change things would have to involve the Resistance to stand a chance.'

'I repeat: opposition takes many forms. There are peace-loving witnesses of conscience and priests who disagree with the regime, let alone revolutionaries, agitators, proto-democrats and the rest. Even the Fellowship of the Righteous Blade's no longer dormant. Did you know they'd reformed?'

'So it's said.'

'Who are they?' Kutch asked.

'They're an ancient martial order,' Karr told him, 'founded on patriotism. Their ranks boast some of the finest swordsmen in the land, and they've helped keep alive a tradition of valour that was once universally respected. They've often appeared in times when this country's independence was threatened.'

'And proved inept, if Bhealfa's present state's anything to go by,' Caldason remarked.

'Perhaps they would have achieved more if they'd had greater support from the rest of us,' Karr replied pointedly. 'At least they're doing something.'

'If you think a bunch of idealists with outmoded notions of chivalry have much to contribute to your cause, I suppose they are.'

'Dissent isn't as black and white as you think. The few politicians of my persuasion need all the allies we can get; we're fleas on the backs of oxen.'

'That just about sums up the size of your task.'

'Even an ox can be brought low by enough flea bites.'

'In your dreams, perhaps.'

Karr expelled a breath. 'You seem less than enthusiastic about the idea of challenging those in power. Given what Qalochians have suffered, that surprises me.'

Reeth visibly stiffened at mention of his birthright.

'Your people have faced massacres and enforced clearances,' Karr continued, 'and what's left of your diaspora has blind prejudice heaped upon it. If any have a grievance against the regime, it's the Qaloch.'

Knowing how sour Caldason could be about his people's lot, Kutch expected a prickly reaction. He was half right.

'The condition of Qalochians is well known,' Caldason said, even-toned, 'yet I see few taking up cudgels on our behalf. Why should we support you?'

'Because it's your fight too. And some of us *have* spoken out about the Qaloch's plight. Myself included.'

'That's made a world of difference, hasn't it?'

'I understand your cynicism, but –'

'Do you?' Caldason's passion began to show itself. 'Have *you* been spat on because of your race? Have *your* settlements been torched, your womenfolk defiled? Have you had your life valued at less than a handful of dirt on account of your ancestry?'

'For my ancestry . . . no.'

'*No*, you haven't. Your safety's in peril, granted, but unlike me you have a choice. You could give up agitation and offer the state no reason to vex you.'

'My principles wouldn't allow that,' Karr bristled.

'I can respect a man who takes a stand. For me there's no option. My blood allows me none. Because when it comes to prejudice and bigotry neither empire has anything to boast of. This land happens to be under the heel of one at the moment. In the past it was the other. The world is as it is.'

'That's where we disagree. I believe we could change things.'

'Gath Tampoor, Rintarah; it makes no difference.'

'I'm not talking about replacing one empire with the other, or trying to moderate what we have. There could be another course.'

'Slim hope, Patrician.'

'Perhaps. But history's stood still for too long. Everything's entrenched. Two-tier justice, blind to the crimes of Gath Tampoorians; Bhealfa's youth conscripted to fight the empires' proxy wars; distant rulers, cut off from the people; extortionate taxes –'

'We know all this,' Caldason interrupted. 'This isn't a public meeting.'

Karr looked mildly slighted at that. 'All I'm saying is that it can't go on.'

'Why not? The empires are stronger than they've ever been. Even if it were possible to defeat one, its twin would fill the void.'

'That's certainly been true in the past. Now I'm not so sure. There are signs that their rivalry is beginning to erode their power.'

Kutch was sceptical. 'Are you joking?'

'I was never more serious. Rintarah and Gath Tampoor are straining under the pressure of outdoing each other. They're hammering at the rights of citizens and subjects both, such as they are, and milking their colonies for all they can get. As to their strength . . . well, a bough's hardy until lightning strikes, and ice is thickest prior to the thaw.'

'Claiming the empires are losing their hold's one thing,' Caldason said, 'proving it's another.'

'I can only cite instinct, and the evidence of daily experience. There's a brutality in the air. Don't you feel it?'

'More than usual, you mean?'

'I can't blame you for mocking. But look around. Disorder's

growing, and at the edges things are drifting into anarchy. We could take advantage of that.'

'You talk of striking a blow, but you haven't told me *how*. Do you wonder I have doubts?'

'No. But perhaps you'll feel differently when you learn more.'

'I don't think we're going to know each other long enough for that, Karr.'

The patrician eyed him thoughtfully. 'Maybe we will. I have a ... proposal for you.' He took in Caldason's wary expression. 'If you'll hear me out.'

Reeth considered, then gave a small nod.

'I need to get back to Valdarr,' Karr explained. 'I've no protection, human or magical. If you could –'

'No.'

'You said you'd listen.'

'I've heard enough. I'm not a wet nurse. I don't join causes or form alliances. If you want protecting, Kutch here can sell you a shielding spell.'

Rightly or wrongly, the boy took that as a criticism of his effort during the ambush. He was hurt by the comment and it showed in his face. The others didn't seem to notice.

'I'm not trying to sign you up to anything,' Karr said. 'All I ask is that you see me there safely. After that we go our separate ways.'

Caldason shook his head.

'You were going to Valdarr anyway, Reeth,' Kutch intervened.

'I didn't say that.'

'Why were you going?' Karr ventured.

Caldason said nothing.

Kutch, feeling reckless after his reproach, dared to answer for him. 'Reeth meant to seek out Covenant. Though I'm not sure he believes it exists.'

'Covenant?' Karr said. 'It exists all right.'

'See?' Kutch reacted gleefully. 'I *told* you so.'

'What business do you have with them, Caldason?' Karr wanted to know.

The Qalochian frowned darkly. 'Personal business.'

'Of course. That's your prerogative. But if it's magic that concerns you, and you won't or can't deal with officially sanctioned practitioners, there are none better than Covenant. Though it must be said that dealing with them has its dangers.'

'Everything to do with magic has dangers.'

'True. It's part of the social glue in an unjust culture. It would be more fairly distributed under the new order I'd like to see.'

'I'd do away with it altogether.'

Karr looked startled. 'Really? And they call *me* a radical.' He would have pursued the issue, but Caldason's expression bode ill for further debate. Instead he declared, 'I can put you in touch with Covenant. It would take my kind of contacts. You stand little chance unaided, believe me. So why not a trade? In exchange for leading you to Covenant, you'll accompany me to Valdarr.'

'And me!' Kutch broke in. 'I've got to have somewhere to go too. I can't stay here.'

Karr seized on this. 'For the boy's sake, Caldason, if nothing else.'

The Qalochian looked from one to the other. At length, he said, 'I'm a wanted man. That has implications for anybody travelling with me.'

'I'm prepared to take that risk.'

'Once we get to the city, Kutch would be on his own. I'd need an assurance he wouldn't just be abandoned.'

'I'll see that he's all right. You have my word on that.'

'Let's understand each other. If I get you both to Valdarr, my commitment ends and we part.'

'So you're saying yes?'

Caldason sighed. 'I suppose I am. But don't take it as meaning I support your cause or whatever this plan is you're brewing. I'm doing it for the boy.'

Kutch beamed. 'Great!'

'Don't get too excited, we're not there yet.'

'Thank you, Caldason,' Karr said.

'Save your thanks. You might end up regretting this. As I've said before . . .' He eyed Kutch. '. . . people around me tend to die.'

'Your enemies certainly seem to.'

That brought to the surface something Kutch had pushed from his mind. He rose to his feet. 'Gods, Reeth, I forgot! Your *arm*!'

Karr joined the chorus. 'Yes, your wound! We're sitting here talking and –'

'Easy.' Caldason waved them back. 'Don't get into a panic on my account.' With no particular urgency he rolled up first the sleeve of his jerkin, then the stained shirt sleeve beneath. His arm was caked with blood. He spat into his hand and began wiping the gore away. The exposed skin was unbroken. There was no wound. 'I said it was nothing.'

Kutch gaped at the unblemished flesh. 'But . . .'

'Sometimes things look different in the heat of a fight,' Caldason told him.

'I could have sworn you took a blow,' Karr said, puzzled.

'A trick of the light maybe. It's of no concern.' He rolled down the sleeve. The action implied a finality, a closing of the subject.

Karr and the apprentice exchanged a look. Neither felt like arguing with him.

'Now get yourselves ready,' Caldason said. 'We're leaving.'

9

Serrah Ardacris didn't care.

It didn't worry her that her stolen boots were the wrong size and hurt her feet. Or that her clothes, snatched from washing lines, scavenged from rubbish tips, were mismatched and ill-fitting. It was only of vague interest to her that for two days she had eaten scraps, drunk rainwater and slept fitfully in doorways.

Serrah hadn't gone anywhere near her quarters, of course, or attempted to contact anyone she knew. She understood how the Council for Internal Security worked; what was possible, what their resources were. So she kept moving. Dirty, exhausted, mending too slowly from her beating, she hobbled as much as walked Merakasa's packed streets.

She was in a curious, befuddled frame of mind, her head full of fluff and dim stars. She felt discorporate, as if observing herself from afar. She was cautious of watch patrols and paladins. But perversely, part of her hoped she'd run into them and make an end of it.

Although she was largely indifferent to her condition, two genuine fears prowled at the edge of her consciousness. One was that she would turn a corner and see Eithne. Or something purporting to be her. In fact, twice she thought she had, and each time her insides gave a giddy lurch before she realised the error. Never mind that she knew her daughter to be in her grave.

Serrah's other dread centred on tracker glamours. The thought of bloodhound spectres and homing revenants penetrated her daze and iced her spine. She wondered whether her former masters wanted her badly enough to justify the expense.

As she roamed, her grasp on reason ebbed and flowed. When the tide was out she had to fight down the urge to scream aloud or pound her head against a wall. To see if anybody noticed. To verify her existence.

In lucid moments she dwelt on the identity of her rescuers and their motive, like a dog worrying a well-chewed bone.

She wandered out of a prosperous area and into a poor one. From citizens parading in finery to beggars with outstretched hands; from bedecked carriages to pigs rooting in the streets. A surprisingly short distance separated the credible, quality magic of wealth and the questionable, second-rate charms of penury.

Here the underprivileged relied on costermongers hawking low-cost spells. Shoddy merchandise smuggled from foreign sweat shops where child labourers toiled in dangerous conditions without proper magical supervision.

There were the counterfeiters' stalls, too. When people couldn't afford to be particular they gambled on fakes. Sometimes the imitation glamours worked. Other times they disappointed, even harmed. Occasionally they proved fatal.

The touts and bootleggers were unlicensed traders, and the penalties for such illegality were harsh. For protection they employed lookouts. Some paid roughnecks to create a diversion should law enforcers happen by. Mostly they guarded their safety with bona fide magical defences; dazzle glamours, ear-splitter banshees, deception clusters and the like.

Serrah could have been a wraith floating through the drab crowds and gutter stenches. But even where abnormality was common, many shrank away from the wild look of her. She was heedless. Because a notion that had been drifting like fog in her brain had crystallised and she knew what she needed.

A weapon.

The marvel was that she hadn't felt the lack before. Two days since her rescuers had made her give up her sword prior to scaling the wall of the redoubt, and only now did she notice the want. The small, quiet voice of what might have been sanity urged her to rectify the deficiency.

She looked around, *really* looked, and studied the current of humanity. Naturally, just about everybody carried at least one weapon. Serrah had little doubt she could take what she wanted from any of them, despite her injuries.

Then she spotted him.

Militiamen invariably patrolled in pairs, especially in a ghetto district. This one was just leaving his partner. Perhaps to take a short walk to a watch station, or to make his way to some off-duty pursuit. He was the taller and by far the strongest looking of the two. That was why she chose him. It was the same kind of contrariness that made people who hated heights go to the edge in high places. In her physical state she should have picked a civilian. But she was spoiling for a fight with authority.

Old instincts took over, a legacy of her training and experience. Slipping into predatory mode, she stalked him.

Wherever he was going, it was with purpose. He moved swiftly, elbowing through the crowd, obliging those in his path to step aside. His manner was haughty, cock of the walk, and he drew glances that mixed deference with contempt.

Serrah followed at a distance, making sure there were plenty of people between them, never losing sight of his broad back.

The militiaman entered marginally quieter streets. Serrah trailed him as he went into crooked lanes, emptier still and rubbish strewn. When he cut into a deserted alley she increased her pace and closed the gap. Her heart was hammering.

She hailed him with, '*Hold!*'

It was the first time she'd spoken out loud since escaping. The gravel-edged sound of her own voice startled her.

He turned, hand on sword.

Serrah stared at the blade like a starving woman spying meat.

'Well?' he said.

She lifted her gaze. 'I want . . .' Speech wavered, dried up. The blood roared in her ears. She just looked at him.

He studied her in turn. Her dark-ringed, intense eyes, ashen complexion and greasy, matted hair. The bruises, sores and grime, underneath which he could see she had been, might still be, quite pretty. He relaxed, judging her no threat.

'What's your business?' he pressed.

Serrah focused. 'You've something I want,' she told him, coming closer.

He wrinkled his nose at the odour her unbathed body gave off, and waved a hand to fan himself. 'And you've something I *don't*.' Then a false understanding dawned. A leer gashed his full-bearded face, revealing teeth the colour of slush. 'Unh,' he grunted knowingly. 'Got a thing about uniforms, have you? Or is it the purse that draws you?' He slapped a bulge at the side of his tunic.

'You'd take me for a whore?' she whispered, righteous anger rising.

'I wouldn't take *you* at any price!' His laughter was coarse, ugly. He dug in a pocket. 'Here. Now move on, trollop, and count yourself lucky.' He tossed a couple of small coins at her.

They lay at Serrah's feet, in the muck, unregarded. She stared at him, darkening with rage. *'A whore?'* she repeated, barely audible.

'And a bloody awful one at that. Now why don't you –' Something about her manner aroused his suspicion. He gave her closer scrutiny. 'Do I know you?'

He might have. They could once have been comrades in arms, in what she already thought of as her old life. But she knew he didn't mean it that way, and didn't answer.

Frowning, he reached into his tunic. His eyes never left her. He took out a flat, square object that fitted in his palm. It resembled a plain hand mirror.

She recognised it instantly. Her fists bunched.

The glamour was light-activated. Serrah knew its reflective side would be blank for a moment, then turn milky. After that, whatever information it held would be displayed.

She could guess what that was.

The militiaman glanced down and his expression confirmed it. His features stiffened. He fixed her coldly and made to speak.

She kicked him in the crotch, as hard as she could.

His face expressed surprise, shock then pain in rapid succession. He let out an agonised yelp and doubled over. The glamour slipped from his grasp.

Striking that blow liberated Serrah's fury. Her chaotic thoughts, her disordered feelings, the weight of her fear; all of it found a focus. She set upon him.

Frenzied, she took swings at his jaw, connecting hard enough to sting her fists. She hurled punches at his chest and stomach, booted his shins and ankles viciously. Little of it had anything to do with what she had been taught, or learned in combat. It was an onslaught, a venting, and it was ungoverned.

At first, her stunned victim didn't do much more than take the battering. Then he overcame his stupefaction and the beating turned into a struggle, centring on his attempt to draw his sword. Shielding himself with a raised arm, he got the blade half out of its sheath. She seized his wrist and gripped it with a strength that belied her wasted appearance. After a moment of wrestling they were mired in a stalemate.

Serrah broke it by delivering a solid head-butt to his brow.

The impact sent a stab of agony through her own forehead, but she was less hurt than him. He cried out and stumbled backwards, letting go of the sword. She hung on to the weapon as it came free of its scabbard. Using the heavy handguard like a knuckle-duster, she cracked him several times across the head. He went down, insensible.

She was breathing hard and shaking. Bending to his unconscious form, her instinct was to finish him. She put the blade to his throat, then hesitated. That small quiet voice had its say again. Whatever else she might be, Serrah wasn't a murderer. Not in cold blood. It hadn't come to that yet. She lowered the sword.

The groaning militiaman carried a dagger, and she took that, too. She stole his scabbard and belt, and clipped it around her waist, tightening it considerably to make up for their difference in girth. After vacillating for a tenth of a minute, she slashed the strings of his purse. As she stuffed it into her pocket she thought how eroded her ethics had become in so short a time. That struck her as funny somehow and she felt like laughing. But she couldn't be sure she'd ever stop. So she took deep, slow breaths to steady herself, and the urge passed.

As she pulled away, she trod on something. It was the glamour he'd dropped, face down in the dirt. She knelt and picked it up. Turning it over, she saw what she expected.

The image seemed to float just above the mirror-like

surface, three-dimensional, crystal clear. It was Serrah, head and shoulders. Her left profile was displayed. That gradually melted into full face. Then her right profile, and back again to left. It was more than a likeness; it was a miniature version of herself, turning slowly to show every feature to best advantage.

Across the bottom of her facsimile, fiery letters spelt out *Fugitive*, followed by the lies *Murder* and *Treason*.

She remembered the image-taking. It had occurred during her induction into the Council for Internal Security. New recruits had to present themselves to the Council's sorcerer clerks, who cast the spell that captured their images for the records division. The session was brisk, business-like, and the clerks shared an officious, unsmiling demeanour. None of the recruits minded that; being accepted into the elite had intoxicated them. She was amazed to recall that it had happened just a couple of years ago. It felt like an age.

Serrah was transfixed by her likeness. She could have been looking at a stranger. Someone robust, spirited, with the prospect of a bright future. An insider, reaping the benefits of the empire's largess. A woman unaware of the coming storm.

Murder. Treason.

The full significance of the glamour hit her. How likely was it that she'd chanced on the only militiaman who happened to be carrying her image? It must have been issued to all the law keepers, which meant hundreds, *thousands* of them in circulation, confirming her status on the wanted list. The authorities didn't do this for every felon, not by a long shot. It was far too costly.

Treason.

She took the thing and beat it against the cobblestones. It gave off tiny, bright blue sparks. The image flickered, dulled, went out. Serrah continued pounding until cracks appeared.

All at once the glamour crumbled into a sandy, reddish dust. A faint luminescence suffused it for a few seconds, then died. Serrah knew it was a futile gesture, but it made her feel a bit better.

Rising, she absently rubbed her dusty hand against her breeches, leaving cherry-coloured streaks on the cheap fabric. Juices were flowing now, her senses were sharpening. She'd lingered here too long. She had to get away.

Shockingly, a sound rang out, a rhythmic caterwauling, loud and harsh. The alley lit up behind her. Serrah spun around.

Through clenched teeth she hissed, 'Shit.'

She'd forgotten about the militiaman's alarum glamour, hadn't checked for his medallion. Now he'd activated it. Or it had triggered itself, if it was that expensive a spell.

The man was still flat on his back, blood trickling from his nose and a corner of his mouth, though he was beginning to stir. No wonder, with the deafening *whoop-whoop-whoop* of the alert. And from a point high on his chest, a beam of concentrated light lanced out to punch the sky. She looked up and saw that, far above, the shaft fanned into a disc. Within it, a wolf's head was taking shape, the universally recognised distress signal. Soon it would be visible over half the city. Then this quarter would be lousy with militia, paladins, government agents, citizens' vigilante groups and the gods knew who else.

Serrah took flight, moving as fast as her aching limbs allowed. From alley to lane, from lane back to bustling streets. In her rush she made no distinction between reality and illusion. Flesh or apparition, she barged through regardless, and to hell with the protocol about damaging other people's glamours. The aggrieved threw curses, shook fists, but nobody pursued her. She looked too dangerous.

After a while she slowed and regained her breath. She

began to be surreptitious, using quieter byways and double-
backs. But she was filled with more determination than at
any time in the last two days.

A plan of sorts had formed.

Once the river had snaked its way through the city's viscera
it opened its mouth to take a bite out of the ocean. The
resultant chunk formed Merakasa's harbour, and it took
Serrah a little over two hours to get there.

A spectacle of masts above the rooftops announced the
port from blocks away. Some of the masts moved, gliding at
a stately pace, pennants fluttering. Higher still, scores of
shrieking gulls wheeled and dived.

It was dusk, but the streets still buzzed with sailors, merchant
seamen, stevedores lugging sacks and barrels, passengers
arriving and departing, handcarts, horses and wagons. A chain
of galley slaves shuffling miserably under the lash.

On the docks themselves longshoremen loaded and
unloaded all manner of cargo. In slings hanging from hoists,
livestock bleated. Fowl beat their wings against the bars of
their tiny cages, stacked twenty high. Fishermen gutted their
catches, scenting the air with a tang that made Serrah want
to retch.

She took care to avoid the customs officials, port guards
and occasional paladin scattered among the crowd. Collar
up, head down, she walked purposefully along the line of
vessels, weighing up their pros and cons.

Hardly a berth was empty, and not all the ships were
mercantile or navy. Private yachts and clippers were moored
here too, their sails bearing the coats of arms of ruling families or the more powerful guilds. In a show of real wealth,
the crests were glamoured. They rippled, shone, slowly
changed colour. The lions rampant, the unicorns, eagles and
twisting serpents pranced and writhed.

Likewise, many a ship's figurehead was magically animated. One, a traditional comely maiden, jiggled ample breasts with impossibly red nipples. As Serrah passed, the wooden effigy gave her a salacious wink. She assumed the craft was a Diamond Isle transport. It was certainly vulgar enough.

At length she came to a three-masted merchantman, a ship of appreciable size. Big was good. It meant the vessel would likely be going somewhere far away, and should be spacious enough to hide her. And it was nearly ready to sail. The last few items of payload sat on the dock, waiting to be stowed. A group of crewmen stood by the prow engaged in conversation, their backs to her.

Serrah looked up. Several hands were in the rigging, and one was climbing to the crow's nest, but she couldn't see anybody on deck.

She seized her chance. Snatching a box, she lifted it to her shoulder, hiding her face from the chattering crewmen. Bent over, moving quickly, she ascended the gangway. She expected someone to shout a challenge, or the sound of pursuing footsteps. Nothing happened.

On board, she discarded the box and surveyed the scene. In front of her was a cargo hold, its deck cover shut and bolted. She made her way astern, keeping low, staying away from the rail. Amidships there was another hold, and this one was open. Creeping to the edge, she peered into the chasm. The cavernous hull was dark, and she could just make out a small mountain of filled sacks directly below. She couldn't see or hear any movement down there. Nor could she find a rope or hauling tackle to help her descend.

So she jumped.

The long drop knocked the wind out of her, and she nearly shouted. At least the sacks weren't full of coal or pig iron.

She scurried down them and onto the floor, wincing. Her joints were still sore. Blinking in the gloom, she tried to get her bearings. The only source of light she could see, apart from overhead, was further to the stern; a doorway shape, faintly outlined. Newly acquired dagger in hand, she headed for it.

Darkness and stacks of cargo got in her way. But eventually, shins and elbows grazed, she reached the entrance. It led to a smaller hold. Smaller, yet probably large enough to build a cottage in. Such light as there was came from a half-open hatch cover, identical to the one she had dropped through. At the far end of this hold were three wooden doors. Skirting the feeble shaft of light, she went towards them.

Opening the first one took mettle. But like the second and third, the room contained only clutter. She thought for a moment. Then, reluctantly because she didn't like the idea of there being only one way out, or the confinement, she slipped into the right-hand room. She left the door ajar so she had weak light to see by.

The chamber was about cabin-sized, but most of it was crammed with chests and bales. She began rearranging them, stopping frequently to listen for anyone approaching. Soon she had a space excavated near the back of the room, just big enough for her to fit into, and a chest ready to plug the entry once she was in. She thought the hiding place would look solid enough to a cursory glance. A proper search was another thing.

A loud crash startled her. The frail light was cut off. They were securing the hatch. She could hear covers along the length of the ship being slammed with an echoing finality.

Serrah groped through the dark and crawled into the cavity. She pulled the trunk into the gap behind her, but left a tiny crack for a spy hole. Not that she could see anything.

Settling as best she could on rough hessian sacks, she made sure her sword and knife were close to hand.

The darkness seemed to sharpen her hearing. She was aware of the hull creaking, and the scratching of rats. More distant sounds, of orders shouted and running feet, drifted to her. She fell to turning events over in her mind.

A nagging thought was that her old masters, the CIS, should have been watching the ports. Serrah couldn't believe they weren't, it was such a basic precaution. Yet somehow she'd got through unchallenged. She hoped it was plain dumb luck and not some elaborate trick. That was a path to paranoia and she forced herself to ponder other concerns, like where she might be going, and what she could do about food and drink.

She felt the ship weigh anchor, then the bumps as it scraped against the harbour wall. Free of restraint, the vessel bobbed gently from side to side. Small pieces of unsecured cargo slid back and forth on the hold's floor. In due course the motion calmed and they were properly underway.

As best she could judge, something like an hour had gone by when she heard a new set of noises. She sat up, alert, grasping her blades. Through her peep hole she saw the glow of a subdued light and a pair of crewmen appeared, one carrying a hooded lantern.

Were they searching for her? Would they notice the storeroom's open door? If the answer was yes, she determined to make a fight of it. Her grip on the blades tightened, though her palms grew sweaty. She remembered her misgivings at entering a place with only one exit, and started to regret the decision.

But the sailors weren't searching. They didn't spot the open door, and they made little effort to be quiet. One sat on a crate, the other rolled a barrel over and perched opposite him. They took out cob pipes and stuffed them with rough tobacco. She realised they were off watch, or simply skiving, and allowed herself to relax a fraction.

They passed a hip flask back and forth as they smoked and talked. She strained to hear their conversation, but caught only snatches.

'. . . thank the gods it's east we're going and not north,' one of them said.

His companion replied, but she didn't catch the meaning.

'Not according to my brother,' the first man went on. '. . . some kind of . . . sweeps aside everything in his way.'

Again, she couldn't quite hear the other man's response, but its tone was sceptical.

'. . . many in the barbarous regions, granted,' stated the one she could hear more clearly, 'but none . . .' Frustratingly, he must have turned his head. Serrah pressed her ear to the crack. '. . . different, you mark me.'

She couldn't get the sense of it. Then she heard a stray word.

'. . . Zerreiss . . .' It was a name she'd heard before, but where or when escaped her.

At least she knew they were travelling east, which was something. The rest of it was too disjointed to mean much, but she carried on listening.

She heard that name again, more than once, as their exchange droned on.

Zerreiss. Where *had* she come across it?

Serrah was trying to remember when exhaustion took her. She fell into a pit of sleep as dark and silent as a tomb.

10

The first glimmer of dawn. Sunlight lanced through the canopy of a great forest, making trees loom ghostlike in the dissolving mist. Silvery dew melted in the warmth, and birds began their morning chorus. The start of a day like any other.

Where the forest ended, pasture lands took over. Farmhouses surrounded by patchwork meadows, cottages sitting prettily on gentle hills. Herds of cows waiting to be milked, fields dotted with sheep softly bleating.

Abruptly, the birds stopped singing. The cattle fell mute. Even the drone of insects faded away.

The silence was so sudden, so palpable, it brought people out of their houses. Frowning women wiped their hands on flour-dusted aprons while youngsters clutched at their skirts. Men shaded brows with their palms to scan the landscape. In the fields, workers straightened, sunshine glinting on the cambered blades of their scythes. They all strained to see what might be causing the unnatural hush.

Very faintly, a sound could be heard.

It seemed to come from deep in the forest. Perhaps from beyond it. The farmers and their kin exchanged perplexed, uneasy glances.

As the racket drew closer they realised it consisted of not
one sound but a mingling of many. And given the distance
it appeared to be travelling, it had to be very loud. Then they
were aware of a weak but growing vibration beneath their
feet. Clouds of birds rose from the treetops, spooked by whatever was approaching.

In fright, the women gathered their children and pushed
them indoors. The men armed themselves with pitchforks
and axes. Everyone stared at the forest's curving rim, for
now they were sure that whatever produced the sounds was
skirting its border. Movement could be seen through the
trees.

Around the lip of the forest came a motley assemblage of
mounted men, wagons, carriages and much larger structures
of some kind, obscured by clouds of dust.

The more perceptive among the farming folk, the more
worldly, guessed what was happening. But it was too late.

A lone rider came ahead of the rest. He slowed his frothing
horse to get his bearings. Those looking on were too stunned
to call out to him. It would have made no difference if they
had; the pathfinder, which is what they realised he must be,
didn't even notice them. After a moment spent reckoning
his course he spurred on, straight across their fields, scattering livestock. The onlookers began to shout then, and frantically waved their arms, but their cries were lost in the din.

Several score cavalrymen arrived with shining breastplates,
standards aloft. Rare grandeur for this rustic backwater. As
they chased the trailblazer, a detail of paladins at least a
hundred strong thundered after them, maintaining strict
formation.

Then the full torrent of chaos flooded in.

A disorderly mob of riders started to come by, many in
diverse uniforms, their numbers impossible to count. Imperial
guards mingled with watchmen and militia. Court sentries

rode alongside detachments of army regulars. There were traders, peddlers, vagrants and chancers in the multitude; itinerant musicians, guildsmen, riderless horses, coach-loads of jovial harlots. Flags, lances and banners swayed above the throng. Bobbing in the flow were merchants' carts, buggies, rigs and wizards' chariots; wheeled cages housing exotic, roaring beasts, pulled by teams of oxen. The noise was indescribable.

The earth shook, and a thousand smells, from roasting meat to dung, permeated the air. Crops were flattened, trampled, churned to mush. Cattle stampeded, fences were levelled. Carried by the tide, haystacks unravelled.

But the farmers' wrath gave way to awe and alarm when they saw what came into view next.

Dozens of fabulous floating mansions and chateaux, drifting like great ships in the ocean of humanity. Magnificent constructions of marble, granite, wood and stained glass, with lavishly decorated facades and twisting spires.

But for all their huge size and splendour they were dwarfed by the structure they surrounded. Like a bloated slug in a column of ants, it was mountainous by comparison. The gigantic hovering palace, an extravagantly embellished confection in marzipan pink, white, blue and black stone, boasted crenellated ramparts, flying buttresses, keeps and balconies. Its numerous towers, cut with arrow slits, were so tall the farm folk cricked their necks trying to see their tops.

Fantastical glamours flew over and about the tremendous palace. They took the form of winged men and horses, dragons, serpents, ladybirds the size of rams, and schools of giant, vividly coloured fish that swam in circles around the towers. Other glamours displayed the royal coat of arms and regal emblems; images drawn in fire on shimmering backcloths of gold.

The lesser palaces ploughed through lone trees and copses.

They crushed hedgerows and demolished barns. Peasants ran for their lives as a floating castle clipped the corner of a farmhouse and brought it crashing down. The castle had an ostentatious watchtower, and its bell clanged at the impact.

Survivors in the farmers' ranks could only cower and witness their ruination.

The inhabitants of the gliding structures looked down on all this with ill-concealed boredom. As though destroying people's homes was a common event. Which, of course, it was.

At the window of a chamber high in Melyobar's travelling palace, one particular observer watched with an expression that was almost vacant.

'How much longer's he going to keep us waiting?' an impatient voice demanded from behind him.

Andar Talgorian, Gath Tampoor's Imperial Envoy, slammed the shutters and turned to the questioner.

Clan High Chief Ivak Bastorran, hereditary leader of the paladins, was above middle years, and his neatly trimmed hair and beard were touched with silver. But his physique was still impressive, the heritage of a lifetime of soldiering, and his eyes were sharp and artful from nearly as long a career in scheming. He wore the clan uniform – red tunic, black breeches, knee-high leather riding boots – as though it had formed around him. Tight, crisp, no creases. His boots shone almost as brightly as the decorations and braid he wore.

'It's getting here at this hour that irks me,' Talgorian complained.

'Nothing special for a soldier,' Bastorran snorted. 'Pity you never had the discipline of a military background.' It was intended as a dig. A small barb in the ongoing mutual loathing between men of equivalent power and differing aims who vied for the Prince's attention.

Talgorian refused to bite and said nothing.

An eavesdropper glamour hung in the air just below the sumptuous anteroom's ornate ceiling. It took the shape of a large brass ear. There was no pretence as to its function, no subtlety intended. Beneath his shirt Talgorian wore a medallion containing a blocking glamour which overrode the eavesdropper. He was sure Bastorran had something similar. Visitors were forbidden to bring spells of any kind into the palace, but it was unlikely anyone would challenge such men.

'The waste of time is what I find frustrating,' Bastorran added. 'I have more important matters to attend to.'

'Such as increased Resistance activity?'

That was a hit. The paladin glowered. 'We try not to call them that. Makes it sound like they have a just grievance. I prefer deviants, hooligans, misfits –'

'However you name them, they *are* more active. In both empires and in the colonies. Not least here in Bhealfa.'

'The clans are on top of it. We have informers in the insurgent ranks, and there's little happening we're not aware of.'

'All interested parties have their spies.'

'Not as highly placed as mine.'

Talgorian regarded that as a bluff, else the paladins would have made better headway with the problem. He tried steering back to the subject. 'Well, *our* sources indicate the rebels are involved in more attacks and criminality than ever before. That has to be of concern to all of us.'

'It'd be less of a concern if we were put in sole charge of dealing with them.'

'You know that would be politically unacceptable.'

'Unacceptable my arse. Politics is a mire. It bogs things down when speed's of the essence. It conciliates when we should be striking without mercy. You're in it by choice. It's your *job* to spew silken words amounting to no more than a pile of horse shit. I wade in the privy out of necessity.'

'Your views on the subject are well known,' Talgorian replied dryly, 'so let's not rehearse them again, shall we? The fact remains that politics is what we're engaged in, like it or not, and that means we practise the art of expediency. It's how we get things done.'

'My point exactly. Expediency. Compromise, concessions, give and take. Allow us a clear path and you'd see improvements in the situation then.'

'I would hardly say that the regime we have now is particularly soft, any more than the penalties meted out by your clans could be called lenient.' He didn't wait for Bastorran to contradict that, and pushed on. 'And you have to admit the paladins are in a delicate position with regard to the Resistance, what with you serving both Gath Tampoor *and* Rintarah. You'll never have a free hand as long as that's the case.'

'Now we have a subject *your* views are plain about,' Bastorran replied heatedly. 'We make alliances. It's our tradition.' He spoke deliberately, as though instructing a dim child. 'The paladins bear arms for anyone who needs our services.'

'Anyone who can pay for them, you mean.'

'Do you do your job unpaid? Or is your patriotism so great your services are given freely? There's no contradiction in what we do. We're stateless, remember, and by choice. Which makes it possible for us to serve and fight without being hampered by ties of nationhood. In any event, no one clan serves both empires.'

'Nevertheless, a paladin of whatever clan is ultimately loyal to all clans.'

'If conflicts of interest arise, paladins withdraw. If that's impossible we serve faithfully, and that includes meeting brother clansmen in battle if need be.'

Which had never been known, Talgorian reflected. And he was far from alone in thinking that if the paladins' stateless condition, a privilege accorded to no other group, wasn't expediency, he didn't know what was. The word mercenary hung in the air, but he had no appetite for using it. He didn't want to make more of an enemy of this man. 'The idea that you could take up arms against yourselves,' he said, 'I always found that difficult to understand.'

'You would, you're a civilian,' the paladin responded, appending, 'With respect,' though he meant no respect at all. 'It's about honour.'

Talgorian raised a cynical eyebrow at that. 'The reality of the situation is that the clans are never going to be entirely . . .' He was going to say trusted. 'The clans are unlikely to be granted the latitude you want as long as you insist on this particular . . . tradition,' he rephrased diplomatically.

'Over the centuries many have tried to persuade my predecessors away from our customs. I very much doubt the present administration, or indeed your good self, is going to have any more success than they did, Ambassador.'

'I would never be so presumptuous, Clan High Chief.'

They exchanged professional, insincere smiles and mentally crept away from the topic.

There was a soft bump as the palace flattened something. A farmhouse perhaps, or somebody's orchard. Nothing of any importance.

Bastorran said, 'I will concede that difficult problems do arise in respect of security.' He noted Talgorian's guarded expression. 'I'm thinking of recent events concerning your Council for Internal Security,' he clarified, 'and the disappearance of a certain special unit captain.'

It was Talgorian's turn to hide embarrassment. 'You suspect the Resistance had a hand in it?'

'She's a reasonably important middle-ranking operative by all accounts. Certainly an asset to them if she has defected, and her escape *was* assisted. On the other hand, things often prove more complicated than they first seem.'

'What's your interest in the matter, beyond the security implications?'

'Several clansmen were killed during her escape. Losing our own isn't something we take lightly.'

'I'm told her escape was purely a criminal matter.'

'Whatever it was it should never have been allowed to happen. The whole affair was a botch from start to finish. When a member of one of the great families gets killed, like this Phosian boy, even if it was incompetence and not assassination, heads should roll. Anything less and the mob loses proper respect for authority.'

'You may well be right. But the fate of a lowly captain isn't what concerns us at the moment.' He nodded towards the pair of elegantly carved doors at the far end of the anteroom. 'It would benefit us both if we had a united front when we see the Prince. I suggest we keep the agenda simple for him.'

'Don't we always?'

'More so today, I mean. By concentrating on one or two issues of special importance.'

'If you're hoping to dominate this audience with your own concerns,' Bastorran rumbled angrily, 'you can –'

'No, no, no, it's not that.' He waved a hand in an appeasing gesture. 'I just want to be sure certain matters that affect us all are given priority.'

'I sometimes wonder why you bother with the pretence of protocol. Gath Tampoor's going to do whatever it wants anyway, isn't it? Given this island's no more than another of the empire's puppet states.'

'*Protectorates*,' Talgorian insisted. 'Unfortunately, in some matters that require Bhealfan co-operation it behoves us to feign legality. Unilateral action could stir up even more agitation among the populace. Something we can do without at a time when our forces are stretched countering Rintarah's ambitions. You know that.'

The paladin nodded. 'Too well. Laws, treaties, etiquette, they're all as bad as politics. They clog everything up. Sweep the lot away, I say.'

The Envoy kept his impatience in check. 'What we have is what we have. Until such time as other, more direct arrangements can be made.'

'Anyway,' Bastorran sniffed, 'what is it that's so important?'

'This warlord we've been hearing about. Zerreiss. By all accounts he's expanding his sphere of influence at an alarming rate.'

'Is *that* all? You're worried about one barbarian chieftain? I thought it must be something important!'

'It might not do to be so dismissive of a possible threat to our borders.'

'Afraid another empire's rising, are you?' He laughed derisively. 'Concerned you could have a rival?'

Talgorian gave him a stony look.

'One tin-pot leader overthrows a few others,' Bastorran went on. 'It happens all the time. He'll fall back into obscurity soon enough. They always do. It's ridiculous to think savages could offer a threat to the might of either empire.'

'Of course it is. But what about some of our more far-flung protectorates? There are northern dependencies that produce valuable resources for us. Seeing the supply of those resources cut off, or worse, having the prize fall into the hands of a warlord, would be another burden for us at a time of unrest.'

'The northern wastes are a long way away. You have one of the two largest navies in the world. Distance and force of arms should be enough defence for you. Anyway, I still think you're exaggerating the risk.'

'With respect, High Chief –' again, none was meant '– I would suggest that the Gath Tampoorian Diplomatic Corps has more of an eye on external affairs than the paladins generally do. And our assessment is that we need to keep a close watch on the Zerreiss situation.'

Bastorran sighed resignedly. 'So what are you proposing?'

'That an expedition be sent to investigate what's going on in the north. We know precious little about this warlord or what his intentions might be.'

'And this expedition's orders?'

'Would be to make contact with Zerreiss, if that's feasible, or to spy out the situation if it's not. But this is sensitive. Sending an imperial flotilla could be seen as inflammatory. We thought a Bhealfan force might be less controversial.'

'A fine distinction, the difference between a Gath Tampoorian expedition and one flying the flag of its . . . *protectorate*. Your barbarian warlord might not appreciate the subtlety.'

'It's not meant for him. It's for Rintarah. We don't want to signal our concerns too obviously and draw their attention.'

'They'd see through it faster than Zerreiss, surely?'

'We might just get away with the pretence that it's nothing more than a Bhealfan trading mission.'

'But in reality you'd have some of your people on board?'

'Of course.'

Bastorran pondered. At length, he said, 'I've no objections to this in principle. But if I back you with the Prince I want to be able to call on your support in turn.'

'Naturally. Do you have a cause in mind?'

'Not yet. Let's just say you owe me, shall we?'

Talgorian nodded.

'I expect to be kept informed of progress,' Bastorran continued, 'and I'd want a few paladins among the crew.'

'That can be arranged. So, we're in accord?'

'On this matter, yes. Have you broached the subject with Melyobar?'

'The expedition, no. Zerreiss, several times.'

'And?'

'There's only one subject on his mind. As usual. That's why we need to work together.' He glanced up at the eaves-dropper and felt a twinge of apprehension, though he knew he was protected by the best counter-magic money could buy. Instinctively, he moved closer to the paladin and dropped his voice a little. 'I assume there's been no news concerning . . . a certain Qalochian?'

'Ah.' Bastorran grew sober. 'None. Beyond unconfirmed sightings and the occasional suspicious deaths of clansmen. You appreciate the unique circumstances surrounding the man.'

'Yes. But . . . I'll be frank. I'm getting a certain amount of pressure from above on this issue.' He momentarily lifted his eyes heavenward.

'The Empress?' Bastorran was slightly awed despite himself.

'Her circle.' They both knew it amounted to the same thing. 'They've been conveying a measure of restlessness, shall we say, at the lack of progress.'

'Do I have to remind you that we have our own reasons for wanting him dealt with? You can't say we lack motiva-tion. Bhealfa might be just an island but it's a damn big one when searching for a single man. And that's assuming he's here. We have reason to think he is, but he could be anywhere in either empire or their dependencies.'

'I appreciate the difficulties.'

'Which are made no easier by the extraordinary restric-tions placed on us as far as this matter's concerned.'

'Our hands are tied. But we have to get the thing cleared up. You know the danger, and the consequences of failure.'

Bastorran was about to respond when there was a knock at the door.

A servant entered. He escorted in another paladin, less than half the High Chief's age and as trimly attired. The family resemblance was unmistakable. But where Bastorran, for all his rigidity and bluntness, was susceptible to at least a degree of reason, Talgorian knew this young man to be bull-headed. As he knew him to be arrogant, and by reputation, brutish.

'I believe you've met Devlor, my nephew,' Bastorran said. It was obvious the older man delighted in the younger. He exuded something like fatherly pride.

'Of course,' Talgorian replied, giving a laconic head bow. 'I trust the day finds you well, Commander.'

'Tolerably.' Devlor Bastorran barely regarded him, while managing to convey indifference and haughtiness in a single word.

The older man beamed indulgently and gave his nephew's shoulder a mock punch. 'The finest swordsman in the two empires,' he boasted. 'I know, I trained him myself.'

Talgorian had heard the brag before, and others concerning the younger Bastorran. He greeted it with a judicious, hollow smile.

'Leave the insubordinates to the likes of Devlor here,' the elder paladin added, 'and you'd see an end to their whining soon enough.'

His nephew flashed a cruel, white-toothed smile of agreement.

'No doubt,' the Envoy remarked.

Ivak Bastorran had no male issue. Rumour held that Devlor was being groomed to take over leadership of the clans when his uncle expired, hence his high rank at such a tender age. If the rumours proved true, Talgorian saw trouble ahead.

His train of thought was curtailed by the functionary's return. Announcing that the Prince was ready to see them, he led Bastorran and Talgorian to the audience chamber. Devlor stayed behind, to the ambassador's relief.

The Prince's suite was disordered. Papers, books, blueprints and bric-a-brac covered every surface, and much of the lushly carpeted floor. The scent from copious bouquets of flowers and pot pourri didn't quite mask the smell of sweat and fear. Near the back of the room was a large object covered by a blue velvet drape.

They were announced and the flunky withdrew. The Envoy and the paladin glanced at each other, then began picking their way through the clutter.

Melyobar seemed hardly aware of their presence. He was on his hands and knees, sifting through documents and blueprints. Several weighty tomes with metal hasps lay open about him. He wore his familiar agitated demeanour. His prematurely greying hair was askew, his sweat-sheened cheeks flushed.

A short bout of discreet throat-clearing made his visitors' presence known. The Prince lifted his head and blinked at them. A degree of recognition dawned and he got up, clutching the back of a chair to steady himself, as though he were a much older man. They refrained from assisting, unsure of his reaction if they laid hands on him, and instead waited with heads bowed.

On his feet, puffing, the Prince said, 'I'm glad you dropped by,' as if this wasn't a long-standing regular audience.

'The honour is all ours, your Highness,' Talgorian responded tactfully. He discreetly nudged Bastorran, who mumbled a similar platitude.

'There are weighty issues to be pondered,' Melyobar declared.

'Indeed there are,' Talgorian agreed, hopeful of a rational exchange for once.

'Do you know,' the Prince confided, 'two or three days ago I thought I had him.'

'Who?' Bastorran asked before Talgorian could stop him.

Melyobar looked affronted. 'Who? Death, naturally. Who else?'

'Oh. Yes. Of course, Highness.'

'It was in a village my troopers came across in the ... south somewhere, I think,' Melyobar related. 'The peasants were harbouring him, I'm *sure* of it. Not that I was there myself, obviously. I'm no fool! But would they give him up? Would they hell! He'd coached them in falsehood. Lies come to him as naturally as truth. More so. He's had greater trade with lies.' He glazed into some kind of reverie.

'What happened, Majesty?' Talgorian gently prompted.

'Happened? They persisted in their refusal to surrender him, that's what. Claimed they knew nothing about him. The sneaks! So I sent an order that had them put to him.'

His visitors were puzzled. 'Sir?' Bastorran queried.

'I had them put to him. You see? Put them to *Death*. See? Eh?' He laughed at his little joke.

They politely echoed his mirth with puny chuckles and thin smiles.

'He escaped me that time,' the Prince went on more gravely, half to himself, 'and it set me to thinking. Were my precautions sufficiently strong? Was simply running from him enough? Could I improve on my defences?' His sickly chest swelled, he eyed them triumphantly. 'Yes, I could!' He moved to the covered object. Grasping a honey-coloured bell rope hanging alongside, he gave it a dramatic yank. The drape rose, lifted by a counterweight and slender wires.

A sizeable cage was revealed. It was robustly built, highly decorated and golden in colour. It may have *been* gold, as befitted the property of a royal personage. But Talgorian suspected it was iron overlaid with gold leaf. Its entrance stood open, the sturdy door held above by powerful spring hinges.

'Well?' the Prince demanded.

'It's . . . unbelievable,' the Envoy whispered.

Bastorran concurred by nodding, but forgot to close his mouth.

'It's *strong*,' Melyobar enthused, wrapping his fist around one of the bars. 'Built by master craftsmen from the toughest materials. And it has spells to fortify it.' He looked at them. 'You can see its function, surely?'

A frozen moment slowly thawed.

Talgorian ventured, 'My congratulations, sir. A remarkably ingenious hiding place.'

'Yes, you'll be unreachable in that, Highness,' Bastorran said, following the other's lead. 'Perfectly safe.'

'*What?*' He frowned at them.

They waited, tongues leaden, expressions fixed.

'For two supposedly intelligent men that's . . . *asinine*!' the Prince announced, staring. Then he laughed. It was a high-pitched mocking bray, almost good-natured. 'It's not for *me*, it's for *him*!' He snatched up a sheaf of papers and rolled them as he spoke. 'Should Death catch up with me, despite all my efforts, he'll be snared. It has a trip, see?' He swatted at the cage with the rolled-up papers. The door instantly fell and snapped shut with an echoing clang. 'Clever, eh?'

'Very,' Talgorian managed, lamely.

'There's just one problem.'

'Your Highness?'

'What do you think I should bait it with?'

11

Dulian Karr said, 'I'll tell you what really happened.'

Reeth, Kutch and the patrician bumped along in Domex's covered wagon. It was pulled by a pair of dappled grey carthorses, with Caldason at the reins. Kutch sat next to him and Karr rode behind in the body of the wagon, his back against a heap of folded sacks. They had travelled through the night, avoiding main roads, heading south towards Valdarr. Now dawn was brightening the sky and they had fallen to discussing Bhealfa's rulers.

'Go on,' Kutch urged, eager for gossip.

'Many stories have been told about King Narbetton's fate,' Karr reminded them, taking up the thread with a hint of relish. 'The official version is that he perished during the chaos when Gath Tampoor drove Rintarah from this island and made it their own, about twenty years ago. Some say he died in the fire that destroyed the old palace. Others that he sacrificed his life heroically, leading a desperate defence against the invading forces. Or took poison, in despair at his kingdom passing from the hands of one occupier to another. They're all lies. Even his state funeral was a sham.'

Caldason glanced round at him. 'You're saying he's still alive?'

'Yes . . . and no. As they withdrew, Rintarahian sorcerers subjected Narbetton to some kind of magical assault. A parting shot, you might say, on a par with polluting wells and sowing the fields with salt. It could have been this that tilted the mind of his only son, Melyobar. Anyway, whatever they did, it left the King in a kind of unconscious state. A condition neither living nor dead, and one in which he apparently never ages. Whether the Rintarahians intended to do this, or if it was a bungled assassination, nobody knows.'

'You ever heard of such a thing, Kutch?' Caldason asked.

The boy looked surprised at having his opinion solicited, and not a little pleased. 'Oh. Well, yes, in a way. There are somnambulist spells, of course, and certain glamours that can put their subjects into trances. But the ones I know about sound mild compared to this, and they can be broken by any able practitioner.'

'This one can't,' Karr replied, 'for all the grand sorcerers in Melyobar's service. Though rumour suggests the Prince may not be as distressed about it as you might think. After all, his father's resuscitation would rob him of his power; and there's reason to believe he never had much liking for the old man anyway. But it's a measure of Melyobar's befuddlement that he's refused to adopt the title of King. Maybe he expects his father to recover. Who can say?'

'Do you know where Narbetton is now?'

'No one does for sure, but the betting has to be somewhere in Melyobar's absurd travelling palace.'

'How do you know all this?' Caldason said.

Karr smiled. 'Just a perk of belonging to the political classes. The story's quite well known throughout the administration.'

'Laying the facts before the people might make Rintarah

even less popular with Bhealfans. Wouldn't that suit our present masters?'

'Yes, but it would also have everyone asking why Gath Tampoor hasn't released the King from his plight.'

'Why haven't they?'

'Perhaps they can't, even with all the powerful magic an empire has at its command. Or it could be that it suits them better to deal with Narbetton's mad, pliable son. Though as the Prince grows more unpredictable that might not last forever. They've certainly benefited from the years of secret legal wrangling over the constitutional implications.'

Kutch had been listening intently. 'The kind of magic you're talking about would have been elementary for the Founders. There are even scholars who say the Dreamtime itself was actually a great spell, an enchantment that turned reality into a kind of illusion, in which everything was malleable. It's thought the Founders could make whatever they wanted just . . . *be*, like in dreams.' He grinned. 'Well, some believe that. There are varying opinions about everything to do with the Founders.'

'But it wasn't Founder magic that bound Narbetton,' Karr said. 'So shouldn't it be possible to undo it?'

'In theory. But there are many strands of magic, and sometimes a spell can be hard to lift because it sort of jams the balance.' He turned to Caldason. 'Like your –' Kutch was about to say problem '– people,' he quickly substituted. 'Your *people*.' Caldason glared at him. 'The Qaloch and their magic, which we spoke about, remember,' Kutch gushed, 'and how it was . . . different from . . . er . . .' Blushing, he felt as though he'd leapt from a hot skillet into a hotter fire.

Stony-faced, Caldason rescued him. 'It's true that the Qaloch have a different attitude to magic, and a different relationship with it. Unlike you, we don't see it as a measure of status.'

Karr didn't seem to notice Kutch's near-gaffe, or he chose to ignore it. 'How strange,' he mused.

With some misgiving, Kutch asked, 'Why are people so prejudiced against the Qaloch?' For a moment he thought he'd made things worse.

But Caldason didn't chide him. 'Maybe a Qalochian's not best placed to answer that. We tend to see the boot, not the reason it's aimed at our faces.'

'I think part of it is guilt,' Karr volunteered. 'After all, the Qaloch were Bhealfa's original inhabitants.'

'That's just a legend, isn't it?' Kutch said.

'Not to my people,' Caldason tautly informed him.

Again, Kutch wished he'd kept his mouth shut.

'Whatever the truth of it,' Karr asserted, 'there's no disputing that Qalochians have been disenfranchised. During my lifetime their last enclaves have gone completely, thanks to Bhealfa's appetite for land.'

'It wasn't just greed for our space,' Caldason told him. 'Look around you, Bhealfa has room to spare.' His manner had begun to be brooding.

'What else would you attach the bigotry to?'

'Our independence. There's little taste for those who don't conform. The fact that we're a warrior race doesn't sit comfortably either. The first thing put into our hand when we enter this world is a sword. Our ideal is to leave it holding one.' What might have been a wistful glow briefly mellowed the hardness in his eyes. 'But if you want to know the real reason we're shunned, it's simply because we're different.'

'People who hate you for that must be stupid,' Kutch decided.

'Never underestimate an enemy. Often it's not brains they lack, it's scruples.'

'Well said,' Karr offered.

For the past few hours they had been travelling through

a landscape of abundant trees and foliage. Now the terrain grew sparser. Ahead, the road forked, with a rougher track going towards the west.

'Turn here,' Karr instructed.

Caldason frowned. 'Why?'

'Just a small diversion.'

'I thought you were in a hurry to get back.'

'I am. But we're still at least two days from Valdarr. We need water and provisions, and we can get them not far from here.'

'How far?'

'A couple of hours at most. Besides, there's something I want you to see.'

'I'm not keen on surprises, Patrician.'

'You might find this one enlightening. Trust me, there won't be much of a delay.'

Caldason said nothing and made the turn.

The road they followed was potholed and overgrown with weeds. On either side the country was more scrub than grassland.

Above an hour later they came to the beginnings of a moor. There were clumps of heather and outcroppings of bleached rock, choked by moss. The few trees were infirm and skeletal. Distant stretches of marsh glistened in the frail sunlight, and the smell of rotting vegetation was in the air.

As they topped a low hill, Kutch remarked, 'This is a godsforsaken place.'

'A location nobody else wanted,' Karr agreed. 'It was all they could find.'

'Who?' Caldason said.

Karr pointed. 'You're about to find out.'

They were coming to a small, shallow valley, housing a

modest cluster of buildings. These conformed to no single style of architecture; a ramshackle appearance was all most of them had in common. Alongside the shacks, lodges and barns there were several thatched round houses, not that different to those Reeth had grown up in.

The settlement, or whatever it was, had no protective walls, ditches or watchtowers. People could be seen; carrying loads, leading animals, conversing in groups.

Karr knelt in the back of the wagon, watching over the others' shoulders. 'Pull up. There're one or two things you should know before we get there.'

The horses came to a ponderous halt, tails swishing, as Caldason tugged on the reins. 'What's going on, Karr?' he demanded.

'That's the Broliad commune, or what's left of it. Named for its late founder, who set it up a decade ago. He was a nonconformist too, Reeth, who persuaded a number of like-minded people to join him. They were a motley bunch, but shared a passion to be free of state interference. Commonly, they're known as the Disobedients.'

'I've heard of them,' Kutch said. 'Aren't they pacifists or something?'

'Mostly. They've tried to oppose imperial domination by non-violent means, and by living as divorced from authority as they can. It's been pretty tough for them.'

'I'm not surprised,' Caldason remarked, gazing down at the commune, 'if they insist on making themselves sitting ducks out here and refusing to fight.'

'Quite so.' Karr paused and added, 'I realise this is going to be hard for you.'

'No, I can respect a peace-loving man who has the guts to stand by his beliefs.'

'Very commendable. But that wasn't what I meant.'

'What did you mean?'

'This is a *pacifist* co-operative, Reeth. That means no weapons. Visitors have to surrender their arms on entering. No exceptions.'

From Caldason's expression, Kutch thought he was going to strike the patrician.

Instead, he rumbled, 'Forget it. Asking a Qalochian to give up his weapons is like . . .' He struggled for a comparison.

'So cheat,' Karr suggested.

'That's the politician speaking, is it?'

'It's common sense. Give up your more obvious weapons but keep something concealed, if you must. Though going armed down there is about as necessary as carrying an axe to defend yourself against a basketful of kittens.'

'They'll take my word that I have no hidden weapons?'

'No. But they'll take mine. They know me.'

'And you don't think that's a betrayal of their trust?'

'If you don't use your weapons it can't be, can it?' Before Caldason could reply, Karr turned to Kutch. 'And you can wipe that smirk off your face, young man. They don't allow magic either.'

To Kutch, this was much more shocking than a weapons ban. 'No magic? *None?* How can they function?'

'They have some sense after all, it seems,' Caldason muttered.

'I thought that would interest you,' Karr said. 'The fact is they don't permit either of the things you pair are wedded to. Live with it, just for a while.'

Caldason gave a resigned sigh and drew a knife. 'What are we doing here anyway?' he wanted to know, slipping it into his boot.

'As I said, I'm acquainted with some of the communards. It was always my aim to connect with them when I came to see Grentor. I have one or two matters to discuss with them. They'll let us have victuals for the rest of our journey, in exchange for a modest swelling of their coffers, and you get to see one way people resist.'

'I've seen plenty of resistance, most of it futile.'

'I'm not saying you'll find anything more effective in Broliad. But I'm honour-bound to meet with these people, and I'd appreciate you both being with me.'

'I'd like to see the place,' Kutch said.

'You've not left us a great deal of choice, Patrician,' Reeth put in.

'You could walk away. Or ride away, with the wagon and team. You're Reeth Caldason, after all. I would have thought an outlaw capable of such a thing.'

Caldason stiffened, his neck and arm muscles visibly knotting. 'Ready?' Without waiting for an answer he slapped the reins smartly across the horses' hinds.

They rattled down the slope in silence.

When they reached the settlement, people came out to meet them. They were dressed plainly in homespun greys and browns. There were roughly equal numbers of men and women, upwards of two score perhaps, and around a dozen children. A small menagerie of unfettered dogs, goats and fowl accompanied them.

Karr's claim that he knew the communards was borne out by the warm welcome they gave him. There was much in the way of hand-shaking, back-slapping and hugs. Reeth and Kutch were introduced only as friends; Karr withheld their names. The greeting they got was naturally less demonstrative than his, but seemed as open. And although Reeth's light olive cast and slightly angular facial bone structure testified to his birthright, no one showed any hostility at having a Qalochian in their midst.

Having handed over his pair of daggers, Karr turned to Reeth. 'You must give up your weapons,' he told him.

Caldason bit down and unbuckled his swords, then took

a sheathed knife from his belt. He dumped them into the outstretched arms of a waiting Disobedient. The man went off with them, smiling. Caldason glowered.

'I have business to discuss with our hosts,' Karr announced, nodding towards a particular group of communards. They were dressed as humbly as the others, and beyond the fact that they stood apart there was nothing to indicate they might have any authority. 'It shouldn't take long. In the meantime, they say you're welcome to go where you please in the commune. Rest, eat, refresh yourselves. I'll join you later.'

Reeth and Kutch watched him go with the communards into one of the round houses. Excitement over, the rest of the crowd melted away.

'Well, that's us dismissed,' Caldason said.

Karr's meeting proved much longer than promised. The morning stretched into afternoon, the afternoon into early evening, without sign of him.

Kutch and Reeth killed time by exploring the settlement. Their first impression was confirmed; the buildings were in a dilapidated state. Doors were off their hinges, corral fences were broken, the pigment used to stain woodwork was blistered and peeling. The animals, both livestock and domestic, looked undernourished. There was a general air of decline.

The communards, who appeared no less gaunt than their stock, left them to their own devices. People occasionally stared, but didn't trouble them.

Given the impoverished state of things, Reeth, and Kutch in particular, felt uncomfortable about asking to be fed. After being led to a refectory, where all the tables save theirs were empty, they were served watery soup, black bread and tart apples. Adequate, if bland fare.

Now, as the evening shadows lengthened, they made their way back to the round house Karr had entered. Its door remained fenced off.

Caldason grew impatient. 'This delay's starting to irk me. How much longer's the man going to be?'

'I suppose they have a lot to discuss,' Kutch replied, shrugging. He'd noticed how his companion's mood had darkened.

'I'll hurry them.'

'That might be thought uncivil, Reeth. Best to wait.'

'Until when? Morning? I'm no man's servant.' He broke away and strode towards the building.

'Reeth, no. Wait!'

Ten paces short, Caldason stopped. The door had opened, a square of light in the gathering gloom. Chattering people disgorged. There was some good-natured laughter. Karr emerged, saw Caldason and hurried to him, cloak flowing, arms outstretched apologetically.

'I'm sorry, truly. It proved much more drawn out than expected.'

'That's all right,' Kutch assured him.

Caldason was less forgiving, and a little sarcastic. 'Part of your grand project, was it?'

'It was important. More than that I can't say at the moment.' He ushered them away from the round house. 'Walk with me, my friends.'

Bunched together, they steered clear of the communards.

'What do you think of the place?' Karr asked.

'We certainly had long enough to form an opinion,' Caldason replied.

'Yes, I said I was sorry. But what do you *think*?'

'The people seem decent enough. As to the set-up here, I'm not too impressed.'

'Kutch?'

'I think the same as Reeth, I suppose. Things don't seem

too efficient, and you'd imagine they would be after . . . What is it? Ten years?'

Karr smiled. 'I agree.'

'You do?'

'Yes. I don't think this place works either. I never thought it would. Right motivation, wrong approach.'

'So why come here?' Caldason said.

'I promised them I would. Besides, I don't say everything they do is wrong. But this isn't the time to discuss it.' He glanced at several passing communards. 'Look, the day's well advanced and none of us got a great deal of sleep last night. We've been invited to stay until morning, and I suggest we accept. Tomorrow we can make an early start.'

Kutch had no objection. They took Caldason's silence as assent.

'We have a choice of places to bed down,' Karr explained. 'There are dormitories, which most of the communards use, or one or two quieter places if you want privacy.'

'I'd prefer something private,' Kutch decided, 'if nobody minds.'

'No problem. But remember the embargo on magic. We don't want our hosts offended by any late night spell-casting.'

'I promise. What about you?'

'I'll take a dormitory.'

'I wouldn't have thought that was what you were used to.'

'Because I'm a patrician?' Karr grinned. 'Don't look embarrassed; you're right. But it's politic for me to enter into the co-operative spirit.' He looked to Caldason. 'You're quiet, Reeth.'

'Just tired.'

'Where do you want to sleep?'

'Out here.'

Karr was perplexed. 'When you have a warm bed on offer? And a roof over your head?'

'I'm accustomed to sleeping outdoors. Stars are the only roof I need.' He indicated a small stand of trees, just beyond the commune's outermost buildings. 'I'll be there.'

The patrician's eyebrows rose a smidgen. 'As you please. Come on, Kutch.'

Kutch bade Caldason goodnight, and felt a little wounded when there was no response. They left him standing in front of the round house.

Karr led the boy to a shack, run-down outside but clean, if spartan, within. It had a reasonably sized cot and a good supply of blankets. The patrician let Kutch know where he was sleeping, closed the door and left.

There were candles on an upended crate, but Kutch didn't bother with them. He realised how tired he was, and took to the bed fully clothed. It was comfortable. In truth, now that a wave of fatigue had hit him, a stone floor would have seemed inviting.

He thought he should at least get out of his jerkin. But he didn't really want to move. And his boots. He should definitely take those off. In a minute he would, when he'd relaxed a bit. He'd just lie here for a while, then undress properly. In a minute or two.

He slipped into a velvety, dreamless sleep.

An immeasurable slab of time passed.

Then somebody was shaking him awake. A figure in the dark he couldn't see properly, looming over him. He tried to cry out and a hand clamped against his mouth.

The figure leaned closer.

'*Help me,*' it whispered hoarsely.

12

Kutch's night visitor must have left the hut's door ajar, because a gust of wind made it creak open a fraction. A sliver of light entered, dispelling the shadows concealing the intruder's face.

Caldason, wild-eyed, dishevelled.

He took his hand away from Kutch's mouth. The boy relaxed a little, though his friend's crazed appearance still made him nervous.

'What is it?' he said. 'What's wrong?'

Reeth put a finger to his lips in a hushing gesture. His movements were uncertain, like a drunk's. But he hadn't been drinking.

Kutch dropped his voice to a whisper. 'What's the matter? Are you ill?'

The last of the sleep ebbed away and he guessed what was happening. 'Is it another of your –?'

Caldason nodded.

'What can I do?'

'I need your help . . . like before. ' His voice wavered. He looked around the sparse room. 'This isn't a good place. Come with me.'

Head spinning, Kutch scrambled from the bed. He saw that Reeth was carrying a coil of thick rope, and that there was sweat on his brow.

'Quickly,' Reeth hissed. He made to leave.

'One second.' Stooping, Kutch rolled up some bedclothes, then covered them with a blanket. Someone taking a cursory look might be fooled into thinking the cot was occupied.

'*Hurry.*'

'All *right.*'

They left the shack, Kutch quietly closing the door behind them.

It was the middle of the night, and the moon was full and fat. They couldn't see anyone about, but crept stealthily, keeping to the pools of denser gloom where buildings overhung.

Caldason walked like a man who'd just run a hard race, breathless and slightly clumsy. Kutch followed, afraid they'd meet somebody and of what Caldason might do if they did.

As they came to the corner of a barn, Caldason motioned Kutch to stop. They peered round at the nearest thing the co-operative had to a town square. It was the confluence of four serpentine lines of buildings, with an open space where their dirt roads met. A gathering area for the communards when group decisions had to be made or a newborn's head wetted. The space was big enough to think twice about crossing if you didn't want to be seen, and some of the buildings around were still burning lights.

'What now?' Kutch mouthed.

Caldason pointed. Just beyond the edge of the settlement was the small copse he'd chosen earlier as a place to sleep. To get to it they had to break cover and cross the square.

'Me first,' he whispered, hoisting the rope over his shoulder. 'I'll signal if it's clear.'

Kutch nodded and watched him go.

Caldason moved in an ungainly way, half doubled over, as though an ache troubled his guts. His progress was sluggish, but he cleared the common without incident. Reaching the far side, he put his hands against a wall and leaned there, head down. That gave Kutch a queasy moment.

Then Caldason raised his head and turned to face him. Looking to the left and right, he waved Kutch across. The boy dashed over to him.

Keeping low, they crept from the settlement. Impacted earth gave way to dried mud and clumps of spongy grass. Now they were in open ground, and twenty paces later waist-high bushes. Then the stand of trees loomed over them, their branches cobwebbing the moon.

Caldason tossed the coil of rope to Kutch. Its weight had the boy staggering back a step, knees bent.

'Tie me,' Reeth ordered, panting. 'To that tree.' He nodded at the biggest. 'And take this.' He bent and fished out the knife hidden in his boot. Kutch slipped it into his belt.

Caldason sat with his back against the trunk. As Kutch began winding the rope around him he said, 'What did you do before you met me?' It was gallows humour, but Caldason took it seriously.

'If I was near the innocent I got as far away as I could. If I was facing an enemy, I didn't bother.'

'What *is* wrong with you, Reeth?'

'Just hurry! And make that *tighter*!'

Kutch finished the knots, with some instruction, and stood gaping at what he'd done.

'Now get away from here,' Reeth said. 'No, wait! We have to stifle any noises I might make. I need something to bite on.'

'Like what?'

'It'll have to be rope. Use the knife to cut a length.'

Taking an arm's length from the coil's end, Kutch severed

it with the razor-keen blade. He fixed it around the tree so that it ran across Caldason's mouth, like a horse's bridle.

'Good,' Reeth said. 'When you've done this, get out of here.' His eyes were starting to roll and he was breathing harder. He bit down on the rope and Kutch pulled it tight, knotting it at the back of the tree. Then he did as he was told and withdrew.

But not very far.

All he knew was pain.

Acrid odours prickled his nostrils. The air stank of charred wood and burnt flesh. A blaze crackled somewhere nearby. Further away, there were screams and shouts.

He must have been on his back, because he could see the sky. It was on fire. Flaming crimson overlaid with streamers of oily black smoke. Ashes spinning in the heat.

Then something obscured his view. A figure, bending over him, blurred, indefinite. Laying hands on him. He glimpsed those hands as they came away and they were bloody.

He tried to speak but couldn't. It was as though he'd forgotten how.

A cup was held to his lips, but he seemed to have forgotten how to swallow, too. The liquid was poured into his mouth. Whatever it was it scorched his throat like molten lead, and when it arrived in his stomach it caused an incendiary spasm.

Pain increased to agony.

The hands were there again. He fancied they made certain gestures over him, complicated arcane movements whose significance he couldn't grasp. His discomfort was alleviated a little. He thought the person tending him might have been an old man, but he couldn't trust his eyes.

Time passed. It was filled with the blushing sky and the burning flesh and the far off screams.

Then he was aware that whatever he was resting on was being lifted. They were moving him, whoever they might be, and the deed brought his body fresh agitation. It made him ache anew, every jolt and bump a thrust from a white-hot dagger. Once more he tried speaking, or to be accurate crying out, but no sound came.

He saw, thought he saw, the tops of burning buildings, and trees alight. And always that sky, churning with flame.

At last he was taken into a sheltered place, exchanging the angry sky for a cross-beamed wooden ceiling. To his relief, the movement stopped.

Those veined and bloodied hands ministered to him. Unable to utter a sound, he could do no more than stare at the buttressed ceiling. Tormented, helpless, misery held sway for an indeterminate period.

Then there was a sudden shift in reality.

What he could see of his surroundings – the wooden ceiling, the hazy figures attending him – was wiped away. Or rather, another scene imposed itself. A dream within a dream.

He stood on the edge of an unimaginably steep cliff.

Below, a vast plain stretched out. Cities blossomed there, as though sown. Fabulous crystalline edifices, shimmering spires, arching bridges no more palpable than moonbeams. Clusters of towers fashioned from solidified light, framed with steel rainbows. Gigantic floating structures, bubble-like, anchored by palpitating tendrils. Municipalities where ice and fire conspired in breathtakingly graceful lines and impossible, vertiginous angles.

All in flux.

Everything was constantly changing, evolving, mutating and reforming. Constructs expanded, compressed or dissolved. New shapes emerged; jagged, forked, rectangular, spiked, pyramidal. Their essences rippled, their surface textures continually altered. The colours attending them danced back and forth across the visible spectrum and beyond.

Nearly level with his cliff-top, but far away, mountains slumbered uneasily. They slowly undulated. Peaks flattened, fresh ones arose. Fissures opened and dribbled lava.

Above, the sky changed colour randomly. From green to grey to orange. Purple transformed to yellow, yellow to red, red was flooded with gold.

Hosts of entities were in the air. Metamorphs, resembling beasts one moment, something like men the next; often corresponding to no known being, or taking on complex abstract forms. All inspired wonder. Many, revulsion.

He knew that everything he saw was animated by energies coursing through the earth. A grid of power, sensed rather than seen, permeating the whole of this world and saturating it with vigour. Power that flowed through him too, throbbing in rhythm with the beating of his heart and the pumping of his blood.

His emotions were contrary. He felt a stranger, an outsider in this place, and was fearful of it, but also that he somehow belonged here.

As he watched the cycle of destruction and creation going on all around, he became aware of a presence. A consciousness, near to hand, seeping depravity and malevolence. The impression was of pure mind. Not singular but many; a vast coupling of intelligences that formed a miasma of spite. He couldn't see it, it seemed to have no substance, but he knew it could snuff him out.

It approached.

A shadow fell over him, though it had no visible source. Its cold touch relayed terror.

He turned and ran.

The black, malignant force pursued him.

He took to the air, lifting as easily and lightly as a bird. It was wholly instinctive. He had no wings; belief elevated him and thought directed his flight. The talent came naturally, and of all the wonders this world had to offer it seemed the least remarkable.

Now he was among the myriad other airborne things, twisting and dodging to avoid them. The dark intelligence was at his back, ready to pounce. He dived, spun, soared, trying to shake it off. His course took him through clouds of the flying grotesques. As he passed,

*they were drawn into the inky embrace of the multi-mind, swelling
its might and rancour.*

*It brought lightning bolts into existence and hurled them at him.
He swerved and spiralled to escape the crackling, dazzling strokes of
energy.*

*Then one struck him. Every particle of his being was ravaged by
its intensity. He plummeted down to the ever-shifting, fickle earth,
and was seized by a power greater than mere gravity.*

*Trapped, defenceless, he could only watch as the manifold black-
ness descended inexorably to engulf him. And he knew that death
was the least it could inflict.*

He screamed.

*Instantly, the fiery sky reasserted itself. Then that was blocked
from view as the wooden ceiling reformed.*

*He was prostrate, staring up at joists and rafters, as the pain
flooded back.*

Again he screamed, until the dark swallowed him.

Late afternoon saw the trio back on the road to Valdarr.

Karr took his turn as wagon driver, with Kutch at his side.
Caldason travelled behind under canvas.

It had been an awkward day. Caldason was taciturn and
troubled looking, only speaking when he was spoken to and
not always then. There had been no time for Kutch to discuss
the night's events with him. Not that the Qalochian seemed
very inclined to do so.

Kutch had watched what happened to Reeth during the
night in horrified fascination. When it was finally over, in
the small hours, he found that the rope gag was almost
chewed through. He got him back to the shack somehow,
only avoiding being seen by sheer luck, and bedded him
down on the cot. For himself, Kutch took the floor, and they
slept erratically for a couple of hours. Naturally they said
nothing to Karr the next morning. And once the communards

had been thanked and their weapons retrieved they made
an early start.

Now Caldason slumped in the back of the wagon looking
exhausted. Kutch, confused as ever about what ailed him,
was lost in thought. Karr seemed his usual self. But Kutch
was coming to realise that in his way the patrician was as
hard to read as Caldason. The difference was that where
Reeth retreated into sullen silence, Karr covered his true
intentions with verbosity. Kutch half suspected the patrician
had some idea of their nocturnal adventure, though he made
no mention of it.

Following some small talk about the commune and its
fortunes, Karr said, 'I wish we'd known this horse's shoe
needed attention before we left there. Still, we'll be at
Saddlebow soon.'

Caldason made one of his rare contributions. 'Can't we go
round it?'

'I don't know where else we can have a horse shod.
Anyway, skirting Saddlebow adds another day to the journey.
But I don't want to linger there any longer than you do.
We'll rest, see to the horses, stretch our legs. No more.' He
turned to Kutch. 'I've been meaning to ask: have you ever
been to Valdarr before?'

'No, nor even Saddlebow. I travelled a bit with my master,
but always to other hamlets and villages. I suppose that makes
me a country boy.'

'Then it's probably good that we're starting at Saddlebow
and working our way up. You could find town and city life
a bit overwhelming at first.' He gave the boy a smile. 'But
don't worry, you have guardians.'

'One of whom's a wanted outlaw,' Caldason said, 'and the
other a target for assassins.'

That put a bit of a damper on things and they rode in
silence until Saddlebow came into view.

It was a sizeable town, full of activity, and when they found a blacksmith he told them he needed a couple of hours to attend to the shoe.

'You won't find another smith less busy,' he promised.

'All right,' Karr replied, handing him some coins.

The man spat on them and dropped them into his apron pouch. 'I'll see to it your team's fed and watered.'

'We could do with that ourselves,' Karr decided. 'Come on,' he told his companions.

They began to walk, looking for a tavern. The streets bustled.

'Is it normally this full?' Kutch asked.

Karr shook his head. 'This is unusual.'

There were watchmen in the crowd, and a few paladins. They steered well clear of them. As they got nearer to the town's centre there were more and more people.

'Maybe we've come on a festival day or something,' Kutch suggested.

'They don't seem in a particularly festive mood,' Caldason pointed out.

He was right. With few exceptions the crowd was sombre and uncommonly quiet for such a mass.

Everybody seemed to be going the same way. Reeth, Karr and Kutch went along with them, partly out of curiosity, partly because they didn't want to draw attention to themselves.

Eventually they came to the town's main square. It was packed with hundreds of people. Peddlers and jugglers worked the throng, but they plied their trade with scant enthusiasm. The tunes the itinerant musicians played were mournful.

Kutch spotted food sellers, carrying their wares on large trays balanced on their heads. 'I'm starving,' he announced. 'Shall we eat?'

'Wait.' Caldason put a hand on the apprentice's shoulder and pointed towards the centre of the square. Kutch and the patrician craned their necks to see.

The crowd lapped up against a long wooden platform which rose above the heads of the onlookers. It could have been a stage, except for several thick projecting posts, about the height of a man.

Kutch looked puzzled. 'What is it?'

'An execution platform,' Caldason explained.

The blood drained out of Kutch's face. 'Oh,' he whispered.

To one side of the platform a small spectators' stand had been erected. It was covered by an awning and held three or four rows of tiered seats. They were filling up with the expensively attired and well fed, presumably local dignitaries. Among them were individuals whose splendid clothing and showy glamoured accessories marked them out as citizens of Gath Tampoor.

A blast of trumpets silenced the murmuring crowd. Then a procession climbed to the platform, led by an official with the self-important look of an over-promoted clerk. He was followed by several other functionaries, and behind them two bedraggled men who were obviously the accused, escorted by militia. Already manacled, the prisoners were chained to two of the posts.

The retinue included a state sorcerer. Swiftly, he cast a spell that conjured an orating glamour. This took the form of a giant mouth that floated high above the dais and acted as an amplifier for the crowd.

Stepping forward, the lead official unrolled a sheet of parchment. As he read from it the hovering mouth aped his lip movements.

'Let it be known,' the mouth boomed, *'that these men stand accused of disturbing the peace of the realm as legally constituted and guaranteed by His Sovereign Highness Prince Melyobar, and*

that through their actions they sought to endanger, subvert and betray the citizens of Bhealfa. Be it recorded, moreover, that they are further charged to be members of proscribed organisations engaged in criminal deeds to the peril of the realm.'

'In plain language, the Resistance,' Karr whispered.

'All here are called upon to witness the indictment of the malefactors in accordance with the demands of law,' the mouth continued, approximating the real speaker but different enough to be unmistakably non-human. *'The degree of their guilt shall be determined, and if their probity be found wanting, let their fate serve as an example. The accused are to be put to the test. Gods save the Prince!'*

The crowd responded half-heartedly, and one or two voices were raised in protest. Mounted paladins and the militia on the platform scanned the gathering, ready for troublemakers.

'What does being put to the test mean?' Kutch asked.

'They'll undergo ordeal by magic,' Caldason said. 'If they pass, they get prison or exile. If they fail, it's death.'

'What does that have to do with proving their guilt or innocence?'

'They're already guilty in the state's eyes. This is by way of public entertainment. Or a warning, depending on the crowd's sympathies.'

'It's a misuse of the Craft,' Kutch seethed. 'Why can't they be allowed a proper trial?'

'Such niceties are available only to our rulers,' Karr told him. 'Though it'll be a chilly day in hell before any of *them* appears in a court. For the rest of us, justice is summary.'

On the platform, the presiding official signalled that the test was to proceed. The sorcerer began a ritual, reciting from a heavy tome held open by an acolyte. Whatever he said was a mystery to the crowd as it wasn't relayed by the levitating mouth.

There was a series of blinding flashes, a fraction of a second apart, and a trio of swirling green clouds appeared on the platform. A collective gasp rose from the onlookers. Rotation slowing, the clouds took on a tangible appearance.

The glamours that formed were identical. Three women, tall, marble-skinned, dressed in silken white gowns that reached the floor. Their hair was spun gold and they wore laurel crowns. Black blindfolds covered their eyes.

They stood in a line before the first accused.

Via the orating glamour, the official declared portentously, *'Behold, the personification of Justice! One holds the key to mercy. The others, annihilation.'* He turned to the first condemned man. *'You have a span of twenty beats in which to make your choice.'* Pointing to each of the statuesque glamours in turn, he counted them off. *'One, two or three. Prisoner, you hold your destiny in your own hands. Let the test commence!'*

An unseen drum began to pound, steady as a heartbeat. Nervously, the accused man's gaze flicked from one motionless glamour to the next. The deathly hush that had blanketed the crowd was broken as people started to call out their favoured numbers.

Karr noticed the anger on Caldason's face, and that he was clutching the hilt of his sheathed sword, white-knuckled. He reached out and stayed his hand. 'No, my friend,' he whispered. 'The odds are too great, even for you.' Caldason glared at him, eyes blazing. 'Think of the boy,' Karr added.

Reeth sobered. He shook free of Karr's grasp and looked to Kutch.

The boy was staring intently at the platform and the unfolding drama. Under his breath he mumbled, 'Two . . . number two . . . pick *two*.'

Abruptly, the drumming stopped. Once more, the crowd fell silent.

'How do you choose?' the official demanded, echoed by the resonant mouth.

The prisoner's hesitant reply couldn't be heard far beyond the platform. The mouth glamour broadcast it.

'He chooses . . . three!'

Those in the crowd who agreed with the choice shouted approval. There were some cheers and boos, but mostly the response was mute.

'*No*,' Kutch groaned, 'it's two. *Two*.'

'Let the named one be revealed.'

The third glamour drifted forward. At a command gesture from the sorcerer it underwent a transformation. Its features blurred and melted, and in seconds it returned to an eddying green cloud. That held for a few seconds. Then the wisps of emerald haze dispersed, showing the glamour reconstituted. But differently.

A roar went up from the crowd, a mixture of disappointment, rage, and a little glee.

The glamour was draped in rags. Her hair was stringy and grey, and the laurel headdress had rotted. The hands and arms were stripped to bone. Where there had been a noble, comely face now there was a bleached skull, a grinning death's head, jaw agape.

'The accused stands condemned! In accordance with the authority vested in this tribunal, the penalty shall be exacted.'

What happened next was at least mercifully swift, if shocking. A brawny militiaman approached the prisoner. As he moved he swung a two-hand broadsword in a high arc. Its blade glinted briefly in the sun, then severed the man's neck. His head sprang from his shoulders, bounced across the platform and came to rest near the edge. The body, hanging by chains, pumped copious blood. It splashed the other, horrified prisoner shackled alongside.

There was uproar in the crowd. A patter of refined applause came from the spectators' stand.

Kutch turned away from the sight, stunned, and in reflex

buried his face in Reeth's side, suddenly more child than man. Taken aback, Caldason gingerly encircled him with a comforting arm.

Matters stood for a moment. Then Karr asked gently, 'How did you know, Kutch? That he'd got the wrong glamour, I mean. You seemed very certain if it was a guess.'

Kutch disentangled himself from Caldason, looking bashful. 'It wasn't a guess,' he sniffed despondently. 'They're using quality magic, expensive stuff, which makes it hard to tell. But not impossible.' He shrugged. 'I recognised it from experience, I suppose.'

'Come on,' Caldason said, 'let's go.'

Before they could push their way out of the mob, the official's surrogate mouth announced the next test. The crowd pressed forward again.

There were three new glamours on the platform. These were male, clothed in white togas and sporting long black hair. They weren't wearing blindfolds; they simply had no eyes, just smooth skin where they should have been.

The second ordeal commenced, the drum began its doleful pounding.

But the accused wasn't going to co-operate. He started to shout, loud enough for some of his words to carry. They were parts of slogans or a speech and the only string they heard was, '. . . freedom! Long live the –'

'Forfeit!' the mouth bellowed.

The militiaman came again and finished his work with the sword. It took two swings this time.

'We should leave,' Karr suggested softly.

The crowd began to disperse, quietly shuffling.

Reeth and Karr each took one of the boy's arms to guide him through.

'It would have been number three that time,' Kutch told them, blinking back the tears.

13

Jecellam, the capital of Rintarah, sprawled in the middle of a fertile plain and was backed by distant snow-capped mountains. Three rivers served the city, one running through, the others looping it. Ranches and farms of enormous acreage surrounded and supplied the metropolis.

The ethos of the eastern empire was collectivist, or at least outwardly so, and nowhere was Rintarah's doctrine more apparent than in Jecellam. Its streets were clean and orderly, with buildings arranged in neat rows. As far as possible, lives were regulated and necessary tasks centrally organised. The city was policed with vigilance, and according to the state was practically free of crime.

Despite Rintarah's egalitarian order, disparities existed, not least in the distribution of magic. The grandest, most expensive products of sorcery were invariably to be found where the affluent lived. And there were such people, whether the system recognised it or not.

The city was predicated on there being a place for everything and everything being in its place. There were residential quarters, and different areas where things were made, youngsters educated, the sick tended.

Officially sanctioned houses of pleasure existed too, well away from the homes of the elite. They clustered in the oldest part of the city, where cleanliness and conformity were less rigidly enforced, and where the unacknowledged poor congregated. Places which respectable citizens, fearing to walk, would visit in carriages with shaded windows.

A particularly notorious street ran adjacent to the docks. The bordellos lining it were said to cater for every taste. Consequently it was one of the few places where the highest and the lowest mingled.

The many establishments the street had to offer ranged from the dismally sordid to the gaudily opulent. One particular building, narrow, tall and outwardly unremarkable, fell somewhere near the middle of this spectrum. Like the others it was always open for trade, as the demand for its services was by no means restricted to the hours of darkness. But around noon few women were working and there was only a trickle of clients. This was a time when the burghers who covertly owned the business saved money by not employing minders.

A visitor to the house, once past its heavy front door, would be aware of shabbiness and neglect. Reasonably luxuriant long ago, the interior was now down at heel. Wall hangings depicting erotic scenes from antiquity and legend were faded. Woodwork was chipped and in need of varnish, rugs were threadbare. The faint odour of rot wasn't quite hidden by incense.

Creaking stairs led to several storeys in like condition, each with half a dozen or so client chambers. On the top floor there were just two rooms, both with their doors shut.

The bigger of the two was very much the same as all the other rooms in the building; grubby and in need of decoration, though a few personal possessions gave a little character to its austerity. Its main item of furniture was a large bed.

A man and a woman occupied it. Naked, entwined.

Mumbling endearments spiced with obscenities, he thrusted feebly. He was old, near bald, with a pepper and salt beard. He had saggy, veined skin and a paunch, and perspired copiously.

The woman under him was putting on a performance, only able to pretend she was enjoying the act because she'd learnt how to disassociate, to put her mind somewhere else.

She had light olive skin and jet black hair. She was strong-featured, handsome and smooth-limbed. But at twenty-eight summers Tanalvah Lahn was growing long in the tooth for her profession.

His exertions seemed to last forever, breath laboured, bony fingers digging painfully into her shoulders. She caught a whiff of his body odour – unwashed flesh and old sweat – and turned her head to one side, keeping a fixed smile.

At last he climaxed and she matched his cries and moans with fake responses. Relief was her strongest emotion, mixed with a revulsion she tried hard not to show.

He rolled off her, panting, red-faced. She hoped he wasn't going to have a seizure. That was always bad for business. He lay wheezing, a trickle of drool snaking from the corner of his mouth.

'You were wonderful,' she lied huskily.

He returned a similarly barren compliment, his interest in her already fading.

She got up, glad to move away from him. On a wobbly cabinet beside the bed stood an earthen basin filled with cold water. She dipped a cloth in it and washed herself. The client rose too and started to dress. She dried off and reached for her own clothes, wriggling into them hurriedly, anxious to be rid of him.

As he put on his garments their finery began to reveal his status; the distinctive livery of a senior bureaucrat. He had a fancy title which, like his name, she'd instantly forgotten.

'So, how long have you been doing this?' he said, negotiating buttons.

It was surprising how often they came out with that question. She suspected his curiosity was feigned, like that of all the others, and he probably only spoke to fill an otherwise awkward silence.

'The governors marked me out at birth. I began work at first blood.'

He winced at her explicitness. Like most men, she reckoned, he didn't want to think about the workings of a woman's body, just make use of it. He covered his embarrassment with flattery. 'Ah, that explains your expertise, my dear.'

She could have told him she never had a choice about the path she trod. Or how sick of it she was. Instead she flashed him a practised, non-committal smile.

A muffled thump and rumble came from the next room. It sounded like Mahba had a lively customer.

'Have you never wanted to do anything else?' Tanalvah's client asked.

It was another standard question. Doubtless to be followed by the time-worn *Let me take you away from all this* that would be forgotten as soon as he'd gone. He was irritating her. She just wanted him to leave. 'Look,' she said, not bothering to keep the annoyance out of her voice, 'it's been good, but time's –'

A shrill scream rang out next door. There were more thuds, and the sound of something breaking.

'Mahba!' Tanalvah exclaimed.

She slipped her hand under a cushion for the thin-bladed knife she kept there. Then she rushed out, leaving her alarmed client hopping with one foot in his breeches.

On the landing she rapped on the door of the next room. The only reply was another round of bumps.

'Mahba!' she called, beating the door with her palms. 'Are you all right? *Mahba!*' There was no answer and it had gone quiet inside. Tanalvah's client joined her. 'Help me!' she pleaded. 'Break down the door!'

The bureaucrat regarded her timidly. 'Surely in this sort of place, with your kind of people, you have to expect –'

'You old *fool*!' she snapped. 'My friend's in there and I need your fucking help!'

'I say, there's no call for –'

A lock rattled, the door slowly opened a crack.

'Mahba?' Tanalvah whispered.

What she saw was a middle-aged man of distinguished appearance. Dressed, though dishevelled, he wore an abashed expression. He didn't speak. Nor did he try to stop her when she reached out and pushed against the door. As it swung further inwards she saw that his white shirt was stained red.

'What's happened?' she said. 'What have you done?'

He only stared at her.

She shoved past him. He didn't resist.

The room was in a shambles, its occupant's few belongings scattered across the floor. A chair was overturned, a broken jug lay on the tattered carpet, a window drape hung by threads.

Tanalvah barely registered any of that. What she saw was Mahba, stretched out on the bed, for all the world like a broken doll, limbs at crazy angles, eyes open, staring. There was a cord wound tight around her neck. Her mouth was partly open, her swollen tongue protruding. Her face was tinged blue, what Tanalvah could see of it through the blood and rising bruises.

'*Mahba!*'

She flew to the bed, discarding her knife. Frantically she began shaking her friend, slapping her cheeks, calling her name. She looked up at the bloodstained man and repeated, 'What have you *done*?'

He spoke then, trying to sound in control, but he couldn't hide the wavering tone of his voice. 'Look . . . this doesn't have to be a problem.'

'*What?*'

'She shouldn't have struggled,' he came back defensively. 'It was only a bit of fun. That's what she's paid for, isn't it?'

'She's dead. Mahba's *dead*! What kind of . . . *fun* is that?'

'We can come to an arrangement,' he snivelled, pulling out his money pouch with a trembling hand.

'Arrangement? You killed my friend, you bastard!' Her dark eyes flashed angrily.

His whining self-justification suddenly evaporated. Genuine wrath took hold of his features. It crossed her mind that he might be ramped; she knew some used it for heightening sexual pleasure. He came nearer, still nervous but his gaze intense.

'Listen, slut,' he snarled, 'I've got contacts. I can make things really difficult for you. I'm talking about big trouble.'

'You're the one in trouble,' she promised.

'And you think the authorities would take the word of a Qalochian whore over that of a man of stature?'

'I have a witness.'

Tanalvah's ageing client, hovering at the door and radiating ineffectiveness, looked startled.

The murderer shot him an artful glance. 'Not unless he wants to be dragged into a public scandal.'

That made the old man's eyes widen. 'No, I couldn't possibly be involved,' he gabbled. 'Absolutely not. I mean, I have to think of my position, my responsibilities. My *family*.' He was backing away. 'But I'll summon help. Just as soon as I'm away from here. I promise.'

'No!' Tanalvah cried. 'Don't go!'

He turned and ran down the stairs, moving with remarkable speed for a man his age. There was no way he was going to risk himself for a prostitute, and certainly not for a Qalochian. She'd seen it in his face, had seen it many times before.

Mahba's killer didn't believe the old man was going for help any more than Tanalvah did. He smiled like a snake. 'Now are you going to see sense?' he said.

'All I see is my best friend dead.'

Far below, the front door slammed with a dreadful finality. She knew there were few, if any, other people in the house.

'You stupid bitch,' he snarled. 'Do you really think I'm going to let myself be ruined over a harlot's worthless life?'

He moved towards her, fury in his eyes. She remembered the knife, lying on the bed. He followed her gaze.

Lunging for it simultaneously, they collided. A struggle ensued as they fought for the blade. Then he backhanded her hard across the face, sending her sprawling to the floor. He had the knife, and came at her with it shouting, his words garbled by rage.

With no time to get to her feet, Tanalvah kicked out at him. More by chance than design she connected solidly with his shin. He lost his balance, almost landing on her. The tussle for the knife resumed, Tanalvah's hands around his wrist, straining to check it. He was more powerful. The blade made steady progress towards her face.

From the corner of her eye Tanalvah saw Mahba's arm hanging limply over the side of the bed. Terror at the thought of suffering her friend's fate gave her the strength of desperation. She fortified her grip and stayed the knife, but couldn't force it back.

Lowering her head, she sank her teeth into the back of his hand and bit deeply. He yelped and dropped the weapon. Tanalvah grabbed it.

'Stay back!' she yelled, scrambling away from him, pointing the knife.

He either didn't see or didn't care about the blade, and flung himself at her.

She felt the impact, and the knife slipping into his flesh.

An outrush of breath emptied his lungs. He made a sound like a sigh. The expression on his face seemed one of amazement rather than pain. As she watched, his eyes glazed.

She was on her knees, supporting his slumped body. Horrified, she pushed him off. He fell weightily. The hilt of the knife stuck out from his chest, a widening patch of crimson where she supposed his heart to be. There was no question that he was dead.

The crossing of that insubstantial line between life and death had happened so quickly she couldn't take it in. Tanalvah wanted to scream, to vomit, to run headlong from this place and hide. For a moment she hung on the edge of hysteria, then gradually fought down the urge for blind flight.

She got to her feet, shakily, and realised she had blood on her dress.

What she was supposed to do was summon the authorities, throw herself on their mercy. She almost smiled. If anybody was going to get the blame for this, she knew, it was her. But she couldn't think of another way.

She looked at the violated, lifeless body of her friend. Then her eye was caught by a particular object in the debris on the floor. The sight of it sent icy fingers caressing her spine.

Stooping, she picked it up. It was an expensive glamour, resembling a thin, red leather-bound book. Mahba had charmed one of her moneyed clients into buying it for her, and it was probably her most precious possession.

Tanalvah opened it, revealing a shiny black inner surface and activating the spell. Tiny glittering specks began to swirl in the core of its darkness. They quickly multiplied and coalesced, forming a vivid three-dimensional portrait, recently cast. The likenesses of two smiling children – a boy of five with tousled ginger hair and freckled cheeks, and a girl of eight sporting long flaxen locks and a slightly serious expression.

What was there for them now? Tanalvah wondered. A state orphanage? Adoption by favoured officials who couldn't have children of their own?

More likely training for farm labour or domestic service. She looked closely at the girl. Or a life like hers, in a brothel.

She had to do something, however slim the chances.

Gently, she laid the glamour on Mahba's chest and folded her already cool hands over it. She lightly kissed her brow. Blinking back tears, she lifted one side of the embroidered bed sheet and covered her body.

There were clothes-hooks on the wall, holding a jacket and a cloak. She searched them and found a key, which she pocketed. Tanalvah took a last look at her friend, and no more than a fleeting glance at her murderer's corpse as she stepped over it. She closed the door quietly behind her.

Back in her own room she splashed cold water on her face, then swiftly changed into fresh clothes. She collected a few of her meagre belongings and stuffed them into a cloth shoulder bag. Lifting a floorboard, she found the purse containing what little money she'd been able to save. She put on a cape, then wound a cotton scarf around her neck so that her lower face was veiled. It was absurdly inadequate in terms of a disguise, but all she could think of.

She left her room and crept down the stairs, avoiding the creaking boards, frightened someone else was there and about to discover her.

Normally, opening the front door would be a time consuming task with its numerous bolts and chains. But they were all undone, presumably from when her client had fled.

The old dolt had been of some use after all. She inhaled deeply a couple of times and stepped outside.

On the street she felt more nervous than she'd ever been in her life. Every passer-by was a potential accuser, every look she drew, an indictment.

She expected the People's Militia to appear and arrest her at any minute. Eyes downcast, she tried to look like an ordinary person going about her business.

She hoped the bodies wouldn't be found until the busy evening period. That might give her just enough time.

Walking seemed the best option. She could have taken one of the public horse-drawn wagons, or spent out on a private hire carriage, even if that ran the risk of her right to do so being challenged. But either would make her feel too restricted, too trapped.

It was an anxious journey, full of dark fancies and false scares. But finally she arrived in a residential quarter and found herself facing the housing block where Mahba had a unit. She knew the inside of the two-storey wooden structure wasn't that different to the rooms in the brothel. Except for what went on in them, of course.

Mahba had been allocated housing outside her workplace partly because she had children, mostly because at least one of them had been fathered by somebody of influence. She had been good at twisting clients around her little finger. Tanalvah had no such connections and lived in the bordello.

She got out the key and entered the building, hoping she looked as though she had every right. Fortunately, Mahba's apartment was on the ground floor. It consisted of just two rooms, one given over to sleeping, the other used for everything else. They were austere, but spotless and tidy. Tanalvah felt like an intruder.

Going to the single window, she pulled back the shutters,

then dragged over a chair and sat down to watch the street.

The hour that followed seemed endless.

Eventually a large wagon appeared, drawn by a team of four horses. It contained benches lined with chattering children, back from kindergarten. The wagon stopped on the opposite side of the road and two tiny figures got off, holding hands.

She dashed to the door and out to the street.

They saw her and ran her way, surprised and delighted. 'Auntie Tanalvah!' they chorused, rushing into her arms. She embraced them, fighting back the tears.

Then came the words she dreaded. 'Where's Mummy?'

'Teg, Lirrin,' she said, 'I've something to tell you. About Mummy.'

14

There had been a deluge of tears, naturally.

Without the children really being able to take in the news, let alone understand it or grieve, they were on the move again. If there was to be a chance of getting away, they didn't have the luxury of time.

Tanalvah Lahn had stayed in Mahba's home only long enough to throw together a few clothes and gather a little food. Now she carried the boy, Teg, and Lirrin walked alongside. They were red-eyed and dumb with shock.

With each hour that passed the risk increased, and it was about to multiply greatly. Because Tanalvah's plan required going back to the docks area, where the bordello was. She couldn't see another way.

Given the heightened tension between Rintarah and Gath Tampoor, and the activities of a resistance movement the state said didn't exist, there were even more uniforms on Jecellam's streets than usual. That made Tanalvah, Teg and Lirrin's journey doubly perilous. They saw many members of the People's Militia, paladins and disparate other law enforcers. Tanalvah accounted it a small miracle every time they passed one unmolested.

The children sank deeper into wretchedness. Only once did they forget themselves for a few moments and their spirits rise. Taking a circuitous route in case they were followed, they entered the fringes of a prosperous neighbourhood. In an avenue of well-maintained dwellings and neatly clipped trees they noticed a small group of youngsters who were being chaperoned by two glamour companions, magical play-mates that also acted as child minders.

One took the form of a man-sized monkey, but it differed from a real simian in having pink fur. Playing a flute and rolling its eyes, it performed a droll, ungainly dance.

The other glamour was a bear. But where the monkey's fur stayed pink, the bear's changed colour, shimmering through orange, purple and green. The quasi-beast stood on its hind legs and a bell on a leather collar around its neck tinkled as it shuffled to the monkey's tune.

The glamours' charges laughed and cavorted and laid down memories.

Tanalvah had to move on, fearful of being seen loitering. Teg and Lirrin's mood soon dipped again.

They entered a much less salubrious district. The houses were mean, and downcast people trudged the streets. There were no expensive glamours here. The quarter lacked the effulgence of quality magic to lighten its gloom.

On a street corner, charity workers were engaged in a magic run. A lengthy queue of the insolvent snaked to the back of their wagon. Each was handed a modest charm – spells that might conjure a transient flock of humming birds or a baby's singing rattle; glamours that produced snatches of transcendent music or sublime visions, to ease the grind of poverty. And for more needy cases, the old and infirm principally, there might be a glamour familiar to relieve an evening's loneliness.

Tanalvah pulled the children away.

Ten minutes later they skirted the block where the bordello stood. There were no signs of unusual activity in the area. That didn't reassure Tanalvah; she knew law enforcers could be sly.

What came next would be difficult. She had to conduct some business, and she needed to do it alone. Teg and Lirrin had to be left somewhere. As their mother had gone to lengths to shelter them from the realities of her profession, Tanalvah hoped they wouldn't be too shocked by what she had in mind.

'Are we going to meet Mummy?' Teg asked.

'No, darling,' she replied softly.

They came to the backwaters and a winding, dismal lane of low repute. A place where street prostitutes could be found, real bottom-of-the-trade working girls. The ones the authorities also said didn't exist.

There was danger here from the militia's regular raids and a clientele that could mete out violence and occasionally murder. The street walkers vied for business furtively, always ready to step back into the shadows. As Tanalvah walked slowly by them, scanning their faces, they returned her stare, wondering how a woman could bring children here.

By luck, or perhaps providence as Tanalvah saw it, she came across the person she wanted almost immediately. At first she didn't recognise her, despite having last seen her only months before. She'd aged before her time. She was woefully thin and had an unwholesome pallor.

'Freyal,' Tanalvah said, approaching her.

'Tanalvah? What are you doing here?' She was guarded but seemed pleased to see her.

'How are you, Freyal?'

'Oh . . . all right. You know.' Her hollow eyes darted to the children. 'But you didn't come here to ask me that.'

No. I . . . *we* need a favour.' She glanced up and down the lane nervously. Other women were taking an interest. 'Can we talk?'

'All right.' Then dryly, 'Step into my boudoir.' She backed into a doorway.

They crowded in with her. Up close, even in the poor light, Tanalvah could see the lines on Freyal's face. Wrinkles that weren't there when they worked together in the brothel, before Freyal had one lapse too many and was cast out, and the other women were forbidden to mention her name.

'Who're these two?'

'This is Teg.' Tanalvah hoisted him. He rammed a thumb into his mouth and gawked, blushing. 'And Lirrin.' The girl, brow furrowed solemnly, gave a small, apprehensive nod.

Gauntly, but with genuine warmth, Freyal smiled.

'I want you to look after them,' Tanalvah said. 'Just for a while.'

Freyal looked doubtful. A strand of greasy hair dangled over her eye. She flicked it aside. 'I don't know, Tanalvah . . .'

'It's for one of our own. Please, I've nobody else to turn to.'

'I'm not sure I –'

'Just for two hours. I'll give you what you'd make during that time.' She peeked out at the lane, empty of all but working girls. 'A damn sight more than you're *likely* to make, in fact.'

'What's wrong, Tanalvah? What kind of trouble are you in?'

'I can't explain now, and maybe it's best you don't know. But believe me, you'd be doing good by taking care of these two for me. Here.' She fished out some coins. 'Take it. You'll have the other half when I get back.'

'Well . . . all right. But no longer than two hours.'

'Good. Just a minute.' She put Teg down. Lirrin immediately grasped his hand. 'I've got to talk to Freyal for a second. All right? You stay there, both of you.'

She took her friend aside, out of their earshot, and whispered, 'If I'm not back in two hours, take the kids and leave them at the door of the Endeavour Street orphanage.'

'You're in *big* trouble, aren't you?'

'It won't happen. I'll be back. It's just in case I'm . . . delayed.'

The lie was poor and neither believed it.

'I know I'm asking a lot of you,' Tanalvah added, 'but I need somebody I can trust.'

'I reckon you must be in a real pickle to ask for my help. And you were always good to me, Tanalvah. So don't worry, I'll take care of them. Just hurry back.'

'Thank you.'

Tanalvah went to the children. 'I have to go somewhere, just for a little while. Freyal's our friend and she'll look after you.' She gathered and hugged them.

'Must you go?' Lirrin asked, near tears.

'Yes, dear, it's important. But I'll see you soon, I promise.'

'You get off,' Freyal said, lifting Teg. 'I'll take them to my place. It's not far and it's safe. We'll be back here in two hours, no later.'

Tanalvah took one last look and turned away.

She moved faster now. Dodging the open arms of leering drunks, ignoring idlers' catcalls, she headed for the docks, fearing that two hours wouldn't be enough.

Again, through providence or chance, she had the advantage. In a tavern no respectable citizen would dare enter, at the table where she hoped and expected he would be, she found the man she sought. He was the captain of a fishing ship, and one of her clients. With persuasion and most of her money, he agreed to take her and the children out of Rintarah. Had the money not been enough she would have paid him another way. And his crew as well, if need be.

She started back by a different route. It wasn't a conscious

decision to go by way of the temple, but Tanalvah was drawn
to it, as she had been many times before.

Although she had never really known much about her
birthright gods, she had no intention of disdaining them. But
temples devoted to the Qalochian gods didn't exist in the
city. Nor was there anywhere she could go to learn about
her heritage; what little she knew came from rare meetings
with her own kind. So Tanalvah had heeded that old saying
about when in Jecellam do as the Jecellamites do, and given
her devotion to a local deity.

In the pantheon of Rintarahian immortals, the goddess
Iparrater did not rank high. There were many in the hierarchy more powerful, dashing, courageous or wrathful. But
none as compassionate. Iparrater's lack of eminence in the
eyes of the state religion was the very reason she was loved
by the poor and disenfranchised. For she was said to favour
the hopeless, the destitute, the weak. She was the patron
and protector of the dregs, and Tanalvah wasn't alone in her
profession in choosing to see that as extending to whores.

Tanalvah had made good time negotiating their passage,
and there was some to spare before she met up with Freyal
and the children. So she decided to go into the temple, just
for a few minutes.

It was small, certainly when compared to those for the
gods preferred by the rich and powerful. That was one of
the reasons she liked it. It didn't make her feel too intimi-
dated. She went through its marble pillared entrance, across
an anteroom and into the darkened hall of worship. There
were several dozen people inside. Some sat on benches, heads
bowed. A few were supplicants, waiting in line before a
perpetually burning flame so they could cast in the scraps of
parchment on which they had written their appeals.

But most simply stood and gazed at the goddess.

Tanalvah understood that the figure on a dais before the

shrine was only a representation of Iparrater, a glamour like-ness tended by her priestesses. That didn't make it any less remarkable. To Tanalvah it was an article of faith that the illusion had an actual affinity with the goddess herself.

There was something almost unbearably sad about the chimerical Iparrater, as was to be expected of a deity that accepted the burden of so much despair. She was a tragic, ethereal figure, swathed from head to foot in grey gossamer, her arms outstretched as though to take on the weight of her worshippers' sorrow. Yet for all the melancholy that attached to her, somehow she was fetching. Her face was veiled, but by some strange quirk of the sorcerers' art or through the transcendent power of the goddess herself, there was an unmistakable impression of her hidden features. A stamp of kindliness, nobility and sublime mercy.

Tanalvah went to her knees. She prayed for Mahba's spirit, for the safety of the children, and lastly for herself. Conscious of time passing, she traced the sign of the goddess, touching her collarbones, left to right, with the middle fingers of her hand. Then she rose and turned to leave.

In a side chapel she paid to light a candle so that Mahba's soul could see its way to the afterlife. And in the annexe she couldn't resist stopping at the oracle. A stone idol, in the form of a scaled-down version of Iparrater's glamour, it dispensed prophecies in exchange for a coin. She dropped one into the dish, reflecting on how fast her money was going, and slipped her hand into the divining slot. A light tingling sensation prickled her fingers.

There was a panel at the foot of the statue, coloured pewter. Its surface swirled and glittered. A few words came into focus.

Interesting times await you.

Tanalvah felt, perhaps heretically, that she could have worked that out for herself.

*   *   *

As promised, Freyal was there with the children. Tanalvah embraced, thanked and paid her. Then she took Lirrin and Teg by their hands and set off again.

She never knew that Freyal would be dead before nightfall.

Her body would be found not far from the street where she worked. The likely cause of death was stab wounds, though she had other injuries that could have proved as fatal. Some put the murder down to a lone sadist. An occupational hazard. There were those who whispered about agents of the state, and of how the girl's condition pointed to torture. She knew a secret, maybe, a piece of information the authorities wanted.

But nobody cared.

On the way to the ship Teg became fractious and tearful, and demanded his mother. He drew unwelcome stares. Tanalvah placated him a little, and Lirrin tried to help calm him, in her perplexed, tight-lipped way. But it was an additional problem Tanalvah didn't need as they moved through byways filled with potential informers and haters of her race.

They were nearly at the moorings when things reached breaking point. The boy was in a tantrum, struggling in her arms, and his sister had succumbed to great wet, gulping tears of her own. Heads were turning their way.

Then a strident noise boomed out above them. They looked up to see a crier glamour far overhead. It resembled an enormous eagle, so big that were it to land its wings would span the width of the road. And it wasn't alone; others could be seen wheeling in the distance.

The voice of the crier, with its distinctive, not quite human inflection, was greatly amplified. But as the glamour was still high in the sky, and circling, only snatches of its proclamation could be heard.

'. . . of a Rintarahian citizen . . . flight from the scene . . . Qalochian . . . Lahn . . .'

'That's *your* name, Auntie Tanalvah!' Lirrin exclaimed.

Tanalvah scooped up the startled children and ran into the nearest alley. She prayed that people on the street were too preoccupied with the glamour to notice. Weaving through the back ways, carrying Teg, dragging Lirrin, both of them bawling, she moved as fast as she could towards the harbour. She'd promised to be with the ship at a specific time, so it could catch the evening tide, and this detour was slowing her dangerously.

Every now and again the crier glamour, or one of its duplicates, appeared low over the rooftops, massive wings beating languidly as it broadcast her description and supposed crimes. Tanalvah expected to be challenged at any moment, to hear the tramp of running boots and feel the thud of a militiaman's cudgel across her back.

But she reached the dockside undetected. And there was the ship, bustling with activity prior to departure. The gangway was still in place, and at its top stood the captain, watching them approach. Tanalvah dashed to it, clutching the children, heart racing. At the foot of the stairs she hesitated, breathing hard. The captain must have seen the criers. Would he want to carry a fugitive?

'Come on!' he yelled, beckoning frantically. *'Hurry!'*

She clattered up the gangway, leaving a trail of bits and pieces that spilt from her open shoulder bag.

'The criers,' she panted.

'I know,' the skipper told her. 'Go with him. *Move!'*

A crewman steered her and the children to the bridge, and out of sight.

The captain bellowed the order to cast off. Crew scuttled along the decks, ropes were slipped from bollards, the gangway was raised. Sails whipping, the vessel moved away from the harbour wall.

Shortly, the captain joined Tanalvah on the bridge.

'We're not clear yet,' he said, 'but I think we'll be all right. Unless they have the navy out. You're not important enough for that, are you?'

'What? Oh. I don't think so. No, of course not. Look . . . thank you for taking us. But why? After the criers, I mean.'

Teg and Lirrin were subdued and tearless now, mesmerised by the captain's weather-battered, generously whiskered face.

'I've no great love for the law myself,' he replied. 'And there's the kids to consider. Besides, a little risk adds spice to life.'

She smiled. 'I think I've had enough to be getting on with.'

'There might be a bit more before we're through.'

'Oh?'

'You were in such a state when you found me at the inn, you didn't even ask where I'd be taking you.'

'No, I didn't, did I? I suppose I was just relieved to be getting away from here.'

'My first thought was the Diamond Isle. Seemed fitting, given your, er, line of business.' He eyed the children. 'But when you mentioned kids I knew that wouldn't have been right.'

'You can say that again. So where are we heading?'

'Bhealfa.'

'But that's Gath Tampoorian territory!'

'It is these days. And they wouldn't take kindly to a Rintarahian vessel sailing into one of their ports, that's for sure. But that's not how we're going to do it. I've arranged to have you transferred to another ship, when we're off the coast. I've dealt with the skipper before and he can be trusted. And as he's a Bhealfan he shouldn't have too much trouble getting you all ashore. But there are dangers, I won't pretend there aren't.'

'You have dealings with the enemy?'

'I deal with men in the same trade as me. They just happen

to be on the other side of a divide because the politicians, the warmongers, say so. And before you ask what dealings I have, let me tell you it's smuggling. It's not what I'd choose to do, but these are hard times for fishermen, what with all the trouble in the fishing grounds up north.'

'Why? What's happening there?'

'Zerreiss.'

'What?'

'*Who.*' The captain smiled wryly. 'Sometimes I forget how little the government lets you land-dwellers know. Whereas out here, on the ocean, and in other climes, we hear things, see things . . . Zerreiss is a warlord, and he's been making some impressive conquests in the barbarous regions.'

'I thought there were many warlords in that part of the world.'

'Yes, there are. But there's something different about this one. Something out of the ordinary.' He took in the faces of his passengers. 'But I'm being a bad host. You look as though you could do with food and drink, and some rest.'

'Thank you, we could.'

'After that, you can tell me why you're fleeing Rintarah, if you're inclined. And I'll tell you what I know about Zerreiss, and why his followers call him the man who fell from the Sun.'

15

By law and convention, Bhealfa's capital was deemed to be wherever the Prince resided. Practicality meant that the old capital, Valdarr, which Melyobar had effectively abandoned, actually fulfilled this role.

The city housed a provisional senate, to handle the day-to-day running of the state. Many regarded it as no more than a sop to the mob and dissident professional classes. Real power resided not with the senate, the Prince, or his puppet Council of Elders, but in the hands of Gath Tampoorian overseers. Most of these were based in Valdarr as well.

At the city's core, the four pillars of Bhealfa's social structure – monarchy, law, religion, magic – flaunted their status in lofty and impressive architectural statements. But under Gath Tampoor, it was whispered, the buildings were more splendid than some of the institutions they represented: the monarchy was mired in insane farce; law enabled repression; religion doled out calmatives. And magic did what magic did.

From the tallest central towers to the coarsest outlying shacks, Valdarr, like any community of any size anywhere, bathed in the glow of sorcery.

A storm was brewing. The sky above the horizon was black and there were flashes of lightning in the distance, followed by dull thunder.

'What do you think of it?' Caldason said.

'Well, it's . . . *big*,' Kutch replied, a little daunted.

'It's a fair-sized city. Nothing compared to Merakasa or Jecellam though, or even some of the other colonial capitals.'

'This is enough for me for the time being, thanks, Reeth.' He looked to the storm. There were more fingers of lightning, far off, and echoing thunder. 'I think it's coming our way.'

'Another good reason for us to get down there.'

Caldason turned and strode to the wagon, standing near the edge of the hill's flat summit. The horses had their heads down, munching grass. Karr sat on the driver's board, watching the sky.

'Still waiting for your sign, Patrician?'

'Yes, but not for much longer, I hope.'

'How will your people know you're here to be signalled?' Kutch wondered.

'They have a rough date for my return, within a few days either way. Assuming I was going to get back at all, that is. Chances are they've sent the herald to this spot several times already. It'll be back.'

Caldason sighed. 'So we have to cool our heels. More delay.'

'It's important, Reeth. There's been a concerted effort to kill me. We need word that it's safe for us to approach my house.'

Karr resumed scanning the clouds. Kutch and Reeth left him to it and ambled away.

After a few moments staring down at Valdarr, Kutch said, 'You promised to show me some swordsmanship, Reeth. Why not now?'

'Well, I suppose it wouldn't hurt you to know some basics.'

'I don't like violence, you know that. But I am interested. Show me a few tricks and I'll swap you some magic.'

'Hardly tricks,' Caldason informed him tightly. 'And you can keep the magic.' Tone lightening, he added, 'So, what do you want to know?'

'Why do you carry two swords?'

'It's a question of the right tool for the job.' He unsheathed the sword at his belt. 'A rapier. Thin, rounded blade, very fine tip. The perfect fencing weapon, providing you're up against an opponent also using a rapier. It *can* be used against an opponent with a broadsword, which is more of a hacking weapon. In fact in some instances it'll give you an advantage.'

'How?'

'There's an old saying among swordsmen: the tip is surer than the edge.' He described a pattern in the air that ended with a blurringly fast thrust. 'Often it's the tip of a blade that can prove decisive in a fight. Here, take it.' He offered the hilt to Kutch.

The boy accepted it gingerly. He waved the sword about a bit. 'It's quite light.'

'Yes, and see how flexible it is? Here.' He took it again, then bent the blade so its tip touched the hilt, making an O. When he let go, the blade immediately snapped back to its original shape. 'A rapier's like a surgeon's knife. It's a precision tool, relying on its point rather than its edge.' He plunged the rapier into the earth and left it there quivering. 'On the other hand . . .' He reached up and unsheathed the sword strapped to his back. 'This is a broadsword. Its blade's flat and it has a sharpened edge as well as a point. Take it.'

Kutch grasped the hilt in both hands and backed a step. The blade thudded to the ground. 'Gods, how do you fight with this thing? I can hardly lift it.'

'The strength needed to wield that kind of blade is why fights often turn on who has most stamina.' He jerked the rapier free, then took the broadsword from Kutch. He held them both up as though they were light as feathers. 'Worked in unison, they can be formidable.'

'Yes, I've seen. You know, this would have interested my brother. He was always martial-minded.'

'You'd do well to follow his example, at least enough to defend yourself.'

'I believe disputes can be resolved by reason and – you're laughing!'

'No, no I'm not. It's just . . . Reason's a good thing, and it should always come first. It's what rational people use to settle their differences. But not everybody out there *is* rational, Kutch. And when you're up against someone who only wants to spill your guts, reason's a poor weapon.'

'Then the Craft's going to be my defence.'

'Don't take this the wrong way, but you haven't mastered that well enough yet.' While that sunk in, he added, 'Were you to use a weapon, I'd suggest the rapier. Its lightness would suit somebody of your build.'

Kutch was bruised by Reeth's candour. 'Even if I did take up a weapon, and I don't want to,' he replied slightly grumpily, 'I'm not sure I'd have the co-ordination. I've seen you fight, and it looked like an awful lot of physical *and* mental effort.'

'Don't you have to do that with magic? Put a lot of thinking into it, that is?'

'In the study of it, yes, of course. But not so much in the doing. For that, practitioners have to cultivate what we call a state of no-mind. You empty your mind and let the energies flow through you. You become a conduit.'

'It's the same with swordsmanship. There's another old adage: the sword is blind. In a way, the swordsman should be, too. It's like saying "try too hard and you fail".'

'When you were fighting those men trying to kill the patrician, you started off with your eyes closed for a few seconds. Is that part of it?'

'I was attuning the instincts you need to fight well. Letting the hand guide the eye and mind, rather than the other way around.'

'I'm not sure I understand that.'

'I'll show you.' Caldason looked around and pointed. 'Gather some of those sticks. The smaller ones. Three or four.' He dug both swords into the earth at his feet.

Kutch collected the twigs from the foot of a nearby oak. The ones he picked were about the thickness of a man's thumb. Laid on his open palm, their length roughly equalled the span between the tip of the middle finger and the wrist. 'I've got four,' he said, tramping back to Caldason.

Karr broke off his sky watch and turned his attention to Reeth and Kutch. There was another distant rumble of thunder.

Caldason glanced at the sticks Kutch had selected. 'They'll do nicely. Now, when you're ready, toss them into the air. Make it a good high throw.'

The boy nodded. He drew back his arm and flung them hard.

Caldason snatched up the broadsword. He sliced the air with it, bisecting the paths of each of the falling twigs. The swishing blade moved too fast to follow.

Kutch knelt to inspect the result. The four sticks were neatly sliced in half, making eight of almost exactly the same size.

'Amazing!' he exclaimed.

'A maximum effect for minimal effort,' Caldason explained.

'How did you *do* that?'

'By not trying.' He brought up the broadsword, flipped it

and re-sheathed it in the scabbard on his back. The rapier was returned to his belt sheath in a similarly matchless, fluid movement.

Kutch's eye sparkled with a competitive gleam. 'Yes,' he stated dramatically, 'but can you do *this*?' He aimed his hand at the tree, fingers together. 'Brace yourselves!' Eyes closed, he began mumbling.

Nothing happened for half a minute, during which Karr inspected his nails and Reeth's gaze strayed to the view.

Suddenly, a frail radiance appeared at Kutch's fingertips. The light throbbed, erratically. A wobbly fireball appeared, about the size of an apple.

Its colour blinked between orange and puce. Kutch grunted with effort. The fireball floated forward a few inches, then flopped feebly to the ground. It fizzled and gently popped.

They looked at it.

'No, I can't,' Caldason replied.

'Damn,' Kutch muttered, deflated and embarrassed.

Reeth laid a comforting hand on his shoulder. 'Persevere in all things.'

Karr joined them. 'Be careful, Kutch. That's not something the unlicensed should be seen doing in Valdarr.'

'An unapproved boy sorcerer, a renegade politician on a death list and a wanted outlaw,' Caldason counted off, 'all about to set foot in a city with the biggest concentration of state and empire forces in Bhealfa.'

'Valdarr's size is our ally,' Karr said. 'There are a myriad places we can lose ourselves down there.'

'Look!' Kutch interrupted.

Something was flying their way, diving at them. It was hard to make out what it was.

'This could be what I've been waiting for,' Karr decided.

'I hope it's kept better time than the last one,' Caldason remarked.

'What if it isn't what we've been expecting?' Kutch asked. 'What if it's hostile?'

Neither of them answered him. But Caldason's hand moved to the hilt of his rapier.

The flying thing rapidly closed the distance, then slowly circled above their heads.

'It's all right,' Karr assured them.

The creature descended and hovered.

This time, the messenger took the form of a giant dragonfly, the size of a large dog. It was fabulously coloured, lustrous blues and greens marking its elongated carapace. Its silvery wings beat so fast they were a smudge. It was grotesquely beautiful.

The dragonfly flitted over to face Karr. It studied him with its bulging, multifaceted eyes, its antennae trembling. Then it let out a loud, preternatural rasp.

'Advance.'

The glamour repeated its message twice more. Then it tore itself apart, disintegrating in a shower of luminous grains scattered by the wind. The glittering particles died as they drifted.

'Time to go,' Karr declared. 'Come on, you two, don't linger!'

When they reached the city's outskirts, Karr, who was driving, pulled up outside a stables.

He told them, 'It's better to continue on foot, so we have to lose the wagon and horses. But, Kutch, by rights this wagon and team are yours, as they belonged to Grentor. Of course the money they fetch will be yours. Any objections?'

'No. I can see the sense in what you're saying. Only . . .'

'What is it?'

'Well, it sounds silly, but they're the last link with my master.'

'No, they're not,' Reeth said. 'You're the link. The person he helped you become, the knowledge he gave you. Your memories of him. That's what keeps somebody alive.'

Kutch nodded, not trusting himself to speak.

'There's a tavern a little further along this road,' Karr explained. 'On the way into town, maybe half a mile. Why don't you two wait there for me? I'll join you once I've made the sale.'

They agreed and set off. The storm was building and drawing closer.

Kutch, apprehensively, asked, 'You will stay a while, won't you, Reeth?'

'I said I would. At least until you're settled, and Karr's made a connection for me with these Covenant people. If he can.'

'I think he can. He seems like a good man to me.'

'From your vast experience of weighing people up, eh?' It wasn't meant unkindly.

'Perhaps I am a bit inexperienced in that way. But he has befriended us, and he's trying to help you with your problem.'

'We'll see. But I'll not be staying in Valdarr forever, Kutch, don't forget that.'

Kutch wasn't too happy, but he didn't say anything.

They encountered more and more people as they penetrated the city. On a broad street corner a group in white robes was holding some kind of vigil. One of their number lectured a small crowd.

'The Thrift Corps,' Caldason explained to a baffled Kutch.

'I've never heard of them.'

'They're afraid the magic will be all used up. They want it conserved by law.'

'It *can't* be used up. The Craft says magic's self-generating and perpetual.'

Caldason looked around, and frowned. A group of militia-men and a couple of stony-faced paladins had appeared. They were eyeing the protest and scanning the crowd.

'We should move on,' he suggested.

Further into town they began seeing Gath Tampoorians. Caldason reflected on how empire citizens always stood out from the peoples they conquered. It was partly the quality and cut of their clothing, especially the magical, ever-changing raiment worn by the richest, and the fact that they often had retinues. But it was also an attitude, a certain bearing, a haughtiness verging on arrogance conveyed by those accustomed to rule.

Reeth and Kutch pushed deeper into Valdarr. They passed men at the roadside selling tokens for the glamour lottery. A board on an easel displayed pictures of the prizes. The top prize was a horn of plenty, which would produce an unlim-ited supply of the finest food for a week. Being magically generated, the food tasted exquisite but had no nutritional value. Some people had been known to favour horn yield so much they gorged on nothing else and starved to death.

At last they came to the inn. It employed a glamour barker to drum up passing trade. This one was a small dragon, about the size of a horse. It sat on its haunches, forked tail curling. Its skin was green, except for its ribbed, pot-bellied stomach, which was white. The glamour-caster had used some artistic licence, incorporating long eyelashes, extraordinarily curva-ceous lips and enormous eyes, yellow with flecks of red, shaped like inverted teardrops. It was an insufferably friendly dragon.

As Caldason and the boy approached the tavern's door, the dragon said, *'Come on in!'*

Caldason ignored it, making no attempt to hide his distaste at being addressed by a glamour.

'Come on in!' the dragon repeated.

'We intend to,' Kutch replied.

'Come on in and have a flagon of ale or a draught of hot toddy!'
The dragon swished its tail and gave them a hideous be-
fanged smile. *'All are welcome! Enjoy a warming cup of brandy
or a goblet of honey wine!'*

'We'd like to,' Caldason growled darkly.

The dragon threw out its arms in a gesture of openness
and hospitality, blocking the tavern's door. *'Eat here! We have
meat, fowl and fish, cooked –'* it breathed a blast of smoky red
flame *'– to perfection!'*

'Thank you,' Kutch mouthed pointlessly.

*'The finest stews, breads, fruit, vegetables, served by genial
apple-cheeked wenches!'* The dragon gave them a lecherous
wink.

Caldason reached for his sword.

'No, Reeth,' Kutch said, staying his hand. 'Come away,
he's not worth it.'

They marched past the dragon to the entrance.

'Come on in!' the glamour parroted. *'All are welcome! Enjoy
a –'*

The door slammed shut behind them.

Inside it was ill-lit and rather shabby. There were no wenches,
apple-cheeked or otherwise. The score or so customers drank,
smoked and conversed quietly in small groups.

Everybody stared at Caldason, but the Qalochian seemed
totally unfazed. His build, weapons and expression dissuaded
anybody who might fancy starting anything, while any
thought the inn keeper might have had of not serving him
was short-lived.

'Brandy,' Caldason said, 'and watered wine for the boy.
Generous on the water.'

'I'm starving,' Kutch announced. 'What's there to eat?'

'Just that.' The inn keeper jabbed a thumb at a platter of
pig's feet. They were green-tinged and fly-blown. He rubbed
a hand on his grubby apron and reached for the plate.

'Er, no,' Kutch said. 'I don't think I'll bother, thanks.'

'Suit yourself.'

He got their drinks and slid them across. Caldason slapped some coins on the distressed counter top.

They sat at a bench in a quiet corner, Reeth facing into the room. The other drinkers whispered and kept glancing their way. It didn't seem to bother Caldason, but Kutch found it uncomfortable.

'How do you put up with it?' he asked under his breath.

'I don't always.'

'You won't kill anybody, will you?'

'I'll try not to. Don't swill that drink.'

They sat quietly sipping, Kutch's face taking on a ruddy shade due to the unaccustomed alcohol.

Eventually, Karr joined them. He refused a drink, and showed them a purse. 'We got a fair price. Here, Kutch.'

'You keep it. I've never had much need for money.'

'You're going to have to learn to use it, you've a new life now.' He crammed the purse back into his pocket. 'Just ask whenever you want it.' He glanced around. 'It's time we moved on.'

'Where to?' Caldason asked.

'I've the use of a house in the eastern quarter. You'll find it comfortable enough. Unlike my main residence, we don't think the authorities know about it. It's a bit of a journey and we'll not be taking a direct route for obvious reasons. So we should be leaving.'

'What about putting me in touch with Covenant?'

'That's going to take a day or two to arrange,' the patrician returned, slightly piqued. 'Be patient.'

They rose and left the inn.

Outside, the dragon was still going through its pitch. The day had grown darker and there were storm clouds directly above. They were laden with rain, but none was falling yet.

Karr strung his cloak tighter. 'It threatens to be a wet journey, I'm afraid.'

He led the way. As they walked, lightning flashed, thunder boomed overhead and a light rain began to fall. People hurried by, expecting a torrent.

They came to a piece of open ground between two houses, like a missing tooth. Only the broken foundations of the absent building remained. They were blackened, indicating the damage had been done by fire, and not recently. The lot was scattered with rubble and choked with weeds.

As the trio passed, there was a blinding flash and a deafening boom. A yellow-white javelin connected sky and ground for a fraction of a second.

The lightning strike stopped them in their tracks. It began to rain the harder. Near the middle of the empty plot there was now a smouldering crater.

'Come on,' Caldason said.

'Wait,' Kutch told him, staring at the crater.

'What is it?'

Kutch paid no heed and started walking towards the pit. They tagged on behind him.

'What's going on?' Karr wanted to know. 'What's the matter?'

Kutch arrived at the edge of the crater and gazed down into it. His expression was rapt. The other two caught up.

Caldason was tetchy. 'What are you doing, Kutch?'

In a kind of daze, Kutch replied, 'It's said they're susceptible to attracting lightning. Particularly when they're close to the surface, like this one.'

Reeth and Karr looked down.

In making its crater, the lightning had fractured something that looked like a channel. Through the exposed duct, at the bottom of the pit, mercury gushed. Or at least it resembled mercury in colour and constituency. It flowed into one side of the crater and out through a fissure in the other. A pool of the stuff was forming. The silverish liquid, whatever it was, radiated intense cold. A kind of crystalline frost was beginning to appear on the crater walls.

Karr, now awed himself, said quietly, 'Is that what I think it is?'

Kutch nodded. 'An energy line. I never thought I'd see one. Do you know how rare it is for it to be exposed like this?'

Although it was summer, their breath could plainly be seen.

Caldason stared at the silvery flux. 'You're saying that's . . . raw magic?'

'Not exactly. It's the carrier for it, the medium. Like an aqueduct. Magic's chariot, the scholars call it. The substance magic uses to manifest itself.'

They saw that the droplets of falling rain were evaporating before they could touch the tide of mercury, disappearing in minute clouds of steam. Yet it was profoundly cold.

'This is dangerous, isn't it?' Karr said. 'Kutch?'

'Hmmm? Oh, yes. Probably.'

Reeth clasped his arm. 'Then it might be a good idea to come away from it, don't you think?'

They pulled back.

For the first time they noticed that other people were gathering. As they moved away, the curious pressed in to replace them. Two men rushed past on their way to the crater, carrying steel buckets. One of them shouted gleefully to the other, 'Think of the value!'

Kutch was alarmed. 'No! They shouldn't do that, Reeth. You've got to stop them!'

'Exactly how dangerous *is* this?'

'The magical energy can manifest spontaneously, and without direction. That could be . . . difficult.'

More inquisitive people streamed past. There was a scrum around the crater now.

A commotion broke out. Cries of alarm, yells and screams resounded.

An eruption occurred. Two bodies, limbs flailing, and two buckets shot high into the air.

'Told you so,' Kutch said.

A series of brilliant flashes lit the crater area. They were succeeded by intense pulsating lights of rapidly changing primary colours. Thick clouds of smoke rose. A strong rotten-eggs smell wafted over the crowd.

Panic set in. People were running and shouting. A jumble of shapes appeared in the foggy confusion at the crater's mouth. Karr, Reeth and Kutch strained to see what was happening.

Suddenly a centaur scrambled out of the hole, rearing and bellowing. It galloped through the stampeding mob, lashing out at people and knocking them aside.

A great swarm of tiny flying creatures emerged and set about plaguing the crowd like angry wasps. They proved to be fairies, their faces screwed into fiendish expressions, with wickedly curved claws in place of fingers. Kutch and the patrician struck at them frantically with flapping arms and balled fists. Reeth took wide, powerful swings at them with his broadsword. Scores exploded and vanished.

Horned demons leapt from the crater pit. Red-skinned, chisel-toothed, with crazy eyes. Goats with babies' heads stumbled into view. Snakes with multiple legs, like centipedes. A flock of white bats, spreading rustling, serrated wings. Enormous indigo scorpions with silver bells for stingers.

'The Dreamtime must have been a bit like this,' Kutch reckoned.

Reeth looked unhappy with the comparison.

'How do we know what quality they are?' Karr shouted. He meant whether they were insubstantial and essentially innocuous glamours, or the more solid and costly variety that could interact and harm.

'I don't know what kind this sort of rupture would throw up,' Kutch explained. 'Probably both.' He swiped at a cluster of vexatious fairies.

'How do we know which is which?'

Kutch shrugged his shoulders.

'Trial and error,' Caldason offered as he decapitated a diving bat. The creature dispersed in a mist of fading embers.

Four or five miniature whirlwinds spun out of the pit. They took off in different directions, gathering masses of leaves and twigs, sucking up bricks from the stubby foundations, battering people aside.

A horde of huge spiders with venom-dripping fangs scuttled over the rim. Some made for the adjoining houses and scurried up their walls. Others began weaving webs of gold to snare the fleeing crowd.

Through the mist and chaos, Caldason thought he saw a mermaid, swimming in air. Gnarled dwarves, malevolent goblins and inebriated pixies hopped from the pit. A pair of black doves soared overhead, cooing impossibly loudly. Fountains of multicoloured sparks burst through cracks snaking out from the crater mouth.

Above the turmoil, the shrill sound of bells could be heard. Several wagons arrived at speed, loaded with men and their gear.

'Thank the gods!' Karr exclaimed. 'A repair gang.'

The crews tumbled off the wagons and began wading through what was left of the crowd. They stepped over bodies on the ground, injured or worse. The crew were shouting, ordering people clear, threatening and shoving them away.

About half the repair crew were sorcerers, wielding

elaborate staffs, and they concentrated on cancelling the magic. Their wands spewed fiery nullifying spells. When the dazzling yellow streaks hit, glamours imploded and dissipated. Steadily, the sorcerers obliterated and corralled their way to the crater and started to surround it. More wagons drew up, and men on horseback. There were militia and, inevitably, paladins among them.

'Past time we were leaving,' Karr suggested.

As they slipped away, Caldason muttered, 'Did I tell you how much I hate big cities?'

16

In the centre of Valdarr the structures of the old kingdom mingled with the newer, more flamboyant edifices of its imperial conquerors. One of the recent additions was a grand stadium. It was the largest covered space in Bhealfa, save the gutted palace, with room for many hundreds of spectators.

For anyone wanting a microcosm of Bhealfan society, the auditorium served well enough.

The private boxes were reserved for Gath Tampoor functionaries, political, military and diplomatic. There were places for wives, concubines, and children with their glamour nannies and companions. Commanders of paladin clans, the priesthood and high-ranking sorcerers had boxes, along with Bhealfan dignitaries favoured by the empire.

Leading merchants, notables from the approved arts, guild masters and usurers occupied the balconies. The stalls were the province of 'ordinary' citizens, albeit the well-connected and those rich enough to afford the prices.

This evening there was standing room only. Except for the Prince's empty box, which surprised no one.

The stage, which was large, was dressed simply but

elegantly. No set or superfluous props, just skilfully arranged layers of coloured velvets, with a rainbow fan centrepiece. Subtle glamoured lighting added its own special glow.

There was just one performer on the rostrum. He was well-built, verging on stocky, as classical singers tended to be, and his height was a little below the norm. His dark hair was short and he had a neat chin beard. He wore a black silk stage costume with a yellow sunburst motif on the chest. At slightly above thirty, he was handsome, in a solid kind of way.

Kinsel Rukanis may not have been the greatest tenor in the two empires, but he was unquestionably a contender for that title. He had rivals more technically adept, and a few who could equal the range and sophistication of his voice. Arguably, none had his interpretative powers. His ability to convey the emotional force of a libretto, to make it accessible, had secured the Gath Tampoorian's fame and fortune.

Rukanis shunned glamour amplification, using only the power of his lungs to cast his voice to the farthest parts of the hushed theatre. He had worked his way through a familiar, much-loved repertoire. Naturally, *After Dark* and *The Story of Your Heart* had featured. His rendition of *Whispering Gods* was received with delight, and *On Wings of Stars* brought an ovation.

Now he performed a song closely associated with him, and one of the most popular: *Far Have I Journeyed in the Realm of Dreams*. For this finale the theatre's special effects enchanters were allowed a hand. Rukanis believed in using such effects sparingly. His attitude was that concerts were concerts, not image shows.

He was into the second verse when the glamour materialised. It was a quality piece of work. An egg-shaped, door-sized loop of linked bubbles appeared in the air next to him. It filled with clouds, puffy white against flawless blue. The vista held for a while as he sang. Then cracks formed, branching out to jigsaw the scene.

A silent explosion, and the loop shattered into a hundred thousand tiny crystal shards, like droplets of brass, lancing off in all directions, catching the light before they vanished. When the dazzle cleared, a figure was floating beside Rukanis, as though gently suspended in water.

She was stingingly beautiful. Her golden hair formed a rippling nimbus and there was fire in her emerald eyes. The silky tendrils of her garments drifted and swayed in unseen currents.

The glamour moved into a lithe, sensuous dance, her dainty feet skimming an invisible plane in a ballet echoing the tragic romance Rukanis expressed in song. His depiction of the lyric's bittersweet sentiments and her exposition had the audience enraptured.

Rukanis came to the story's culmination, the point where its fated lovers are compelled to part. As he reached the climax and its portrayal of loss and hope, rapture and heartbreak, the glamour began to weep. Not tears, but diamonds. They flowed from her remarkable eyes as silvery liquid. Rolling down her marbled cheeks, they solidified and fell as twinkling gems, pattering onto the stage in increasing abundance. They glanced off, some bouncing into the orchestra pit, a few over the first rows of the stalls, but evaporating before they landed.

Voice soaring, Rukanis brought the piece to an end. Tears dried, the glamour turned and blew him a kiss. Then she vaporised, her essence sinking as fine silver rain towards the stage, but never reaching it. Rukanis bowed.

For the span of a heartbeat, there was complete silence.

Then the audience roared. They clapped and cheered, and leapt to their feet in tribute – energetically in the stalls, with restraint in the balconies and boxes.

Several shy little girls, daughters of the worthy, appeared from the wings with bouquets. Real bouquets, not glamours. It was more of a compliment, according to current fashion in the perverse world of culture. He took the flowers, kissed the girls' cheeks and acknowledged the deafening adulation. Grinning, giving small bows, he clutched the masses of flowers to his ample chest.

To an upsurge of applause, he slowly backed away from the edge of the stage. The curtains swept in and concealed him. As was well known, he didn't do curtain calls, no matter how insistent the demands or the calibre of the audience. He puffed his cheeks and expelled a relieved breath.

No sooner had the curtains drawn than a small mob of colleagues and backstage workers moved in to congratulate him. They slapped his back, pumped his hand, showered him with praise, and he took it with good grace.

He passed the flowers to someone, gratefully, then thanked them all and headed for his dressing room. Somebody handed him a towel. He accepted with a smile and dabbed at his sweating brow.

A stagehand he passed called out, 'You've a visitor in your dressing room, sir.'

'Any idea who it is?'

'A man. It was the name you left at the stage door, I think. Geheim, was it?'

'Ah, yes. Thank you.'

Geheim. The standard name they were using at the moment. He hoped that in coming here the man had been careful he wasn't followed. Rukanis dismissed the thought. They were experienced at this kind of thing and knew what they were doing.

When he entered his dressing room he found someone he'd never seen before. He was young and robust looking, clean-shaven but with an unruly mop of blond hair.

'Geheim, I presume,' Rukanis said.

The stranger smiled. 'For our purposes, yes.' They clasped hands. 'That was one hell of a performance.'

'Thank you.' Rukanis locked the door. 'You were in the audience?'

The man was still smiling. 'Hardly. I heard some of it from back here.'

'Of course.'

Geheim glanced around. 'I take it this room's safe?'

Rukanis fished an anti-glamour pendant from inside his shirt.

'Good. But you shouldn't warrant eavesdropping, should you? A man like you must be above suspicion.'

'I'm not sure anybody's exempt from suspicion these days.'

'Indeed. We appreciate how risky this is for you.'

'I'm prepared to do what I can for the cause, short of violence. Do you mind if I change?'

'Go ahead.'

Rukanis began riffling through a rack of clothes. 'What do you need from me?'

'Two things, if possible. First, the usual.'

'Message carrying.'

'Yes. We'll need several delivered to our people in Gath Tampoor. I'll arrange to get them to you before you leave. Is that all right?'

'It's not a problem. And second?'

'The reception tomorrow night. There are going to be lots of important people there –'

'And you want me to keep my ears open.'

'It's surprising what they can come out with when they think they're among their own. But there's something in particular we'd like you to listen for this time. Have you heard anything about some sort of Bhealfan trading expedition to the northern wastes?'

'No.' He was pulling on a fresh shirt.

'We've had whispers. But there's something not quite right about it. Seems like it's more an empire mission than Bhealfan, and we'd like to know why.'

'I'll be alert for it. Though I wish I could do something a bit more substantial.'

'Don't underestimate the value of intelligence gathering. The Resistance is grateful for what you do, believe me. Not least the money you give. As to anything else . . . Well, your pacifism's well known and respected, but it does tend to limit the kind of operations we can involve you in.'

'I understand.'

'One last thing; your contact point here in Valdarr. Directly opposite the northern corner of Tranquillity Square there's a street . . . well, not much more than an alley really, called Falcon's Way. There's a leather tannery near the far end.' He smiled again. 'Ask for Geheim. Have you got all that?'

'Yes. I don't expect to need it.'

'I hope you never do. But remember it's a safe house as well as a drop point. It's as well to cover all contingencies.'

Rukanis nodded.

'I have to go,' Geheim announced.

'And I'll take a short walk, I think. I always like some air after a performance.' He wrapped a cape around his shoulders and selected a wide-brimmed hat from his assortment.

They left the theatre together.

Outside the stadium the streets were busy. They stood for a moment watching the flow.

Rukanis breathed deeply. 'Aaah. It's a nice evening. I'm for wandering down to the harbour.'

'Take care. And don't forget about the safe house. You're clear on that?'

'Perfectly.'

They said their goodbyes and parted.

Rukanis rather liked this Geheim. It would be interesting to know more about him. But of course that was impossible.

Even dressed in ordinary street clothes Rukanis would be easily recognised by some of the passers-by. He pulled down the brim of his hat and headed for the harbour.

There were many ships anchored, and a lot of activity, despite the lateness of the hour. He strolled along the moorings, savouring the air and the solitude. After a few minutes he stopped just short of a bridge that spanned a narrow part of the inlet. Leaning on a wall, he looked out at the vessels coming and going, and the distant gleam of navigation lights.

But he only half saw the view. His mind was on the direction his life was taking. On how he was getting in deeper with the insurgents, and how much further he might feel compelled to go with them.

He heard a scream. Or thought he did. Could it have been his imagination? A gull, perhaps? He listened for a few seconds, shrugged and slid back into his reverie.

Another scream, nearer and unmistakable this time.

Rukanis looked around, trying to see its source. His eye was caught by movement on the bridge. At least one figure was running over it, coming his way. Perhaps a hundred paces behind it a number of pursuers were visible. He couldn't make things out too clearly in the poor light. Concerned, he began walking towards the bridge.

He got to its entrance as a woman rushed off. She was tall, raven-haired, and she carried a child under one arm, like a parcel. Another, older youngster clutched her hand. They looked terrified. Faced by him, they stopped, breathless and fearful, the children tear-stained.

'What's wrong?' he asked.

The woman stared at him, then seemed to make a decision. 'Help us,' she breathed, and there was true desperation in her voice.

He looked along the bridge. Four men were dashing across it. They were near enough for him to make out their uniforms. Two harbour watch, a militiaman and, alarmingly, a paladin. Further behind them, at the bridge's opposite end, a bigger group followed.

'Come on,' he said, scooping up the second child, who was too frightened to object.

The woman seemed shocked, unable to believe she might have an ally.

They started to run, each with a child in their arms, aiming for the warehouses and the tangle of narrow lanes adjacent to the harbour.

Their pursuers clattered off the bridge and sped after them.

Serrah felt strange being on dry land again.

She was glad to see the back of the ship, and getting off it had proved easier than she feared. Looking around the harbour, she wondered what to do now. She knew no one in Bhealfa.

Getting away from the docks quickly was her first priority. Ports were usually well guarded, and she couldn't expect the same luck she'd had leaving Merakasa. If it was luck. She began trotting towards the mean streets.

Turning a corner, she nearly collided with a small group of people. A big, bearded man in a cape and hat, along with a dark-haired woman, Qalochian probably, and a couple of kids.

They were agitated, fearful even, and for a moment she thought it was because of her. In truth, she must have looked a sight after being cooped-up on board for days. But she soon saw that wasn't the problem. Somebody was chasing them, and these people didn't look in a fit state to run much further.

Four men were homing in, swords drawn. Serrah recognised their uniforms.

The Qalochian woman gazed at her and whispered, 'Please.'

The man said nothing. He didn't look the running or fighting type. But his expression spoke volumes. The children were obviously petrified.

Serrah moved to stand between them and their advancing hunters.

The four men slowed at the sight of a bedraggled, wild-looking woman with her arms crossed, barring their way. They came on warily, blades lifted.

One of the two harbour watchmen took the lead. The paladin, who would be expected to take command in a situation like this, held back a little with the others.

'Out of the way,' the watchman demanded.

'Since you ask so nicely,' Serrah replied, 'no.'

'Official business. Move.'

'Look, I don't know what this is about, but –'

'*Stand aside, bitch.*'

She drew her sword in a fast, smooth motion. Everybody tensed. There was an intake of breath from the man with the hat. The younger of the two children, the boy, whimpered quietly.

'Stick your nose in what don't concern you,' the watchman advised menacingly, 'and it's the last thing you'll do.' He edged forward and shouted to the others, 'Come on, she's only a fucking woman.'

Serrah instantly lunged and struck out at him. Her blade travelled in a sweep up his face, slicing through flesh. The man screamed, dropped his sword and pressed his hands to the gushing wound. His bloody nose bounced wetly across the cobbles.

'Try sticking that,' she told him. She looked demonic.

Shocked gasps and muffled screams came from the couple and their children. The other three armed men were equally stunned, but they held.

'Move him!' the paladin ordered, taking over. The second watchman pulled his wailing comrade aside. 'And watch them!' the paladin snapped. The militiaman did his best to stand guard over the family while not actually challenging Serrah.

His path cleared, the paladin came at her. Their swords met with an echoing clash. Serrah relished the sound. Her pent-up fury needed sating.

He was good. The combination of passes he sent her way was faultless. But his classical style, while impressive, was also a potential weakness. Those trained traditionally, as the likes of paladins tended to be, found it hard coping with unpredictability. Serrah had traditional training too, but her work with the CIS unit meant she also had street-fighting skills. It was the difference between fighting to win and fighting to win at all costs.

The paladin directed a low stroke at her legs, hoping to bring her down. Serrah rapped that aside and the pass she returned had him pitching backwards to avoid a gutting. She followed on, hammering at his blade frenziedly. He managed to hold her at bay, but only just, his smug expression vanishing.

In a matter of seconds Serrah had turned her opponent from attack to defence. Her next move was to finish him, and quickly. But a new element foiled her. Seeing the paladin stumble, the militiaman decided to join in. Now she had two foes to contend with.

His first couple of swipes showed that the militiaman had energy but little expertise. She parried them easily. For a moment she swapped blows with both men alternately and held them off. But deadlock didn't suit her. With a series of wide sweeps and deep jabs she drove back the paladin. Then she spun to the other man and mercilessly hacked at him, to the extent that when she feigned an opening he took it recklessly. She knocked his blade clear, breaking his guard.

The gap was all she needed. Her sword sank into his chest. He staggered and fell.

As Serrah pulled away she glimpsed the family, huddled at the wall, horrified expressions on their faces.

The paladin was onto her again. After what he'd just seen he was fuelled by desperation. His strategy was simply to batter her into submission, and the way he dealt out steel verged on the careless. Serrah liked that. An unruly enemy was a gift. She soaked up everything he threw at her, letting him tire. When fatigue set in, she went for him.

While she pounded, Serrah was aware of the two watchmen. They were a dozen paces off, the wounded man sitting on the ground, hands to his streaming face. His partner knelt beside him. But he was staring at Serrah, and she thought he was about to move.

A crack from her blade prised ajar the paladin's guard, and she would have finished him, but the second watchman chose that moment to spring at her. He came with his sword slashing in great arcs. She ducked a pass from her main opponent and turned to face this new one. Expertly she blocked the side of his speeding blade with the edge of her own. It ruined his rhythm and rocked his balance.

Another cross to the paladin kept him clear. With her full attention on the watchman she engaged again, targeting his sword arm. Two swipes skimmed his flesh. The third connected, ploughing the length of his forearm, spraying blood. He yelled in agony and his fist spasmed open, releasing his weapon. She thrust hard and pierced his heart. The watchman sagged and dropped. His injured comrade, one hand to his face, quickly crawled to him.

Serrah powered back into the fight with the paladin. If anything, he fought with more intensity, forcing her to retreat a step or two. She barred his onslaught and reversed the trend. They fenced back and forth along the lane, some of his traditional skills resurfacing. Their blows and counter-blows fell like metal hail.

At last she drew him out with a fake offering of unpro-tected flesh. He gulped the bait, moved in, ready to evis-cerate this mad, troublesome female.

She swerved, hammered his blade out of play and ribboned his chest. He shrieked, slashed wildly in her direction, and took the full impact of her follow-up. Her sword burrowed between ribs and ruptured a lung.

Spitting crimson to match his tunic, the paladin went to his knees, then pitched forward. He lay still, bar the twitching.

Serrah took a long breath. She looked to the watchman who'd lost his nose. He crouched next to the partner she'd killed. The man was frozen, transfixed by the sight of her. She walked over to him, gently swinging her sword. He cowered.

'No!'

It was the big man, his hat comically askew. She stayed her hand, stared at him.

'There's no need,' he explained, talking rapidly. 'He can't do us any harm. Leave him. Please.'

The dark-haired woman was nodding agreement and mouthing some kind of plea to back him up.

But it was the faces of the children that decided Serrah.

She bent down to the quaking watchman and wiped her bloody sword on his jerkin, making him flinch. Then she straightened, re-sheathed and strode to the others. They watched her coming with eyes wide.

'We have to get out of here,' the man said.

'There are more coming,' the woman reminded him, clutching the children tighter.

Serrah scanned the harbour. 'Any ideas for a good hiding place? I'm new in these parts.'

'Yes,' the big man told her, 'I think so. Come with us. But hurry!'

He began hustling them away.

Serrah got a good look at him. 'Don't I know you?'

He looked pained. 'Can we discuss that later, please?'

They fled, leaving a trembling watchman and three bodies in spreading dark pools.

17

'Are you sure you'll not take some wine?' Karr said, offering the flagon again.

Reeth shook his head.

The patrician eyed Caldason's modest platter of dry bread, cheese and a few grapes, which he was picking at with scant enthusiasm. 'You're not exactly eating extravagantly either.'

'I take a sufficiency.' He was in a brooding temper.

Kutch, tucking heartily into his heaped plate, asked, 'Can I have some of that, please?'

Karr smiled. 'You seem to have developed a taste for the stuff since Reeth took you into that tavern. Here.' He poured a little wine into a cup, then topped it up from a jug of water. When he passed it across, Kutch's look of gratitude was tempered with just a smidgen of disappointment at the dilution.

They went back to eating in silence.

The large, solid table they sat around stood in a sizeable kitchen in a spacious house on the edge of Valdarr. Sitting on a small rise and surrounded by a high wall with stout iron gates, the house was located at the end of a road with open fields beyond. There were several exits. When he first saw the place, Caldason correctly assumed it had been chosen because it was defendable.

Since they had arrived, a stream of visitors had been discreetly coming and going. Karr introduced some of them to Reeth and Kutch, usually by name only, with few if any personal details. But mostly he didn't. Other people seemed to be permanently based in the house, acting as staff and bodyguards.

Sighing, Karr finally put down his knife. 'This sort of atmosphere can affect a man's appetite. What's on your mind, Caldason?'

'What do you think?'

'Covenant.' He said it with the air of a man who'd heard the word too often.

'It has been a couple of days now. And you did –'

'Promise. Yes, I know. I'm trying, Reeth, believe me. They're not the easiest group to contact and they don't exactly advertise their presence.'

'You said you've dealt with them.'

'So we have. We're in an alliance with them, in fact, as we are with other like-minded groups. But it's early days and communication tends to be on their terms.'

'Nevertheless, we had an agreement.'

'And I'm doing my best to honour it. I have somebody working on this right now as a matter of fact. But to put it bluntly, Reeth, I have problems other than yours to sort out. Plenty of them, just in the couple of days we've been here.'

'It feels longer,' Caldason remarked acerbically.

Karr decided to ignore that. 'I've seen people who want my help because they've had their children taken away by government officials, or their brothers have been unjustly sentenced. People who've caught diseases after being forced to work in the eastern mines, had their sons conscripted, or their property seized to house Gath Tampoor's bureaucrats. To mention just a few.'

'Do you normally get so many requests?' Kutch asked.

'Their numbers climb the more the empire encroaches on personal freedoms. On top of that,' he added, warming to his subject, 'we've just learnt that Ivak Bastorran himself is in Bhealfa, along with his sadist of a nephew. We're trying to find out if such high-ranking paladins are here for a special reason, something we should know about.'

Mention of the clans brought a harsh set to Caldason's eye. 'All right, so you're occupied with other people's problems,' he conceded, 'but you can farm out the routine work to aides, can't you?'

'To some extent, yes. But now and again something comes up that's out of the ordinary. And we've just had not one but three . . . oddities, I suppose you could call them. I think at least one of them might be of interest to you, Reeth.'

'Oh?'

'There are three stories, as I say, and they're quite a tangle. But I'll try to tell them simply. If you want to hear them, that is.'

'*I* do,' Kutch said.

Caldason said nothing.

'They do make for intriguing table talk.' Karr wore the slightly smug expression of someone about to impart a good tale. 'Recently, a member of one of Gath Tampoor's leading families met an untimely death in Merakasa,' he explained. 'The regime blamed a captain of one of the special units run by their Council for Internal Security.'

'What are special units?' Kutch asked.

'Like a lot of things the empires do, officially they don't exist. In reality, they're small groups of elite fighters whose job is to assassinate enemies of the state. That can mean dissidents, revolutionaries, opposition members, bandit gangs . . . whoever's causing enough trouble to be worth eliminating.'

Kutch looked shocked.

'Anyway,' Karr went on, 'this captain was held responsible for the young man's death. Dereliction of duty, they called it. Whether that's the case or she was a dupe, we still don't know. The Resistance in Merakasa saw her as a potentially valuable asset. Their thinking was that if her bosses had turned against her she might be inclined to talk, or even to join the dissident ranks. So they got her out of jail, and right under the nose of Commissioner Laffon too, though they took heavy losses.'

'What happened to this woman?' Caldason wanted to know.

'No sooner had they made good her escape than she got away from them and disappeared. Only now she's popped up again. Here, in Valdarr. But her story's just a third of it, as I said. The woman in the next story couldn't be more different from her. She's from Jecellam, but she isn't a Rintarahian. She worked as a courtesan in a state-controlled brothel, apparently.'

A reddish tint flared in Kutch's cheeks.

Karr drove home his point. 'And this is the part you might find interesting, Reeth. She's a Qalochian.'

Caldason was typically hard to read.

'She had some involvement in the deaths of two people,' Karr continued, 'including a middle-ranking state administrator. She's fetched up here as well, along with two children, not her own. The Rintarahian Resistance told us she got away without their help.'

'You mean the Resistance here and in Rintarah talk to each other? They're connected?'

'Don't look so surprised, Kutch. Resistance is universal. It straddles trifling political differences.'

Caldason brought the conversation back on line. 'You were telling us three stories.'

'Yes. The third concerns a Gath Tampoorian quite prominent in his profession; a pacifist who quietly supports the Resistance. When these two women crossed his path, here in Valdarr, there was more violence, and possibly an end to his career. Though that still has to be determined.'

'Why are you telling us about these people?' Caldason asked.

'Because the underground has given all three protection. Lost lambs brought into the fold, you might say. And it's possible that before too long you'll be making their acquaintance yourselves.'

'Why?'

'No particular reason. But you never know what the future might bring, do you?'

'Stop trying to drag me into your schemes, Patrician. Don't even think about it. You know what I've said about –'

A soft knock at the door interrupted them. The man who entered was one of the many unnamed people who acted as helpers and guards in the house. He went to Karr and whispered something in his ear. Karr nodded and thanked him, and the man quietly left.

'Well, you've got your wish, Reeth. You're to be granted an audience with Phoenix himself, it seems.'

'About time.'

'And he wants you there too, Kutch.'

'Me? Why?'

'That's something you'll need to ask Phoenix.'

'I'm not sure about the boy going along,' Caldason said.

'Oh, come on, Reeth!' Kutch complained, face twisted in youthful angst at the prospect of missing a treat.

'It might be dangerous. Anyway, I'd prefer privacy.'

'Apparently it's a condition,' Karr pointed out. 'Both of you or not at all.'

'It makes no sense.'

'Well, you've come this far . . .'

Reeth considered it. 'All right. When?'

'Today. They're sending someone to pick you up now.'

Covenant were as good as their word.

Within the hour their emissary arrived. He was short and bony with an orderly beard, and he used words sparingly. They were told to call him Ockley. He didn't know or wouldn't say why Kutch had been included in the audience with Phoenix. Nor was he forthcoming about exactly where they were going.

Another hour later they found themselves on the opposite side of the city from Karr's safe house. They were in a bustling, run-down neighbourhood mostly given over to small manufacturers of clothes, cheap furniture, minor glamours and other daily necessities. A market shared the neighbourhood, adding to the traffic. Streams of people on foot weaved around wagons and mules being loaded and unloaded. Tradesmen lugged sacks of vegetables and crates of fish.

As always, there were men and women in the crowd who regarded Caldason with contempt, if not plain hostility. It wasn't uncommon for children to share their distaste and to show it.

'How much longer before we get there, Ockley?' Caldason wondered.

'Not far now. Naturally we're taking an indirect route.'

'Can't we move a bit faster?'

'We're to do nothing that might attract attention to ourselves,' their guide replied sternly. 'I would have thought you of all people could understand that.'

Reeth and Kutch slowed and fell back a few paces. They conversed under their breath.

'Jolly soul, isn't he?' Kutch reckoned.

'I can see the need for caution, but this endless dawdling isn't to my taste.'

'You're not very fond of cities, are you?'

'Not greatly. Such places are cut off from nature, and that goes against the way my people see things. And cities have the biggest concentration of magic.'

'I think that's one reason I'm starting to like it here. Anyway, there's no contradiction between magic and nature. Magic's *part* of nature.'

'I don't dispute that. It's the use it's put to I don't like.'

A passer-by stared rudely at Caldason. He returned the gaze levelly and the man looked away.

'Aren't you excited about meeting another Qalochian? I mean that woman the patrician told us about.'

'Would you be excited about meeting another sorcerer's apprentice?'

'Well, interested might be a better word.'

'That's more or less how I feel.'

'But I'm excited about meeting Phoenix. Aren't you?'

Caldason didn't answer.

They carried on without talking, watching Ockley's back. Then he stopped abruptly by a wooden building whose side was covered in handbills.

When they caught up, Reeth said, 'What is it?'

Ockley nodded at the mass of posters. They announced events, advertised goods, denounced and championed causes, pleaded for lost things and people. Layers were plastered over each other, with the older flyers peeling and in places defaced. One of the newer posters, still smooth and unruffled, read:

WANTED
REETH CALDASON

Felon. Traitor. Outlaw At Large
A substantial reward is offered for the apprehension
of Qalochian Reeth Caldason, murderer, agitator
and disturber of the peace.

It is the duty of any citizen knowing the whereabouts
of the said Caldason, or having knowledge of his
activities, to report to the authorities without delay.

Warning is hereby served
that any found wilfully harbouring the fugitive
face punishment as laid down in law.
Contact your local watch-house or paladin garrison.

By Royal Proclamation

Underneath, there was a glamoured, three-dimensional representation of Caldason. The picture showed someone older, heavier and fully bearded.

'It's nothing like you!' Kutch exclaimed.

Caldason shushed him. 'I've seen few that were. Maybe because I've managed to avoid having my actual likeness taken. These things are always an approximation.'

'There's little chance of you being identified from that,' Ockley agreed. 'But it's freshly pasted, and that underlines the importance of us proceeding with caution.'

Kutch started scraping at the poster's upper edge with his fingernails, trying to tear it down.

'Leave it,' Caldason said, 'it won't be the only one.'

'Come,' Ockley instructed them curtly.

Yes, sir, Kutch mouthed behind his back, pulling a sour face.

They resumed their journey.

Ockley insisted on maintaining his serpentine route. It took them through crowded squares, roads lined with merchants' stalls and noisome cobbled lanes. They came to a narrow street where the buildings had jutting upper storeys and a virtual sewer flowed underfoot.

Somebody threw a pail of slops from a window above, barely missing them.

Gales of laughter and hoots of derision came from across the way. A group of drunks were tumbling from an inn. One staggered a few paces to relieve himself against a wall. The others shouted abuse at Caldason and his party, their insults centring on his race. He stopped and stared at them. The jeers increased in volume and spite.

'Come along,' Ockley sniffed like a prissy school marm, 'ignore them.'

Caldason didn't move.

The two most vociferous of the drunks stood out from the rest. They were worlds apart in appearance. One was a weasel of a man with shifty eyes and bad skin. The other was melon-headed and built like a mountain. But muscular, not fat.

Passers-by were taking an interest now.

'We don't need this attention,' Ockley hissed.

'*Qaloch shit!*' the weaselly man yelled.

His huge friend, indicating Kutch, shouted, 'Your butt boy, is he?' Bending over, he pointed to his own enormous rear.

The drunks roared.

Caldason stepped into the road.

'*Reeth!*' Kutch begged. 'Leave it. It doesn't matter.'

He paid no heed and walked slowly towards the mob. To a chorus of catcalls and urgings from their cronies, weasel and the man-mountain moved to meet him.

They came face to face on the boardwalk outside the inn. The other drunks seemed content, so far, to simply watch and voice their mockery.

Weasel man, wiry and street-wise, took the lead. 'Got something you want to say to us, trash?'

Caldason gave him a benevolent smile. 'Nothing you're bright enough to understand, my friend.'

'Yeah? Well you ain't no friend of mine. You're a fucking Qalochian bastard. Understand *that*?'

'Ah, but there's one difference between you and me. I'm proud to be a Qalochian and I'd never change it even if I could. You, on the other hand, can't do anything about that broken jaw.'

Weasel-face looked puzzled. 'What broken jaw?'

Reeth's left hand shot out and grasped the man's throat. A powerful tug brought him straight into the Qalochian's flying right fist. The crack was audible. Weasel gave an agonised snort, hands to chin, eyes screwed up in pain.

'That one,' Caldason said.

It happened so quickly nobody had time to react. Now the other drunks fell silent, smirks frozen. Weasel sank to his knees, groaning.

Man-mountain looked down at his stricken companion, then over to Caldason, fury lighting his dim eyes. 'You're gonna regret that, you Qalochian scumbag,' he rumbled.

Caldason still wore his agreeable smile. 'Make me, lard barrel.'

The mountain seethed. Veins in his bull neck stood out like knotted rope. 'You better get ready to use them fancy swords, little man. Not that they'll do you any good.' He was bunching his rock-sized fists.

'I don't think I'll bother. Not with you so outclassed already.'

Any restraint snapped. The man-mountain bellowed and lumbered at Reeth, swinging his fists as he came. Sliding out of his path, Reeth swiftly turned and delivered a double-handed blow to the mountain's side. It felt like hitting granite. His opponent looked more annoyed than hurt.

Caldason ducked as one of the ham fists soared his way. He went under it and in, pounding the man's belly with a series of deep, weighty jabs. That had more of an effect, but not much. The mountain lunged, tree trunk arms spread wide, trying for a bear-hug. Reeth backed off fast and escaped it.

Moving with more speed than Reeth would have credited, the mountain threw another punch, and this one connected. The blow glanced off the side of Caldason's head. He was fortunate not to take the full impact; the partial hit was almost heavy enough to down him.

He went straight in for a counter-attack. Aiming high and hard he got in a series of punches to the jaw. Right fist, left, then right again. Now the mountain staggered, blinking watery eyes, footing unsure. His guard was a sham. Caldason stooped and punched beneath it, pummelling the man's stomach again. Then he quickly pulled back, avoiding a reprisal swipe.

A blur of movement in the corner of Reeth's vision made him turn. Weasel was charging him, anger outweighing the pain in his jaw. He ran low, keeping his vulnerable chin down and offering a minimal target. Reeth spun aside, getting him clear of the mountain and putting him at a right-angle to his rushing comrade. His goal suddenly removed, Weasel was unable to slow himself. He would have over-shot, except for the solid kick Reeth landed on the side of his head.

Weasel was sent cart-wheeling, limbs akimbo. He went down with a hefty, bone-breaking jolt, bounced several times and came to rest senseless.

Enraged, the mountain ploughed in again. Reeth dodged a roundhouse punch that would certainly have felled him. By way of payback he turned himself around and viciously booted the back of his foe's knee, not once but twice. That brought pain home to the mountain, and threw him off his balance.

Caldason intended finishing it then, but the man was stubborn about standing.

It was the mountain who went on the attack. Swerving from him, Caldason saw a wooden pail on the boardwalk. It was filled with soil and some anaemic flowering plants. He swept under the mountain's latest pass, threw himself across the walk and grabbed the bucket's handle. The pail was reassuringly heavy. He swung it with all his might in a wide arc that intersected with the mountain's advancing head.

When it struck, with a meaty *thunk*, the onlookers winced aloud. The mountain swayed. Reeth swung again, then once more, scattering soil and petals. Vacant-eyed, the mountain plodded a pace or two before going down like a felled oak.

Caldason tossed aside the bucket and looked over to the rest of the drunks outside the tavern. They were an appalled tableau.

'Next!' he barked.

They stood mesmerised and open-mouthed for two whole seconds before fleeing, ignoring their fallen comrades as they scattered.

Kutch and Ockley hurried to Reeth and began hustling him away.

'We do not need this kind of attention,' Ockley complained.

'I don't back down from anybody,' Caldason told him. There was something about his manner that brooked no comeback.

Ockley steered Reeth and Kutch into the back ways of Valdarr again.

It took half an hour to reach their destination. Caldason suspected it would have been a lot less but for Ockley taking an even more roundabout route. The Covenant man was silent but obviously angry at Caldason's antics. Caldason himself was growing visibly impatient.

Then Ockley discreetly indicated a particular building. A large warehouse, obviously disused, its windows were shuttered and the doors nailed up. It spoke of neglect.

Alert to watchers, they took an alley that went to the rear of the warehouse. If anything, the back of the building was even more decrepit than its front. Lumber and rubble lay in heaps, and a harvest of weeds had sprung up. Again, doors and windows were blocked.

Incredulously, Kutch asked, 'This is Covenant's headquarters?'

'Just for today,' Ockley assured him.

He crept to a door and rapped out a series of knocks. Nothing happened immediately, then it opened a crack, and a second later was thrown wider. There seemed to be more than one person inside, but it was too dark to be sure.

'Come,' Ockley commanded. 'Quickly.'

Caldason paused for a beat and glanced at Kutch. Hand on sword, he stepped inside. Kutch and Ockley scrambled after him. No words were spoken by the people who let them in. The door was slammed and secured. An instant passed in total darkness.

Then the whole place lit up. Illuminating glamour orbs hovered far above their heads, giving out a strong, bright light.

Squinting, eyes adjusting, Reeth and Kutch saw that apart from Ockley there were half a dozen other people in the room, facing them in a large semi-circle. Dressed in simple grey robes, with masks covering all but their eyes, they had no obvious weapons. None of them spoke or moved.

The room was vast, layered in dust and festooned with cobwebs. Apart from a few empty crates and some innocuous clutter, it contained nothing in the way of furnishings or any indication of the business once carried out there. The air was musty with the smell of wet rot and general dilapidation.

'This way,' Ockley said, directing them to a door set in the far wall. The six masked guardians stayed where they were.

On the other side of the door there was a narrow wooden staircase, dimly lit by radiance from above. Spurred by Ockley, Reeth and Kutch began to climb the creaking treads.

Two turns of the staircase brought them to a landing. Off this, a doorless entrance opened into another room, much smaller than the one below and also glamour-lit. Unlike everything else they'd seen, it was clean here, the floorboards having recently been scrubbed. In the centre of the chamber there was a large table and several mismatched chairs. The sweet aroma of incense pervaded the room.

'What now?' Caldason asked.

'Please make yourself comfortable,' Ockley replied. 'Phoenix will be with you in a moment.' He nodded towards a door they hadn't noticed before. It was no more than a faint outline in the opposite wall, and it had no handle.

Caldason began to ask another question, but when he turned, Ockley had gone.

'Probably glad to be rid of us,' Kutch quipped. But there was an anxious edge to his voice.

'The feeling's mutual.'

They moved into the room. Caldason checked it out suspiciously, scrutinising every drab detail. He went to the near-invisible door and tried pushing it, with no success. It was hung flush, so he couldn't get the purchase to prise it open either. He gave up and joined Kutch by the table.

'I can't believe I'm going to meet Phoenix,' the boy confided, speaking low.

'He's just a man.'

'Well, yes, but an exceptional one if you believe all the stories.'

'You'd heard stories about me too, remember.'

Kutch smiled. 'Having seen you in action, I'm not sure they were so farfetched.'

'So what do these stories say about him?'

'They're not all consistent, to tell the truth. But they do agree he's a great magician, and very old. And that in some way he defies death, or in the more colourful versions, that he can't be killed.'

'Ah, yes,' Caldason responded thoughtfully.

Kutch didn't notice this moment of introspection and carried on. 'He's said to be very wise. Which I suppose you'd expect from someone really old.'

'Don't count on it. In my experience that isn't always the case.'

'Well, I'm dying to find out. I hope he doesn't keep us waiting too long.'

'I think your wish has just been granted.'

The door was opening. Slowly, inch by inch, and it was dark on the other side. They could make out somebody in the shadows, but no detail. All they could say for sure was that the figure was surprisingly short.

It came into the light, and whatever they expected, it wasn't this.

Standing before them was a child, a girl of about ten years old. She was thin, with almost stick-like arms and legs. Her hair was in pigtails. She had azure eyes and long blonde lashes. Her clothing consisted of a white smock embroidered with tiny flowers, and shiny black, buckled shoes. Not pretty by any stretch, her looks weren't improved by the deep-set scowl on her freckled face.

Kutch gaped at her.

Caldason reacted irately. 'What *is* this? Another trick? More delay?'

'That's not a very polite way for a guest to speak,' the girl replied. Her voice had a high-pitched, sing-song tone, and she sounded annoyed. 'Particularly after Phoenix was kind enough to grant you an audience.'

'Is this some kind of *joke*?'

'Reeth,' Kutch murmured, 'I think –'

'And Phoenix isn't happy about you brawling in the street,' the child went on, 'like some common gutter ruffian. Especially when you were told to be cautious on your way here.'

'To *hell* with Phoenix and his opinions! I didn't come here to be lectured by a child.'

'Er, Reeth,' Kutch said, 'you might find –'

Caldason ignored him. 'I thought we were supposed to be meeting with the head of this . . . *sect*. If I'd wanted to be rebuked by a kid I'd have gone to a kindergarten and avoided all this nonsense.'

'You're not a very nice man,' the child decided, huffily.

'We came here to see Phoenix,' Caldason explained, adopting a speciously reasonable manner, 'at his invitation. I don't know who you are, little girl, his grandchild perhaps, but why don't you run along and bring him here?'

'You want to see Phoenix?'

'Yes.'

'Now?'

'*Yes,*' through gritted teeth. 'Or else we're leaving.'

'Very well.' For the first time, she favoured them with a smile. It was so unlike a child's grin, so *abnormal*, that they both thought they preferred the scowl.

Then something started happening to the girl. Something strange.

As Reeth and Kutch looked on in astonishment it became very strange indeed.

18

The girl began to mutate before their eyes.

Her features seemed to melt, to become malleable. She was enveloped by a haze, like the agitation heat currents make in air, and light played around her. The swirling mist and sparkling illumination grew fierce, so much so that Reeth and Kutch couldn't see what was happening.

As the light faded, the haze started to dissipate. They could make out a shape, a heap of what could have been flesh, pulsating on the floor. Then there was a crouching figure, shaking itself the way a dog does when it comes out of water. The figure rose, and it was much taller than the child had been. Its features clarified.

A very old man stood before them. He was white bearded and rangy. Uncountable wrinkles creased his seasoned face. He wore a deep blue ankle-length robe with silver trimmings.

Caldason had his sword half unsheathed. 'What the hell –?'

'No, Reeth, wait!' Kutch exclaimed. 'I think . . . I think it's all right.'

'Heed him, Qalochian,' the old man said, 'there's no danger for you here.' His voice was like aged rum and warm honey.

He stretched, fists bunched, shoulders back, as a man might when he's just woken up.

Reeth clacked his sword back into its scabbard. 'You're Phoenix, I take it.'

'I am. Forgive my little deception.'

'I'm not in the mood for jests, sorcerer.'

'It was no jest,' the old man informed him in a starched tone.

'You call that charade serious?'

'My *intent* is deadly serious. It's to escape capture or worse at the hands of our enemies. A plight I believe you're familiar with yourself. My appearance is known to the state, making a mask necessary.'

'An odd choice of disguise.'

'But particularly effective. It also has the virtue of amusing me.'

'How did you *do* that?' Kutch blurted out.

'Ah, the apprentice.' He fixed the boy with an unwavering gaze. 'I think you might be able to explain as well as I.'

Surprised, and a little overwhelmed, Kutch stammered, 'Me?'

'Why not try?'

'Well, Mage . . . *sir* . . . I imagine that the spell you used didn't actually compress you to child size. It made you . . . invisible, which is to say glamoured, so it gave the *sense* of invisibility, and the image of the child took your place. It's basically, er, an illusion, as all magic is on one level. But a . . . uhm . . . complex, impressive illusion. Very advanced Craft. Sir.' Kutch completed his explanation with a hesitant smile.

Phoenix flashed unexpectedly white, even teeth. 'Excellent! Wrong in every essential, but top marks for inventiveness.'

Kutch's face fell.

'There's always more to learn, boy,' Phoenix added, his brusqueness softening a degree or two. He turned to

Caldason. 'Look, we've got off on the wrong foot and that wasn't the idea at all. I know you're here seeking help for a grievous malady, and –'

'What do *you* know of it?'

Phoenix, ruffled at Caldason's curt manner, went back to brisk himself. 'Would you like me to speculate on the symptoms? Let's see. You have fits that are violent and dangerous to others, and when unrestrained you fight like a berserker. You hear voices. If wounded, you heal remarkably quickly . . . Will that do for a start?'

'You seem a damn sight better informed than me. But I don't hear voices.'

'Oh, haven't they started yet? Give it time.'

'Are you trying to mock me?'

'No, Caldason, I don't want to provoke you or make fun of you. I'm just saying that your condition, or something like it, isn't entirely unknown to us.'

Hope stirred in Caldason. It showed in his normally unreadable face.

'Truly?'

'I wouldn't lie to a man with your burden.'

'Can you help me?'

Phoenix sighed. 'Perhaps. But before we go into that . . . It would be good if you didn't misinterpret what's about to happen.'

'What do you mean?'

'*Come!*' Phoenix called.

Two men entered the room. One was a stranger, ruggedly built, perhaps thirty, clean shaven but for a moustache, and he was armed. The other was Dulian Karr.

Kutch was taken aback. Caldason scowled suspiciously.

'What is this, Karr? What are you doing here?'

'Forgive me, Reeth. But please, listen to what we have to say.'

'This was supposed to be a private meeting. Now half of Valdarr's trooping through here. What can you say to me now that you couldn't have said before?'

'Plenty, as it happens. Only here it can be said with more authority. You've met Phoenix.' He turned to the stranger. 'This is Quinn Disgleirio, representing the Fellowship of the Righteous Blade. A man who can be trusted.' Disgleirio nodded. 'And I hope you know by now that you can trust me, Reeth,' Karr went on, 'and those I've brought you in touch with.' He spread a hand wide, indicating Phoenix and Disgleirio. 'What we have here is a three-pronged alliance. A union of dissident magical, martial and political forces.'

'I'm honoured,' Caldason returned sarcastically.

'You should be. If you can contain your anger and not storm out, you're going to be told things few others have the privilege of knowing. We intend putting an enormous amount of trust in you, Reeth. It's time we were completely honest with each other.'

'You assume I have any interest in your plans.'

It was Disgleirio who answered. 'We're offering you hope, man. You've searched long and hard for a solution to your troubles, and it could be in your grasp. Don't walk away from that. Hear us out.'

'And if what you say doesn't suit me?'

'Some of it may well not,' Karr told him. 'But if once you've heard us you feel you don't want to take things further, then we'll go our separate ways. We'd be content to trust you with our secrets, and wouldn't hinder you.'

Caldason pondered the offer. 'I'll hear you. But I don't need a debating society. Keep it brief.'

There were relieved smiles all round. At Phoenix's bidding they moved to the table and took seats.

'Thank you, Reeth,' Karr said. 'You heard Phoenix say he

might have a bead on your problem. We propose starting with that.'

The wizard fastened his steady gaze on Reeth. 'The patrician spoke of honesty, Caldason.' He nodded Kutch's way. 'Don't you think the lad deserves to know the truth about your ailment? He's stood firm with you, and the rest of us mean to do the same. Let us in.'

'There are aspects of it that tend to . . . unsettle people.'

'Not us,' Karr assured him.

Kutch added softly, 'I don't know what's going on here either, Reeth, but I'm sure you're among friends.'

Caldason scrutinised their faces. He said nothing.

'I claim no special insight into your condition,' Phoenix explained. 'The patrician told me about your seizures.'

'I knew when we were with the communards, Reeth,' Karr admitted. 'You were seen. How could you hope not to be?'

'The rest fell into place,' Phoenix went on, 'once I examined the annals for other cases matching your symptoms. Such cases are very rare, but with diligence they can be found.' He paused to consider his next statement. 'It's said that I can defy death. This is untrue.' Fleetingly, his grin flashed again. 'Perhaps not even Melyobar can do that. I confess I haven't discouraged tales of my longevity. They have value as far as Covenant's image is concerned. But what of the enduring nature of *your* life, Caldason? Would there be some justification if such tales were told of you?'

'As you said, my wounds heal quickly. Broken bones re-knit. I never get ill.'

'Never?'

'I came through the black spot epidemic in Shalma, and the outbreak of rotting sickness in Deeve. Other plagues at other times left me untouched too.'

Kutch stared at him in wonderment, and with not a little apprehension. 'You mean you're immortal?' he whispered.

'No. Extremely resilient rather than indestructible is the way I'd put it. There seems to be a limit. If I had a severed limb, I can't imagine it would re-grow, for instance. I guess I'd die if someone pierced my heart or parted my head from its shoulders. Then again, I was poisoned once and survived.'

'Who gave you poison?'

'I did.'

A moment passed in silence while they took that in.

Phoenix broke it by asking, 'Do you age?'

'Imperceptibly. My appearance hasn't changed much over time.'

'How long have you been like this?'

'Since the last great massacre of my people, at Keskall Pass.'

Karr didn't hide his astonishment. 'That was seventy years ago!'

'Seventy-two,' Reeth corrected.

'That makes you older than my master was when he died. Yet you look . . .' Kutch faltered.

'I know.'

'Is it some kind of curse?'

'It certainly feels like one. But I don't think it is in the way you mean, Kutch.'

'Now I understand what you meant about your friends dying in ways other than violently.'

'I've seen too many age and pass from this world. I'm not keen to repeat the experience.'

'But what *happened* to you?' Phoenix pressed. 'At Keskall.'

A pained expression wreathed Caldason's features. 'I . . . I don't know. I survived the massacre somehow, though I took wounds. Wounds that should have been fatal. Somebody helped me. I'm not sure about much else. It's confused, jumbled in my mind. There are holes in my memory. Though, sometimes in dreams . . . Well, not dreams really, more like visions or . . .' He shook his head, defeated by the challenge of explaining.

Karr said, 'Isn't it true that historically the Qaloch had good relations with the rulers of Bhealfa?'

'Yes. Our independence was respected and our borders were inviolate. Something changed that.'

'And the paladins broke the treaties and all but wiped out your people.'

'They were the instrument of our ruin, and for that I've tried to make them pay. But for all their power they weren't the masters. I've never been able to find out who the Qaloch were such a threat to that they'd engage in genocide against us.'

Disgleirio had proved a man of few words. Now he said, 'It's been my honour to have Qalochians as comrades in battle, and in resisting the tyranny of the empires. They were the most courageous and skilled fighters I've ever known.'

Caldason gifted him the slightest of nods, and a fleeting, dilute smile of gratitude.

'These are deep waters and we may never get to the bottom of them,' Phoenix pronounced.

'I need to,' Caldason told him.

'I understand. But best to concentrate on your affliction for now.'

'An affliction,' Disgleirio echoed thoughtfully. 'Yet immortality, or at least a version of it like yours . . . isn't that something people would kill to have?'

'Rather than try killing themselves because they had it, you mean?' Caldason replied. 'That depends on whether you see it as a privilege. I don't, because it's a trade-off, and I fear the ultimate cost will be the loss of my mind. It makes me feel like I'm connected to something . . . malevolent, and incredibly powerful.'

'I told you that Covenant knew about conditions similar

to yours,' Phoenix reminded him. 'It would be more accurate to say that we've heard of such things rather than actually encountered them.'

'What have you heard?'

'Enough to suspect that Founder magic could be involved.'

'But Founder magic's dead,' Kutch broke in.

'You know better than that, boy. It's all around us. It's the Founders who are dead. Their heritage is the magic we take for granted.'

'How does that help me?' Caldason said.

'Founder magic was the most powerful ever known. Our skills are petty compared to theirs. Your search for a cure was always doomed because no magic we have could lift your burden. But perhaps, just perhaps, there might be a Founder solution.'

'How could there be? The Founders and all their works disappeared before recorded history.'

'Covenant is very old. Some believe that our creed's antecedents go back to the Dreamtime itself. I don't know whether that's so. But we've studied the Founders for a very long time. We've tried to find out as much as we can about them and their ways. It's one of the reasons we're so frowned upon by the authorities and approved sorcerers.'

'There can't be much left for you to study.'

'Precious little. The achievements of the Founders moved from history to memories. Memories became stories, handed down by our barbarous ancestors. The stories slipped into legends, and the legends ripened to myths. Our harvest of knowledge, after centuries, is piteously small.'

'Have you learnt anything that could help me?'

'It's more that we have an inkling of where such knowledge might be found. If we're right, and if we can master it, there's hope for you. For all of us.'

'That's a lot of maybes.'

'More than you have before you now, I daresay.'

'Be clear about this knowledge. What is it, and where?'

'There aren't straightforward answers to such questions. I'll try. One of the most persistent legends about the Founders is that they left certain legacies apart from our system of magic. These include something we call the Source, which is the way we refer to the vast repository of knowledge they must have had. That knowledge would be of immeasurable value to us. After all, the Founders used the same earth energies we employ. So it must have been in their *techniques* that they were so advanced over us.'

'What form would this hoard of knowledge take?'

'That's one of the difficulties,' Phoenix confessed. 'We might think of such a thing as a grimoire, a tome of spells or the like. A whole library. But it's important to understand that the Founders didn't think like us. It could well be something quite different. Something we can't imagine.'

'Whatever it is, you're saying it could help me?'

'*If* it exists that would be one of its lesser miracles.'

Caldason looked dejected. 'You don't even know if it's real or just another fable.'

'Granted we're not entirely sure. For a long time we were convinced it was only a story, with no substance. Lately, our researches have led us to doubt that. If we're right, the benefits would be enormous, not least in breaking the shackles of the empires. A great tyranny requires a great counter force to combat it.'

'It all ties together, Reeth,' Karr added. 'You'd have a chance to lift the hex from your shoulders, and with Founder magic the Resistance would have a weapon that could give us a fighting chance against both empires.'

'All right, I see where you're going with this. But still no one's told me where this source is.'

'Have you ever heard of the Clepsydra?' Phoenix asked.

Caldason shook his head. 'No. Another fairy tale, is it?'

The magician chose not to be affronted. 'We think not.'

'I've heard of it,' Kutch offered. 'It's known to everyone with an involvement in the Craft.'

'What is it?' Caldason said.

'A myth.'

'Don't be so hasty,' Phoenix cautioned. 'We believe it might be real. As to what it is, it's possibly the Founders' most abstruse remaining artifact. Assuming it does remain. As near as we can tell, it's some kind of device for measuring the passage of time. Not the trifling time of everyday concern, not the hours, days and weeks we're ruled by. Oh, no. It's said that the Founders had ways of divining when the world would end, and they created the Clepsydra to mark off the eons to the Day of Destruction. It may even have been intended to prevent that catastrophe.'

Caldason was growing visibly restless. 'What's the connection between this thing and the Source?'

'There are stories linking the two. They could be together. Then again, the Clepsydra might *be* the Source. It's said to have more than one function, a combination of what seems to be a practical and a religious significance.'

'*Could* be together, *might* be the Source. More ifs and buts.'

'Short of laying out for you all the research material we have concerning this, which would take weeks, for the moment you'll just have to take my word. The evidence is circumstantial, but convincing.'

'What good is any of this if you don't know the Clepsydra's whereabouts?'

'That's just it. We think we might have traced its location.'

The Qalochian looked very interested indeed. '*Where?*'

'I'll show you.'

Phoenix rose. Swiftly, his hands described a conjuration. A mass of green luminescence appeared in the air above the table. It formed itself into the shape of a large sheet or rug, wafer thin. At a further gesture it drifted down to the table top and floated just above it.

'Bhealfa,' the sorcerer announced.

Now that he'd identified it, the image made sense. A bird's eye view of the island state, its lines and contours traced out in glowing green. The glamour map rippled gently in a breeze perfumed with incense.

'We believe the Clepsydra is located off the northern tip of Bhealfa.' Phoenix indicated the area. 'Up here somewhere, in this scattering of islands.'

'There are scores of them,' Kutch said.

'Hundreds, actually, though most are tiny. It's a very inhospitable region, subject to storms, treacherous tides and no end of other natural perils. Plus it's quite likely to be defended in some way, perhaps by Founder magic.'

Caldason stared at the dusting of emerald specks. 'Then that's where I'm going.'

Disgleirio responded with, 'We, which is to say the United Revolutionary Council, want you to be part of finding it. You have the necessary skills and certainly the best motivation.'

'I don't need your permission,' Caldason told him.

'Think, Reeth,' Karr said. 'Even if we managed to narrow down the location, how would you reach it unaided? Even if you did, you wouldn't know what you were looking for, or how to utilise it in the unlikely event of being successful. No, this has to be an organised, combined effort.'

'What are you suggesting?'

'The Resistance will undertake an expedition, properly crewed and provisioned, with adequate fighting forces and a complement of sorcerers on board.'

'When?'

'We're as anxious as you to find this thing. But it takes

time organising something like this, particularly as it all has to be done in the greatest secrecy.'

'How long?' Caldason insisted.

'I can't give you an exact answer. Weeks, certainly. Perhaps months.'

'That's not good enough, Karr.'

'Not good enough be damned!' the patrician flared. 'The Resistance has other tasks that have to be carried out as a matter of urgency. Our resources are stretched. You'd get there no quicker under your own power, believe me.' He calmed, and continued reflectively, 'We have a deal to propose. We'll move with all speed on mounting the expedition, and we guarantee you'll be part of it. In turn, you undertake to help the Resistance.'

'I'm not looking to be part of any movement.'

'You're a loner, we know that. But there are times when things can only be achieved through co-operation. And this makes sense because our interests coincide. You just have to have patience.'

'That's a counsel easier to deliver than receive. What is it you'd have me do as my half of the bargain?'

'Chores well within the capabilities of a man like you, though I won't pretend they wouldn't be dangerous.'

'A little more detail would be useful.'

'That will be provided as and when you need to know it. You really don't have a choice, Reeth, you must see that. Are you in?'

After a pause, Caldason replied, 'I'll think about it.'

'Do that, my friend. Can we expect your decision soon?'

'Give me a while to weigh the odds on all this.'

'That's fair.'

Kutch, still nervous at being in such exalted company, indicated the splash of dots on the map. 'Er . . . Phoenix, how will you go about finding the Clepsydra's island?'

'A good question,' the magician replied, 'and opportune as it brings us to our next topic.' With a wave of his hand the map collapsed in on itself as though crushed by a giant invisible fist. Then it faded and vanished. 'One of our methods would be magical sensing. You know about that, don't you?'

'Well, I've read about it, and my master –'

'I meant knowing in a more personal way.'

'I don't understand.'

'I believe we have two people with exceptional abilities here today, Kutch. Our Qalochian friend –' he nodded towards Caldason '– and you.'

'What . . . what do you mean?'

'You were quick to see through my little illusion when you first arrived here. That, and what Patrician Karr told me about the executions you witnessed in Saddlebow, makes me think you could have a very rare and special gift.'

'Me?'

'I believe you could be a spotter.'

Kutch didn't speak. But his face told a story of puzzlement and disbelief.

'Is somebody going to tell me what a spotter is?' Caldason asked. 'And what the hell's magical sensing?'

Phoenix smiled. 'Magic gives off a distinctive psychic aroma, for those who can detect it. Such people are very few, and the skill is a birthright; it can't be taught. The way in which these sensitives perceive the gist of magic varies. Rarest is the gift of spotting. A spotter can see through magic, literally. They can tell glamour from reality, no matter how sophisticated or expensive the spell. It's an incredibly uncommon ability.'

'Do you have it?'

That caused the wizard to laugh. 'No! But what I wouldn't give for just a *taste*!' He continued more soberly. 'Covenant actively seeks those with magical sensing gifts, and currently the number in our ranks could easily be counted on the fingers of one hand. I'd think myself extremely fortunate if I found one more in the whole of this new alliance we've formed.'

Kutch, still looking confounded, muttered, 'It can't be.'

'When we first saw the patrician,' Caldason remembered, 'back in your hamlet; you knew he had a protective shield long before I did.'

'Perhaps I just have better eyesight, or . . .' Kutch trailed off, lacking conviction.

'Can we do anything to establish this, Phoenix?' Karr asked.

'With the boy's permission: a test. It's not to be taken as definitive, but it's a good indicator. Do you mind, Kutch?'

'No, I'd like to find out.'

'Very well.'

The magician left the room by its smaller door. Seconds later he returned. Behind him filed the six masked, grey-clad guardians they had seen downstairs. They lined up against a wall, facing the table. Kutch stood and moved a few paces towards them. Phoenix laid a hand on his shoulder.

'Five of these men are genuine, flesh and blood members of Covenant,' he explained. 'One is a glamour. Can you tell which?'

The half-dozen were absolutely identical, and seemed very real. They all had sweat on their brows. They blinked with normal regularity. It was even possible to see their face masks creasing slightly as they breathed in and out.

For Kutch, the test had unpleasant echoes of the executions he'd seen, which made it hard for him to clear his mind.

Perhaps Phoenix realised this. 'Relax,' he advised, 'take your time. There's no penalty for failing.'

Kutch studied the unmoving figures, his eyes sweeping the line. He looked from one to the next, taking in everything about them. At last he said, 'That one,' and pointed. 'Second from the right.'

'You're sure?'

The boy nodded.

Phoenix made a complex gesture. Slowly at first, but with gathering pace, the chosen figure loosened its hold on quasi-reality and flew apart, so many billion grains of golden sand. The flaming particles dissolved.

At Phoenix's signal the remaining five guardians turned and quietly left.

'Not conclusive, as I said, but certainly indicative. How did it feel? I mean, what was it about the decoy that made you pick it?'

Kutch frowned. 'Nothing special really. It just seemed . . . obvious, I suppose. Like recognising a lame horse in a herd.'

'This was why Domex apprenticed you,' Karr said. 'He saw that you had the gift. Sadly, he didn't live long enough to help you develop it.'

'Now we can do that,' Phoenix promised. 'Covenant could train you, discipline your power and teach you to hone it.'

'And there'd be a place for you in the Resistance as well, Kutch,' the patrician added. 'The plan we hatched, the one your master was instrumental in drawing up; you can be a part of that, if you'd consider it.'

'He's only a boy,' Caldason complained, an edge to his voice. 'Don't push him.'

'There are younger in the Resistance. Anyway, the decision is his. What do you say, Kutch?'

'Well . . .'

'You should have time to think on it, like Reeth. Will you do that?'

'Yes . . . yes, I will.'

'Good. And perhaps what we have to tell you about the greater plan might help you both make up your minds.'

'You'll never get your precious revolution started,' Caldason reckoned. 'Even with the prospect of this fanciful old-time magic and child spotters.'

'Revolution? Who said anything about a revolution? Gods, no. We have something much more creative in mind.'

19

'It's time you kept your half of the bargain and started being honest with *me*,' Caldason said. 'If not an uprising, what *is* your plan?'

Kutch, Phoenix and Disgleirio, also seated around the ancient, solid table in the abandoned warehouse, fell silent. They looked to Karr.

'Not just my plan,' he corrected mildly. 'Many have contributed.'

'Whoever dreamed it up,' Caldason came back impatiently, 'what is it?'

'Let me put it this way . . .' the patrician began, making Caldason sigh. 'When one's homeland is conquered and occupied, the first instinct is to fight, to throw the invaders out. You know that feeling, Reeth. But how do you do it when the enemy's too powerful? And when another, equally powerful, is waiting to step in and take over? Fighting against one empire is really fighting against both, do you see? That's why a much larger slice of the populace isn't actively with the Resistance. They don't see the point.'

'The politician's curse; long-windedness,' Caldason grumbled. Karr took that in good part and smiled. The Qalochian added, more seriously, 'What you've just said sounds like a counsel of despair.'

'No, it's simply expressing the problem. If giving up isn't an option, and it isn't with any of us here and thousands of others, then another solution has to be found.'

'And you think you've found it.'

'Yes. Many of us don't want to be under the rule of either empire. Well, then, we won't. We'll take ourselves out of the picture.'

'Life's not a kids' ball game. You can't say you're not playing anymore.'

'We're aware of that,' Karr replied, adding stingingly, 'As are the families of many who have given their lives for the cause.'

'All right, cheap gibe. Sorry. But what *do* you intend doing?'

'Simply put: not to stay and fight, but to go.'

'Go?' Kutch said, plainly confused. 'Go where?'

'Some place where we can concentrate our dissident forces and stand apart from the influence of both empires.'

'That's insane,' Caldason reckoned. 'Where's the sense in making sitting ducks of yourselves?'

Karr was unruffled. 'Remember the commune I took you to? They're good people, but they got it wrong. You can't be apart while surrounded by hostility. Not if you expect to prosper, anyway.'

'Exactly my point.'

'And you're right. It was the lesson I hoped you'd take from the communards. Success or failure turns on location.'

'I'd like to know how you expect to get around it.'

'We've given this a lot of thought, Reeth, and while we're not saying it would be easy, we think it can be done.' He leaned closer, elbows on the table, hands knitted. 'Let me explain.'

Phoenix raised a hand and stifled Karr's flow. 'Your pardon,' he said. 'But before any more talk I thought refreshments might be in order.'

Nobody objected, and he called in one of the grey-clad acolytes and instructed him. The man returned with the rest of his company, bearing platters and flasks. They laid bread, fruits and meat on the table, alongside wine, ale and water. Everybody helped themselves to food and drink. Caldason took only water.

Karr sipped his wine and resumed. 'Our original thought was to annex a chunk of land somewhere here in Bhealfa. Something remote, maybe with a shoreline. We rejected that quite early on, for obvious reasons.'

'At least you had that much sense,' Caldason commented dryly.

'Then we looked at the possibility of somewhere beyond these shores; part of another country. But of course we'd need control of the whole area we occupied. So it had to be an island.'

'It may have escaped your attention, but we're already on one.'

'It can't be Bhealfa,' Disgleirio told him. 'There are too many forces to be overcome here. As well as being somewhat too large for our purposes at this stage.'

'Wherever you choose you'd still face opposition on every side. More so on an island because you'd leave yourself open to being cut off and starved out.'

'Not if we're totally self-sufficient,' Karr said.

'Do you really think the empires would leave you alone long enough to achieve that?'

'We're counting on them not knowing what we're doing until it's too late. This whole operation is being conducted in absolute secrecy.'

'It'll be a hard secret to keep, Patrician, given the number of people who'd have to be in on it.'

'Just about everybody's on a need to know basis. And the Resistance is organised on a cell system. There are plenty of cut-offs.'

'All it takes is one captive with a vital piece of information being put to torture. Then the empires are going to piss on you from a very great height.'

Disgleirio impaled a piece of meat. 'Aren't they doing that now, with our tacit connivance?'

'Your longevity's made a pessimist of you, Reeth,' Karr put in.

'I prefer realist. More so than you, if you believe you can get away with a plan like this. You're talking about nothing less than the creation of your own state.'

'And a rallying point.'

'Think of what a functioning state needs.' Caldason began counting off on his fingers. 'An army, or at least a militia, to defend it; armourers, smiths, wheelwrights, farmers, herdsmen, butchers, bakers, builders, healers, tailors, cobblers, administrators inevitably, not to mention a navy to get everybody there and –'

Karr held up his hands to quieten him. 'Enough! You're right, we'd need all those skills and more. Do you imagine we haven't thought it through? This is the culmination of a lifetime's work.'

'Gods, man, how many people would it take to do this thing?'

'That depends on where we do it. But many thousands, naturally. And those thousands are all about us, and willing.'

'Perhaps Reeth's right in doubting you can pull it off,' Kutch said, eyes shining, 'but I think the idea's . . . *amazing*.'

'It does have a certain fascination, doesn't it?' Karr allowed, grinning. 'The sheer complexity of putting together something like this, something that's never been done before, is intriguing. The puzzle-solving, the problems that have to be confronted; it's all quite satisfying in its way.'

Caldason seemed interested despite himself. 'What about the intangibles? Politics, religion, that kind of thing.'

'You see? It *is* an engaging subject. Would we have a state religion? Probably not. We'd leave that to individual preferences. What kind of political system would prevail? One with as much participation as possible by the citizens, obviously, though we're still working on how we could achieve that.'

'Some things you can't plan for,' Disgleirio contributed. 'Given the chance, people decide for themselves what sort of life they want.'

'What about magic?' Caldason said.

'What about it?' Phoenix asked.

'Starting afresh would be a good opportunity to ditch it.'

The magician couldn't hide his dismay, or didn't bother. 'We'd as soon get by without water to drink,' he asserted, stern-faced.

Karr attempted to smooth over the disagreement. 'We all appreciate that magic has harmed you, Reeth, but you have to be realistic. It's too fundamental a need.'

'A *need*? I see it as fetters and chains. It doesn't liberate; it reinforces bondage.'

'Not everybody thinks like those communards. Or like you. To most people, magic's a daily necessity, and we're not about to deprive them of it. We're trying to oppose a dictatorship, remember, not become one ourselves.'

'You're wrong about this. It's doing people no favours.'

Karr was growing irritated. 'Its value as a weapon alone makes it a vital element in our defence. Would you have us stand unarmed against the sorcery of the empires?'

'You're not taking the neutrality of magic into account,' Kutch reminded Reeth. 'You know it has no morality. Magic's only as good or as bad as those who channel it. I think the Resistance can be trusted to use it virtuously.'

Phoenix backed him. 'Well said, lad.'

'If magic wasn't here in the first place,' Caldason responded, 'there'd be no issue of whether it was used for good or ill.'

'You could say the same about your swords,' the magician argued. 'About all weapons. If they didn't exist, where would the temptation to misuse them be?'

'No,' Caldason stated flatly. 'There's something clean and honest about sharpened steel. Magic's base deception, and corrupt.'

'We're not going to agree on this,' Karr decided. 'Let's drop the subject.'

'So much for participation.'

'If you feel so strongly about it,' the patrician snapped, 'join us and work to change our minds. But for now, let it rest.'

Caldason glared at him.

Disgleirio noisily cleared his throat. The effect was theatrical, but it got everybody's attention. 'Time is short and we all have pressing business elsewhere. Not to mention the risk of staying here too long. So, unless there's anything else to be said . . .'

'Only this,' Karr replied. 'When I took my first uncertain steps in politics, I was lucky enough briefly to have a mentor. Old and venerable he was, yet he still burned with radical zeal. He told me, "Don't do anything for history, for posterity. Do it for yourself, and for the benefit of others. Because no matter how big your gesture, even history will forget you in time." That always struck me as a kind of truth, and I commend it to you all.' He turned his attention to Reeth and Kutch, and his usual ebullience seemed to be back. 'There's a lot more we could say about the plan, and we will. But

now there are others I want you two to meet. It might make
your decision about whether to join us a little bit easier. Are
you game?'

Karr, Reeth and Kutch made their farewells and left together,
discreetly. A carriage was waiting for them close to the
derelict warehouse. There was nothing special about it or its
anonymous driver. It had blinds on its windows, which they
left half-drawn.

   As they set off, Kutch asked, 'Where are we going?'

   'Another safe house,' Karr said. 'Well, not a house exactly.
You'll see.'

   'Is it far?'

   'Edge of the city. Shouldn't take us too long.' His attention was on Valdarr's bustling streets.

   Eventually the city began to blend into countryside. Roads
gave way to tracks and houses were sparse.

   They came to a low hill; little more than a mound, in fact,
and certainly man-made. Standing on its plateau was a wind-
mill. It was very tall and white, though its paint was peeling.
Its four great sails turned slowly in a light wind.

   'You conduct your business in some interesting places,'
Caldason remarked.

   'Needs must,' Karr. returned.

   The coach was dismissed and they crunched up the gravel
path leading to the mill's entrance. They heard the wind
crackling the fabric covering the ribs on its sails. Wood
creaked, and there was the low, rumbling sound of grinding
cogwheels. When the trio reached level ground they saw
that a cluster of squat outbuildings attended the mill.

   There were no obvious signs that they were being
observed, yet Caldason wasn't alone in feeling watched. With
a gloved hand, Karr rapped loudly on the door's sturdy
planks. It was opened almost immediately, liberating a blast

of mechanical noise. A company of armed guards met the
visitors, and recognising Karr, waved them through.

At the centre of the large circular room were three inter-
meshing toothed wheels, enormous and made of iron, which
clacked and rumbled as they turned. The chamber was lit by
glamour globes, lessening the risk of fire. A dozen or more
hovered close to the high wooden ceiling, like bulbous,
glowing fungi. Their intense light showed up the fine flour
dust in the air.

The place was crowded with people, their murmured
conversations rivalling the machinery's clamour. Most were
men, of all ages, but there was a fair sprinkling of women
and children. They sat on crates, heaps of sacks or the odd
bench and chair. Many stood. Some of the youngsters were
curled up on the floor, asleep.

A woman emerged and made her way to Karr and the
others. She was middle-aged and of a chunky build, with
severe hair, and looked as hard as hell. But the smile she
wore on seeing the patrician softened the effect.

'This is Goyter,' Karr said. 'She's overseeing this little
group.'

He swapped greetings with her, then indicated his guests.

If Caldason's name meant anything to her, she didn't blink.
'Good to meet you both. Here for the investiture?'

'Not as participants,' Karr answered for them. 'But hopefully soon.'

'Investiture?' Caldason queried.

'Everybody here has been accepted for Resistance membership,' Goyter explained. 'We make a small ceremony of the
induction, to mark the event.'

The Qalochian looked at the waiting conscripts. 'The movement seems to attract a varied membership.'

'Oppression casts a wide net,' Karr replied. 'Some are here
as a matter of principle. Others have more direct reasons for

joining us. Come and meet a few. You as well, Kutch.' He nodded to Goyter and she went back to her duties, the smile blinking off.

Karr led Reeth and Kutch deeper into the room. They stepped over reclining bodies and outstretched legs, skirted knots of chattering postulants. He spotted someone he knew and made for him. The man was probably just into his twenties. He was clothed poorly, but looked fit. Karr didn't introduce him by name.

'Would you mind telling why you're here?' he asked. 'For my friends?'

'No, sir.' The young man was hesitant. He struck them as a doer rather than a talker. 'Suppose it's simple, really. I always wanted to do something of service to the country, like my father before me. He was regular army, sir. So I put in for the militia. But what they made me do, and the things I saw . . .' The memory clouded his face darkly.

'Such as?' Caldason prompted.

'Lawful protests put down with uncalled-for brutality, people terrorised into becoming informers, suspects tortured or murdered . . . no end of things a peace-keeping force shouldn't be doing.' A flash of zeal animated him. 'I joined to safeguard people's freedom, not to steal it.'

'Tell us how it came to the crunch for you,' Karr said.

'One bad order too many, sir. It was as plain as that. I had to disobey it, and that's something you don't do in the militia. So I deserted. My father would have been *scandalised* by that. But I reckoned I'd serve the people best by siding with the Resistance rather than the empires and their puppets.'

Karr clasped the young man's hand. 'Your integrity does you credit.'

As they turned from him, a woman approached. Her careworn face and sorrowful eyes spoke of some tragedy that had aged her. She was evidently someone else Karr knew.

Once they'd greeted each other, he asked her the same question he'd asked the deserter.

'Why am I here?' She seemed genuinely perplexed. 'Where else could I be after what happened?'

'What was that, ma'am?' Kutch inquired, his tone courteous and soft.

The woman stared, as though seeing him for the first time. After a beat, she said, 'Lost two boys. One not that much above your age, the gods bless you.'

'How did they . . . ?'

'War did for the eldest. One of those pointless wars against people we've no quarrel with. State killed the youngest.'

'Executed for cowardice,' Karr elaborated. 'I knew him. If he was a coward I'll walk naked into a barbcats' den.'

'Speaking his mind was his only crime,' the woman judged, 'and they took his life for it. That's why I'm here, bringing what I can to the cause.'

Karr thanked her and she reclaimed her place on a patch of floor.

Nearby, he found another woman he recognised. Life had wearied her too, though her youthful looks remained more or less intact.

The patrician related her story himself. 'You lost your home in a forced clearance, so a palace could be built for a Gath Tampoorian overseer. Isn't that right?'

She nodded. 'But that wasn't the worst of it. When the people in our quarter united to object to the plan there was a bloodbath. My husband and my brother were . . . butchered.'

'They sent paladins in,' Karr supplied.

'*Bastards*,' the woman hissed. She noticed Caldason's sympathetic expression, and studied him with shrewd eyes. 'You're a Qalochian?' she asked.

He confirmed it with a slight bob of the head.

'Then you know all about suffering at their hands. For my money, anyone who goes against those clan swine deserves a medal. I say more power to their sword arm, and good luck to them.' Her smile had little warmth but a great deal of canniness in it.

The remark was pointed enough to make them pretty sure she'd guessed who Caldason was. They left it hanging and moved on.

'See him?' Karr indicated a bearded, stocky individual, perched on a barrel. He wore a wool cap and was dressed in a heavy, dark blue long-coat. 'Another defector. Navy, in his case. Second in command on a slave galley, would you believe. Hated the brutality and came over to our side.'

Every step seemed to elicit a tale. Karr pointed out more volunteers.

'That pair standing by the door – reformed bandits. Some very useful skills they've brought us. Him. See? A priest. Broke his vows over a matter of conscience. The couple over there – a merchant and his wife. They –'

'I think we get the point,' Caldason interrupted. 'You have a groundswell of support.'

'Yes, the Resistance is drawing from a wider pool than ever before.'

'So all these people will be going to your island paradise?'

Karr gave a small laugh. 'It'll hardly be that. But perhaps some of them will. We'll see.'

Caldason scanned the room. 'It's a motley crew.'

'I think diverse is a better way of putting it. They have a range of expertise we need. More important, they've got something not easily measured. Passion. You can move mountains with that.'

'Moving the empires might prove tougher.'

Karr bristled. 'Why do you always have to –'

'*Ssshhh!*' Kutch had a finger to his lips.

Goyter was standing on a crate. Now she called for order. Two men went to the conjunction of cogwheels in the middle of the room. They grasped a massive lever. Muscles working, they wrestled it down. The wheels slowed, their clinking grew lazy, then they squeaked to a halt. A final shudder released falls of fine white powder from somewhere above.

With the machinery and chattering stopped, the silence felt strange. Everyone was standing by this time, and looking Goyter's way. Karr, Reeth and Kutch found themselves at the back of the crowd, which suited them.

'You all know why we're here,' Goyter boomed, 'so I don't intend making this any longer than it should be. You've taken a decision that's going to alter your lives. And that's maybe going to alter the way we live, for the better. It's a decision you can't go back on after tonight, so be sure. Are there any here who don't want to go further?'

Not a hand went up, and nobody moved.

'No one's backed out yet,' Karr confided in a whisper. 'I'm not sure what we'd do if anyone did at this stage. Have them killed, I suppose.'

Reeth and Kutch exchanged a glance, almost entirely sure he was joking.

'Good,' Goyter continued, her strong, clear voice filling the room. 'For what it's worth, I think you're doing the right thing.' She looked from face to face. 'This is an uncommon moment, and one you won't forget. Savour it.' Following a reflective moment, she added, 'It's time to take the oath. Raise your right hand and repeat after me.' Needing no written reminder of the pledge, she began reciting it from memory. 'Of my own volition and free of duress . . .'

She paused every so often to let them repeat the words. Caldason took in the chanting crowd – young, old, middle-aged. Even a few children, too young to understand, with their hands raised and wearing solemn expressions.

'... *I hereby swear allegiance to* ...'

Some looked earnest, or ardent, excited, apprehensive, jubilant, glassy-eyed. A few were tearful. One or two seemed bored.

'... *oppose those who subjugate us and cause us* ...'

He glanced at Karr and saw that he was silently mouthing the oath, gazing unwaveringly at Goyter.

'... *vow my mind, my body and my spirit to the* ...'

Kutch was transfixed too, fascinated by the flow of lofty ideals and noble phrases.

'... *to protect the weak, fight for the downtrodden, speak out for the voiceless* ...'

Had the emotions in that room been uniform, had sentimentality and pious conviction been the crowd's only mood, Caldason could have dismissed it all.

'... *the inalienable right of all* ...'

But it seemed to him there were as many reactions as there were different types of people present. That somehow gave a power to what was happening. Not a power he was unfamiliar with, but one he hadn't felt for a very long time.

'... *nor rest until freedom* ...'

Widely different people – *diverse*, Karr had called them – yet sharing a connection, an affinity of common purpose. The feeling it gave him dredged something from the pit of his memory. It rekindled the trace of a dream.

'... *This I do swear and affirm.*'

The end of the oath brought a hubbub. Clapping, subdued cheers, the resumption of chatter. Caldason refocused on the here and now.

'Quieten down!' Goyter shouted, dampening the new conscripts' noise. 'Those of you making your way back to your homes and families will be leaving here in small numbers and not all at once. The guards at the door will take care of that. Those who aren't going back, just stay where you are and your group leaders will come to you. Let's do this quietly and sensibly, shall we, folks?'

She got a smattering of applause.

'Aren't going back?' Kutch echoed.

'Some have been selected to work clandestinely,' Karr explained. 'They'll give up the lives they've known and be swallowed by the underground. New identities, new objectives. Others serve best by staying in the roles they occupy.'

'It all sounds very organised.'

'We're still learning. It's taken us years to build the movement's structure. But now this new alliance means we have access to an even greater network.'

'It's quite exciting, isn't it, Reeth?'

'You see this as very romantic, don't you, Kutch?' Caldason replied. 'A bit of an adventure.'

'Well, I suppose –'

'It's not. It's about real people taking real risks and maybe dying because of it. It's about somebody's wife or brother or father being maimed, tortured or worse. Why don't you tell the boy about that side of it, Karr?'

'You, sir, are a cynic.' The patrician said it with good humour, though he couldn't keep a mild undercurrent of genuine criticism out of his voice. 'It's all those things, yes. People will be hurt, and die, and misery's unavoidable. It's a dangerous enterprise. But Kutch is right, too; it *is* an adventure. Probably the greatest we'll ever see. As for romance, what grander than the romance of liberty?'

Caldason didn't answer.

People were leaving, let out in ones and twos by the poker-faced guards. Those who stayed were being shepherded into units by their minders. Goyter moved among them, urging, smoothing tempers, answering questions.

'What now for us, Karr?' the Qalochian finally asked.

'One more task. Though I hope you won't see it that way.

I thought it was time you met those people I told you about earlier. The little band of escapees who washed up on our shore. *Ah.'* He turned to the door.

There was a minor commotion there. A small group was being brought in, cloaked and hooded. Several of the newcomers were obviously seasoned Resistance members, acting as guides and protectors. Their charges were a man, two women and a pair of children. Even at first glance they seemed an oddly assorted bunch.

Diverse, Reeth thought.

No one, least of all Caldason, knew everything was about to change.

20

The new arrivals rolled back their hoods and doffed their cloaks.

At least, the women did. Both of them shook loose their hair, releasing a cascade of blonde and raven locks. Caldason immediately recognised the brunette as a Qalochian. Such meetings were rare enough to mean something to him, and he thought she had the same feeling. The children, who proved to be a boy and a girl once unwrapped, and quite young, looked bone tired. They all did.

The man, on the short side and well-built, kept his cowl in place. There may have been a good reason for this, but all it did was arouse interest.

Caldason was intrigued by the prospect of meeting another Qalochian. He was curious about the man who remained hidden. But he had eyes only for Serrah Ardacris.

He instinctively knew another warrior, and would have even if Karr hadn't already spoken about her. She had the effortless grace common to good dancers and good fighters – athletic, supple, light on her feet, with a muscular potency that didn't submerge her femininity.

There was a certain comeliness, too, under the wear and

tear. It was to do with strength. Caldason knew that when people spoke of character it was usually strength they meant, and this woman's face was etched with it. She had a *presence*, a bearing that spoke of confidence shot through with wilfulness. And maybe a dash of something a little like insanity.

From across the room, she studied him in turn. A natural process when two people who live by violence recognise each other. Her gaze was unblinking, but not devoted exclusively to him. She constantly surveyed her surroundings and the people, seemingly relaxed but actually alert. It was the way of Caldason himself, though he was better at concealing it, having practised for so much longer.

Somebody released the lever and the cogwheels started up again.

'This is not the place for a meeting,' Karr shouted over the racket, 'even if we are among our own. We need privacy.' He gestured to Goyter. After a hasty, whispered consultation, he said to Reeth and Kutch, 'One moment, please.' Then he went to the newly-arrived group at the door.

Reeth glanced at Kutch. 'Been a long day, hasn't it? Lot to take in.'

The boy nodded.

'Are you all right with it?'

'Yes. Well, kind of. A bit overwhelmed. Knowing I might be a spotter, hearing the Resistance plan . . . finding out about *you*.'

'After a flurry of events, things have a way of settling down.'

'They never seem to when you're around, Reeth.'

As Karr said something to the new arrivals, they all looked Caldason and Kutch's way. What Reeth noticed most was the stare Serrah gave him. Proud, penetrating. That strength again.

Karr rejoined them, the fresh group in tow. 'Come on, there's somewhere we can go.'

Caldason and the boy fell in behind the newcomers and Karr led everybody to a small door on the far side of the room. He opened it and ushered them through, slamming it behind him at the last.

'That's better,' he announced.

It was quieter, and cooler. They were in a storehouse; a long, low building with sacks and barrels piled along each side of a central aisle.

Glamour globes gave light here too, though there were fewer than in the mill, making it shadowy. Caldason quickly scouted, satisfying himself that they were alone.

'I think you can remove the hood now, Kinsel,' the patrician said.

The stocky man did so, revealing an amiable, neatly bearded face. 'Thank goodness for that.' His voice was bass and smooth. His open smile was genuine.

Karr returned it. 'Time for introductions, I think.' He gestured to the others. 'Reeth Caldason, Kutch Pirathon.'

Kutch said hello. Caldason gave one of his small, almost indistinct nods.

Karr indicated the other group. 'Serrah Ardacris, Tanalvah Lahn.'

Serrah said nothing, and remained perfectly still. Tanalvah smiled and greeted them, adding, 'And this is Lirrin and Teg.' The children clutched her hands and studied the floor.

'Hello, kids,' Kutch returned. He got a shy peek from the youngest.

'And Kinsel Rukanis,' Karr continued. 'Who you may already be familiar with.'

'Not me,' Caldason stated bluntly.

Rukanis took no offence. 'I'm very pleased to make your acquaintance.'

'I know about you, Master Rukanis, sir,' Kutch volunteered. 'I saw a likeness of you once. I've never heard you sing, but people say you're very good.'

'Thank you, Kutch. I hope you'll have the opportunity to hear me some time.'

'Kinsel is one of the most respected and talented classical singers in the empire,' Karr explained.

Rukanis tried waving away the compliment, cheeks colouring.

'Oh, yes,' Caldason said. 'The pacifist.'

'This isn't exactly luxurious accommodation,' Karr cut in, 'but, please, sit down.'

Tanalvah perched on a crate, Teg in her arms, Lirrin beside her, holding Tanalvah's dress and bashfully sucking a thumb. Kinsel lowered himself onto another crate nearby. Kutch choose a heap of plump sacks. The patrician settled for a barrel. Caldason and Serrah remained standing, eyeing each other.

'So, how have things been for you?' Karr asked the newcomers. He added, 'It goes without saying, by the way, that everyone here is to be trusted, so we can speak freely.'

Serrah Ardacris took him at his word. 'We've been dragged from pillar to post and back again,' she informed him crisply. 'How do you think we feel?'

'Yes, my apologies.' To Reeth and Kutch he explained, 'It's been necessary to keep our friends moving since they sought our help.'

'It would be good to stop,' Tanalvah said, glancing at the siblings, 'for the children's sake if nothing else.'

'Of course. We have secure accommodation for you now. You'll be going there soon and you can rest properly.' He turned to Rukanis. 'But your situation's different, Kinsel, and we need to discuss it as a matter of urgency.'

'Do they know the circumstances?' the singer asked, nodding at Reeth and Kutch.

'Some of it.'

'I've been involved with the Resistance for seven years,' Rukanis told them. 'I won't bore you with my reasons, though they're simply enough expressed in terms of my beliefs about liberty and freedom. My creed, as you pointed out, Caldason, is one of non-violence. I don't think that means I'm any the less useful to the cause. My profession involves a lot of travel, and access to certain echelons of authority, and that has been of benefit to the Resistance. Everything went smoothly until . . .' He looked to Serrah. 'I . . . *all* of us owe a debt of gratitude to this woman. We wouldn't be here without her.'

'And we're profoundly grateful to her for that,' Karr stated. Serrah showed no recognition of the compliment. 'But the circumstances in which you all met could have created problems,' he went on. 'From what our intelligence tells us we think no suspicions have been aroused about you, Kinsel. After all, you've been out of circulation for only a short while. But that doesn't mean you haven't been compromised.'

'Your advice?'

'It has to be your decision, but I think this may be the time to consider giving up your public persona and letting the underground protect you. You've had a good run, let's not tempt the fates.'

Rukanis sighed heavily. 'I've thought about it, to be honest. The thing is, my day-to-day work. I have responsibilities there, too. People depend on me. I can't just disappear and leave them in the lurch.'

Karr smiled mischievously. 'It couldn't be that you're loath to give up the glamorous life you lead?'

'It's nowhere near as glamorous as it might seem. And important as singing is to me, my work with the Resistance is more so. Anyway, who said anything about giving up singing? I fully intend performing under our new order.'

'So you'll think about joining us full time until then?' Karr persisted.

'I don't want to address any of this until after the reception tonight.'

'Might be best to forget that, Kinsel. Too risky.'

'More risky than not turning up and snubbing some powerful people? And what about the information you wanted me to be alert for? Isn't that still important?'

'We can find other sources. Think of your own safety.'

'Listen to him, Kinsel,' Tanalvah cut in. 'You don't seem to realise how dangerous this all is.'

The children's wide-eyed gaze went from her to Rukanis.

'I'll be all right, Tan,' he assured her gently, 'I can look out for myself. You mustn't worry.'

'We're not going to change your mind on this, are we?' Karr realised. 'You always were your own man, Kinsel. Go ahead and attend the damned reception then. I'll have some of our people reconnoitre the place beforehand, and they'll stay nearby in case of trouble.'

'What's so special about this reception?' Caldason asked.

'All gatherings of top state officials interest us for the unguarded comments that tend to be dropped. This one's particularly important because the commanders of the fleets are going to be there.'

'Why do they interest you?'

'We've heard rumours about an expedition that's about to be mounted. It's supposedly a trade mission, though there seems to be a lot of military involvement. We suspect the Bhealfan flag's being used to cover some empire adventure. The whisper is that the flotilla's heading north, so we think it might have something to do with Zerreiss, the warlord.'

'The man who fell from the sun,' Tanalvah said.

Karr frowned. 'What?'

'I heard him called that, in the ship on the way here. They say his own people gave him that title. I don't know why.'

'I knew he had some fancy names, but I've never come across that one before.'

'I've heard something similar,' Serrah added. 'That came from seamen, too, and they're usually a good source of information. When they're sober. And back in Gath Tampoor my unit had a briefing on him.'

'I'd be keen to hear about that.'

'Don't get too excited; it was pretty basic stuff. No more in it than you probably already know.'

'I think I see where this is going, Karr,' Caldason said. 'You're hoping to make this warlord your ally. An asset to the Resistance, like Founder magic.'

'It's crossed our minds. My enemy's enemy and all that. But equally, we'd be concerned that Zerreiss might make an alliance with Gath Tampoor. An accommodation could suit both sides, and we'd have another force ranged against us.'

'What's to stop them doing the same with this Clepsydra thing and what you call the Source? They must have heard of them. Why haven't they located them and turned Founder magic against the Resistance? Not to mention against Rintarah. Come to that, why hasn't Rintarah tried finding them?'

'We have no answer to those questions.'

'An obvious one would be that these artifacts don't exist and the empires know it.'

'Or that they believe they're just legends and haven't bothered looking. Or they have searched and they're just too hard to find. We still think there's everything to play for, Reeth.'

'Then the sooner you get me out there the better.'

'We'll be working on it, believe me. But you're forgetting something. We're putting ourselves out for you, so you could at least meet us halfway. Why not do the same as Serrah here, and Tanalvah, and join the Resistance formally? I know you wanted to think on it, but really, what's there to think about?'

Caldason looked from one face to another, lingering just a little longer on the impassive Serrah.

'All right,' he said.

Taken aback by Reeth's sudden change of mind, Kutch exclaimed, 'Don't forget me!'

'Excellent,' Karr enthused. 'You can both have your own impromptu swearing-in ceremony, right here.'

'Just make good use of me,' Caldason told him. 'I'm growing bored with inaction.'

'Don't worry about that. You're going to be earning your keep from now on, believe me.'

Caldason was only half listening. His attention was on the inscrutable expression Serrah wore.

21

A lot happened in the course of the next few days.

The social gathering Kinsel Rukanis attended passed without incident. But it was disappointing in intelligence terms. He learnt almost nothing about the supposed trading mission to the north, except that it was due to depart in a matter of weeks.

Nobody was greatly surprised when Kinsel and Tanalvah Lahn set up home together, living with Teg and Lirrin as a family.

Kutch began his training as a spotter, supervised by Phoenix himself. It proved harder than he expected, leaving him exhausted after most sessions and sometimes uncharacteristically fractious.

There was a riot in one of Valdarr's poorest quarters, sparked by a dispute over the provision of clean drinking water. The authorities' heavy-handed response left eleven dead and an uncounted number of injured. Somebody burnt down a militia staging-post later the same day, bringing more reprisals.

A small group of insurgents, using a customised bootleg enchantment, managed to conjure an enormous flying pig.

Hovering above the city, it spewed a multicoloured alphabet that arranged itself into a coarse limerick featuring a local official. Sorcerers had to be brought in to neutralise the pig with anti-glamour bolts. But not before the anatomically impossible feat described in the limerick had amused a wide swathe of the population.

An obscure member of the Bhealfan royal family was attacked in the street by a man with a grievance. The man was downed by bodyguards wielding glamoured shock sticks. A district organiser with the Resistance disappeared, presumed captured or dead, and there was talk of betrayal. A mid-ranking military chief was assassinated on his own doorstep by an archer hiding on a rooftop opposite. A magical brawl between groups of licensed and unlicensed sorcerers started a fire that gutted half a dozen riverside houses and an inn.

And Reeth Caldason and Serrah Ardacris prepared to commit a robbery.

The United Revolutionary Council had ordered the formation of a special operations unit, similar to the one Serrah had commanded in Merakasa. But Serrah wasn't made its leader. That role was pressed on a reluctant Caldason, for reasons best known to the council. If Serrah resented demotion to second-in-command, she didn't show it. Perhaps because she allowed herself to reveal little in the way of emotions. Or because, in practice, she and Caldason led the group jointly.

Beneath them in the band's command structure were two 'subalterns', with eight 'privates' forming the pyramid's base. Half the membership was drawn from the ranks of the Resistance. The other half came from the Fellowship of the Righteous Blade, hand-picked by Quinn Disgleirio. All were seasoned fighters. But the unit lacked a thirteenth member, due to the scarcity of combat sorcerers.

At the end of a hard day's training in a small wood beyond the city limits, Reeth and Serrah were summoned to Karr's hideaway. No one else was present at the meeting. It took place in a cellar whose entrance was concealed by a glamour that mimicked a solid wall. Used for planning and briefing sessions, the cellar was brightly lit and well appointed.

They sat at one of several large benches, taking refreshments. For Serrah and Caldason, who shared frugal appetites, that meant light fare and plain water. Karr allowed himself a goblet of diluted brandy.

He swallowed a mouthful and said, 'Is everything going well with the band?'

'Seems to be,' Caldason replied. 'They work together and take orders. No problems so far.'

'You being a Qalochian isn't an issue? I should hope it isn't, of course, but prejudice can exist even in our ranks.'

'No more an issue than Serrah being a Gath Tampoorian, I'd say.'

'Good. So, you think the band's ready to be put to the test?'

'Ready as it'll ever be.'

'Serrah?'

She nodded. Her eyes were less hollow, there was more colour in her face. Rest, nourishment and having a purpose had begun to revive her. 'Ready and eager. Particularly if there's a chance of doing some damage to my old masters.'

'Then I think you'll approve of what we have in mind.' Karr took another drink. 'It's no secret that one of the ways we finance ourselves is through stealing. Not from the common people, of course. We take from the masters, the imperialists who squeeze their vassals dry. You might call it ethical robbery. It's something of that kind I'm proposing for your unit.'

'A politician involved in criminal enterprises?' Caldason gently mocked. 'Whatever next?'

Karr laughed. 'Does beggar belief, doesn't it?' More soberly, he added, 'But there's a real contradiction, of course. No decent public servant should be forced into illegality, no matter how deserving the cause. There comes a time when the disparities are too difficult to balance. I think that's where I am now.'

'What are you going to do about it?' Serrah asked.

'The day's close when I'm going to have to give up so-called legitimate politics. To do what I urged Kinsel to do and get out. Things have gone too far for lawful opposition to make much difference now. Direct action's the only path I can see.'

'I'm surprised you've stuck it out this long,' Caldason said.

'You hold on to your illusions, you know? Once, politics seemed to make a difference. Somehow you lose sight of the fact that it doesn't anymore. You don't see the piecrust promises and downright lies, and go on believing that the platitudes matter.'

'You've changed your tune. Not that long ago you were saying politics still had a value.'

'Partly it was seeing Kinsel come so near to grief. That was sobering. But mostly it's the general situation. The more we kick out at the state, the more they ratchet up their oppression. That's only to be expected, but it makes it harder to achieve anything through official channels. It certainly makes it more difficult for me to live two lives.'

'So you're going underground.'

'Probably. But I've not officially made the decision, so keep it to yourselves, will you?'

They nodded.

'I've got us away from the subject,' Karr went on, businesslike. 'First priority is your mission. And it's the sort we particularly favour; a redistribution of some of the taxes leeched from the provinces.'

'Redistribution,' Serrah repeated, quietly pleased with the word.

'Yes. It doesn't all go back to the people, but we pass on as much as we can after our needs.'

Caldason raised an eyebrow. 'So *you're* taxing them.'

'They give it willingly, Reeth, believe me. Look at it as the state collecting donations on the Resistance's behalf. And the collection we're concerned with happens once every three months. That's how often they bring in the tithes from outlying districts. In this case, from quite a wide area to the east of the city. That's rich farming land, several good-sized towns and a lot of villages, as you know. Should be a hefty take.' He produced a large rolled parchment and nodded at the bench. 'Clear that, would you?'

They swept aside the food and drink. Karr unravelled the parchment, which they weighted at the corners.

'A paper map,' Serrah muttered. 'Quaint.'

It showed an edge of Valdarr where a hamlet was being absorbed by the spreading city. The effect was like the profile of a face with an absurdly long nose. A smattering of buildings thrust out from the urban mass into virgin countryside. The farthest end of the captured hamlet, the tip of the nose, met a small river, with a few buildings on its far side. At that point there was a bridge. When the road it carried reached the city side, it turned sharply and narrowed, threading its way through a cluster of houses and tree-lined lanes.

'That's the only bridge for miles,' Karr informed them. He didn't have to spell out the potential for ambush.

Caldason pointed at the map. 'You're sure they'll go that way?'

'They vary the route every time, but we have good intelligence that it's going to be along here.'

'When?'

'That's the thing. This evening. In about four hours.'

'Gods, Karr,' Serrah exclaimed, 'that's cutting it a bit fine, isn't it?'

'Yes. But the tip-off just reached us. It's tonight or in another three months, and next time we might not know the route.'

'What sort of numbers are we talking about?' Caldason said. 'How's it protected?'

'One or two wagons for the load. Escort party of between twelve and twenty, going on past form. Certain to be paladins among them.'

'They outnumber us.'

'I'm sure you can be inventive on that score. And maybe we can bleed their number with a few diversions.'

'Hmmm,' Serrah mused. 'They're going to be well glamoured, aren't they?'

'Chances are they'll have standard magical ordnance. But so will you. Only you won't have a trained sorcerer on hand to work it properly. This is a dangerous mission, I won't pretend it isn't. Which is why I have to be sure your band's up to scratch.'

'It is,' Caldason assured him. 'We can deal with this.'

'I wouldn't be quite so hasty,' Serrah said. 'This is all last minute, we're going to be outnumbered, the band's untested, and –'

'Oh, come on. You know we can do it.'

'*Planning*, Reeth. It's the key to any successful operation. How much preparation can we do in four hours? What's our strategy if things go wrong?'

'It looks pretty straightforward to me. It's perfect terrain for waylaying a convoy and we'll have the element of surprise.'

'Rushing in blindly's a lot worse than not doing it at all, believe me. Remember, I've had experience running units

THE COVENANT RISING 273

like this. The least we should do is give the rest of the band the choice of coming along or not.'

'This isn't a temple picnic, Serrah. We're supposed to be a disciplined unit. We can't give people the option of backing out. You're worrying about the band too much; they'll be all right.'

'*You'll* be all right, you mean.'

'Pardon?'

'You've got this invulnerability thing, haven't you? Well, the rest of us don't have that luxury. You might keep that in mind when the lives of our band are on the line and you feel like behaving recklessly.'

'I'd trade what I've got with you any time,' Caldason replied icily. 'And I'm not invulnerable. I can still be killed, or maimed if the wound's bad enough.'

'So you say. I'm just thinking about the safety of the group.'

'Oh yes, that's something you know all about, isn't it?'

She glared at him. 'What?'

'They say you got a rich kid killed over in Merakasa. One of your band, wasn't he?'

'They say you're a murderer of innocent women and children.'

'That's horse shit.'

'Right.'

Karr watched them as though they were a game of pass the ball.

'I'm not careless with lives,' Caldason rumbled.

'And *I* am?' Serrah returned.

'I didn't say that.'

'*When* are you respectful of other people's lives? When you're having one of your uncontrolled berserks, maybe?'

'That's not fair. I have no –'

'*Excuse me,*' Karr grated. 'Can I have your attention, please? Thank you. If you two can't work together I'll have to disband your unit. Which would be a shame because we see this mission as a rehearsal for more ambitious assignments. And not only will it increase our funds, it'll get you that bit nearer to the Clepsydra, Reeth. So why don't you both turn your little creative tensions towards the job at hand?' He beamed at them. 'What do you say?'

They looked at each other. Serrah shrugged.

'Fine,' they chorused.

It was dusk by the time they got to the site and in position. That left about a quarter of an hour before the convoy arrived.

The point they chose was on a tight lane. One side was lined with outbuildings and abandoned properties. The other fronted the boundary of a wood, where a pair of cottages stood in a small roadside clearing.

Caldason and Serrah, on horseback, had hidden themselves on the wooded side. The bridge was to their right, but couldn't be seen. What they could see was a lookout, stationed at a bend in the road, who had a clear view of the approach.

To their left was the city, sparkling with its usual dizzy magic. Light bursts, lancing beams, glamours born and dying like a million swarming fireflies. The distant urban roar.

Out here on Valdarr's hinterland there was little in the way of magical discharge. Hardly anybody was about. A mild breeze carried the scent of honeysuckle, and grass after a recent shower. It was quiet, except for the sound of axes biting timber.

The sky was turning the colour of lemons and blood as the sun sank. Stars glinted against spreading purple velvet.

Serrah took a deep breath and let it out slowly, as though savouring a fine tobacco. The distraction of the mission seemed to have lightened her earlier testy mood.

'At least the air's better in these parts,' Caldason remarked.

'It's not something I'm usually aware of.' She added by way of explanation, 'I'm a city girl.'

It was the first time he'd known her volunteer any kind of personal detail. 'I prefer the reality of the countryside,' he confided.

'That's an odd choice of word; *reality*.'

'It's the Qalochian way of seeing the world. To us, cities seem an unnatural way to live. Unreal.'

'You've never got used to them? Even after all your . . .'

'Years? No, it gets worse. More people buzzing pointlessly about more buildings. More self-deluding magic. None of it's restful to the spirit.'

She glanced in the direction of the lookout. 'Change happens. You can't fight it.'

'Live as long as I have and you realise that, believe me. But some things never change. People don't, not really. They wallow in ignorance and always have an appetite for cruelty.'

'I'd like to think there was some kindness and wisdom, too.'

'So would I.' His tone didn't allow for any.

For a moment it looked like Serrah was going to take issue. Instead she steered him back to the mission. 'It can't be much longer now,' she said, checking with the lookout again.

Two of their band appeared on low rooftops opposite. They lugged coils of rope.

There was a sudden absence of noise as the axes fell silent.

'At least they got that done in time,' Serrah muttered.

Late birdsong swelled to fill the void.

She dug into her saddlebag and brought out a cylindrical glamour. It was barely longer than the fist she clutched it in.

'I don't know why you need a wailer,' Caldason grumbled. 'A blast from a horn should serve.'

'Do you *have* a horn?' she came back acerbically. 'Could you play one if you did?'

'You don't play it, you blow it.'

'I'd rather not put that much reliance on your lungs. This is surer. Nobody's going to miss hearing it.'

He had a finger to his lips. 'Listen.'

The sound of a drawn out, unbirdlike whistle reached them. They turned to the lookout. He was waving frantically.

'They're on their way.' Serrah wrapped her horse's reins around one hand. She held the glamour ready in the other.

The men on the roofs ducked out of sight.

Caldason drew his broadsword. 'Everybody should be in place by now. Sit tight.'

Several minutes dragged by. Then the lookout signalled again before concealing himself.

The clip-clop of hooves could be heard, and wagon wheels rattling on the bridge's planks. Then the head of the convoy appeared: two mounted paladins, followed by a quartet of militia. An enclosed wagon came next, a four-hander, with driver and bowman guard. Another pair of militia rode behind, ahead of the second wagon. The caravan rounded off as it began, with the four militia–two paladin combination.

'What do you think?' Serrah whispered. 'Eighteen, maybe twenty?'

'About twice our strength, yes. Could be worse.'

The whole convoy was on the straight now. Alert to the danger of a narrowing road with cover on either side, it began upping its pace to get through quicker. Soon it would reach Serrah and Reeth's hiding place.

'Easy,' he cautioned, eyeing the glamour she clutched. 'Watch the timing.'

'All *right*,' she hissed. 'I know what I'm doing.'

'And plug your ears.' He offered her a small ball of wax. She had to slide the glamour into her armpit to free a hand.

The escort was scanning both sides of the road, wary and

nervous. Caldason worried that the convoy's gathering speed might just get it through before his men could do what had to be done.

A second later the two lead paladins hit the trigger point.

'Now!' he yelled.

Serrah struck the base of the glamour hard against her thigh, setting it off. The wailer gave out an ear-splitting scream, a note so shrill and intense it cut to the bone. Reeth and Serrah had to restrain their horses from bolting. From all around, flocks of screeching birds took flight.

The convoy's mounts shied and faltered, too, slowing progress. Their shocked riders struggled to control them in the confusion. Several had the presence of mind to draw weapons, and the bowmen nocked arrows.

Serrah's glamour expired and she tossed it away. The abrupt silence was almost as painful as the din itself. She aped Reeth and gouged out the earplugs.

The wailer was supposed to act as both a distraction and a signal to the rest of the band. But nothing seemed to be happening, and the convoy was still moving, though in disarray. It was almost level with Reeth and Serrah's hide.

'Damn it!' she snapped. 'What the hell's keeping –'

A new sound rent the air. The crack of splintering wood and a growling creak as something ponderous slowly toppled.

Ahead of the convoy a massive tree crashed down and blocked its path. Taller than the road was wide, the tree's upper third smashed through a barn on the far side, completely demolishing it. Branches bounced as they struck the road and swirling clouds of dust were liberated from the crushed building.

The charging convoy struggled to rein in, drawing up just short of the roadblock. The sudden stop made the first wagon slew to one side, finishing at an angle across the lane. One of the militiamen following on was unsaddled.

At the rear of the convoy the riders tried turning their horses about. But they were still churning and shouting when there was another thunderous crash. The band had felled a second tree, cutting off retreat and boxing in the convoy.

'Let's go!' Caldason spurred his ride and burst out of cover. Serrah was right behind him, whipping her blade free.

If they'd been privy to each other's thoughts, they would have known they shared a similar feeling at that moment. It was as though their senses were as keen as blades.

Band-members erupted from their bolt-holes. They rode out of the trees, emerged from buildings, came in from front and rear. A small force, but well placed to strike at the trapped tax gatherers.

An archer on the second wagon reacted swiftly. The shaft he released whistled past Serrah's ear. He quickly drew and shot again. This time the bolt was intended for Caldason, missing him only when he ducked with a fraction of a second to spare. The arrow buried itself in an oak, quivering.

'He's mine!' Serrah shouted, heading for the wagon.

Caldason had his own goal. One of the band had been wounded and pitched from his horse. As he struggled to his feet, a paladin was moving in to finish him. Reeth galloped their way, knocking aside the paladin's descending blade with his own. The band-member scrabbled clear. Leaning out from their saddles, Qalochian and paladin began trading blows.

The archer Serrah targeted was obscured by fights that had broken out around the wagon. A militiaman appeared from the melee clutching a barbed spear. Holding it level, he rode at her. She swerved, avoiding the strike. As the rider passed she lashed out with her sword, slicing the lance in two. Enraged, he discarded the broken shaft, drew his sword and came around for a second charge. Serrah bobbed and his blade glided harmlessly above her head. Hers hacked into his chest. He screamed and fell. The riderless horse stampeded on.

Caldason was locked in a tit-for-tat exchange with his paladin foe. They battered each other, blocking passes, chasing an opening. Their spooked horses snorted and pawed. Reeth broke the deadlock when he got through and scoured his opponent's sword arm. A swift follow-on saw his blade in the paladin's heart. Slumped on its bolting horse, the corpse was carried off, scattering allies and enemies.

Serrah cracked the skull of a militiaman. As he went down, she saw the archer clearly again. He was alone on the wagon, the driver having been sucked into the fray. His drawstring was taut and he had a bead on one of her comrades. There was no time to act. The arrow flew to its mark, ending a duel the band-member would have won.

She flipped her sword from her right hand to her left. From her belt she plucked a snub-nosed throwing knife. She aimed and flung it hard. The blade thudded into the wagon's wooden enclosure, a handspan from the bowman's head.

He looked around wildly, spotted her and reached for his arrow sheath. She felt for another knife. He teased out a bolt and notched it. She drew back her arm. He pulled on the bow. She lobbed the blade. He loosed the arrow. It sailed over her right shoulder. Serrah could swear she felt its plume tickle her as it passed.

The archer still stood. But she realised that was just temporary. The hilt of her knife stuck out of his collarbone. A red patch was spreading across his grey tunic. He swayed, then toppled.

She goaded her frightened horse towards the wagon. Somebody on foot rushed over and tried to pull her down. Kicking out, she booted him back into the scrum. At the wagon, she scrambled onto the driving board. The bow was there, along with the quiver. Serrah took it and looked to the brawl going on all around her.

In the thick of it, Caldason was facing two opponents. He had a mounted paladin alongside and a militiaman on foot harrying him with a mace. His defence had to be alternate, swiping at the rider one minute, the mace-man the next. He was holding them off but making no progress.

Then an arrow came out of nowhere and struck the paladin in his back. As the man fell, Reeth glimpsed Serrah standing on the wagon, directing bolts into the fracas. His attention went back to the man with the mace and he disarmed him with a couple of downward strokes. Caldason's next swing proved a killer blow.

A moment's lull, as strangely happened in even the most furious of engagements, allowed Reeth to snatch an overview. He judged that his side had the better of it. There were fights everywhere still, but the tide seemed to be running in the ambushers' favour.

He noticed one of the remaining paladins, on foot and moving away from the convoy. In his hand was an object that looked very much like a distress glamour. That was something they could do without. Reeth headed for him.

Serrah had one arrow left. She singled out a likely target. It winged the man, spun him off his feet and dumped him in the road. She dropped the bow, took up her sword and leapt into the battle.

Reeth's duel with the paladin was frenzied and short. Wrenching his sword from the body, he looked around for the glamour. He found it in the long grass at the road's edge and ground it under his boot. It gave off blue sparks and wisps of orange smoke as it died.

He turned and saw that all but six or seven of the convoy's escort had been downed. The holdouts were bunched together, on foot, in front of one of the lane's shabby buildings.

They were retreating in the face of an advancing semi-circle of band-members. As Caldason made his way over, the beleaguered group had their backs to the wall.

In the short time they had to plan the ambush, Caldason and Serrah had thought about speed. They had a contingency to help overcome the guards as quickly as possible. Reeth signalled the men on the roof and set it in motion.

The fading light obscured what was happening up there. Something was tossed from the roof – for a second it looked like a mottled black cloud. Instantly it descended, dome-shaped as it fell.

A large weighted fishing net came down on the surviving escorts. They yelled and flailed in the tangle. The band rushed forward and subdued them with sword butts and clubs. They disarmed them and secured the net with rope. So many flies in a giant spider's web.

Serrah was at Caldason's shoulder. 'Seems like letting them off lightly.'

'Would you rather we tethered them to a team of horses and sent them off over a cobbled road?'

She smiled. 'It's no more than they deserve.'

'Maybe. But I've always tried not to stoop to their level. I reckon you feel the same.' Before she could answer, he went on, 'We need to move fast now. Let's go.'

The band gathered their wounded, and their dead, and lashed them to horses. Some were put into the wagons. All hands set to hauling clear the tree blocking the way ahead. The other was left where it was, to hinder any pursuit. They weren't brutal with the enemy wounded, which might not have been the case if things had gone the other way. The prisoners were simply left, securely bound, to await rescue; and no doubt punishment for allowing their consignment to fall into Resistance hands.

A rendezvous had been fixed a mile or two on, where the

spoils would be loaded onto smaller vehicles and dispersed.

Caldason took the reins on the lead wagon himself. Serrah sat beside him.

'Our first successful mission,' she said.

'Think so?' His voice was suddenly cold.

'Don't you?'

He didn't answer, and they made the rest of the journey in a stiff silence.

All the while, Caldason's eyes were on the city's glittering splendour and phoney rainbows.

22

A fiery streak sliced the heavens. It could have been a shooting star. More likely it was somebody flaunting their wealth.

Seen from the summit of an outlying hill, Valdarr met the horizon and appeared to blend seamlessly into the night sky. The powdering of stars above silently mirrored the rippling colours and bursts of radiance below.

Two people sat on a pallid, long-dead tree trunk. They had little interest in the view.

'What do you mean, *not good enough*?' Serrah demanded.

'We lost three men,' Caldason reminded her.

'And twice that many got wounded. I'm aware of that. It's tragic, but they knew what they were signing up for. There are always casualties.'

'You were the one so concerned about losing lives.'

'I was worried about them being lost *recklessly*.'

'Didn't you feel bad when you lost members of your team, back in Merakasa?'

Serrah looked pained at that.

'Sorry, of course you did.' He added, 'I didn't mean it to be a dig about what happened to you, either.'

'All right.'

'But it's a question of responsibility and –'

'Yes, I know. Naturally I felt responsible if any of my band got killed or hurt. That even goes for the fool who landed me in this mess, although I've no reason to blame myself. But I have to say that for a man so used to combat you seem pretty troubled about this.'

'You don't understand. It's to do with . . . I suppose you'd call it control.'

'You're right, I don't understand.'

'When the Qaloch were being cleared from their land, when we were being massacred, I was helpless. Not just for myself; I couldn't help anybody else. People I was honour-bound to stand by and protect were slaughtered in front of me. I had no control.'

'How could you? I don't know the details of what happened to your people, but I do know the odds against you were crushing. And you were taken unawares, stabbed in the back.'

'You sound like somebody who knows about betrayal.'

'I wouldn't be here without it, trying to adjust to everything that's changed in my life.'

'Exactly. Betrayal's a form of powerlessness too.'

'In the sense that I had no control over what happened, yes. But in the end it might be liberating, for all the pain involved. It made me see the world in a different way. Made me realise the true nature of the system I was serving.'

It seemed to Reeth that she was trying to make the best of it. He kept the thought to himself. 'I've never been blind to the order of things,' he said. 'Or been part of it.'

'Then you should be perfect for the Resistance.'

'So everybody tells me.'

'At least freedom's more than just a word to them, Reeth.'

'In the end they're only another kind of system.'

'But a much better one than anything we've got. Potentially, anyway.'

'So you're a prime candidate for the Resistance too?'

'As long as it suits me.'

'That's more or less the way I see it. Not that I'm finding it easy, and today didn't make it any easier.'

'Ironic, isn't it?' A mellow smile played on Serrah's lips. 'I'm having to learn to accept a different kind of authority, and you're having to learn to accept *any* kind of authority. I wonder if either of us are cut out for it?'

He left the question hanging and asked one of his own. 'What do you think about this grand scheme of Karr's?'

'An island state? I don't suppose I know any more about it than you do. You could call it visionary, I guess. Utopian, even. But it does have a certain attraction.'

'You'd go there, be part of it?'

'You're assuming I'd be invited. If I was . . . well, I really don't know. I'd need to be told a lot more about it. Would you go?'

'I'm not convinced Karr's dream will ever happen.'

'Yet here we are helping the cause.'

'Or helping ourselves.'

'It sounds less than charitable when you put it that way.'

'Perhaps.'

Tethered nearby, their horses had their heads down, grazing the long grass.

'Whatever the reason we're here,' Reeth said, 'the band's got to shape up.'

'We can always be better, I suppose.'

'They're relying on me. I don't want any more . . .'

She was staring hard at him. 'Guilt?'

'Is that so strange a thought?'

'No . . . no, it's not.' Her expression was distant and grave, and didn't seem to welcome inquiry.

He steered clear. 'You're right, we can be better. I want to keep down the chance of losses.'

'At least we've got a good crew.' She'd broken out of her reverie. 'They're keen, fit, quick to learn –'

'They'll have to be. When Karr hinted that today's robbery was a dry run for other missions, you can bet he started us on something basic. Whatever's coming is going to be a lot harder. We've got to be ready for that.'

'Don't worry,' she told him, 'you'll have your control.'

The stars couldn't be seen from the centre of the city. There was too much competition from the glare of magic.

On the balcony of an unpretentious mansion in a moderately affluent quarter, another couple sat and took in the view. She revelled in the soft, warm night air. He poured honeyed wine from a carafe. They touched their cups together in a silent toast.

Valdarr glittered and throbbed, a pageant of illusion that could have been for their sole benefit. Every so often a gush of sparks flared briefly in the streets below, marking a glamour nativity. Or an ebbing spectre drifted by, its magical charge used up. The rhythm of supernatural creation, mutation and destruction was incessant.

Yet for Tanalvah Lahn this place was a haven.

'I didn't realise,' she said, 'that I'd never really felt safe before.'

'It's good to hear you say that,' Kinsel replied. 'Oh. I don't mean good that you –'

'I *know* what you mean.' Smiling, she lightly caressed his cheek. 'We're protected, thanks to you. Our saviour and our champion.'

He kissed her palm. 'I think you're giving me too much credit.'

'No. You're a virtuous man, Kinsel. You could have walked

by. Instead you gave hope to me, and to those poor children. You don't know what that means to me. The only men I've known before were . . .'

'Yes.' He nodded his understanding, saving her the torment of recounting bad memories. 'But that's over now. You don't have to do anything you don't want to do, not anymore.'

'I find it a wonder that my life from before doesn't seem to worry you. You really don't think the less of me for it?'

'Of course not, Tan. You had no choice. I look at it as being like the countries the empires occupy.'

That puzzled her. 'How?'

'Because the conquerors can take land and chattels, but they can never possess people who long to be free.'

'In the bordellos of Jecellam, the other women used to say that the clients can have your body but not your mind, your soul. Not the real you.'

'That's my point; and that's how it is with the Resistance, too. The most important thing we have is the *idea*. Our enemies can't own that, or destroy it. It's our greatest weapon, whether we have Founder magic, warlord allies or anything else.'

Grinning, she said, 'You look terribly serious.'

'Do I?' He was a little abashed. 'Well, I *am*. I've always believed in the Resistance ideal. It's a passion with me.' His expression grew earnest for a moment. 'One I hope you'll come to share.'

'I think I'm beginning to. But what chance is there of Karr realising his plan? Can there really be somewhere for us that's truly free?'

'I just told you, there already is.' He tapped his forehead. 'Up here.'

'You know what I'm saying.' Her tone was mock stern, a smile breaking through.

Kinsel returned it. 'Yes, I think the plan can happen. We

have to *make* it happen, though it's going to be hideously difficult and cost dear in lives. What choice do we have?'

'You had a choice. You could have stayed in your privileged world and never risked yourself.'

'I didn't start out there, Tan; I was born low. My gift raised me. But not before I'd learnt how things are. In fact, my earliest memory was seeing . . .' He stopped himself. 'Well, they say the first bite's taken with the eye, don't they?'

'Must we have secrets?' she asked.

'No, there should never be any between us. These are wounds, not secrets, and I'm not ready to pick at them just yet.'

She squeezed his hand. 'I'll be here when you are.'

He nodded his gratitude, then took up the thread. 'Even if I had been born with a silver teething ring in my mouth, I like to think I'd still have chosen the same side. But who can say? Perhaps being raised in affluence would have smothered my conscience. As it was I wavered for years before throwing my lot in with the Resistance.'

A watch of nightingales casually flapped past. They were luminous and of assorted colours, and gave off discordant, unbirdlike noises.

'Are you going to do as Karr said and give up your public life?' Tanalvah asked.

After a pause, he answered, 'In time.'

'I'm afraid for you. Accept the protection of the Resistance and go underground, *please*.'

'I can't. Not yet.'

'You could easily have been exposed when you stopped to help us, and it would have been my fault. And the fact that you suddenly seem to have acquired a family must surely arouse people's interest. You're in such a dangerous position.'

'It *wouldn't* have been your fault,' he insisted stubbornly, 'and we didn't get caught.'

'That's not the point. You're running a tremendous risk. Give it up, Kinsel. For the sake of me and the children, if nothing else. There are other ways you can serve the cause.'

'That's just it; there aren't. The most valuable contribution I can make is the one I'm making.'

'Surely there must be something you could –'

'No, hear me. There are few people sympathetic to the Resistance who have access to the higher echelons of government. I'm lucky enough to be one of them, and the intelligence I gather can be vitally important. That's particularly true as we get nearer to achieving Karr's plan. I can't pull away now.'

'The patrician would find another role for you,' Tanalvah persisted, 'I'm certain of it.'

'My pacifism greatly limits what I could do.'

'There are many in the Resistance who share your opinion.'

'Doing clerks' jobs, essentially. There's nothing wrong with that, but it isn't as important as what I'm doing now. I'm an asset; why turn me into a quill-pusher?'

'You're not going to change your mind on this, are you?'

'For now, my love, no. But you shouldn't be anxious about me. I'm always careful and I know the hazards.'

She looked far from convinced. 'Something else concerns me,' she said.

'You really are a worrier, aren't you?' he gently teased.

'I've just found you; I don't want to lose you again.'

He planted a light kiss on the side of her face. 'What is it?'

'Your pacifism.'

'You don't approve?'

'No, no, it's not that. Far from it. It's just . . .' The words tumbled out. 'You know I killed someone. I didn't mean to, it was an accident, or at least unintentional. But how can you respect me when I'm a murderer? Being a whore was bad enough, but –'

'Don't ever call yourself that. Nor are you a murderer. And believe this, Tan: I can't think ill of you, whatever you might have done. You took a life, and that pains me, but I see it as righteous self-defence. If you hadn't . . .'

'I know. The thing is, I have a code, too. I follow Iparrater, who values the sanctity of human life above all else. I've violated that precept, which must mean I've cast myself out from her protection.'

'Not if the goddess's reputation for compassion means anything. She'll understand that you acted through necessity, and that your motives were pure.' He sighed reflectively. 'People think trying to live non-violently is an easy option. But my actions have put lives at risk, and no doubt caused the loss of some. All any of us can do is what we believe to be right, for a greater good. You've no more reason to blame yourself than I have.'

'That gives me comfort. Though I wonder if your opinion's clouded by your feelings for me.'

'Possibly. But I think not. I've found life to be a series of moral compromises. That's as true for you as anyone else. There should be no burden of guilt for you to carry.'

'Would you say the same of Serrah Ardacris?'

'Serrah? Yes, I believe I would. Why do you ask?'

'From what I know of her she made a profession of murder.'

'That's too harsh. I'm sure she thought she was doing the right thing, too. I can't approve of what she did before coming to Bhealfa, but I'm grateful to her for helping us.'

'So am I, don't get me wrong. It's just . . . she seems so troubled. As though she shoulders some awful weight.'

'Do you know anything about her background?'

'Only that she was an assassin.'

'She commanded a special forces unit. Her superiors saddled her with a member of one of Gath Tampoor's more powerful families; little more than a boy, who fancied himself a warrior. When he was killed they made a scapegoat of her.'

'She must have been bitter about that.'

'There's more to her misery. Karr told me a little of the intelligence he had about her. Apparently she lost her daughter a few years ago. Due to ramp.'

'That explains why she appears so tormented. She's forfeited everything. How sad.'

'One thing you'll learn about the Resistance is that it attracts strange bedfellows. Unhappy and even bizarre stories aren't uncommon.'

'I've seen something of it already. That young sorcerer's apprentice, for instance.'

'Kutch.'

'Yes. There's a boy who's been through bad times for one so young. But he seems to have kept his innocence. I think he's sweet.'

'And Caldason?'

Her smile evaporated. 'Ah, that one. In my line of work I saw many men who were hard-hearted and callous. Men who had no respect or real liking for women. The worst of them gave off a kind of dangerous coldness. But I never came across any like him. He frightens me.'

'I'm surprised to hear you say that.'

'Why? Because we're both members of the same race and should have so much in common?'

'Well . . .'

'People have stopped me on the street and asked about Qalochians I've never heard of. They think we all know each other! Every Qalochian is bound together by blood and our history. But that's not to say we have to like each other. I mean, do you get on with all the other *singers*?'

Kinsel had to grin. 'Now that you come to mention it, no, I don't.'

'They say he has fits, did you know that? Violent, crazy, frightening outbursts when he's a menace to himself and others. A berserker.'

'Yours *is* a warrior race.'

'It goes far beyond that, from what I've heard,' she said, frowning. 'There's something about him, Kinsel. The way he's supposed to have lived so long, yet doesn't look it. And those *eyes* . . . Do you know what I think?'

'Go on.'

'I think he wants to give to others what he can't have himself. Death.'

'But there's no need to fear him. He's on our side, remember?'

'Men like Caldason have only one side: their own.' She shrugged. 'Or perhaps being a prostitute made me too cynical about everything.'

'Let's forget all that for now. This is our first night together in our own home. We should celebrate.' He reached under the table and brought out a small wooden box. It was chestnut, smoothly lacquered, and had no catch or hinges. Its top bore the red outline of a heart. He set it down in front of her.

'What is it, Kinsel?'

'It's for you. Go ahead, open it.'

'How?'

'The heart.'

Tanalvah stretched a hand and lightly touched the heart with her fingertips. The box took a breath, or so it seemed, and she drew back.

A criss-crossing of fine lines appeared on the lid, all bisecting the heart. The lines marked segments in the wood, which began to rise, like the unfolding petals of a flower. They revealed an interior of brilliant white light.

Tanalvah stared, enraptured. Kinsel watched her, gladdened by her wonder.

The white light dimmed to a softer glow. With the improbability of magic, the fully-opened petals formed not a serrated bloom but a perfectly round, flat disc. It resembled a mushroom, and the base of the box its thick stem. A little smoky eruption occurred in the disc's centre. The turquoise cloud blossomed, spreading outwards and up into a swirling pyramid. That held for a second, then popped. Vanished.

Leaving two miniature figures, tall as a man's hand. Male and female, dressed in flowing gowns of choice silk. Music rose. Soaring strings and dulcet voices laid over a leisurely but insistent rhythm. The tiny man bowed as his partner curtsied. They moved together, clasped hands, and began to dance.

'It's beautiful,' Tanalvah whispered, eyes shining.

The petite dancers reeled and weaved, glided and swayed. Their discreet jewellery caught the light and flashed brilliantly. The hems of their gowns floated as they spun.

'Oh!' Tanalvah exclaimed, recognising the figures. 'They're *us*!'

'Yes, except he dances better than I ever could.'

'We'll have to see about that!' Laughing, she began dragging him to his feet.

'No, no,' he protested. 'I'm a terrible dancer!'

'You're blushing!'

'So would you if you danced as badly as I do.'

But now she had her arms around him, and his around her. They melted into a shuffling imitation of the little people moving about their pure white dais.

It seemed to go on for a long time, music directing their footfalls, the large mirroring the small. Then a sound more demanding cut through their reverie.

'Ah,' Tanalvah said, 'they're awake.'

A child's voice called from inside again. The words were muted but the tone was clear enough; the anxiety that follows a bad dream.

'I'll go,' Kinsel offered.

'Sure?'

'I'd like to.'

They lingered for a moment, locked in a tender gaze, then kissed and parted. She sat to enjoy her glamour. He went into the house.

Teg and Lirrin shared a room, their beds side by side. The girl was sitting up.

'What's the matter?' Kinsel asked.

'Had a nightmare,' Lirrin replied, massaging her eyes with balled fists.

'It's all right,' he soothed, sitting beside her. 'It's not real.'

'Really?'

'Yes, really. Dreams are just little plays that go on in our heads when we're asleep. They can't hurt you.'

'I can't sleep either,' Teg piped up.

'Why not?'

''Cos *she* had a bad dream.' He pointed an accusing finger at his sister.

'All right, settle down, both of you.' Kinsel tucked them in. 'Tanalvah's here and so am I. We'll keep the dreams away.'

'How?' Lirrin asked with a child's shrewd logic.

'Well, I know a song that can keep you safe. It's one my mother sang to me when I was about your age, Teg. Would you like to hear it?'

They consented, sleepily.

He began the lullaby, singing softly, bathing them in the warm comfort of its words. Soon, their eyes grew heavy.

Outside, the nightly display lit up the metropolis.

23

Anybody noticing them would assume they were siblings running an errand.

A little girl, nine or ten years old, wearing a flowered apron and buckled black shoes, her blonde hair in pigtails. She walked with a gangling, older boy, nearly a young man, clutching his hand. In the way of growing lads, this was naturally very embarrassing for him.

'What about that one?' the little girl exclaimed loudly, pointing across the road to a man loitering outside a tavern.

'Please, Master,' Kutch appealed in an undertone, 'I do wish you wouldn't draw quite so much attention to us.'

'Nonsense!' Phoenix snorted. 'People can mind their own business. Now do as you're told. The man over there. Yes or no?'

Kutch studied the target and made his decision. 'Yes.'

'Good!' Phoenix snapped his fingers in a dismissive gesture.

Opposite, the glamour posing as a man vanished. It left a cascade of expiring sparks. A pedestrian walked through them, absently waving a hand to clear the fug.

'Stay alert, boy, stay alert!' Phoenix barked.

A passing stranger gave them an odd look, and slowed down to rubberneck.

The bogus child glared back at him. 'Move along there! There's nothing to see!'

Head down, the man hurried off. Kutch went scarlet.

They walked on, scanning everybody and everything on the streets. At last Kutch said, 'That one.'

'No! Only those with my signature. Not the cheap, counterfeit stuff. Just the ones I've conjured.'

'That one isn't real. On the bench.'

'Even I can see that,' Phoenix came back testily. 'Remember what I told you. What are the two cardinal rules of spotting?'

'Look and Don't Believe.'

'Precisely. Carry on.'

The streets were as crowded as Kutch had ever seen them. And now Phoenix was *skipping* along beside him, tiny feet pattering, ponytail swinging. The boy's discomfort returned.

Phoenix caught the look. 'Well, you wanted me to act more naturally, didn't you? Keep watching. Do your job.'

Kutch sighed.

A moment later his eye alighted on something. He dismissed it, looked again and muttered, 'Oh, clever.' Indicating it, he said, 'That.'

'Well done.' The sorcerer made a swift, complex hand gesture.

A citizen's transport wagon drew level with them. Four horses pulled it, and it was full of passengers. The wagon, drays and passengers, the driver and his mate, all turned transparent for an instant. There was a glimpse of the skeletal structure of the horses and the people, attesting to the thorough job Phoenix had done on the casting. Then everything turned into smouldering motes and drifted away. A small inrush of air could be felt, as was common when large glamours expired. It caused some small inconvenience to the other road users, but nothing they weren't used to.

'You saw, didn't you?' Phoenix said. 'Not only that the wagon was a glamour but also the signature I'd woven into the spell.'

'Yes, Master. It was a bit like . . . I don't know . . . a watermark on a piece of parchment.'

Phoenix nodded and allowed himself a small smile, crinkling his freckles. 'You're making a little progress, my boy.' Then sharper: 'Come on, come on! I've conjured plenty more.'

'We're supposed to be at the meeting.'

'We'll be there in time if you don't dawdle. I've planted more likenesses along the route, so look about you, lad, and doubt. Look and Doubt.'

Carrying on at a faster pace, Kutch pointed things out and Phoenix either nodded or berated. To onlookers they were merely a brother and sister, bickering on their way home. With an unusually large number of glamours expiring in their wake.

They approached Karr's hideout more soberly. Slipping in one at a time, they ran the gamut of precautions that established they were who they appeared to be.

In a corridor somewhere between the front door and the cellar, they paused so Phoenix could resume his normal form.

When they got to the subterranean conference room they found Caldason, Serrah, Karr and Quinn Disgleirio waiting for them.

'Good, now we can start,' Karr said. 'Please.' He invited them to sit with a sweep of his arm, and everyone gathered at the largest table. 'I take it we're cloaked against eavesdropping?'

'I did it myself,' Phoenix assured him.

'Reeth's band did well yesterday,' Karr began, 'and made

a valuable contribution to our coffers. It's to be regretted that this was achieved with the loss of three band-members, and the wounding of five others.'

'I take full responsibility for that,' Caldason volunteered.

'I'm not criticising you, Reeth,' the patrician replied evenly. 'I'm merely reporting, and commemorating the fallen by mentioning them here. The losses are unhappy, but we judge the mission a success.'

Caldason seemed to accept that. Serrah shot him a side-ways glance. As usual, his expression was unfathomable.

'The coin you liberated yesterday,' Karr went on, 'after we return some to the people, won't all go into Resistance war chests. In fact, most of it won't. You're here today to be told what the money bought. But first . . .' He gestured towards the open door.

Several helpers brought in trays of drinks and sweetmeats. Setting them down on side tables, they hurried out. The door was secured.

Karr raised a cup and eyed the company. 'Your good health.'

'And confusion to our enemies,' Phoenix added.

Caldason took a desultory sip of his drink. Serrah faked conviviality. Kutch wished he had less water in his wine.

Putting down his cup, Karr continued, 'You know, it's funny, but one of the most important things about the empires is an aspect we tend not to notice.' He had their attention. 'What we forget about Gath Tampoor, about both empires, is that for all their military might and economic muscle, at base they're bureaucracies. They have to be, there's so much to administer.'

'I can confirm that from my encounters with the clerks in Merakasa,' Serrah offered.

'All existing states are built on mountains of paper,' Karr stated.

'What's this got to do with us?' Caldason asked.

'Plenty. It provides a weak link in their chain of occupation, and in striking at it we can do ourselves some good.'

'How does targeting paper-shufflers help us?'

'It depends on what they're shuffling,' Disgleirio told him.

'That's exactly the point,' Karr agreed. 'Gath Tampoor's Bhealfan minions generate vast amounts of information daily. Most of it's administrative stuff of little interest to us. But some of it's vitally important to them and us. I'm talking about the records they hold on individuals and groups they regard as enemies of the state. I think you can verify that too, Serrah.'

'Yes. The CIS holds many files on criminals and political activists. My unit relied on them when we were planning operations.'

'It's the same here in Bhealfa. There are whole armies of information gatherers compiling files on dissidents. Almost certainly they have files for everybody in this room. With the possible exception of young Kutch here. Sorry to disappoint you, lad.' There was a little laughter at that, mostly from Disgleirio. 'But if we could get to those records –'

'You're obviously saying you've found a way,' Caldason reckoned.

'I think we have. The bulk of the money you and your band seized yesterday was used as a bribe. I'm about to show you what for.' He nodded to Phoenix.

The sorcerer produced a small cube and rapped it against the table. A glamour materialised, covering almost the entire table top. It was a meticulously detailed scale model of a section of a city. Even the houses in a dilapidated state were portrayed as such. There were minute cracks in the paving stones and the towers had flags.

'You might recognise this as part of central Valdarr,' Karr explained. 'It contains a perfect example of how the orderly minds of our rulers work in our favour. They have all the records that interest us in one location. Here.' He pointed at a building.

It was an ornate structure, boasting several spires.

Kutch said, 'That's a temple, isn't it?'

'Apparently. Actually, it's heavily glamoured to look that way. Its real appearance is somewhat different. If you'd be so kind, Phoenix.'

The sorcerer lightly smacked the cube. What had been a temple melted into a much plainer, more functional looking building. Even on this scale it was possible to see that its doors were hearty and its windows barred.

'What about worshippers?' Kutch asked. 'Don't they get suspicious?'

'It poses as a private place of worship, only for the influential. Ordinary people aren't encouraged to go there.'

'How are *we* supposed to get in?' Serrah wanted to know.

'This way.' He signalled Phoenix again, who manipulated the cube once more.

The building expanded to the size of a rich child's doll's house, filling the table. All the other buildings and streets were pushed away, and vanished.

Then the building disappeared too, leaving a three-dimensional representation of its foundations. It was riddled with tunnels.

'What you're seeing is the sewage system, and the channels that bring in fresh water from artesian wells, here and here. All the modern conveniences.'

'It's a maze down there,' Serrah said. There was a hint of disquiet in her voice.

'Yes, but we've plotted a course through. That was Quinn's responsibility, so I'll let him explain.'

Disgleirio took over, using a dagger to point things out. 'This large channel here is the key. As you can see, a lot of lesser conduits branch out from it. The trick is to find the one that feeds directly into the building. That's here.' He jabbed the blade at an underground junction.

'How big are these tunnels?' Serrah asked.

'They vary. Some are surprisingly large, others tight. All of them seem to be of a size that people can move through, though it'd be a bit of a squeeze in some.'

'We'd be using what?' Caldason said. 'Water or sewage tunnels?'

'Sewage.'

'Sounds pleasant,' Serrah mumbled.

'Fortunately they tend to be the larger tunnels,' Disgleirio explained, 'and most have narrow walkways along their edges. See?' He pointed to one.

Caldason studied the model. 'How do we get into the system in the first place?'

'This big outlet tunnel passes underneath several adjoining buildings. One of them happens to be a place we have access to. The outlet runs directly under its cellar. That's been verified; we've already broken through to the tunnel.'

'Serrah's right about it being a labyrinth. It'd be easy getting lost down there.'

'You'll have a map. And of course there's no light so you'll need glamour illumination.'

'What part of the building do we come up in?'

Disgleirio nodded to Phoenix. The building reappeared, transparent this time. Disgleirio indicated an area on the ground floor, near the back wall. 'Just about here. We reckon that should be the easiest place to get through the flooring.'

'Why is so much of the inside of the building blank?' Serrah said. 'What's on the rest of the ground floor, and the upper floors?'

'We don't have a plan for any more than you're seeing now,' Karr answered. 'Our informant couldn't supply that, no matter how greedy he might be. What we're told is that the ground floor doesn't contain much of interest except a guard room. The upper storeys are where the records are kept.'

'You can't be entirely sure?' Caldason prompted.

'Not completely, no. But you can be certain there are glamour alarums and traps in there. Quite apart from any human opposition you might meet.'

Serrah exclaimed, '*Might?* The place is going to be crawling with people, isn't it?'

'Normally it would be. But remember what's coming up in a couple of days.'

Disgleirio supplied the answer. 'So-called Freedom Day.'

'Precisely. The day when demonstrating our loyalty and great love for the occupiers is compulsory. None of the clerks are going to be working in this repository, and there'll only be a skeleton crew of guards, if that. Not to mention that the streets will be full of the usual dragooned parades and marches. That should provide a nice diversion and tie up most of the security forces.'

'You're sure about all this?' Serrah queried.

'Our intelligence unit's been working on it for nearly two years. It'll be a heavy blow to the authorities if we can pull it off, so naturally we've tried to plan for every eventuality. But that doesn't mean it isn't very hazardous. That's why we're asking you to go, not telling you. Everybody has to be a volunteer.'

'There's the question of getting your band back up to strength,' Disgleirio added. 'We can do that with Righteous Blade members. It means you'll be going in with new men you haven't had time to gel with. There's no way round that. All we can do is give you our best.'

'Before you make up your minds,' Karr returned, 'there's another consideration. I said this place is going to be well protected magically. That means you need to have a sorcerer with the band, and for preference a spotter. They're in short supply, as you know. So what I'm proposing is that Kutch fills that role. Under normal circumstances I wouldn't ask this. But these aren't common times.'

Kutch looked thunderstruck.

'Wait a minute, Karr,' Caldason rumbled. 'He's just a boy, and this is a dangerous situation we'd be getting into. His inexperience could put all of us at risk.' He turned to Kutch. 'Sorry, but that's how I see it.'

'I think Kutch should make the decision himself, don't you? Go ahead, Kutch. What do you think?'

The boy had coloured from being the centre of attention, and at first stumbled over his words. 'I want to do whatever I can to help. I know I haven't got much experience, but I learn fast. Don't worry about me, Reeth, I wouldn't let you down.'

Caldason asked Phoenix, 'Is he fully trained as a spotter yet?'

'Nowhere near.' The magician held up a hand to still the protest. 'But he's made good progress and he can do the job. Besides, as the patrician said, we've little option. Spotting is incredibly rare, and having a spotter with you could make the difference between success or failure for this mission.'

Reeth pondered that. 'Are you sure, Kutch? Do you know what you'd be getting yourself into?'

'I have a much better idea of what violence is all about since knowing you, Reeth.'

'Er, I'll take that as a compliment. All right. Kutch is included only on condition that once he's done his job he's out of there. I don't want him exposed to any more danger than necessary.'

'Work it out in whatever way you think appropriate,' Karr told him.

'What about you, Serrah? Are you in for this one?'

'I'm in.'

Caldason sighed. 'Assuming the rest of the band volunteer too, which I'm sure they will, that seems to settle it.'

'Excellent, Reeth.' Karr beamed benevolently.

Kutch wore an expression of cheerful self-importance. Caldason seemed less happy.

'So, what's the plan once we're inside?' Serrah said.

'Arson,' Karr replied. 'Phoenix's people have developed some concentrated flammables. Light enough to carry but strong enough to do the job.'

'I bet it'd be interesting to see what those files say,' Kutch speculated.

'We'd all be intrigued to find out, I'm sure,' Karr smiled. 'But that's a pleasure we'll have to forgo, I'm afraid; removing even a percentage of them would be impossible. No, we have to destroy them, and get our satisfaction from knowing we've struck a heavy blow against the oppressors.'

'Does this mission get me any nearer to my goal?' Caldason wanted to know.

'It does. Trust me.'

'Then we'd better start preparing ourselves, hadn't we?'

24

There were fires all over the plains, reddening the night sky.

A township was burning. Buildings collapsed, cattle stampeded. The crops in surrounding fields were ablaze, trees converted into huge flaming torches, smoke driven by chill northern winds. Choking, tear-stained, the vanquished streamed from the settlement, herded by their conquerors.

The town's last enclave had fallen. It was adjacent to the final battlefield, which was littered with defending and invading dead. The first far outnumbered the second, as was to be expected given the winners' advantage. Already, scavengers were moving through the carnage, gathering loot and ending misery with sharp blades.

The new master watched it all from a commanding clifftop.

He was The Awakened. Emperor of the Barbarians. Shadow of the Gods. The Man who Fell from the Sun.

He was Zerreiss.

Nothing he wore distinguished him from the lowliest of his soldiers; no finery, no golden armour. If anything, he was less well built than was the norm for his race, and no taller. He had still to reach his middle years, and retained a measure of youthful looks, which his rugged complexion and beard failed to conceal. His features were even, average, ordinary.

Yet he was phenomenal.

He had a quality some called presence. Others said authority, charm, allure, seductiveness, charisma, strength. But, in truth, words were too feeble to describe his singularity. For he had all these traits and something more. Something indefinable. It was as though he embodied a nameless force of nature. A power that left an indelible brand on all who came within its range. It beguiled, inspired, and never failed to excite awe. Fanatical devotion or dread were kindled by it.

This day, the warlord had come with the gift of darkness.

Only true fire ravaged the mesa; there was no longer any synthetic illumination. The lights of his invasion fleet, anchored in the shallow bay, were fuelled by oil and tallow. His horde, their numbers blackening the plain, held aloft genuine brands.

They gloried in his latest victory, chanting his name as though it were an incantation. It sounded like a great sea swell crashing against rocks. The rhythmic pulse of a hundred thousand hearts and voices, laced with pounding drums.

His guards brought him the chieftain of the defeated. The man dropped to his knees, in supplication and terror.

'Get up,' the warlord said, speaking softly, 'I have no need of idolatry.'

The captive met a gaze that seemed all-knowing. 'You've brought us to waste. Where else should I be but on my knees?'

'Your people fought well. Do not abase yourself.'

The chieftain slowly rose. 'We posed no threat to you. Why make war on us?'

'What other option did you leave? Had you united with me this could have been averted.'

'My people want no truck with devilry.'

The warlord laughed, not unkindly. 'You think me evil?'

'Look about you.' The chieftain swept an arm to take in the violated landscape, his ruined fiefdom. 'Isn't this bad enough to count?'

'No. This is restraint.'

'You consider yourself a *benign* conqueror?'

'I don't consider myself a conqueror at all. I've come to set you free.'

It was the chieftain's turn to laugh, cynically, and notwithstanding his plight.

Zerreiss smiled, easily and in good nature. 'So, how are we to proceed?'

'With my death,' the chieftain replied, his chest swelling.

'You can join me yet. Many have.'

'I expect no mercy.'

'Your bravery does you credit. But why throw away your life? I offer pardon for you, your family and kinsmen. For your people. You have only to swear fealty to me.'

'And live in shame?'

'You would be part of a great enterprise. What shame is there in that?'

'A great madness, more like.'

For an instant, the warlord's eyes were stone. 'Look at my army. See how many different bloods it holds. They do not think of themselves as subject.'

'But why are you building this massive force? What goal do you have beyond subjugating your neighbours?'

'I told you. Liberation.'

If the chieftain hoped for clarity he was disappointed. The warlord's expression was enigmatic. 'They say you're wise beyond your years,' the chieftain said, 'and your skills as a general can't be doubted. Yet you pursue some grand scheme whose aim you do not state.'

'You need only know that what I bring cannot be resisted.'

'I must be more simple-minded than I thought. All you say is a riddle to me.'

'Rally to my banner and everything will fall into place.'

'I can see one thing already; that you push ever south. Soon you'll be in the domain of others not so easily overcome. Then you'll meet powers greater than your own, Zerreiss.'

'We'll see.' The warlord was unperturbed. 'But you still have to decide. Should my army be fire-raisers or firefighters? Are you with me or –? *Wait.*' He closed his eyes and tilted his head, as though interrupted by a sound only he could hear. 'It comes,' he mouthed.

'What?' The prisoner looked around at the warlord's retinue. They resembled a carved tableau, frozen mid-task. Listening. The army below had also fallen still, and silent. Although well accustomed to the northern climate, the chieftain shivered.

'Let your decision rest on this,' Zerreiss told him.

The chieftain could feel it now. A bass sensation in his bones; a sound too low to be audible. The distinct impression of events about to collide. He gazed stupefied at the warlord. 'Who . . . *what* are you?'

'I am Doubt, made flesh,' Zerreiss proclaimed.

And the Earth began to shake.

The royal palace in Merakasa was a vast bubble of tranquillity in an ocean of foaming disorder.

Away from the city's glamoured chaos, inside the palace's innermost walls, another world turned. Paths wound gently through sumptuous grounds which were thick with trees. The colour of every bloom delighted the eye. But no birds ever sang there.

Nearer the palace itself, the pastoral met acres of white

marbled courtyard. Here there were arbours, arches, and benches no one ever sat on. Where grass ended and flagstones began the tradition of marking subterranean power channels was respected. Coloured lines, unerringly straight, homed in from all compass points. A spider's web of red, black, peach, blue and a dozen other shades, all kept freshly tinted.

The vivid stripes continued inside the palace itself, running the length of corridors and under walls, cutting across the floors of rooms. They intersected deep in the palace's heart, in the *sanctum sanctorum* which only Gath Tampoor's ruling dynasty had ever entered. A massive vaulted chamber, ringed by impossibly tall pillars, lit by radiances whose source could not be seen. Quietly opulent in its decoration, sparely but tastefully furnished, it was perfumed by rare essences smouldering in iron braziers.

Entering from every direction, the lines gave up their rectilinear courses, curved, intermingled and flowed into an enormous circle upon the floor. Their colours blended too, and became glistening silver. Within the circle, and linked to it, shimmered the burnished emblem of Gath Tampoor: the pyramidal teeth of a stylised sunburst, enclosing a magnificent dragon. Permanently glamoured, the coiled, scaly beast belched sheets of orange flame.

One of the dragon's great eyes was a hollow cavity. A smooth-sided pit large enough to comfortably drop a stagecoach into. The content of all the channels fed the pool at its bottom. Magic's chariot, quicksilver with the consistency of honey, coursed and blended there. The pool's shining surface, agitated as the liquid ebbed and fluxed, would often settle and take on the properties of what might best be described as a window. A window that showed images from a myriad elsewheres.

Not that most people would recognise the images as such, or indeed the window.

A small group clustered around the eye. One of them held
the most powerful position in the empire. The others had
blood ties to her. They dressed in spectacularly expensive
glamoured raiment, and several were accompanied by
chimera companions. These were beautiful or repulsive in
the extreme, as dictated by taste.

Empress Bethmilno XXV was very old. Though assuming
she was senile could prove fatal. She wore thick white face
powder. Her lips were a scarlet wound, her eyes and lashes
heavily lead blackened. Artificially dark, her hair was piled
up and lanced with long silver pins. Her garb was light-
coloured and delicately glamoured, so that its continuously
shifting display of patterns changed subtly.

The group studied the recess, seemingly untroubled by the
intense cold it gave off.

'There!' the Empress exclaimed, pointing to a stir of
shadows in the quicksilver. 'And again, there.'

'Does it have the same source, Grandmother?' a young
man asked.

'Yes, the barbarous lands. Though not so far north this
time.'

'These disturbances in the grid grow stronger and more
frequent,' an older man remarked. 'It beggars belief that one
human being could have such an effect.'

'Yet it appears so,' Bethmilno said, 'for all that he's an
ignorant savage.'

'Is there any precedent?'

'None.'

'This should have been nipped in the bud,' another grumbled. 'It's past time this upstart was dealt with.'

The Empress viewed him sternly. 'You can't honestly
believe the warlord could endanger us in any way. When
has any threat from the people ever done that? To interpret
this as some kind of hazard to the imperium would be to

take it too seriously.' She paused, and added, 'We have not come this far, however, by being incautious. And there are considerations beyond the problems a single warlord may bring us.'

'Rintarah,' the grandchild supplied dutifully.

The Empress smiled indulgently. A sight which, to an outsider, might appear grotesque. 'I could wish others were as focused on realities as you, my dear. It should never be forgotten who the true enemy is.' She looked to them all. 'Rintarah. Of course. *Always* Rintarah. An alliance between them and the barbarian could seriously upset the balance.'

'As could a union with the insubordinates,' the first man suggested.

'We are alive to that possibility. Although for my part I consider them more a nuisance than a threat. A disorganised rabble.'

'Not everyone holds that opinion.'

'I am aware of that. We take every precaution.'

'But still they strike at us.'

'The way a gnat might attack a buffalo.'

'Surely the real danger is the possibility of the Resistance and Rintarah uniting against us?' another of her kin offered. 'It would make sense, backing one side against the other.'

'I consider that the least likely option. The insurgents are equally opposed to both empires, and their movements in both are linked. No, Rintarah wouldn't unite with them any more than we would.'

'The Resistance shows signs of greater organisation. That must be a cause for –'

'There's something you should try to understand about them,' the Empress stated, every inch the condescending matriarch, 'however long it takes you. And it applies to all our subjects. Anarchy is their natural state. Look at how they treat the magic we permit them. They resent control, yet,

save a minority, have never marshalled themselves sufficiently to oppose it. They are cattle, and cattle don't have
the imagination to run the farm.'

'True. Though some are of hardy stock.'

She waved away the qualification. 'The bulk of their
fellows can be relied on to drag them down. Don't underestimate the power of apathy. Overwhelmingly, the people
are too preoccupied with the baubles we throw them to
bother us. But don't take that to mean we ignore the so-
called Resistance. Steps are being taken against them, and
this renegade warlord.'

'What steps?'

'We're continually tapping the essence,' she nodded at the
pit, 'for a clue to the nature of his power. In addition, there's
the fact-finding expedition to the northern wastelands we've
decreed, under the Bhealfan flag. As a precaution, the crew
will be allowed higher grade glamours as part of their arsenal.'
She noted her family's apprehensive expressions and made
to reassure them. 'That's not a matter for concern. The magic
will be supervised by trusted servants, and is sorcerer-specific
and non-renewable. There's no chance of it proliferating.'

'And the Resistance?' someone prompted.

'I've ordered that action against them be more draconian.
The paladins are proving a useful tool in this respect, and
they'll be given greater overall control of strategy. We're
increasing infiltration of the dissidents' ranks, too, and that
policy is already paying dividends.'

'What if things come to a head with the warlord despite
these efforts?'

'I grant we may well have to meet him in open conflict.
Be assured, that would be a long way from our borders, and
the outcome would not be in doubt.' As she spoke, the
Empress absently worried a tiny scab on the bridge of her
nose. The flap of skin detached. She looked at it, flicked it

away. 'As far as our own subjects are concerned, that could
be a bonus. There's nothing like a war to distract the populace.'

Someone who hadn't spoken before cleared his throat and
ventured, 'There is one possible aspect to all this we haven't
considered.'

The Empress raised a quizzical eyebrow. 'Oh?'

'The Qalochian,' he replied hesitantly.

Her gaze narrowed at mention of it. There was a general
shuffling of feet. One of the chimeras, emotionally linked to
its owner, briefly transformed from comely to hideous.

'What of him?' she asked tightly.

'You know that our intelligence indicates he may have
fallen in with the insubordinates. Potentially, that's the most
perilous development of all.'

'I know that. The situation is under review.'

'But this isn't as straightforward as our other problems, is
it? Given the rules of engagement that must be followed in
respect of this man, our hands are tied.'

'It's time that was re-examined, too,' someone muttered.

'You know that's impossible,' Bethmilno snapped.

'So we're to let him run loose and do as he pleases? Until
he realises the real extent of the havoc he can cause?'

'No,' the Empress stated flatly. 'Reeth Caldason will be
dead before we allow that to happen.'

The quicksilver pool swirled darkly.

At the core of Jecellam's regulated, well-policed streets,
there was an extensive walled compound. In its outermost
ring of joyless buildings the distribution of food, laws and
lies was overseen. The structures forming the complex's
nucleus were devoted to governance and power. It was here
that the Central Council met, in chambers only they
frequented.

Where Gath Tampoor followed the western tradition in choosing a dragon as their emblem, Rintarah drew on its eastern heritage. Its symbol of state was a shield embellished with an eagle in flight, wings outstretched, lightning bolts playing in the background. The image was everywhere: on flags, mosaics, public transportation vehicles and the stained glass of temples.

But its most striking manifestation was reserved for the few. This was to be found in the grand council chamber, a cavernous hall where sunlight never intruded. As in Gath Tampoor, the colour-coded lines of power were here too, penetrating the inner sanctum from every bearing. Each of the lines ran to one of the sturdy legs of a mighty table, big enough to seat forty with ease. The table was fashioned in the shape of the Rintarahian shield, with the eagle and lightning motif etched into its surface. Glamour energy animated the portrait, so that the bird's immense wings slowly flapped as the lightning rippled.

On this occasion the council was not seated at the table; their deliberations were taking place at a far end of the room. This section housed an aperture not unlike the one in Merakasa, except it was plainer, the sole concession to ornamentation being the waist-high brass rail surrounding it. In every important respect, however, it was the same: a smooth-sided well into which the channels bled liquid metal that made a churning pool.

In styling themselves a council, the rulers of Rintarah may have given the impression that some kind of equitable process was involved in their selection. This was not so. Every councillor was related, and there was no nonsense about democracy. This day, perhaps a quarter of them were in attendance, staring down at the agitated quicksilver.

The council's Elder, a position matched in power only by Gath Tampoor's Empress, was Felderth Jacinth. In common with Bethmilno, he was of very advanced years. He was tall and rangy. His skin was unblemished and he retained a full head of hair, though there was more than a hint of the unnatural in these assets. The richly coloured brocade he wore lent him a touch of the grandiose. It was certainly a counterpoint to the severity of his surroundings.

'I have grave suspicions,' he announced, studying the disturbance in the matrix, 'that Gath Tampoor could be behind this.'

'How can they do something we can't?' a kinsman wanted to know.

'Some breakthrough, some new application of the Craft . . . Who knows?'

'One we haven't discovered ourselves? How likely is that?'

'I find it easier to believe than the idea that an ignorant conqueror's causing this. These events are becoming increasingly recurrent, and they're growing in strength. Something more powerful than a lone man has to be involved.' He was gripping the rail, white-knuckled. Although that was probably due to thin blood.

'Perhaps another alliance is responsible,' somebody suggested.

'Those who style themselves the Resistance, you mean.' The Elder snorted derisively. 'How could that be? What power do the citizens have beyond what we gift them? No, the people are sleepwalkers. If it weren't for the fact that their usefulness to us marginally outweighs their annoyance value I'd advocate a cull.'

'Who's going to keep the lawns trimmed for us then?' a wag opined.

There was laughter at that.

Elder Jacinth remained sour. Almost to himself, he said, 'These fluctuations in the energy could be a ploy, of course. Some ruse on the part of Gath Tampoor.'

Another of his kith was sceptical. 'A trick that can affect the essence? That's just as hard to believe. And to what purpose?'

Frustrated, the Elder sighed. 'This isn't getting us any nearer to dealing with the warlord, whoever he may or may not be allied with.'

'What about the expedition our spies told us about?' the sceptic pressed. 'From Bhealfa to the northern wastelands? If it really is exploratory, doesn't that indicate the Gath Tampoorians know as little about this Zerreiss as we do?'

'*If* it's exploratory. It could be a bluff, misinformation to throw us off the fact that they already have a pact with him. Or it could be the aim of this expedition to forge one.'

'But if they're as much in the dark as us, sending such a mission is exactly what they'd do, isn't it?'

'I concede that as a possibility,' Jacinth replied, stony-faced.

'In which case, shouldn't we mount our own expedition, and with all speed?'

'I confess I've been thinking about doing just that. Up to now I've been reluctant to do so on the basis of rumours about a Bhealfan expedition. But in view of these ever more violent disturbances to the essence, I think perhaps you're right about this. I'll order preparations at once.'

'That means we could find ourselves in a race with Gath Tampoor,' a councilman mused.

'There's more than one way to win a race,' the Elder reminded him. 'Whatever they may have offered the warlord, we'll top it. We can always renege later, when he's served his purpose. He's only a barbarian who's been lucky, after all. Let's not forget that.'

'Bhealfa seems to come up a lot these days in terms of problems.'

'It's one of the hotbeds for dissidents, there's no denying that.'

'I was thinking more in terms of a specific problem,' the councillor said. 'The last sightings we have of Caldason are in Valdarr. If he's linked up with the Resistance –'

'He's not demonstrated a leaning towards them before.'

'As far as we know.'

'Are you suggesting some connection between the Qalochian and the warlord?'

'I don't know. But look at the sequence of events. Caldason turns up in Valdarr, and apparently begins associating with known dissidents. That's what the paladins tell us, at any rate. At more or less the same time, the warlord's power reaches new heights.'

Jacinth pondered the idea. 'Hmmm. Caldason is the only individual we know of who just might be able to affect the matrix in the way we're seeing.'

'Can he really do that?'

'Should he come to an awareness about himself, he possibly could, yes.'

'If ever there was a neck worthy of stretching on a rope, it's the Qalochian's.'

'Him and his whole damned race. I'd love to be able to take the gloves off and deal with Caldason. I've often been tempted to go against the protocol and have him killed.'

'Is that possible?'

'Which proposition?'

'Both. Can the protocol be breached and is it possible to kill him?'

'Ending his life would take special measures. As to the protocol . . . well, that would prove a lot harder.'

'But not impossible?'

'Who can say? These are uncharted waters. Though it might be prudent to see what steps could be taken to that end.' There was a nodding of heads all round. 'But for the time being, more immediate matters require our attention.

The hour has come to contact our principal agent in the Resistance ranks. Make ready the grid.'

With a fluidity that came from ample experience, two of his cohorts swiftly enacted a silent conjuration. Instantaneously the essence made connection with some other node elsewhere in the matrix. A spume of cold fire erupted from the well, shaped like an enormous candle flame and made up of a billion vivid sparks. Slowly at first, a shape began to form in the boiling flame. In seconds it solidified and became the image of a recognisable human figure.

Elder Jacinth stepped forward and greeted his spy at the heart of the Resistance.

25

It was said that, outside of the empires, the paladin clans owned more property than anyone else. They kept lodges wherever they operated, and they operated everywhere bar the northern wastes. Often these properties were fees or rewards from their governmental clients. Not uncommonly, the provision of land in perpetuity in exchange for their services was part of the clans' covenant. This was a contrary situation for a supposedly stateless fraternity, albeit a very lucrative one.

In Bhealfa, the paladins' headquarters occupied a prime slice of Valdarr real estate. A fortress of some grandeur, it was no less impressive than the state buildings surrounding it.

As dawn broke, golden light glistened on its stone facade, damp from a recent shower.

A labyrinth of tunnels riddled the belly of the fortress. Two men, one nearing old age, the other no longer a youth, made their way through the echoing passageways. They walked close together, conversing in hushed tones, occasionally passing guards who stiffened to attention.

'We've had too many sightings for it to be beyond doubt,'

Devlor Bastorran insisted. 'He's here, in the city. What do you find so difficult to understand about that, Uncle?' His tone was exasperated.

Clan High Chief Ivak Bastorran would normally resent being spoken to in such a way, but devotion to his nephew moderated his irritation. 'He may well be here; it wouldn't be the first time he's entered Valdarr. All I'm trying to say is that going against him without sufficient forces and planning is extremely dangerous.'

'That's part of our job, isn't it? Dealing with outlaws.'

'Caldason's no ordinary criminal, you ought to know that much by now.'

'He's been a thorn in our side for years. I'd have thought you'd be eager to have a reckoning.'

'I'm keener to punish him than you know. But this is one outlaw we have to capture, not kill. He has to be engaged only under certain special conditions.'

'Where's the sense in that? Why treat this scum with kid gloves?'

'You don't understand, Devlor.'

He scowled petulantly. 'Too right I don't.'

'You're not leading the clans yet, boy. When . . . *if* you do, you'll be privy to more than you are now. Perhaps you'll understand better then.'

'What does *that* mean?'

'It means that we hire out our services to clients, and in Caldason's case those who pay us, handsomely, I might add, have laid down certain rules in relation to him. The clansmen he's killed have died because they've gone against him not knowing who he is, or because they thought they could best him and were insubordinate. They paid with their lives.'

'We're the clans. We can do anything we choose. Why should we abide by other people's rules when they're so nonsensical?'

'We have a great deal of autonomy, but there are limits even for us. If we try to get too big for our boots certain parties will feel threatened. That could put our independence at risk, and I don't want that to be my heritage. If you want to succeed me you'll have to curb that impatient nature of yours.'

They carried on in silence for a moment. More guards snapped to attention. They turned a corner.

'Tell me about the new intelligence reports,' the uncle asked.

'The dissidents are cooking up something. I don't know what it is yet, but it looks to be important.'

'Who are you thinking of delegating it to?'

'I'd like to handle this one myself.'

Ivak thought about it. 'All right. But play it by the book. It'd be a feather in the dissidents' bonnet if they were to bring down somebody of your status. Not to mention a blow to the clans, and to me personally.'

'I'm not a fool, Uncle.'

'I know. But you can be headstrong. I made certain promises to your parents, the gods keep them, and your safety was one of them.'

'Do you honestly believe anybody could better me?'

'With a blade? I doubt it. But there are other ways a man's life might be put in peril.'

'Have no concerns for me. I can look after myself.'

The passage they trod was sloping upwards. They were approaching a set of open doors and daylight.

Bastorran the elder moved the conversation to more mundane matters. 'How many are there today?'

'Oh, a score or so.'

'I do find this a tedious chore,' he sighed.

'I'll send them away if –'

'No, don't do that. We've occasionally reaped benefits from

granting these people an audience. I suppose it's the usual motley bunch?'

'More or less. There's one who might be of real interest though. A sorcerer called . . .' He took out a folded parchment and consulted it. '. . . Frakk. I'm told he's come up with some useful innovations in the past, of a minor kind.'

'Any idea what he has this time?'

'No. But he says . . .' He looked at the parchment again. 'He says it's something revolutionary and potentially of great use to us.'

'They all say that. We'll have him up first, see what he has to offer.'

They emerged into a large courtyard with high walls on every side. Clansmen were combat training, their clattering swords ringing crisply in the morning air. Others fought with staffs, or loosed arrows at straw targets.

The group of postulants had been kept well away from these activities. They sat on benches at the far end of the quadrant. As the Bastorrans came into sight they got to their feet, and some tried to push forward. Guardsmen held them back, blocking their way with staves.

'Let's get through this as quickly as possible, shall we?' Ivak said.

Devlor nodded. He called out to the guards, 'Send over the sorcerer Frakk!'

The man in question came out of the crowd. A short, plump individual with a red face, he looked discomposed. He was accompanied by a skinny youth, taller than him and no more than a third of his mass. Some of the others waiting grumbled under their breath.

Guards shoved the pair forward. The sorcerer approached the paladin leaders diffidently. He respectfully whipped off his wide-brimmed floppy hat, revealing a bald pate and nearly tripping on his overly long cloak in the process. The boy came after him, struggling with a large, obviously heavy leather bag.

Reaching the Bastorrans, the wizard performed an ungainly bow. 'Gatleff Frakk at your service, masters.'

The boy stood open-mouthed, until a swipe from Frakk's hat had him bobbing too. He dropped the bag.

Frakk glared at the lad. 'And this is my apprentice, Mudge.'

The boy blushed.

'All right,' the elder Bastorran told him, 'you can cut the formalities. Our time is short. What have you to show us?'

'With your permission, Clan High Chief.'

'Yes, yes, get on with it.'

The wizard beckoned to a group of burly helpers at one end of the courtyard. They stood by an unhitched wagon. At his signal there was a flurry of spitting on hands and rolling up of sleeves. Then they set to pushing the wagon in his direction. It trundled to a halt in front of the wizard and the paladins. Frakk's helpers backed off.

'I'm about to demonstrate a radical development in both the potent art and ambulatory warfare,' the sorcerer announced. He looked to his dopey young assistant. 'The bag, boy. The *bag.*'

Mudge snapped out of it. 'Oh. Yes, master.'

He bent and undid the bag's fastening, then strained to lift something out of it.

Ivak Bastorran sighed loudly.

The sorcerer moved to help his apprentice. There was a moment of muddle and an irritable slapping of the boy's wrists. At last they removed a weighty cube, the colour of red ochre. It had runic symbols carved on all its sides. Tottering to the wagon with it, heaving and puffing, they manhandled it onto the tailboard. Then Frakk produced a wand and proceeded to tap it rhythmically against the cube. Next he circled the wagon, tapping each of the wheels in like fashion.

Ivak grunted. Devlor folded his arms.

Frakk cleared his throat and resumed his pitch. 'No one before has thought to utilise the power of magic in quite this way. That cube –' he pointed at it '– has been charged with magical energy, and I have developed a unique spell for dispensing it. Shall I proceed?'

'Do,' Ivak told him.

The sorcerer drew himself up to his full height, such as it was, mouthed an incantation and dramatically jabbed his wand at the wagon.

Nothing happened.

He waved the wand about a bit more, then shook it. The paladins looked on disdainfully.

'Er, just let me try that again,' Frakk said.

He went through the spell once more, ending with another thrust of the wand.

Everything stayed the same. The wagon remained a wagon.

Then they heard a creaking sound. Wood softly groaned and metal gave a tiny ping. The wagon shuddered.

Slowly, ever so slowly, it began to move. Gradually it gathered momentum, until it was moving at a leisurely walking pace.

Frakk whooped in triumph.

The wagon trundled across the courtyard, rattling and squeaking, until it neared a wall. A quick pass from the sorcerer's wand stopped it.

Smiling proudly, he brandished the staff again, in a kind of summoning gesture. The wagon began rocking, then started to reverse. As before, it moved fairly slowly at first, the speed building the further it travelled.

When it went by Frakk and the other observers the wagon was travelling fast enough to give off a little rush of displaced air. They noticed its spinning wheels were suffused with a purplish glow that crackled about the spokes. As the wagon headed down the courtyard, bumping and juddering, it picked up even more speed. By the time it came within range of the wall at the other end of the courtyard, it was going about as fast as it would if horses had been attached.

Swelling with pride, looking just a touch smug, Frakk flourished his wand, commanding the wagon to stop.

It kept going.

He waved the wand again, his smile growing forced.

The wagon didn't slow.

The wizard became frantic. Swishing the air with his staff, he jumped up and down and took to shouting.

With a loud crash, the wagon hurtled into the wall. Wood splintered, metal twisted. A wheel detached, bounced, spun. The sheen of purple radiance that enveloped the wreckage sputtered and went out.

Silence descended.

'He's invented a horseless carriage,' Devlor said.

'A horseless carriage,' his uncle repeated.

They looked at each other. Then burst out laughing.

Laughter instantly spread across the courtyard. The other petitioners on their benches began to laugh, and the guards with them. Clansmen practising combat lowered blades and bows to join in. The men who pushed the wagon, armourers, blacksmiths, servants, everybody started to laugh.

The wizard, bewildered, started to laugh. He nudged his apprentice and he started to laugh, with an effort.

Ivak Bastorran, racked with laughter, eyes damp, turned to the sorcerer. 'I should . . . have you . . . flogged . . . for wasting our time.'

The sorcerer stopped laughing.

'What a *stupid* idea,' Devlor agreed, gulping air and dabbing his eyes. 'Who's going to use something like *that* –' he cocked a thumb at the demolished wagon '– when we've got horses?'

'It's the most feeble-minded notion I've ever come across,' Ivak spluttered.

'Thank you, Frakk,' Devlor said, slapping the back of the wincing sorcerer, 'you've brightened my day. Have you thought of selling it to the Diamond Isle as a novelty attraction?'

'Even better,' Ivak wheezed, 'see if Melyobar wants to buy it!'

Frakk desperately tried to cling to the last shreds of his dignity amid the roars of mirth.

Elsewhere in Bhealfa that dawn the Prince's court was roaming through a sparsely inhabited strip of coastland. The royal household, its retinue and uncountable camp followers were moving along a lengthy, golden beach.

Swarms of spy glamours hovered far above, keeping pace. They belonged to both friend and foe, and occasionally attempted to annihilate each other with negating bolts. But even from their height, the flying eyes could barely take in the procession in its entirety.

The palace itself, in the centre of the crawling mass, might have been a sizeable island. Accompanying residences, the manses and castles of courtiers, occupied less acreage but were still titanic. Bustling around and between these lumbering colossi was an army of horsemen, and vehicles of every conceivable kind. Such was the size of the company that its flanks splashed through waves on one side and bumped over scrubby sand dunes on the other. Nothing of the beach could be seen.

The royal palace had no foundations in the conventional sense, for obvious reasons. Yet it did have a subterranean level. This was achieved by the simple expedient of having no windows or other apertures on its lowest three or four storeys. Anyone transported to this area of the palace would see no difference to being genuinely underground. Though few would welcome the prospect.

Although he couldn't cite an example from memory, Prince Melyobar had always felt the victim of treachery. Consequently he took many precautions to defend himself, and one manifestation of this wariness was his praetorian guard. They were a hand-picked elite, their loyalty subject to terrible oaths and hourly testing. He didn't trust them, of course, because he trusted no one. But he relied on them a little more than most.

Up much earlier than was his usual practice, he was accompanied by two of these worthies as he moved through the palace's lower reaches. They passed numerous other sentinels, and negotiated many secure doors. At last they came to a door defending a section only the Prince would enter. He dismissed his escort and watched them leave.

The door was substantial; layered steel and hardwood, thick as a mature tree trunk. It bore the moulded face of a lion.

'Let me in,' the Prince demanded.

'*I require proof of identity,*' the lion replied. '*Place your hand in the receptacle.*'

Melyobar slipped his hand into a wall slot. He felt a slight tingling sensation in his fingers.

'*Welcome, your Majesty. Please enter.*'

Had the Prince been an impostor he would have lost his hand, followed shortly by his life.

There was the sound of stout locks uncoupling. The door slowly swung open. As Melyobar stepped inside, glamoured lighting came on, then the door closed behind him with a weighty thud and its locks re-engaged.

He was in the royal treasury. The chamber was the first of a series of spacious, interconnecting vaults, with arched openings leading from one to the next. The riches stored here had been estimated as a quarter of the realm's wealth. But that wasn't what interested him.

The first room he passed through was given over to coin. Untold sacks of currency were stacked like sandbags, floor to ceiling, with narrow paths between the rows. A profusion of loose, burnished coins had been scattered on a polished oak table. They all carried his profile, a flattering version of his younger self.

Next he came to a vault dedicated to silver. Piles of ingots in massive blocks, head-high. A profusion of statuary, chalices, picture frames, cutlery, objets d'art. The lustre of cold moon metal.

A stark contrast to the room that followed, where gold was stored. Warm yellow bars criss-crossed in heaps the size of chicken coops. Jewellery, helmets, breastplates and greaves, goblets and plate. Flaxen idols, precious to the sun.

The room after that held precious and semi-precious stones. Twinkling blues, reds and greens on racks and shelves. Pearls, sapphires, rubies, emeralds, amethyst, jade, beryl, jet. Necklaces, bracelets, brooches, daggers inlaid with jasper and agate.

In the adjoining chamber the lights had been dimmed, lest its treasure blind the unwary. Diamonds of all sizes, some as big as hen's eggs, nestled on black velvet trays, and in settings, as crowns, coronets, tiaras and fiery chokers. Multifaceted jewels winking like a million stars.

Next he entered the room where rare, expensive glamours were kept. These came in a variety of shapes and sizes: phials, tablets, cones, cubes, rounded stones, pyramids and spiky wheels. Charms for love and death, elevation and calamity, revelation, concealment and a thousand other grand illusions. Frozen spells laid down like vintage wine – of which there was also a vast quantity in the adjacent cellar. Tiers of cobwebbed bottles, ranks of flasks, jeroboams and methuselahs. Beyond that, an apartment containing artworks: paintings, tapestries, statues, carvings and friezes.

Melyobar weaved through this hoard with little regard, except to run his finger now and again across a dusty surface. He lingered only once, in the penultimate chamber, a room filled with nothing save worthless bric-a-brac.

Here he found some resonance with the contents of an open, battered box. It held a ball, a hoop and stick, and a hand puppet.

Finally he came to the innermost apartment. It was quite unlike all the others. What it housed was something most precious to him, and which he feared nearly as much as Death himself.

He gathered his courage and entered.

There was a smell of sweet decay. Not putrescence, but an aroma of flesh gradually slipping into irreversible decline. The scent of over-ripe ambition and lost hope.

The room was uncluttered. Its spare furnishings consisted of a chair, a bureau and a four-poster bed. An almost completely transparent glamour bubble enclosed the bed. On it lay the body of his father.

King Narbetton looked the way a king ought to: majestic of mien, strong-featured, face lined with the wisdom gained from age and experience. He had the physique of a warrior, still apparent despite time's ravages. He was dressed in finery, with a gold crown upon his brow. His orb and sceptre had been laid out on one side of the wide bed, his ornamental broadsword on the other.

The King had been in magical stasis for the best part of two decades. An endless parade of sorcerers had tried to break the spell. In recent times it seemed Melyobar had come to have second thoughts about this, and the succession of enchanters dried up.

Narbetton seemed to be asleep, though it was near

impossible to detect his breathing. His hair, beard and nails had kept growing, which added a kind of leonine magnificence to his appearance.

The Prince crept into the bedchamber, like a child again. Dragging over the high-backed chair, he sat, steepled hands in his lap.

'How are you today, Father?' he asked, speaking in a near whisper as though fearful of angering his parent.

'Ah, good, good. I'm glad to hear it.'

He cocked an ear. 'What was that, Father? Oh yes, all's well with the realm. There's nothing that need concern you about the governance.'

Melyobar listened again, intently. 'No. As I said, everything's – Hmm, yes. Of course, but –'

The Prince slumped back in his chair and minded his father. 'Why? Well, I wanted your advice about something. You're the only one who really – No. *No*, Father. I won't let him take you, I promise.'

There was a further pause. 'But that's why I'm here. It's to do with him. It *is*. If I can explain? Can I, Father? *Can* I? Thank you.'

Melyobar composed himself. 'As I say, I need your counsel on this very subject. I've been thinking about it quite a lot lately, and – He can. He can, Father. I think you'll find that he can. All right. Now, may I . . . ? Very well. My best efforts have been directed to finding a solution to the problem, as you know. I keep on the move to outpace and confuse him. I've surrounded myself with an iron wall of security. I send out hunting parties, though always without success, because I know I have to take the fight to him. But just lately I've come to realise that I can't see for looking. Hmm? What do I mean?'

He thought about it, expelled a breath and said, 'Imagine I'm looking for a particular kind of tree in a forest. What kind of tree? Oh, I don't mind. It doesn't *matter*. Father, *please*. Let's just say there's only one of this particular kind of tree, whatever it is, but I can't find it because of all the *other* trees it's mixed in with. Now, think how easy it would be if all those other trees died, and just the one I was looking for was left standing.'

There was a long pause. 'Don't you see? Father, you *must*. Look. I can't find Death because he's hidden amongst all those living people. Millions of them. If they weren't there, he'd really stand out, wouldn't he? After all, he'd be the only one left alive. So to speak. And me. And perhaps my personal guard to deal with him now he wouldn't have anywhere to hide. Yes, Father, you too. Of course. *Of course* you too, Father. You know I meant you as well, I just forgot to say it, that's all. I wouldn't let him take you. I promise. Trust me. What was that?'

Melyobar nodded. 'Yes, that's right. And who knows? Perhaps he'll be so pleased at having that many dead people slapped on his plate he'll grant me a pardon. Yes, and you too, Father. I hadn't forgotten.'

The Prince took in the King's next comment. '*Exactly*. I knew you'd get to the nub of it. Well, I thought of ordering them all to kill themselves. A royal proclamation. But I regret to say that not all my subjects can be relied on to follow orders, and it only takes a few not co-operating to ruin things for everybody else. Subjects can be very selfish. I considered the possibility of setting up groups of assassins with orders to kill everyone. Then I'd order them to kill each other. But you can't trust assassins. I wondered whether there was some kind of spell that could annihilate everybody, but I don't think there is such a thing. I've contemplated the idea of poison, except I don't know how I'd get them to take it. Tell me, Father, how *do* you kill off the entire population?'

Prince Melyobar listened intently to what the King had to

say. 'I knew your advice would be sage. It sounds no easy task, but needs must. I'll begin work on it right away.' An abstracted look came to his face, and it darkened. 'I wish it could be tomorrow. Tomorrow's Freedom Day. Huh! What freedom have I, trying to avoid his clutches? They'll be parading themselves like fools. Anarchy and uproar. Shielding *him*. What I'd give to cut down that forest.'

He smiled at his father's motionless form. 'Yes, I wish it could be then.'

26

By mid-morning Valdarr was warm and sunny. The few clouds were as pristine white as icebergs, navigating a perfectly blue sky.

On the balcony of Kinsel Rukanis's mansion, Kutch had joined the singer, Tanalvah and the children. The young sorcerer's apprentice was showing off his growing skills as a spotter.

'Over there.' He pointed to three figures, a man and two women, strolling along an avenue. 'He's real, they're not. And that bird, on the roof opposite. That's a glamour, too.'

'Amazing,' Kinsel said. 'There's no way I could have told the difference.'

'Well, you have to take my word for it, of course.'

'Don't worry, Kutch,' Tanalvah laughed, 'we believe you!'

'What about that one?' Lirrin piped up, pointing at something that looked like an oversized gremlin prowling about on the balcony of an adjoining building. Teg watched wide-eyed and uncomprehending.

'Afraid not, dear,' Tanalvah told her. 'Or rather, *yes*, it's a glamour, but we can all see that. I mean, we know there are no such things as gremlins, don't we? So we can guess that something unusual like that has to be magic. Kutch can see things that don't *look* as though they're magic.'

Lirrin and Teg listened intently, wonder on their plump, shining faces.

'I know next to nothing about the workings of magic,' Kinsel admitted. 'Like most people I just take it for granted.'

'Me too,' Tanalvah agreed.

'So, how do you do it?' Kinsel asked. 'More to the point, *what* do you do? If it's not some dark secret, that is.'

'It's not a secret. But explaining spotting isn't easy, because a lot of it's kind of . . . instinctive. My training's to do with sharpening that instinct. I can tell you the theory of spotting, though.'

'I'd like to hear it. Let's sit down.'

They retreated to the table. The children ran off for a game of their own.

'Don't break anything, you two, and keep the noise down!' Tanalvah called after them.

'Yes, Auntie Tanalvah!' they chorused, dashing into the house and slamming doors.

'I don't think they find grown-up talk very interesting,' she explained, smiling.

They poured themselves tumblers of thick, sweet fruit juice.

'So, how does it work, Kutch?' Kinsel repeated.

'I'm still a neophyte, remember, so I might not be able to answer all your questions.'

'You're a damn sight better qualified than we are!'

'All right.' He took a sip of his drink. 'The basic principles of spotting are all to do with the basics of magic itself. Understand the one and you'll know something about the other.'

'Don't forget you're talking to two people who don't know anything about either,' Tanalvah reminded him.

'Most people don't. Why should they? Not everyone's cut out to be a sorcerer. Anyway, the thing to bear in mind is that because the system draws on the inertia of belief, magic's an everyday reality.'

'I think you've lost me already,' Kinsel confessed.

'I'm certainly in the dark,' Tanalvah said. 'You must think us terribly slow, Kutch.'

'Of course not. I mean, I don't know the first thing about what you two do. Your singing, Kinsel, or your –' He locked gazes with Tanalvah. A moment's embarrassment washed over them. Kutch cleared his throat emphatically. 'It might be useful,' he hurried on, 'to tell you the way my master, Domex, used to put it.' His hosts exchanged secret grins. 'He said that our perception of magic is a bit like the way language must have been born.' He saw them looking baffled again. 'It's quite simple really. Imagine a time, long, long ago, when our ancestors were still incredibly primitive.'

'Would that have been before or after the Founders?' Tanalvah wondered.

'After, I suppose. We don't know. The Founders are a mystery wrapped in an enigma. We don't even know if they were human in any sense we understand.'

'That's a chilling thought. Sorry, I shouldn't interrupt.'

Kutch smiled. 'That's all right. But it's probably best to leave the Founders out of it. They tend to complicate things. Just think of when people were very primitive, and imagine how language might have started. Chances are, somebody pointed to a tree, let's say, and made a noise that marked out trees from everything else. Then if everybody agreed that *tree* meant big leafy thing, trees had been named. Same with anything else: sun, moon, river, mountain, barbcat, whatever you like. When everyone agreed on the sounds, the words, that described them, we were on our way to creating a vocabulary. A language. The philosophers call the process concord. It just means everybody agrees on reality.'

'Those of us who believe the gods created people,' Tanalvah said, 'know that they gave us our tongues.'

'Yes, but they wouldn't necessarily have created us with the ready-made ability to communicate in words. Any more than we were created with the ability to . . . oh, I don't know, tame horses. The gods gave us brains so we could learn and develop. Otherwise, why didn't they just cause us to be perfect in the first place?'

'To better ourselves and become enlightened certainly seems part of the gods' design.'

'This is all very interesting,' Kinsel said. 'But what has it to do with magic?'

'The parallel's about perception,' Kutch explained. 'Put bluntly, we perceive magic because we collectively agree that magic's there to *be* perceived. But we do it totally unconsciously, of course.'

The singer pondered what he'd just been told. 'Isn't that like saying magic doesn't exist?'

'No. The tree's still there, whether we give it a name or not. It's the same with magic. We've developed a kind of vocabulary for magic in the same way we've named things in the world around us, that's all.'

'How does this connect to spotting?'

'It seems to be the ability to get back into the primitive mind before things were named, and before we had a collective agreement about magic.'

'That's fascinating.'

'You're a very smart young man, Kutch,' Tanalvah told him.

The boy flushed at the compliment. 'I've a long way to go yet. And it really isn't to do with intelligence; it's luck. Being able to spot is very rare. I'm just lucky enough to have it.'

'But it must be in all of us,' Kinsel reasoned, 'from those ancestors before they started organising the world. Mustn't it? Deep down.'

'I suppose so. I guess spotters just find it easier to get in touch with that primitive state of mind. So maybe being able to spot isn't an advance but a throwback. A lack of something rather than something extra. I don't know. Nobody does. It's just there. The same way some people can dowse or predict the sex of babies.'

'So you can hone this ability but not develop it from scratch?'

'It has to be there in the first place. Sometimes, training brings it out more.'

'And you train how?'

'By looking but not believing. Not taking for granted. They're the basic tenets of spotting. Look and Doubt. I can't explain it any better than that. I expect Phoenix could.'

'How are you getting on with him?' Tanalvah wanted to know. 'It must be hard adjusting to a new master.'

'He's *a* master, not mine. That will always be Domex. It's the way. I can learn from others, but never call them by that name, except as a courtesy. Phoenix is very inspiring. I think he might be a bit insane.'

They all laughed at that.

Kinsel said, 'How much longer will you have to train?'

'Forever. Magic's a lifelong commitment.'

'And is that what you want?' Tanalvah asked. 'After all, your late master brought you into the Craft when you were too young to make the decision yourself.'

'I'm so glad he did. It's what I've always wanted, though I didn't know it then. I'm very grateful to Domex. He was a good master, and kind.'

'You do him credit,' Kinsel replied, 'and that's as fine an epitaph as any man could want. Look, as you know, I'm singing tonight. Eve of Freedom Day concert. Complete farce, but I'm obliged. Tanalvah and the children will be there. Why don't you come too?'

'Oh, sorry; no, I can't. I have to get ready for tomorrow.'

'The mission. Of course. Stupid of me. You'll be needing a good night's rest.'

'There are some preparations I have to go through with Reeth before that.'

'He worries me, that one,' Tanalvah stated bluntly. 'I hope he's the right man to lead this mission.'

'Tan!' Kinsel protested.

'I mean no insult by it. But he brings harm wherever he goes.'

'But you're both . . .' Kutch began.

'Qalochians, yes.' She shot a glance at Kinsel. 'I seem to have had this conversation before. The fact that we're the same race doesn't come into it. All I'm saying, Kutch, is that Caldason's known for a dangerous man. And he's *different*. His malady, the years he's lived . . . Be careful is what I mean.'

'I think he's the most honourable man I've ever met.'

'I'm sure he is. But he has a darkness in his soul.'

Kutch didn't take offence on Caldason's part, because in truth he knew her to be right. What he said was, 'I don't think he believes in the gods. Or if he ever did, he seems to have lost it.'

'Nevertheless, I will pray for him.'

They stood in silence for a moment before Kutch announced, 'Time I went. Thanks for your hospitality.'

Kinsel took his hand. 'Good luck for tomorrow.'

'Yes, take care of yourself, Kutch.' Tanalvah planted a kiss on his cheek.

'It seems I have a rival,' Kinsel joked. 'Teg! Lirrin!' he called. 'Come and say goodbye to Kutch!'

The siblings rushed out and marauded around the adults' legs.

'What about *that* bird?' Lirrin demanded, jabbing a finger at the sky.

'We're not playing that game anymore,' Tanalvah said. 'Kutch has to go.'

'It's all right,' Kutch told her. 'That's just an ordinary bird, Lirrin. Now, that black and white cat down there is definitely a glamour, and –' He froze. Intently, he gazed down at the streets, then lifted his head to take in the scene more generally. He stared like a newborn seeing a rattle for the first time. Closing his eyes and looking again didn't change his expression of uneasy bewilderment. He put a hand to his brow, and swayed.

'Kutch!' Kinsel exclaimed. He reached out and took his shoulders. 'Kutch, what's the matter?'

There was no answer. He simply stood there, unfocused, as though in a daze.

Tanalvah was growing anxious. 'What's wrong? *Kutch?*'

The children were starting to get frightened.

Kutch appeared to be aware of them again. He blinked, shook his head, took a breath. 'Sorry.' He managed a weak, unconvincing grin.

Tanalvah laid her palm gently on his chest. 'What is it, Kutch? What's wrong?'

'I thought . . .' He shook his head again. 'No, it was nothing. Nothing at all.'

'Your face. For a moment there –'

'I'm all right. Really.'

Kinsel remained concerned. 'Are you sure? Look, sit down for a moment, have a drink and –'

'No. Thank you. I'm just tired, that's all. Too many late nights, too much spotting.'

'You should look after yourself,' Tanalvah said. 'You're

taking on some big responsibilities for one so young. You hear?'

'Yes, Tanalvah, I hear.' He disentangled himself. 'Sorry, but I'll have to go now. Reeth's expecting me.'

He had no idea how he came to be in this place. Or where this place might be. But he did have a sense of who he was.

It seemed he was in a clearing in a forest or wood. The trees were thick, so it wasn't possible to see very far through them. They were tall and crowded inwards, so only a small circle of blue sky was visible above.

Caldason realised that he had a sword in his hand. He looked down at himself. He was bare chested, and bore the scars of brutal wounds. But they were mending, so he knew time had passed.

He had no conception of what was going on, yet it all felt familiar.

Someone was standing in front of him. He didn't know why he hadn't noticed them before. The figure was unclear. He strained to bring it into focus.

It was an old man. Someone he thought he recognised but couldn't place. Like a memory at the edge of his mind.

He wanted to speak, to say something to him, but he couldn't. It was as though the gift of speech was another memory he couldn't quite summon. Nor could he move towards him. His legs wouldn't obey.

The old man was impassive. Neither smiling nor grave, and totally still.

Then he did move. He lifted a hand, his fingers in some odd configuration.

There was a sound, which made Caldason realise that there had been none before. Now he distinctly heard air being displaced, the kind of noise arrows made in flight.

Something was coming his way. A swarm of somethings, flying low out of the forest. He saw that they were knives, a dozen or more, soaring towards him. Coming too far, too fast, too hard to have been lobbed by any mortal hand. Stranger still, they seemed to be moving consciously, varying their speed and trajectory.

The leading knife zeroed in on him. Instinctively he brought up his sword. The knife struck the side of his blade and bounced away. Then he was in a storm of hurtling metal. He batted at the incoming blades, deflecting, blocking, swiping them aside.

They attacked high and low, and as he swatted them they shot off in all directions, emitting a shrill whistle before disappearing. He needed his wits and reflexes at their quickest to keep the shiny, wickedly sharp blades at bay. One nicked him, slicing painfully across his shoulder. It wasn't a deep wound but it spurred his senses further. None of the others hit.

The knives were gone as quickly as they'd appeared.

He looked about to see if any more were in sight. There was no sign.

Touching the gash on his shoulder, his fingers came away covered in blood. He tasted it, the warm, salty tang caustic on his tongue.

The old man was still there, staring at him with that enigmatic expression. There was no doubt he was responsible for the flying knives. But Reeth found it hard to believe his intention was malicious, crazy as that seemed.

Caldason blinked and the old man was gone.

Or rather, he was replaced. Four men now stood where he had been. They were obviously much younger, though their faces were masked with all-over hoods, only their eyes showing. Each wore different coloured garb: red, brown, white and blue. They were all armed in various ways.

The one in red came at him, brandishing a staff. And somehow Caldason was holding a staff too, not the sword. He had no time to think about it. Red was attacking.

Caldason met the first jarring blow, their staves cracking together loudly. There was a brief tussle as they disengaged, then Red tried knocking the Qalochian off his feet with a powerful low sweep. Reeth leapt over it and countered with a stroke to his opponent's head.

That missed by a hair's breadth and they set to exchanging potent blows.

His attacker's three comrades looked on, not trying to join in or interfere.

The fight stepped up a notch in ferocity, each man delivering bone-juddering raps in turn. Its pace increased too, their staffs travelling with eye-blurring alacrity.

At last, Caldason forced an opening, his staff knocking askew Red's latest blow. The follow-up smashed meatily into the man's midriff. As he reeled, Caldason brought down the staff squarely on his skull with all the force he could muster. Red fell, and kept collapsing until he was nothing more than a cloud of crimson motes. A puff of non-wind scattered them to oblivion.

Reeth stepped back, panting.

Without pause, the man in brown came forward, armed with two wooden stocks joined by a long, sturdy chain. Caldason wasn't surprised to find that he had a flail in his own hands.

A quite different form of combat ensued. They circled, seeking a breach, lashing out with their flails. Brown whipped one of his stocks at Caldason's face, and would have had his way if the Qalochian hadn't swiftly dodged. Reeth replied, scoring a hit on Brown's chest that had him retreating a staggered step or two.

With flails, it was inevitable it would come to close-quarter fighting. They moved together simultaneously. Caldason aimed a stock at Brown's head. It was off target, missing by a whisper. As he tugged it back, his outstretched arm was briefly exposed and Brown took the chance, flung out his own flail and saw it wrap itself around Caldason's forearm. He pulled hard, jerking the Qalochian into an iron embrace. The fight became more like a wrestling match, each struggling for advantage.

Exerting every ounce of strength, Reeth managed to reach his flail with his other hand, and transfer it. Then he used it as a club, battering the side of his foe's head until the hold was broken. Brown reeled, and Caldason went in like an assassin, his chain a tourniquet.

He looped it over the other's head, twisted it and applied choking pressure.

Brown floundered and kicked impotently. Caldason tightened his grip. As Brown's efforts grew weaker he began to sink to the ground. But before he reached it he started to lose substance. He transformed into a tan cloud and vanished, leaving Caldason empty-handed.

The figure in white came forward, holding out a pair of knives. Reeth found that he was clutching a pair too, as he had come to expect.

They whirled and ducked, their blades scything the air in search of flesh. Occasionally they clashed with a metallic ring, the impact grazing Caldason's sweating palms. White drove him back with a series of ever wider swipes, promising a gutting if they connected. Reeth side-stepped, and raked White's unprotected flank as he charged past. It was a deep wound, enough of a distraction to allow an uncontested follow-through.

Reeth wasted no time. Spinning, he arrived at his perplexed foe's back and sank both daggers into it. White stiffened, head thrown back, and shattered into a thousand milky-coloured shards. They drifted to extinction as fine dust.

Caldason felt a weight form in his hands. He carried a two-handed butterfly axe. So did Blue, and he was swinging it as he advanced.

All Reeth could do to avoid the initial onslaught was drop. The axe sliced the air where his neck had been. He scrambled on all fours, crabbing himself out of range. Then he rolled, regained his feet and rose just in time to meet another blow. Their axes resounded mightily as they collided. They both stood their ground, taking great swings at each other, chipping steel, swerving from the returns. It was combat as aching drudgery. Blue ventured a base stroke, designed to hamstring. Reeth withdrew fast, feigned, went back in, swinging his axe.

It severed the man's head.

The body stood for a second or two, swaying, before it was consumed by a turquoise miasma. Ten feet away the parted head underwent its own shift to blue-misted nothingness.

*Caldason was breathing hard, muscles burning from his efforts.
He had sweat in his eyes and an ache in every bone.*

*The old man winked into existence again, and this time he was
smiling. Still he didn't speak, though it looked as though he
was going to, because he opened his mouth. Instead he spat fire.
Fiery clods of it, rosy-yellow and hellishly hot.*

*Reeth had no weapon of any kind now. He could only try avoiding
the fireballs with speed and dexterity. He ran, jumped, cart-wheeled
out of their path, feeling their searing heat as they roared by. Some
hit trees, instantly igniting them. Others skimmed the ground,
bouncing, leaving footprints of flame wherever they touched.*

*They stopped coming. The inscrutable old man had closed his
mouth. He raised a hand again.*

*Caldason held a sword once more. He looked around, wondering
what else was in store.*

*There was a disturbance in the ground nearby. An area of grass
rose, like a swelling dome, then split. Something broke through. It
was deathly pale, leathery, wet. Large and palpitating. The thing
undulated out of the earth and reared up.*

*At first, Reeth took it for an enormous worm, thick as a man.
While it certainly resembled such a creature, it was as much snake
and millipede. It had a huge maw, filled with long needle teeth. Its
eyes were black orbs, riddled with yellowy-green veining.*

*The thing heaved more of its bulk out of the hole, its terrible,
drooling mouth agape. Its frightful eyes were fixed on Caldason.
They expressed sheer spite, and hunger.*

*He judged the time right to go against it, while the creature was
still only partially out of the ground. Though the gods alone knew
how much more there was to come. Charging in, he set to hacking
at the monstrosity's writhing, pulpy flesh. What passed for the beast's
blood gushed out; black, thick as treacle and steaming.*

*The creature let out an awful, ear-splitting roar, part bellow of
pain, part howl of murderous defiance. Stunningly fast, it brought
its great mouth down and snapped at Reeth. The stink of its breath*

was overpowering. As he scrambled clear, Caldason hit out with his blade. More by chance than design, the sword struck one of the monster's teeth, breaking off half its length. That cued more bellowing and wild, slimy contortions.

As Caldason zigzagged about the clearing, the creature's head jabbed down to peck at him. When the jaws slammed shut, narrowly missing him, there was a loud crack as the razor-keen fangs came together. Reeth kept moving, rushing in to harry the brute at every opportunity. He was inflicting more wounds, but knew that wasn't enough. So when the head swooped down again he held firm. For a moment, his vision was filled with nothing but the hideous face of the worm thing.

He raised his sword two-handed, then thrust it with all his might into the creature's eye. A viscous green fluid erupted, showering him. As he retreated, the worm rose up to almost vertical, taking the sword with it.

Roaring again, great shudders ran through its sinuous body. It twisted, contorted, fell with a tremendous crash. Briefly it twitched and quivered, and was still.

The carcass began to shrivel, letting off a foul stench, before caving in on itself like the ashes of parchment. What was left drifted away.

Caldason wiped the putrid muck from his eyes. He spat it from his mouth. Turning, he faced the old man, who still stood placidly by. He wanted to scream at him, to demand to know what was happening and why he was being subjected to these torments.

A shadow fell across Caldason.

The old man nodded at him, just slightly, and looked up. Reeth followed his gaze.

An eagle descended. But no ordinary bird; it was the size of a mature bull. Its wings stretched from one side of the clearing to the other. It had talons to rival ploughshares and a bill to accommodate a dray horse. Before he could move, the eagle swooped on Reeth and snatched him up. For all the good they did, his struggles could have been those of a babe.

The bird climbed fast. Caldason's weight seemed no kind of burden for it. Soon they were high in the sky, the wind lashing him unmercifully. Far below, the forest shrunk to the size of his fist.

Banking sharply, the eagle chose its course and increased its speed. Reeth had a dizzying glimpse of fields, streams, woods, plains, distant snow-topped mountains. And at last a river. A silver cord at first, then as they swooped, a wide, vigorous torrent. The eagle flew ever lower, until the river was all that was under them and its banks were too far away to see.

The bird released its claws and dropped him.

Reeth cried out as he fell. The world spun, and most of it seemed to be water.

He hit hard, the impact and the cold knocking the breath out of him. Down he went, momentum slow to decay in the river's covetous grip. He did surface again, carried up by the turbulence and his own frantic kicking, but briefly. The undertow took him, and this time it held on, dragging him down. His hair a black flame, Reeth was sucked ever deeper.

His lungs were bursting, his limbs were too feeble to raise him. Yet something else had greater hold of his attention.

Through the murky, churning waters he beheld another scene. He saw that place he had glimpsed and feared before. The domain of living architecture and dark flying entities. The place where everything was in flux. Where a special kind of malevolence, utterly alien, waited to claim him for its own.

He was drowning.

He jerked awake, fighting for breath.

It took him a long moment to remember where he was. He sat up and perched on the edge of the bed, sweat-sheened, his head in his hands.

'Are you all right?'

Caldason looked up quickly. Kutch was there, standing in the shadows on the far side of the room. Staring at him.

'I heard you,' the boy said. 'So I came in. Was that . . . another one?'

Caldason nodded.

'Is there anything I can do?'

Caldason shook his head. He stood. Whatever his eyes were focused on, it wasn't the room they were in. He looked terrible. 'We have things to do for tomorrow. Let's get on with it.' His words were flat, distant.

It didn't seem a good time for Kutch to tell him about what he thought he'd seen earlier.

'Come here,' Tanalvah said.

Teg reluctantly trudged forward. She licked the corner of a silk handkerchief and rubbed at his cheek. 'Hold still.' The child grimaced. 'There.'

The boy retreated, face screwed up. He wore a smart new outfit. A long-sleeved overshirt and trews in midnight blue, and highly polished black ankle boots. Lirrin had on a new dress that was also blue, but a much lighter shade.

'You two look lovely,' Tanalvah told them. 'Don't they, Kinsel?'

'They certainly do. And so do you.'

'Thank you, kind sir.' She gave a little twirl to show off her new evening gown again. The black spider-web silk wafted as she moved. 'These clothes are wonderful. The nicest we've had.'

'Only the best for you.'

'You look pretty good yourself, Kin.'

He smiled and absently fingered his velvet cravat. 'We'll be the centre of attention tonight.'

She went up on tiptoe and kissed his cheek. 'I can believe that.'

'And not just tonight. In future, we'll –'

'Dare we? Make plans, I mean. It almost feels like tempting fate.'

'Yes, we can.' He took her hands. 'This is a new life, a better life. For all of us.'

'It won't be better if we're late. That carriage should have been here by now.'

'It is!' Lirrin shouted from the window.

'Come on then, you two, let's be off.' Tanalvah herded the children.

The singer, the whore and the two orphans swept out of the room and bustled down the stairs.

Across the way was a house that directly faced Kinsel's. On its second storey, behind a window disguised by a deception glamour, two men were watching. They saw the group leave their house and climb into the waiting carriage.

'Well?' Devlor Bastorran said.

The companion he addressed wore the uniform of a harbour watchman. In every respect but one, he was perfectly ordinary. The exception was his nose. Where it should have been he wore a black leather contrivance, the equivalent of an eyepatch. But solid and padded out, so that it mimicked a nose. 'Yes, sir,' he answered, 'that's them.' The way he spoke was, of necessity, a little strange.

'Are you sure?'

'I am, sir. You tend to remember things like that.'

'And the woman?' the paladin asked.

'She and the brats were there at the docks, too. But she isn't the bitch who did this to me.' He touched his false nose, gingerly, as though it might come off.

'No doubt she'll be known to us soon enough.'

'Can't be quick enough for me, sir. And what then?'

'Then they'll pay.'

27

Freedom Day celebrations, albeit reluctantly for a goodly segment of the population, started early. Valdarr was bedecked with streamers and bunting.

The city hosted military marches, parades and floats. There were street entertainers and speeches. All in the name of bogus fellowship with Bhealfa's conquerors.

Not everyone joined in the festivities; and for some, they proved a good cover. The bulk of Caldason's special operations unit, along with other Resistance fighters, were stationed around the records office, mingling with spectators.

Three blocks from the fake temple stood a school. In common with all other public buildings and most private enterprises, it was closed on this special day. In the preceding week, Resistance agents posing as government officials had gained access to the school's cellars. In an unused, neglected section, they had broken through to the main sewage channel running under the building.

Caldason, Serrah and Kutch, along with four seasoned band-members, stood by the cavity. Except for Kutch, they were heavily armed. All of them carried two or three flasks of flammable oil in specially made belt pouches.

Reeth pointed to one of the band-members. 'You'll be staying here to guard this end. The rest of you are going through with us.'

Kutch thought that, despite the obviously unnerving experience Caldason had undergone the day before, he seemed typically unfazed. He wasn't so sure about himself.

'As for you, Kutch,' the Qalochian went on, 'once we're safely in the records office you're coming back here. I'll have somebody escort you.'

'But, Reeth —'

'Lesson one: don't argue with an order.'

Kutch looked humbled.

'You three —' Caldason indicated the band-members '— will take this tunnel upstream until you reach the first junction. You'll stay there until Serrah, Kutch and I join you. Got that?'

They nodded.

'Go.' He turned to the man designated as a guard. 'Position yourself over by the door.' The man went off.

A rope dangled into the hole, tied off around a ceiling beam. The three men began lowering themselves down it.

'Mind those flasks!' Reeth called out to them.

Serrah was putting on a black headband. Kutch shuffled nervously.

'Ready, Serrah, Kutch?'

'I am,' the boy replied.

Serrah glanced at the cavity. 'No.'

'What?'

'Kutch,' she said, 'would you excuse us for a moment, please?'

'Er, yes, of course.' He looked mystified.

She drew Caldason to one side.

'What's the matter?' he demanded.

'Do you think such a small group's enough for this

mission?' There was a lack of conviction in what she said. She seemed tense.

'We decided on it days ago. You know that. What's really on your mind?'

'I . . .'

'Serrah, we can't afford any hitches now. If there's a problem, spit it out. Are you ill?'

'No. It's just . . . You won't ridicule me for what I'm going to say?'

'Why should I?'

Her eyes flicked to Kutch and the guard, then back to him. Words didn't come easy to her. 'It's just . . . I don't like underground places. Anything confined, closed in, makes me feel terribly helpless. It was bad enough when I was in that cell in Merakasa, but this . . .' She actually shuddered.

'Why didn't you tell me before?'

'I didn't think it'd be a problem. I reckoned once we got going it'd be all right.'

It crossed his mind that it wasn't in her character to show the world a weakness. He could relate to that. 'If you back out now we'll be under strength and I'll have to abort the mission.'

'I'm not backing out!' she hissed.

Kutch and the guard looked her way.

'I'm not,' she repeated in a hushed tone. 'It's just that going down there . . .' She looked at the cavity in the floor. 'I don't relish it.'

'Do you want to change places with the guard and stay here?'

Her teeth pinched into her lower lip as she weighed the offer. 'No. All I need is a minute to get used to the idea.'

'We don't have too much time.' Kindlier, he added, 'Think on this. You won't be by yourself down there, and the channel's quite big. Tall enough to stand in.'

'And after that?'

'There are a few beyond it that are a bit tighter, it's true. But we should move through the system pretty quickly. We've got maps, remember. Look, why not try coming part of the way and seeing how you feel? If it's too much for you, you can come back and swap with the guard. What do you say?'

She swallowed. Then nodded.

'Good. Come on.'

They rejoined Kutch.

'Everything all right?' he asked.

'Yes,' Caldason assured him. 'Just a bit of last minute strategy. We have to move. You're going down first, Kutch. It's not that deep, and at the bottom there's a ledge. The others have already placed some lights down there, and we've got these.' He tapped the amulet Kutch wore. The glamour lit up. 'Think you can do that?'

'Yes, Reeth.' He looked pale, but was keeping his apprehension in check.

'Serrah's next, and I'll follow on. Let's go!'

Reeth steadied the rope for Kutch as he climbed down.

A few seconds later he called, 'I'm there!'

Caldason turned to Serrah, holding out the rope for her. She hesitated only a fraction of a second, took it and scrambled down at speed, hand over hand. Reeth nodded to the guard, then descended himself.

He joined the other two on a narrow ledge, part of a walkway that ran along beside the sewage channel itself. They were all relieved to find there was one. The water was flowing by sluggishly, and the atmosphere was dank. But while the smell was unpleasant, it wasn't too bad. The tunnel had a curved ceiling and walls, and was just about high enough to walk upright in, as Reeth had said. They could see the distant glow of lights where the other band-members were waiting.

Caldason glanced at Serrah. To them both, he whispered, 'Take it easy and follow me along this ledge to the others. It's not far.' That wasn't entirely true. The junction was probably three or four hundred paces away.

They set off, edging their way along, Kutch in the middle, Serrah bringing up the rear. The walls were slimy and spotted with lichen, and took on an eerie luminescence under the glamour orbs' light. There were occasional sounds of scurrying, presumably from unseen rats.

At one point Kutch nearly slipped. Serrah grasped his arm. 'Easy,' she advised. 'You wouldn't want a dip in that.'

They pushed on, Kutch more gingerly than before.

At last they came to the junction of tunnels where the three men were stationed on a wide stone platform. They all scrambled onto it. Here, the main channel split into two, with feeder tunnels running north-west and north-east. The new tunnels were smaller than the one they'd just left. They still had walkways, but they were narrower.

'We want that one,' Caldason said, pointing to the north-east tunnel. 'It's a bit of a trudge, but eventually it takes us to another junction. You three lead the way. Kutch, Serrah and I will bring up the rear.'

They resumed their journey, more slowly now because the ledge was so much more confined.

When the three band-members and Kutch were out of earshot, Caldason asked Serrah, 'Well? Are you up to going on?'

'I'll be all right.'

'You're sure?'

'I want no special treatment,' she came back irritably.

'You're not getting any. My concern's the success of the mission.'

'All right. But there's no need to keep asking me how I am.'

'I don't intend to, Serrah. After this stretch there's no going back.'

'I understand.'

'All right, let's catch up with them. I'll be right behind you.'

As they started, she suddenly said, 'Is Kutch all right?'

'Why do you ask?'

'He seems . . . preoccupied.'

'He's bound to be, isn't he? He's never done anything like this before.'

'I thought it might be something more than that.'

'I'll keep an eye on him. You look after yourself. And keep moving.'

They caught up with the others.

This time the trek was much longer. The tunnel was unvarying and seemed to go on forever. All that broke the monotony were one or two places where the walkway was eroded and chunks had broken off. None of the breaks were large and no one got their feet wet.

It was perhaps half an hour before they came to another, more complex junction, where no less than four tunnels met in a high-roofed chamber. This had a wider walkway skirting it. About halfway round, metal rungs were set in the slimy wall, leading up to a wooden trapdoor in the ceiling. The roar of water was much louder here.

'Most of the distance we have to cover is over,' Caldason told them. 'But the journey gets a bit trickier from here on.' He nodded at the ladder.

'Do we know we can get through that trap?' one of the band asked.

'According to the source who gave us the plans it's secured with nothing more than a bolt. We'll see.'

He led the way to the rungs and began climbing them. Once at the top he pushed at the trapdoor. It didn't open, but the wood was damp and flaky, the rusty hinges loose, and there was a lot of give in it. One of the band-members handed him a mallet and he set to battering. The trap lifted an inch or two. Reeth moved up another rung and pushed hard. The trapdoor flipped open with a crack and a little shower of pulpy splinters had him blinking.

'Got it!' he called down. He hoisted himself through the hole.

He was in another tunnel, about the same dimensions as the one they'd just left. But there was no walkway here; they'd have to wade through the gently flowing waste water. Luckily it was only a few inches deep. He could see, about thirty paces on, yet another junction.

Caldason helped the others up. They sloshed to the new junction. Three tunnels met there. On a stretch of wall there were two further openings, about head height. Discoloured water trickled out of them, and moss grew around their mouths. They were the smallest channels they'd yet seen.

'It would be really easy to get lost down here,' Kutch decided.

'Don't forget we've got these.' Caldason took out his map and consulted it to be sure. 'Yes, thought so. We need the right-hand outlet.'

He caught a glimpse of Serrah. If the prospect of entering such a confined place worried her, she was hiding it well.

'We have to go through it bent double, maybe on all fours,' he explained. 'So I hope you're not wearing your Freedom Day best. It probably isn't going to be that pleasant in there, but according to the map we don't have to put up with it for long. Are we ready?'

There was a mumbled chorus of assent.

The group paddled over to the outlet. Caldason told the others to go up first. He wanted to check on Serrah again, no matter what she'd said.

Two band-members gave the first a leg-up, then he hoisted them after him. Kutch was next.

While that was going on, Reeth looked to Serrah. She gave him a brief, emphatic nod, and he acknowledged it before she clasped outstretched hands and was pulled up.

Reeth jumped and caught the edge of the drain. With the others hauling and him scrambling, he soon joined them.

He'd been right about the size of the tunnel they'd entered. They could only move through it single-file and bent very low. They set off, loping like apes. But before long they came to something unexpected and unspecified on the map.

The tunnel suddenly became even smaller.

Serrah, in front of Reeth, looked over her shoulder at him. Her expression was unreadable, but he could guess what she felt.

They had to proceed by crawling, and the tunnel was so much tighter that their heads still only just cleared the ceiling. Progress slowed greatly. The crawl seemed to go on forever, and Reeth could only imagine what Serrah was making of it. He was ready to reach out a comforting hand, if need be.

In due course there was a whispered exclamation from up ahead. It sounded positive. Soon after, the tunnel joined another passing it at a right angle, a much larger one it was possible to stand in.

Once they were out, Serrah took deep breaths and stretched. She didn't speak, and Reeth didn't say anything to her.

Kutch looked askance at the muck on the front of his breeches and the sleeves of his coat. 'Are we nearly there?' he asked.

'Not far now,' Reeth said. 'And according to this –' he waved the folded map '– the rest of it's nothing like what we've just been through.' He noticed Serrah staring at him, and thought he detected relief on her face. In the poor light he couldn't be sure. 'We go round this bend here on the left.'

He started off. The group followed.

They found themselves at the confluence of two more tunnels.

'There,' he said, indicating the next stage of their journey.

As they walked towards the fresh tunnel, Caldason took the opportunity of seeing how Kutch felt.

'You all right?'

The apprentice nodded. 'Fine. You?'

Caldason nodded back. 'Your part in this hopefully won't take much longer. There's just one thing. If you had to find your own way back, could you?'

An alarmed expression came to the boy's face. 'Yes, I suppose so. Do you think I'll have to?'

'No, don't worry. Just covering all the possibilities. But it makes sense to note where we're going. Just as a precaution.'

'I think I'm all right with it so far.'

'Good. Not long now.'

Kutch thought again of telling his friend what he'd seen yesterday, but immediately realised this was definitely the wrong time and place.

The tunnel they entered had a flat roof consisting of stone blocks. It was low enough that they had to stoop slightly. They hadn't gone very far when it made an acute turn to the right. Caldason stopped them.

'What needs doing next has to be fairly accurate,' he spelt out. 'According to the map, from this corner it's between twenty and thirty paces. Obviously we'll call it twenty-five. That should take us directly under where we want to be. Let's be sure about this. I'll start pacing; a couple of you do the same.'

He began a deliberate walk, counting his steps. When he

arrived at twenty-five the others were right behind him. There was no argument about the spot.

Reeth looked up. He was almost exactly beneath a square roof block. 'That one looks as good as any. Let's get started.'

They got out the tools they'd brought: mallets, chisels and crowbars. Then they set to chipping away at the join around the block, a task made much easier due to the low ceiling. Mortar and stone chippings began to fall.

Eventually they were able to insert crowbars in the fissures they'd made. After a brief struggle the whole block suddenly fell, shattering loudly on the sewer floor. Everyone kept absolutely silent for a moment, listening. Apparently there was nothing to hear.

Inside the opening they could see planks of wood. They went to work again, chiselling their way through them, passing down chunks. When that was removed they found another layer of planks, supported by joists.

'That's the actual floor of the building,' one of the band-members confirmed.

'This is the acid test,' Caldason said. 'If Karr's informant's to be trusted, there's nobody up there. If he's wrong, or lying, we could be walking into a trap. Stay alert, and be ready to fight or run.'

In ten minutes they'd exposed a layer of thick, coloured fabric.

'Presumably that's a carpet,' Reeth judged. 'We're just a cut away now.'

'I'd like to be the first one up,' Serrah volunteered.

He imagined that was because she was anxious to get out, but asked, 'Why?'

'That hole looks a tight squeeze. I'm the smallest here, and maybe the most agile, so it makes sense. The smallest bar Kutch, that is, but I'm assuming he's not frontline.'

Kutch started to say that he'd be glad to do it.

'No,' Caldason interrupted, 'Serrah's right. We need an experienced fighter for this, just in case. Your skills are too precious to risk.' To her he added, 'You're first up, then. But straight back if there's a sign of anybody up there, right?'

'Right.'

Two of the band-members crouched so she could clamber on their backs. She went up with a knife and started cutting. Scraps of carpet dropped down.

'I'm through,' she reported.

She poked her head through the hole. Shortly, she bobbed down again. 'There doesn't seem to be anybody about. I'm going in.' Her legs and feet disappeared.

A moment later her head popped through the hole. 'It looks clear. Come on.' Once more she vanished.

'Right, everybody up,' Caldason ordered.

His crew scrambled through the hole.

They emerged in a grand hallway decorated with marble pillars and wood panelling. A mosaic of the Gath Tampoor dragon emblem occupied a section of wall, giving the lie to this being a place of worship – unless it was the worship of colonial masters.

Serrah was at the hallway's far end, examining a pair of huge doors that presumably led to the outside. There were a number of other doors in the hallway.

'I don't want anybody going too far,' Caldason decreed. 'Not until we're a little surer of what the set-up is. Kutch, time to earn your keep. Can you sniff around for alarum glamours, sentinels, booby-traps, that kind of thing? And be careful!'

Kutch started to creep along the hall, gazing about intently.

Reeth turned to the three band-members, and picked one. 'I want you to guard our exit. If anything happens try letting us know. Use a wailer if you have to. At some point I'll be sending Kutch back here. When he arrives get him out, quick as you like, and get away yourself, too. Got it?'

The man nodded.

'You can amuse yourself by spreading your oil around the place.'

'You'd think there'd be some kind of security in here,' one of the others remarked.

'It's guarded on the outside. That's where they'd expect someone to try something. Anyway, don't assume there isn't security. There's bound to be, and in a place like this it's going to be good.' He looked around. 'There's supposed to be a guards' station here somewhere.'

'It's over there,' Serrah reported. 'Deserted. Kutch's checking it out.'

Even as she said it, the apprentice reappeared.

'Well?' Caldason asked.

'I haven't spotted anything yet. But I've only checked this hallway and the guards' station.' Up close and quietly he added, 'Remember, Reeth, I'm still only a novice at this. I can't swear I'd spot everything.'

'I know. But we're still a damn sight better off with you. Now just relax and do your job. We'll check the rooms down here first.'

He insisted that they stick together for this, while the guard remained at the hole. They took the doors right to left, from the end of the hall where the street doors were back to where they'd broken in. The first couple opened onto nothing more interesting than offices and other mundane utility rooms. Kutch detected no hint of magical duplicity in any of them.

The third door, a double set, led to something a little more striking. A huge room filled with clerks' benches and high-backed stools, hundreds of them. It was an administrator's paradise.

'Karr was right about the bureaucracy,' Serrah remarked.

They entered other doors and found nothing special. All

the rooms were without windows, and none of them were locked. Serrah commented on this.

'It confirms that they've concentrated all their defences on the outside of this place,' Caldason thought. 'They didn't consider an attack from within. As you said, the bureaucratic mind.'

The last set of doors opened onto a wide staircase.

'It seems we were informed correctly,' Caldason said; 'upstairs is where the records are kept. Be extra alert, all of you. Kutch, you'll lead with me.'

Kutch looked a little daunted, but he was game.

They started up the staircase. It curved, so their destination couldn't immediately be seen. The walls were lined with impressive glamoured portraits of empire dignitaries – generals and admirals saluted, royal luminaries and politicians struck courtly poses.

As the party turned the bend they saw that the stairs terminated on a wide landing. On either side of the top step were two tall, square pillars of pinkish stone, decorated with gold stencilling.

'Wait,' Kutch said.

They froze.

Caldason laid a hand on his shoulder. He couldn't help but notice that the boy was shaking. 'What is it?'

'Has anyone got a knife?'

'Of course,' Serrah replied.

Kutch eyed his comrades and the small armoury they toted. 'Oh, yes. Silly of me. Do you have one of your throwing knives, Serrah?'

She plucked one from her sleeve scabbard. 'This do?'

'Could you hit that door up there, opposite the top of the stairs? And can you throw through the pillars?'

'Sure.' She drew back her aim and lobbed the blade.

The throw was true, and would have struck the door. But

as the knife soared between the pillars something like lightning instantly crackled out of them. Undulating crimson whips seized the knife in flight and annihilated it with a loud report.

'I think you just earned your place in the band,' Serrah told Kutch.

'What's the extent of the thing?' Caldason wanted to know. 'Are we going to have to climb up another way?'

'I don't think so,' Kutch replied. 'Serrah, can you oblige again, please?'

'Another knife? This is getting expensive. These are good blades, you know.'

'If I'm right, you won't lose this one. Try throwing it low this time. Get it to go through the pillars about knee height.'

She went up a few more steps and threw again, underhand this time. The knife reached the pillars and carried on through, embedding itself in the door.

They resumed their climb and, one by one, went through the pillars on hands and knees. Now they faced the door, from which Serrah retrieved her knife. It was the only door in the corridor, although the corridor was very long.

'Picking up anything here, Kutch?' Caldason asked.

'No, I don't think so.'

They found that the door was locked.

'Careful now,' Reeth cautioned as the band-members moved in with their crowbars.

Everyone stood ready, weapons drawn.

The door opened with no trouble. Behind it was a dimly lit corridor with another set of doors at its end. They headed for them.

'Do you get the feeling this mission never seems to get anywhere?' Serrah wondered.

'Wait!' Caldason exclaimed.

They stopped, blades raised.

Kutch was puzzled. 'What is it, Reeth?'

'Down there.' He pointed towards the floor.

Kutch couldn't see anything until they turned their glamour globes on it.

Then a thin, almost invisible strand of wire stood out, stretched across the corridor at ankle height.

'Obviously not all the traps here are magical,' Reeth said. 'Everybody back off.'

They retreated a few paces.

He stepped over the wire. Nothing happened. He beckoned and the others queued to skip it.

'I wonder what it does?' Kutch said.

'I'm glad we didn't find out. Let's try and remember it on the way back, shall we?'

They reached the second door and repeated their careful procedure for opening it. It wasn't even locked. That took them to an iron balcony, part of a walkway that went around the entirety of the massive room they were looking down into.

It was filled with hundreds of rows of shelving. Every available area of wall space was shelved. There were shelves up on the balcony level where they stood, floor to ceiling. All these shelves and racks were crammed full with what looked like books. But they were entirely uniform: tall, bound in brown leather and with neatly labelled spines. They numbered many thousands.

The Gath Tampoorian imperial emblem was here too. This time it covered a large part of the ceiling, probably because there was nowhere else to put it.

'I think we've finally arrived,' Caldason said.

The walkway they were on had a number of staircases joining it with the records hall below. He started out for the nearest.

'Stop!' Kutch yelled.

Everybody froze again.

'The floor,' the boy explained, pointing ahead of them. 'It's not right.'

'It looks real enough to me,' one of the band-members reckoned.

Kutch reached over and pulled one of the bound books from a shelf. It was obviously heavier than he expected. He threw it at the floor. It went straight through. For a fraction of a second the glamoured surface disappeared before reforming itself. Long enough for them to see that the drop was much further than just to the next level. There was some kind of shaft or well directly beneath.

'The gods know what's at the bottom of that,' somebody remarked.

'As long as it isn't us,' Reeth said. 'Well done, Kutch.'

They turned around and made for the next staircase. Everybody moved very carefully.

Once they were down in the hall, the enormity of the place struck them fully. The towers of shelving and endless files crowded in.

Caldason told Kutch to examine the place as thoroughly as he could, and sent the two remaining band-members to accompany him.

That left Reeth alone with Serrah. He took the opportunity to ask how she was feeling.

'Not bad. Thanks for being considerate about . . .'

He nodded. 'It's all right.'

They took in their surroundings, trying to make sense of the mountains of information all around them.

Kutch returned. 'Everything in the immediate area seems all right. But it's a big place. I can't guarantee I haven't missed anything.'

'We have to get out of here soon anyway. Why don't the three of you prime for a fire? You know where best to put the accelerant. We'll take care of this end.'

Kutch and the others went off again.

Reeth and Serrah began throwing the liquid around. They sprinkled it on files, books, piles of parchments, anything that might burn.

Kutch called out, from not far off. They jogged over to him. They found him and the other two men staring at a blank wall.

'The fact that it had nothing on or against it was what attracted my attention,' Kutch explained. 'Must be the only bit of blank wall in the place.'

'A deception glamour,' Serrah said.

Kutch nodded and started to walk towards it. 'Come on, I'll show you. It's safe.'

He led them through the wall. They felt no more than the gentlest breeze as they pierced the illusion. They discovered a big recess, fenced in with bars. Inside the cage, there were more racks of files. Several hundred at least.

'The special stuff,' Serrah reckoned.

There was a gate in the cage, but it didn't stand up to their battering. They went in and had a quick look around.

Reeth read some of the labels on the spines of files. 'Practically nothing here means anything to me,' he admitted. There was a murmur of agreement from the others. 'Anyway, we haven't got the time, interesting though it might be. Let's get on with it.'

The others moved out. He lingered for a moment, splashing the inflammable liquid around. As he was about to leave, a small rack of bound files caught his eye. They were in alphabetical order. ABBROM, ADAZE, BARAMAK, BEKKLE, BURR, CAID . . .

CALDASON.

He slid the file from its shelf. His full name was written on the front. Sweeping a table of its clutter, he laid it down and opened it.

All the pages had been cut out.

He pulled a couple more for comparison. They were complete. He stared at his.

'Reeth!' Serrah shouted. 'Come on!'

Caldason scattered the last few drops from his flask and left the cage.

They were waiting for him near the staircase.

'Serrah, help me set the fuses. The rest of you go. There's nothing more you can do here. We'll meet up later.'

Kutch started to say, 'Are you sure I can't –?'

'No. You've done well. Now follow orders and get out. And all of you: watch for those traps on the way back.'

They turned and clattered up the stairs.

'Let's see those fuses,' Serrah asked.

Reeth dug into his pocket and produced three or four of them, holding them out on his palm for her to see. They were small cylinders of thin metal with a join in the middle.

'One end has a highly inflammable oil. The other's filled with vitriol. When you put pressure on both ends it breaks a seal and the acid starts burning through to the oil. When it reaches it, it ignites. Very violently. Ingenious, eh? Phoenix's people made them.'

'How long does it take for the acid to burn through?'

'About twenty minutes.'

'Tight.'

'We'll be all right as long as we're in the tunnel by then. Here.' He gave her a handful of the fuses. 'You start that side, I'll start at the other. Just squeeze the ends and scatter them.'

They parted to sow their fire-makers.

A couple of minutes later they reunited across from the staircase.

'Now we move,' Caldason told her.

They made for the stairs.

Something came from behind a rack and blocked their path.

The barbcat was a big, fully mature adult. Longer than Reeth was tall, maybe three times his weight, it had claws the size of daggers and curved white fangs. As well as the rancorous attitude common to its species.

The cat was tensed, as though ready to spring. It studied them with yellow, famished eyes. White foam flecked its jaws.

'Oh, don't worry about that,' Serrah announced airily. 'I've been here before.'

'What?' Caldason whispered.

'It's a sentinel glamour. You get to recognise them.' She went to move forward.

'Wait. If it's a glamour, how come Kutch didn't spot it?'

'He's still learning, he said so himself. Or maybe it was out of range or something. I'll go and shoo it.'

'No. This is an empire building. They'd have the best defences, and what better than a genuine barb? That's real wealth.'

'Don't be ridiculous,' she snorted. 'People use glamours like this for security all the time.'

The barbcat's fur was bristling. Its mouth was open in a toothy snarl. They could hear the rumble of its purr.

'If that's a real barb,' she declared, 'then I'm a –'

The cat let out a thunderous roar. It raised itself up and casually side-swiped a stack of bound records. The barb's claws slashed them like a scythe cutting through a snowdrop. A little shower of fluttering leather and shredded paper spilled across the floor.

Serrah said, 'Shit.'

Then the barbcat charged.

28

The barbcat raced towards them with eyes blazing and slavering jaws. It moved with the legendary speed that made its species notorious.

Serrah threw herself to the right, Reeth hurtled to the left. They'd barely moved when the cat ripped through the space they'd vacated. Roaring with frustration, it skidded on the polished floor and half turned, ready to leap. The sudden absence of its prey baffled the creature. It looked around, stupefied.

Reeth and Serrah had put distance between themselves and the cat, and their swords were drawn. They stood at opposite ends of the hall, in sight of each other, the barb between them. This finally dawned on the beast. Its great shaggy head went from right to left and back again, trying to work out who it should go after.

'Don't move, Reeth!' Serrah yelled.

Well-meant advice, but delivering it was a mistake. The cat's head snapped her way. It made up its mind about which morsel to go for. Springing forward, it loped in her direction.

Serrah dashed into the tangle of storage racks, weaving her way through the tiers. The cat arrived and commenced to stalk her, whiskers prickling. She crept about the maze, trying to put as many turns between them as possible.

While the animal was preoccupied, Caldason stealthily made his way to Serrah's end of the hall. He couldn't see the barb, but he could hear it – snuffling, growling, over-turning things that smashed and rattled. He heard Serrah too, running on the balls of her feet to keep the sound down. A forlorn hope. If he could hear her, the barb's sensitive ears would have an even better chance.

Reeth got to within three or four rows of where he thought the beast was. Serrah's location he was uncertain about. He tested the stability of the rack he was hiding behind by gently shaking it. Then he saw that it was bolted to the floor and seemed solid enough. Carefully, he began climbing the shelves.

Serrah was a mouse, doing her best to throw the cat off her scent. She trod a devious route, a turn and turnabout to shake the barb. Playing the animal at its own game was hope-less, of course, and she knew it.

She tiptoed to the corner of a line of shelving and poked her head round, just as the cat did the same at the other end of the row. They saw each other. No more than a second passed, though it felt like a century. Then the barb dashed at her. She hastily withdrew and sprinted the length of another tier, turning sharply and running down the next row. The pursuing cat roared its fury.

Reeth was on the top of his rack. He could see Serrah now. She was crouching just a couple of tiers away. The barb was two rows further along, sniffing the floor.

He took a chance. 'Pssst!'

He had to do it again before she heard and started looking around for the source of the sound. It didn't occur to her to look up. So he gambled again. 'Up here!' he hissed.

She saw him.

So did the cat. Again, it was transfixed, with two meals in sight. Serrah made a break for it, heading Reeth's way, and that meant abandoning cover. The cat came after her. She made it to Caldason's rack and scrambled up it, the creature snapping at her heels. Reeth caught her hand and hauled her the last few feet. The barb looked up at them, its eyes flashing emerald.

Serrah panted from the exertion. Between breaths, she said, 'This is . . . stupid. We can't . . . stay up here . . . forever.'

'Or very long at all. Not only are the fuses set but . . . cats can climb, can't they?'

'Damn!'

The barb was on its hind legs, its front paws mauling the shelves, trying to get a climbing hold. Serrah leaned over and slashed at it with her sword, but she couldn't reach far enough. Undeterred, the slobbering animal was starting to scale the rack.

Caldason grabbed a stack of bound files and threw them down at the beast. They showered onto its head, making it leap back to the floor. The cat was growing ever more enraged. It began circling the rack, jumping up every so often with gnashing teeth, or trying to climb the shelves to get at them. They carried on pelting it, just about holding the brute at bay.

'It's going to get up here sooner or later,' Reeth said.

'And we're going to run out of these.' She hefted a file and tossed it at the barb. It bounced off its snout, adding to its impotent fury.

'Don't worry, the place's going to go up soon. That should take care of it.'

'This isn't the time for jokes! What are we going to do about it?'

'Barbs aren't the smartest of animals, and we've seen this one can be confused.'

The rack shuddered under the impact of the heavy animal trying to climb up again. Files cascaded from the shelves.

'What are you saying? That we can baffle it to death?' She was hanging on now as the rack continued to shake.

He aimed another book at the cat, drawing a satisfying whimper. 'We need to distract it so we can make a break.'

'Easier said than done, Reeth. That thing's fast. Gods, I've just thought.'

'What?'

'Suppose it got Kutch and the others after they left us?'

It had occurred to him, too. 'I think we would have heard it. And if it did get any of them I reckon it'd be sated now and not so interested in us.'

'There's a nice thought. So what are we going to do?'

'If it's got two targets to go for maybe we can confound it long enough to get away.'

'I was afraid you were going to say that. What's the plan?'

'Plan? We get off this thing and run like hell in different directions.'

'And that's it?'

'Can you think of anything better?'

'No, damn you, I can't.'

'There's no point in getting uppity with me, Serrah. After all, you were the one who thought –'

'I know, I know. Don't rub it in. If . . . when we get clear, we head up there, right?' She pointed to the balcony at the top of the staircase.

'Yes, the way we came in. If we can get those doors shut behind us we stand a chance.'

'Stairs aren't going to be any hindrance to this thing.'

'You're right. Getting there first's our only hope.'

'It isn't just going to stand by and watch us go.'

'Perhaps we can slow it a bit. How many of those throwing knives have you got left?'

'Six or seven. But I'm not sure one of them would be enough to kill a barbcat.'

'I'm certain it wouldn't. It could give it something to think about though.'

The rack shook again, heavily. They knew it wouldn't take much more to bring it down.

Serrah dropped another pile of files on the maddened cat's head. 'Whatever we're going to do, let's do it soon, shall we?'

'Right. You distract it with a knife throw and we'll get running.'

'We won't be able to head straight for the stairs, will we? It'd outrun us easily.'

'I know. We'll have to take roundabout routes. Ready?'

'There's no time like the present.' She drew a snubbed throwing knife from her sleeve.

The cat was pacing below, wary of being bombarded again but determined to reach its tormentors. Its constant movement made it a difficult target, but she took a bead on its head and lobbed the knife.

While it was still in flight the barb leapt at the blade and caught it in its teeth. It shook it, as a cat might shake a dead bird, and the knife flew out of its mouth, clattering across the floor. The barb ignored it and resumed its pacing. It was even more irate.

'Under normal circumstances that would be quite a neat trick,' Serrah observed.

'Try again, but after I've given it another diversion. Avoid its head this time.'

Serrah took out a second blade.

Caldason grabbed a file from the ever-decreasing piles. 'Be ready,' he warned.

Serrah nodded.

He didn't try throwing the book at the animal this time.

He aimed over its head and beyond it. The file soared through the air. The cat, head up, watched it go. Before it landed the barb was after it like a dog with a stick. Serrah flung her knife.

It struck the beast on the side of its front left leg, sinking deep. The cat bellowed pain and fury.

'*Now!*' Caldason yelled.

They dropped to the floor and instantly streaked off in different directions. The barb hesitated for a second, head swivelling. Then it decided on Caldason and took after him. The knife was still lodged in its leg, and the barb had a slight limp, which perhaps slowed it a fraction. Whether that would be enough they were about to find out.

Caldason ran like fury towards the far end of the hall. He didn't know what had become of Serrah. But as there hadn't been any screams he assumed she was all right for the moment.

Then he picked up the sound of the animal chasing him – the weighty thumps as it ran, its claws on the wooden floor, its hard, wheezy breathing.

He looked over his shoulder. The barb was closing.

He wanted to avoid climbing another rack and being back in the same position he'd just got out of. As the thought occurred, he passed one that was free-standing. Dashing behind it, he applied all his strength. The rack swayed. Files rained down. Then it collapsed with a loud crash in the barb's path. A cloud of dust went up.

But it only slowed the cat for a heartbeat. It jumped the obstruction with ease, despite the knife in its leg, leaving a sprinkling of blood over the upset files and general debris.

By this time Reeth was on the move again, trying to navigate a circuit that would take him back to the staircase. Or failing that, any of the other stairs leading up to the walkway. He ran a zigzag course, hoping to gain some small advantage. But still the barb was nearly on him.

'Reeth!'

He glanced the way of Serrah's shout. She'd got herself to the walkway and was running along, following the chase. When the cat came near she hurled a knife at it. But it fell short and buried itself in the wooden floor. She threw files into the cat's path, along with small pieces of furniture and anything else she could lift.

The snarling barb was learning to keep its distance. It was still after Caldason, but its pursuit had been slowed a little.

For his part, Reeth ran as if all the demons of hell were after him. He was awarded a small bonus. The cat slid in a pool of the flammable oil they'd splashed around. Slippery paws brought a short respite.

'Here!' Serrah cried. 'Here!'

She was indicating a staircase he hadn't noticed in his flight. He headed for it.

'The floor!' she cried. 'Remember the floor!'

He realised that these stairs were the ones that led to the glamour trap with the pit beneath. He put on a renewed burst of speed. As he hit the steps the cat was only a few paces behind. Reeth dashed up, running as fast as he could, then leapt for all he was worth.

He didn't know if he'd make it. He wasn't sure where the false floor ended and the real one began. He readied himself for a dizzying fall.

His feet landed with a slam on solid iron, and he practically fell into Serrah's arms. They looked around and saw the barbcat's fuzzy head appearing at the top of the stairs. Then the whole animal was in view. The knife was still sticking out of its leg, though it looked as if it had worked itself out a bit.

The cat stopped.

'Come on,' Serrah urged under her breath. 'Come on . . . Just take another little step, you bastard.'

The cat studied them slyly. It stared at the floor and for a moment seemed undecided. Then it turned and disappeared down the stairs again.

'Would you credit it?' she said. 'It's given up!'

No sooner were the words out than the cat reappeared, coming up the stairs very fast. It leapt, its great muscles releasing energy that made the jump appear easy. The barb sailed over the deception and landed with a clamorous thunk on their side.

'Move!' Caldason bellowed.

They spun and ran along the balcony, the cat at their backs.

The set of doors they'd come through was in sight. They put on a spurt to reach them, and made it by a literal whisker. Tumbling through, they seized the doors and began closing them. The barbcat hit the other side with a crash. The impact was so strong it nearly knocked them off their feet. They struggled for a moment trying to shut the doors on it, but its strength was overpowering.

'We can't hold this,' Caldason said, strain in his voice.

'Run?'

'Run.'

They turned and sprinted for their lives. The barbcat burst in behind them, the doors smashing back against the walls.

A realisation hit both of them at the same time. 'The trip wire!' they yelled simultaneously.

They jumped it. But Serrah landed awkwardly, stumbled and fell. Reeth stopped and dragged her to her feet. The cat was catching up. They weren't going to get clear. Reeth fumbled for his sword. Serrah cried out.

The animal blundered into the trip wire. It stretched tautly across its front legs. There were a few seconds of bewilderment as the barb surveyed this new irritation.

A mechanical rumbling started up somewhere. On either wall and across the ceiling a narrow slit appeared. Suddenly, a huge pendulum swung out of the right-hand wall, suspended by a rod from the ceiling slit.

The razor-keen blade sliced straight through the barbcat.

It happened so quickly the animal didn't even have the time to make a sound. The gory pendulum carried on and disappeared into the corresponding slot in the opposite wall. It left a scene of blood and ghastliness, and one very dead barbcat.

'Now we know what it does,' Serrah said.

He pulled her to her feet. 'Come on!'

They stumbled along the rest of the corridor and through the next set of doors. Negotiating the pillars, they thundered pell-mell down the staircase.

There was no sign of anyone in the ground floor hallway.

'Let's hope the others got out all right,' Serrah panted.

She looked at the hole they'd cut. Her expression needed no elaboration.

'We haven't a choice,' Reeth reminded her. 'Unless you want to try walking out the front door.'

They began their descent.

In the paladins' headquarters, not far from the records office, Freedom Day was like any other. There were no celebrations here, beyond those required as a diplomatic sop to the clans' Gath Tampoorian paymasters. It was business as usual.

This applied just as much in the depths of the fortress, where the dungeons and other unpleasant facilities were located. These included several state-of-the-art torture chambers. In one, Devlor Bastorran had enjoyed observing the morning's work.

A ruined body lay on a bloodstained slab. Nearby stood one of the clans' most experienced inquisitors, wiping his hands with a cloth, his butcher's apron stained crimson.

Devlor was pacing impatiently. 'Where is he? I'll have that messenger's head!'

The door swung open and Ivak Bastorran strode in.

'At last!' Devlor exclaimed. 'This is of the utmost urgency, Uncle.'

The Clan High Chief glanced at the mutilated corpse. He was untouched by the sight. 'What's going on?'

Devlor jabbed a thumb at the slab. 'This man was detained while trying to board a ship out of Bhealfa. His travel documents proved to be false, and he was found to be carrying a large amount of money.'

'This concerns us how?'

'Two ways. On close examination the documents turned out to be of a kind we know the rebels manufacture. More importantly, it was discovered that he worked as a clerk in the secret records office here in the city. Though we have to assume it's no longer a secret.'

That got his uncle's attention. 'Go on.'

'Considering the sensitivity of that position, we arranged to have the traitor brought here. As you can see, it was necessary to subject him to a thorough interrogation.'

While he spoke, two minions entered and took the body for disposal. The torturer threw a bucket of water over the slab.

'And the result of this questioning?' Ivak asked.

'He confessed supplying the rebels with certain sensitive information. We know what they're doing and how they're doing it. I told you they were up to something big!'

'It's to do with the records office?'

'Yes. Destruction or theft, the clerk didn't know. I think we can assume he was telling the truth on that score.'

'What was the nature of the information he passed to them?'

Devlor produced a folded square of parchment. 'This. It's

a map of the sewage and water system for central Valdarr, with particular emphasis on the records office.'

'Damn!'

'The prisoner didn't know when they were going to make use of this information, but what better time to strike than today?'

'Say no more. Take charge of this personally and draw on whatever forces you need.'

'I've a bad feeling about this, Uncle. We have to get there with all speed.'

'On Freedom Day, with the streets clogged? They've planned it well in that respect.'

'Then we'll just have to persuade the crowds to let us through. It's a question of national security, not to mention the clans' reputation. I won't tolerate delays.'

'Go then, and show the renegades no quarter.'

His nephew summoned an aide. The man snapped to attention.

'Saddle me a fast horse!' Devlor barked.

In a house not far from the phoney temple, and with a view of it, Kutch and the other four band-members sat and waited.

They had encountered no problems getting out of the tunnels, or the school. Mingling with the crowds, they'd made their separate ways to this safe house, to clean up and change their soiled clothes.

Now they fell to wondering how Serrah and Caldason were faring. They should have been here by now and there was no sign of them.

Kutch in particular was worried. He hadn't wanted to leave his friends. Not that he could have done much to help if things had gone wrong. But that didn't make him feel any less guilty. He couldn't help thinking about his late master and how he hadn't been there in his hour of need.

The others were kind to Kutch, and did their best to reassure him. He thought they were putting a brave face on it.

One of the men, standing at the window, interrupted the apprentice's reverie. 'Something seems to be happening down there.'

They all rushed over to join him.

A large force of paladins was arriving, their wagons ploughing through the crowds. Mounted clansmen bowled people aside. Their comrades on foot whipped celebrants out of the way. There were militiamen too, dealing with the revellers no less brutally. An ugly scene was brewing.

'Looks like we've been found out,' someone said.

'How did they know?' another wondered. 'The place hasn't started burning yet.'

'Maybe it won't if they're in time to stop it.'

They watched as paladins, accompanied by a knot of sorcerers, raced towards the fraudulent temple. Seconds later, the glamour camouflage disappeared, revealing the much plainer building beneath. Cries of astonishment went up from the turbulent crowd.

'Reeth and Serrah!' Kutch exclaimed. 'We have to warn them!'

'That's beyond our power now, son,' one of the men told him. 'We can only hope they got out too.'

The force of paladins didn't bother with niceties when it came to entering the records depository. They had sorcerers quickly cleanse the doors of prohibition spells, then they battered them down.

As they poured in, an officer barked orders. He dispatched wizards to negate booby-traps. Clansmen were sent to find trespassers, or to nullify any harm they'd planned.

They discovered the flammable oil that had been splashed

around the lower offices. A squad prepared to investigate the hole cut in the hallway's floor.

The officer led the biggest contingent up the staircase, with sorcerers moving ahead to kill the glamours. They came across the dead barbcat, skirted it and flowed onto the walkway. Men hurried down into the hall of records and began a frantic search.

It was apparent from the oil about the place that the intruders intended starting a fire. As no obvious means of ignition were evident, the officer wondered if they'd been disturbed before they could finish the job.

Then a subordinate approached and reported that a quantity of unusual objects had been found strewn about the place. He handed one over. The officer examined the tiny cylinder. He worried at the groove running round its middle. He shook it, held it to his ear, tried easing the two halves apart.

Finally he stared at it, puzzled, as it lay in the palm of his hand.

At which point the fuse went off.

The explosion instantly turned him into a blazing fireball. It did the same to everybody else within a ten-foot radius. The streaks and puddles of oil burst into flame. Fire raced to stacks of records and set them ablaze.

Fuses were exploding everywhere, showering fire and vitriol. Burning men shrieked and blundered, spreading the conflagration. Rows of files took light, the flames jumping from tier to tier. Choking clouds of oily black smoke filled the air.

Those who were able ran for the stairs. The fire had climbed before them and taken hold of the records stored around the walkway. Heat and smoke funnelled along the corridor where the barbcat lay, filling the main stairwell with haze and sparks.

A host of fires had broken out on the ground floor, too. The offices and the great clerks' chamber were infernos. In the hallway itself, the crew who were about to explore the breached tunnel had abandoned their post.

Fragments of burning wall tapestries spiralled in the updraught, smouldering furniture burst into flames. Fuses continued to go off with loud reports.

The survivors staggered to the massive front doors, gagging and retching, acrid smoke stinging their eyes.

They disgorged onto streets where the populace was rioting, outraged at their treatment at the hands of the authorities. With Resistance members helping to stir the pot, the city's firefighters had little chance of reaching the scene.

Devlor Bastorran had no idea any of this was happening.

He stood in the school basement, accompanied by an elite troop of bodyguards and a clan sorcerer. They had lanterns and glamour globes, and they were examining the excavation.

Devlor noticed the wizard pulling a face. 'What's the matter, smell too ripe for you?' he mocked. 'It'll smell a lot worse if the rebels are down there.'

'Yes, sir.'

'Have you got it?'

'I have, sir.'

'You've made sure we're protected?'

'Yes, sir. But, sir, I'm obliged to point out the dangers inherent in the course of action you're proposing. In a confined space particularly, it could –'

'Are you daring to defy me? Hold your tongue and just do as you're told! And hurry!'

The cowed sorcerer nodded. He began a faltering incantation. As he spoke, he removed a smoked-glass bottle from one of his robe's voluminous pockets.

When the incantation was done he carefully removed the

cork. Then he stepped to the edge of the hole and, holding the bottle at arm's length, tipped it, as though pouring something.

What came out was a white glutinous substance, like tree sap or gum in texture. It left the bottle slowly as a continuous globular strand. The leading end developed a protuberance not unlike a peeled onion. And on this bulge was a tiny pair of black eyes.

The strand grew longer, more elastic, and as it dribbled nearer to the hole it began to expand. In seconds it had filled out to match the size of a man, and the eyes were like saucers. But it had no mass.

It started to emit a sound unlike anything easily described. The nearest comparison was rasping breath, crossed perhaps with the noise an insect's carapace made when crushed by a boot.

When the last of it emerged from the bottle it didn't fall. It sank through the air as though it were water. Still expanding, it disappeared into the hole.

The tracker glamour had gone hunting.

29

Caldason and Serrah were less than halfway through the tunnel system when they heard a faint rumble.

'Was that the place going up?' Serrah wondered.

'I reckon so.'

A few minutes later the water around their ankles grew warmer. It ran with odd colours and tiny pieces of debris.

'Now all we have to do is get out of here,' Caldason said.

They trudged on through the humid sewers.

'Do you think Kutch and the others got out, too?' she asked.

'I don't see why they shouldn't have. And no, I don't suppose the barb ate them.'

She smiled as they splashed into one of the tunnel junctions.

A little further on, she said, 'Why are we taking these risks?'

'What do you mean?'

'I don't know about you, but I seem to have fallen in with the Resistance almost without realising it.'

'From what I know of you, you're not averse to risk.'

'*Controlled* risk; and I was doing something I believed in. Or thought I did.'

'You've changed sides. That must take some adjusting.'

'It was more that I left my side, rather than setting out to join the Resistance. And of course they rescued me in Merakasa. Not that I knew it at the time. I owe them something for that.'

'I never had a side. I'm with them for a reason.'

'This Clepsydra, the Source, whatever it is.'

He nodded.

'So I'm here by mistake and you're here because you want something. Isn't there more to it than that, Reeth?'

'We've had this conversation before.'

'Things change.'

'In a couple of days?'

'They can change in a minute, believe me. But what I meant was that the more I get to know the Resistance and understand their cause, the more I can see they've got something worth fighting for.'

'Maybe. But I'm not one for causes.'

'I'm not sure I believe that.'

They continued in silence for a moment.

'Did you ever have a family?' she asked.

There was such a long pause before he replied she thought he wasn't going to. Then he said, 'My people were killed in the clearances.'

'Yes. But since then. In all the years after.'

'No. You?'

'Yes.' Now it was her turn to keep him waiting. 'I don't really want to talk about it.'

'Why bring it up then?'

'Because I thought I could talk about it.'

He wasn't sure he fully understood that, so he held back from answering.

A minute later, she said, 'What's the worst thing about living so long?'

He gave a little snort of laughter. 'You're all questions today.'

'I like to understand people. I guess it's a hangover from having to lead them. Not that I've always done *that* well. But what is the worst thing?'

'You really want me to tell you?'

'Yes.'

'Memories. The weight of them. If that makes any sense.'

'I think it does. Though I'm not sure you need to live overly long to carry that kind of weight.'

She seemed in a strange mood, as though she might be slipping into some kind of melancholia. Perhaps it was her apprehension about being in confined places. He didn't press her, and they focused on the journey.

Another four or five minutes passed. Then they heard something.

It was a sound hard to describe, like a drawn-out howl or screech, although neither word did it justice. The echoing confines of the tunnels added to its eeriness. It was striking enough that they stopped to listen. A moment later it came again, and seemed nearer this time.

'What was *that*?' Serrah said.

'I'm not sure. But . . . That sound we heard earlier. Perhaps it had nothing to do with the fire.'

'That'd crossed my mind, too.'

It was as though neither of them wanted to voice what they suspected.

The sound repeated. It was longer, louder and spine-chilling.

'It's a tracker, isn't it, Reeth?'

'I think it might be. Ever heard one before?'

'Just once. That was enough. They say they suck the life out of people.'

'They do. I've seen it.'

'They're relentless, Reeth. They *never* give up. If they've
sent one after us –'

'I know.'

'What are we going to do?'

'Keep our heads for a start. Trackers are just glorified blood-
hounds, after all.'

'They're more than that and you know it. Gods, they make
that barb look like –' Her eye was caught. She stared over
his shoulder.

He turned to see what had distracted her.

At the end of an adjacent tunnel there was a bend, and
something was rounding it. Wispy white tendrils came first,
seeming to caress the corner. They dragged a greater bulk in
their wake. It was like a cloud, but one that constantly
changed shape and was more liquid than misty in appearance. Its interior had a kind of nimbus, reminiscent of a dim
lamp inside a tent, and there was a dark, palpitating inner
core.

A thick stalk jutted from the top of the sac. At its end was
an outgrowth that bore a pair of filmed eyes, similar to those
of a toad. The stalk moved from side to side. Searching.

Some people called trackers thinking fog. Caldason had
heard its shimmering appearance referred to as heavy light,
which seemed as good a description as any.

He grabbed Serrah's arm. 'Come on!'

They set off at speed. When they looked back the tracker
was still some way behind, but closing. Its abominable cry
came again.

Soon they were in sight of the narrow tunnel, the one
they had to crawl through.

Serrah surveyed it with unease. 'I have to tell you, Reeth;
the idea of going through that with a tracker after us . . .'

'It'll follow us wherever we go, you know that.'

'I'd rather it didn't catch us *in there*.'

'There might be another way. Not necessarily an easy one, but –'

'What are you talking about?'

'Trust me.' He hurried her towards a branch tunnel they hadn't been through before.

'Where are we going? What's happening?'

'I've got an idea.'

'Want to tell me what it is?'

'You're not going to like it.'

'I'll be the judge of –'

'Just a minute, I have to check something.'

He pulled her to the side, got out the map and studied it. 'Right, this way.'

They moved off and entered yet another jumble of tunnels.

The sound of the tracker was constant now, and its wail was mixed with a guttural snuffling.

'Do you have any notion what you're doing?' Serrah asked.

'Bear with me.' He consulted the map again. 'If this is right, there should be –'

'*Reeth,*' she whispered.

'What?'

'Behind . . . us.'

Slowly, he turned.

The tracker was coming towards them. It floated along just under the roof, its ribbon arms probing the tunnel walls as it moved. The black, glistening eyes were fixed on them.

'This way!' Caldason yelled.

They ran, spattering brackish water. The tracker increased its speed. Its body compressed and elongated, the better to move faster, the lengthy tendrils streaming behind like a comet's tail.

Reeth and Serrah sprinted the harder, arms pumping.

'Where are we going?' she said.

'We want that.' He pointed ahead to a door set in the tunnel's wall.

'Let's hope it isn't locked.'

They hit the door at the same time, and both of them grasped the handgrip. The door opened and they piled through.

The tracker had caught up; outlined by the doorframe it made a repulsive portrait. Its tendrils snaked towards the entrance, the eyed stalk bent to study its victims.

They slammed the door. There were bolts on their side, which they quickly shot. They gasped for breath.

'That won't stop it,' Serrah panted.

'No. But it's gained us a minute or two.' He brought out the map again.

The tracker began seeping through the edges of the door. White gloop dribbled in at the top, sides and bottom, and there was a distinct odour of brimstone.

'These areas shaded in red,' Caldason explained, tapping the map, 'they mark places that should be avoided.'

'Why's that?'

'They're dangerous. A lot of fumes accumulate down here. They get siphoned into these red sections.' He nodded along the new tunnel. 'And there's an entrance to one just over there.'

Serrah was about to say something, but he'd set off. She caught up. 'How does this help us? Trackers don't breathe, if you were thinking of poisoning it in some way.'

'I had something else in mind.'

Bar a few particles, the tracker was almost entirely through the door. It was beginning to re-form.

They arrived at a trapdoor. It didn't seem to be locked.

Reeth crouched next to it. 'Under here there's a stretch of tunnel a couple of hundred paces long. According to the map, there's another trapdoor at the far end.'

'But how does it help us?' she repeated, misgiving creeping into her voice.

'How long can you hold your breath?'

'*What?*'

He glanced back at the tracker. It had nearly reconstituted itself. 'We've no time, so listen. The gas down there comes from waste; it's highly inflammable. If we can get out the other end while the tracker's still behind us, then ignite the gas –'

'Are you *crazy*?'

'There's only one outcome if we stay here.'

'Do you know if we can go through it without choking to death?'

'No.'

'Or getting blinded by the stuff?'

'Not really.'

'Or whether the trapdoor at the other end isn't locked?'

'No idea.'

'Or if the tunnel's big enough for us?'

'No.'

She took a deep breath. 'Let's do it.'

He ripped a piece off the front of his shirt and tore it in two. Then he dunked the scraps in the not entirely filthy water trickling past. He handed one to Serrah. 'Keep it over your face, it should block some of the gas.'

'Ugh.'

'Let's go.' He reached for the rung on the trapdoor.

'Wait! How we are going to set off the gas?'

Reeth dug his hand into a pocket. He brought out one of the fuses they'd used earlier.

'I thought they needed twenty minutes.'

'I've already started it.'

'When?'

'When we first heard the tracker. I figured it could be useful. I knew I could always get rid of it.'

'Reeth, how long ago did we first hear the tracker?'

'I haven't really been keeping track.'

'Oh, *great.*'

'There's a more pressing reason not to dawdle. Look.'

The tracker had reconstructed itself and was racing their way.

'Gods, Reeth, I hate you for this.'

'Brace yourself.'

He grasped the trapdoor's ring. They both took deep breaths, then clamped the sodden cloths to their mouths and noses.

The trap was stiff and heavy, and took an effort to lift. Once it did, a cloud of foul-smelling, obnoxious gases billowed out. Hardly able to see, their eyes already watering, Reeth and Serrah quickly clambered down. The trapdoor thudded shut above them.

It was all they could do to make out their hands in front of their faces, even with the light from their glamour medallions. The space in the tunnel was very restricted and they had to go on hands and knees to enter it.

Overhead, the tracker arrived at the trapdoor and immediately set to investigating it with strands of milky ectoplasm. The trap was a tight fit, the cracks around its edge almost impossible to see. That was no bar to the tracker; it sought out the tiniest of clefts and started to infiltrate.

Reeth and Serrah were making slow progress. The fumes were so dense they felt like they were moving through an abrasive fluid. If there had been more than one way to go they would already be lost. Their skin was growing itchy and tender.

Not far to their rear, the tracker was oozing into the tunnel. It penetrated faster than it had with the earlier door, despite the smaller gaps. Trackers learned from experience and adapted accordingly. The spell that bound them was predicated on maximising their efficiency as hunter-killers.

Serrah's lungs were bursting. She could barely see Reeth, crawling along ahead of her. Her mind was on how she was going to die. Most likely the tracker would catch them in this horribly confined tunnel. Or they'd find the other trap-door sealed and be asphyxiated by the gas. She wasn't opposed to the idea of death, but had definite preferences about the method. Given the present options, she'd prefer the fuse to go off. She wondered, fleetingly, if that would be enough to kill Reeth.

The tracker proclaimed its triumph over the trapdoor by letting out one of its dreadful wails. Untroubled by the gas, unhindered by poor visibility, it resumed its pursuit.

They couldn't fail to hear the tracker's caterwauling; it reverberated around them like a stone in a shaken metal bucket. Serrah could just about turn her head enough to look back along the tunnel. She didn't expect to see anything. Yet for all its abundance, the haze couldn't quite obscure the glow of the thing tracking them.

Reeth was moving more rapidly, and she forced herself to match his pace. Her shins and palms were painfully sore. The cramped space made her want to scream.

The sound of the tracker was so ear-splitting she was sure it was at her heels. She considered the possibility of cheating it by cutting her throat.

Reeth stopped, and she almost collided with him. Then he was standing, which meant they must have reached the tunnel's end. Serrah prayed they'd get out. There was no way she could hold her breath any longer.

Suddenly, Reeth was up and stretching a hand to her. She hauled herself, feet kicking, and came through the trap-door. He dragged her free. Serrah gulped for air, her eyes streaming.

Down below, bleached tracker flesh came into view, its feelers climbing to the opening. Reeth had the fuse. He flung it along the tunnel at the advancing tracker. Then he slammed the trap and both of them fell across it.

She thought the impact might have set off the fuse. But nothing happened. They lay there, breathing hard.

The tracker attached itself to the underside of the trapdoor and began burrowing. It toiled patiently, inflexible determination as much a part of its nature as bloodlust.

An intense flash of light illuminated the tunnel. A blink later it was filled with fire, burning with the vigour of a furnace. The tracker was blown to atoms, devoured, pulverised by blast and heat.

The force of the explosion lifted the trapdoor, even with Serrah and Reeth draped over it. There was a rank odour in the air.

They lay still for a while.

When they finally climbed to their feet, Serrah said, 'Get me to where I can see the sky, for pity's sake.'

Devlor Bastorran and his group were gone from the schoolhouse cellar before the explosion.

A breathless messenger had arrived. 'Sir! The records depository's in flames! There's unrest on the streets. The High Chief wants you to oversee pacifying the mob.'

'Those Resistance bastards. Damn their eyes! All right, all of you, out!'

Timidly, the sorcerer asked, 'What about the tracker, sir?'

'If any rebels were still down there it would have got them, wouldn't it? We were just too late this time. There's no point wasting ourselves here.'

And so they left.

But they hadn't gone very far when Reeth's head poked out of the pit. The coast clear, he and Serrah climbed up.

'You have no idea how good it feels to be out of that cesspool,' she said, stretching her arms.

'I didn't exactly relish it myself. But we're not home yet. If that tracker was deliberately set on us, if it wasn't a defence glamour we tripped, then they knew we were using the tunnels.'

'Why no guards here then?'

'Maybe they were relying on the tracker doing its job.'

'That's reasonable, considering they always do.' She added, 'That was a smart move, Reeth, even if it did age me a decade.'

'You might not have finished ageing. We've still got to get out of here and to a safe house.'

'Reeth, what if the tracker was in the tunnels when Kutch and the others came through?'

'That thought had occurred to me. But when trackers finish with their victims they leave them as husks. We didn't see anything like that down there.'

'Doesn't mean to say –'

'No. But there's nothing we can do about it now. We have to concentrate on getting ourselves out.'

'Right. And once we're on the street we should separate.'

'Agreed. Ready?'

They crept from the cellar. There was nobody on the stairs or in the corridors they walked. But it was a different matter when they reached the open door to the street and peeked outside.

The street itself, a wide avenue, was streaming with Freedom Day celebrants. Their mood had a sour edge, fed by ripples from the trouble several blocks away. They were still bent on enjoying themselves, though their revelry was likely to take a form the state hadn't intended. Militiamen were trying to shepherd them.

Of more concern to Reeth and Serrah was the cluster of

paladins at the foot of the schoolhouse steps. One of them was a commander, high-ranking.

'What now?' Caldason wondered.

'Look along the street. See those horses, by the wagon? There's only the wagon driver guarding them.'

'It's not a good day to ride.'

'They'll get us a few blocks, then we can lose ourselves in the crowd.'

'What about them?' He nodded at the paladins.

'Simplest is best.'

'Let's get going.'

They sprinted down the stone steps and bowled into the group of red jackets, scattering them. Then they ran for the horses. The paladins dashed after them, and others began running in to intercept.

Serrah made it to the horses first. The wagon driver leapt from his seat to challenge them, sword drawn. Still moving, she deftly tossed one of her knives. It struck the man's shoulder, spinning him aside and out of their path. She grabbed a horse's reins, put boot to stirrup and swung into the saddle.

'Hurry!' she called.

Reeth was a few paces behind. 'Go on! I'll catch up!'

She hesitated for a second, then spurred her mount and galloped into the flow of revellers. Several paladin horsemen went after her. It was additional entertainment for the crowd, and a cry went up.

As Reeth clambered onto a horse a pursuing militiaman loosed his bow. The arrow skimmed the animal's head. Unhurt but spooked, it reared, dumping Reeth in the back of the open wagon. He fell awkwardly, bruising his ribs and winding himself. As he rose, somebody vaulted in beside him.

It was the paladin commander, a sword in his hand. Reeth

wiftly drew his own weapon and met the attack. In the
melee a wide stroke from the paladin cuffed the wagon's
rake handle. The team of four horses, unsettled by all the
noise, were already champing. There was a lurch and the
wagon swayed.

Then, to a roar from the crowd, the horses bolted.

30

The panicked, driverless team of horses broke into a full gallop. Revellers, paladins and militia scattered in their path.

In the back of the wagon, Caldason and Devlor Bastorran fought furiously.

Caldason had no idea who his opponent was, but he quickly discovered that he faced a swordsman of rare ability. Even in the hostile environment of a runaway wagon the paladin fenced with exquisite skill and remarkable agility. He displayed a streak of recklessness, too, which Reeth suspected was inherent in the man's style. Good fighters were often prey to over-confidence, and sometimes it could be turned against them.

But that assumed the careering wagon didn't come to grief first, a prospect that grew more likely by the minute.

It went over a pothole, its wheels briefly leaving the ground. Both men held on with their free hands. The wagon came down with a bone-jarring crash and they immediately resumed their duel.

The paladin unleashed a series of blows that took all of Reeth's dexterity to counter. He repaid with a succession of blistering strokes that would have downed a lesser foe. The frenzy of their combat stepped up a notch.

A mounted paladin appeared beside them. He matched pace with the charging team and stretched a hand to the bridle of a leading horse, hoping to halt the stampede.

The speed, the uncertain way ahead and the irascible team all conspired against him. He over-reached and lost control of his own steed. Bucking with fright, the animal tossed him from the saddle. The paladin spiralled past, his cry swallowed by distance. His horse bolted and ran off into the heaving throng.

Unstoppable, the wagon's team plunged headlong into the even more crowded heart of the city. The masses of people and the cacophony of sounds added to their alarm.

A thick column of smoke rose from the city centre, marking the spot where the records office burned.

Reeth and the paladin battled on. As far as swordplay went, it was a contest of equals. Each doled out ever more complex combinations of thrusts and parries. Neither could broach the other's guard. Their swinging and hacking grew wilder.

Pedestrians dashed screaming as the lawless wagon ploughed on. Exotic, abnormal or plain ordinary glamours with no sense of self-preservation were slower to move, and the team rode through them, converting their forms to shimmering dust or golden implosions. The more expensive models re-formed themselves afterwards.

Bastorran didn't know who he was fighting. But as the man was obviously a Qalochian, and given his facility with a blade, he could guess. The probability that it was Caldason spurred him to greater effort, and to hell with special orders concerning the man.

The world went by in a blur, its noise one continuous clamour.

Up ahead, a marching band was crossing from one side of the street to the other. At the sight of the runaway horses they fled, many dropping their instruments. The wagon thundered through the diving bandsmen, crushing lutes and pipes under its wheels, sending drums rolling in all directions. Open-mouthed fist-wavers saw off the renegade. Yells and curses were aimed at its disappearing tailboard.

The duellists' swords continued to flash, despite the bumps in the road that threatened to dislodge them. They knew nothing but conflict. It was the centre of their universe, no matter how turbulent the surroundings or desperate their plight. They fought on, steel hammering steel, sweat beading their brows.

The wagon team, mouths foaming, rumbled across a small park. Walkers jumped for their lives, picnics were ground to mush, clods of earth flew left and right.

Then the wagon entered a narrow lane, bouncing and rattling over the cobbles. Mothers snatched children to safety, people flattened themselves against the walls. Here there were flagpoles sticking out of upper windows. Reeth and Bastorran's duel was punctuated with ducking, lest they be struck. Hanging ensigns slapped their heads.

The wagon hurtled into a broad avenue and met a parade containing horse-drawn floats bearing larger-than-life caricatures of imperial and Bhealfan notables. One of the floats, transporting an enormous wood and papier-mâché representation of Prince Melyobar's head, half blocked the wagon's path.

Swerving by instinct, the team almost missed it. But clipping the float's corner was enough. The nation's foremost head slipped its moorings and thudded to the road, then it trundled towards the onlookers and downed a swathe of the crowd like tenpins.

Still the wagon travelled on, a posse of mounted paladins and law enforcers in its wake. In the back, its passengers continued their affray unabated.

They shot along the avenue, cutting a trail through
revellers, causing rigs and carriages to collide. Brave, foolish
or drunk people occasionally ran out in front of the wagon
and tried to stop it by waving their arms. At the far end of
the avenue stood Bhealfa's Royal Mint. The road turned at
an acute angle to avoid it. Whether the wagon would do the
same was debatable.

Even Reeth and Devlor Bastorran took note of the hazard.
Their slashing and swiping continued unabated, but was
seasoned with glances ahead.

The maddened team raced on unswervingly. The sober
edifice of the Mint loomed larger.

At the very last moment they turned. But too fast and too
sharply. One side of the wagon lifted off the ground, causing
the combatants to clutch at handholds. It moved along on two
wheels for a second, then flipped and smashed into the road.
Caldason and Bastorran half jumped, were half thrown clear.

The horses broke loose and kept going, trailing tackle that
jangled.

Reeth hit the road and rolled. Dazed and bleeding, he got
to his feet. The paladin lay nearer the wrecked wagon. He
wasn't moving.

A small army of mounted pursuers was almost at the scene.
Reeth limped to the crowd and melted into it.

Friendly hands found him and spirited him away.

Serrah had no such trouble.

She was chased for several blocks, but had little difficulty
losing her pursuers. At the first opportunity she left the horse
tied to a hitching rail and blended in with the crowd. Then
she spent some time waiting for Caldason to arrive. She didn't
know he'd been taken in the opposite direction.

Finally she gave up and decided to make her way to Karr's
house in the hope that Reeth might be there. It was a long

way to her destination, and the packed streets didn't make the journey any easier.

Serrah had been in Bhealfa only a short while and knew hardly anyone. So the odds against her meeting one of the few people she did know, especially in such dense crowds, must have been astronomical.

But as she was making her way along a crammed street someone lightly touched her shoulder. Hand to sword, she spun round, expecting denunciation, exposure, arrest.

Instead she found herself facing Tanalvah.

'What are *you* doing here?' she blurted.

Tanalvah smiled. 'I might ask you the same.' She leaned closer and whispered, 'Is everything all right?'

'Yes. Though I seem to have lost Reeth somewhere in this mob.'

'He can look after himself.' She looked Serrah up and down. 'If you don't mind me saying, you seem rather hot and bothered.'

'I've just come from a hot and bothersome place.'

'I understand. It might be an idea to clean up a bit before going further. And getting off the streets sooner rather than later could be a good plan.'

'What do you suggest?'

'I was about to go in there.' She nodded at a temple. It was an impressive pile dedicated to the hierarchy of gods, not any one in particular.

'You could freshen yourself inside. Kinsel's going to pick me up later in a carriage, though goodness knows when in this crush. We can take you back.'

Serrah looked at the temple. 'All right.' She didn't really know Tanalvah, but somehow she was glad she'd run into her.

They weaved across the crowded sidewalk and went through the portal.

Serrah hadn't set foot in a temple for years. Not since before she lost Eithne.

Beyond the gates there was a courtyard, the temple itself standing a little further on. The place was busy. Public holidays tended to bring out the spiritual side in many people.

There were several fountains in the courtyard. Armed with a dainty handkerchief supplied by Tanalvah, Serrah washed her hands and face. She wasn't the only one doing it and nobody paid much attention.

Tanalvah watched her in silence, then said, 'Do you believe in meaningful coincidences?'

'I don't know. I've never really thought about it.'

'I do. I think there are times when the gods place something we need in our path. We just have to recognise it. That's how I see Kinsel and me coming together, for instance.'

'What's your point?'

'Meeting you outside this place, amongst all these people, in a city the size of Valdarr; that's stretching coincidence quite a way, don't you think?'

'Life's full of chance meetings and random events.'

'If you choose to look at them that way, yes. But if you see them as signs, opportunities –'

'You think that us bumping into each other was some kind of sign?'

'You must tell me to shut up if I intrude too much. But ever since I first saw you I've felt that you carry a great sadness. I thought that even before I knew anything about you. Now that I know a little of your past, I think I can guess what your burden might be.'

Normally, Serrah would have deflected Tanalvah's concern, but at this moment her words seemed to reach her. That in itself was a wonder to Serrah. She had been thinking about Eithne a lot, the last few days in particular. Her daughter had invaded most of her waking thoughts, and visited in dreams.

'Come in with me,' Tanalvah offered, indicating the temple.

'No, I don't think –'

'I've found that it helps. Let it out to the gods if you can't do it any other way. If nothing else it might give you a moment of calm.'

For some reason, perhaps because Tanalvah had caught her at a susceptible moment, Serrah heard herself saying, 'All right.'

They moved into the temple proper. It was large, with its great hall divided into sections, each devoted to a different god or goddess. They all had their own altar, some elaborate, some plain, with a glamour representation of the deity on a raised dais. The air was cloudy with incense.

'I follow Iparrater,' Tanalvah explained. 'I've found her a comfort. Do you have a favourite?'

Serrah shook her head.

'My goddess welcomes all who are uncertain or feel lost. You could do worse than unburden yourself to her.'

Serrah shrugged. She reckoned one deity as good as any other, as far as any of them had any worth at all. Instantly she regretted the irreverent thought in such a holy place. That reaction surprised her, too. It was like a throwback to her childhood and the way she was brought up.

Tanalvah made her devotions to Iparrater and knelt to pray.

Serrah felt awkward and simply stood there, staring at the hooded likeness of the goddess.

When Tanalvah finished she rose and went to the little stone oracle at one side of the chapel. She put a coin into the collecting dish and inserted her hand in the augur slot. Unlike the oracle she was used to in Jecellam, this one issued its prophecies on small gold-edged cards. When hers popped out of another slot she read it carefully then slipped it into a pocket.

She realised Serrah was watching her. 'Why not ask for guidance?'

'No coins.'

'Here.' Smiling, she handed her one. 'It helps to have a question in your mind while you're doing it.'

'Thanks.'

'You go ahead. I'll be here when you want me.'

Serrah felt gauche again. She didn't really know why she was doing this. Nevertheless she dropped her coin into the dish. But she had no idea what question to ask. So she closed her eyes, hoping something would come. It did, immediately. Her question was *Will I ever be free of my despair?* She put her hand in the slot.

When her card came out, the answer was short and to the point. She stared at it for a long time.

Tanalvah rejoined her, and seeing her expression said, 'I don't know what you asked, but sometimes the answers aren't what they seem. My own question concerning Kinsel got a rather unclear answer. Often it takes a while to make sense.'

'Yes,' Serrah replied quietly, putting away the card.

She said nothing after that, except to give monosyllabic responses when Tanalvah tried talking to her. It was the same when Kinsel arrived, and all the way back to Karr's house she remained wrapped up in herself, scarcely uttering a word.

Reeth got to Karr's hideaway some time after Serrah. He was told that she'd gone to her room and didn't want to be disturbed.

But he was glad to see that Kutch was there, and well.

Karr joined them, and Caldason recounted what had taken place in the records depository.

'They could only have known about the raid if they had inside information,' the patrician concluded. 'We know there are informants in our ranks, but this points to a source high up. We're going to have to look into this, and without delay.'

'But it doesn't explain my missing file, does it?' Caldason said. 'I mean, if they knew we were going to get into the records office –'

'They wouldn't simply have destroyed your file. They would have been waiting for you inside.'

'Exactly.'

Karr frowned. 'I don't know, Reeth, this goes deeper than I can figure out.'

'Did you tell Reeth about Devlor Bastorran?' Kutch wanted to know.

'What's that?' Caldason asked.

'The paladin you fought in the back of the wagon,' Karr said. 'It was the younger Bastorran, no less, heir apparent to the clans leadership.'

'I'm flattered. He was a damn good fighter, I'll give him that.'

'He'll be an even more implacable enemy now, believe me. Apparently he took a harder tumble than you did, but he'll be mended before long. That's when you'll really need to watch your back.' His expression lightened. 'Anyway, I think we can judge the mission a success. And your contribution was particularly valuable, Kutch.'

'Thank you, sir.'

'If you'll excuse me, I've things to do,' Karr told them. 'Join us up on the roof later and we'll toast the day's successes.' He paused at the door. 'I have a piece of news for everyone, so be sure to come.'

When he'd left, Reeth said, 'He's right, Kutch; you did well. I'm proud of you.'

'Thanks, Reeth.'

'Why the frown? You should be pleased.'

'I am. It's just . . . there's something I want to tell you about. Well, ask your advice about, really. I've wanted to talk to you for several days. This is the first time I've seen you alone or when you've not been preoccupied by other things.'

'You've got my attention now. What is it?'

'It's to do with spotting, sort of.'

'You know what I feel about magic, and I'm certainly no expert. Maybe you should talk to Phoenix.'

'I will. Though I admit I've been putting it off. I'm worried that he'll stop my training, you see.'

'All right. Whatever it is, get it off your chest.'

'It's hard to explain. But, a couple of times now when I've been practising the spotting, I've . . . seen something.'

'That's what it's supposed to be about, isn't it?'

'No, I don't mean I saw through the magic. It was more like seeing *beyond* that. Catching glimpses of . . . somewhere else.'

Caldason's interest was whetted. 'Tell me about it. As much as you can remember.'

Kutch did.

He had never seen Caldason rattled before. But that was how he seemed now.

'What is it, Reeth?' he begged. 'What's the matter? Was it something I said?'

'It was everything you said.'

'I don't understand.'

'What you've just told me is something I'm very familiar with.' He stared hard into the boy's eyes. 'Kutch, you're seeing my dreams.'

'*What?*'

A scream sounded, somewhere in the house. They leapt

to their feet and made for the door. When Caldason pulled it open, Tanalvah was there. She was in a state of distress.

'Quick!' she pleaded. 'It's Serrah! In her room. She . . .'

Reeth elbowed past her, Kutch at his heels. They dashed the length of the corridor, turned a corner and came to the open door.

Serrah was hanging. The thick rope about her neck was secured to a ceiling beam. There was an overturned chair.

'Her legs!' Reeth yelled. 'Hold them up, take her weight!'

Kutch did as he was told. Caldason quickly righted the chair, jumped onto it and slashed through the rope with his knife. Serrah's body fell, and Kutch struggled until Reeth joined him and took the strain. They laid her on the bed.

'Serrah!' Reeth called, slapping her face. *'Serrah!'*

Other people came into the room. They heard Tanalvah crying. 'I was only trying to help,' she moaned, and Kinsel was comforting her and saying, 'You mustn't blame yourself.'

Reeth was shaking Serrah now as well as slapping her cheeks, and he kept calling her name.

Her eyelids fluttered. She took a rasping breath.

When she opened her eyes and saw Reeth, she whispered, 'Bastard.'

Kutch noticed a little gold-edged card on the floor. It had writing on it. He bent and picked it up.

The card read, *Not in this life*.

That evening they gathered on the flat roof as they said they would, but it was a much more solemn occasion than anyone had expected.

Valdarr was marking Freedom Day with pyro-glamours. The sky hosted starbursts, soaring golden streaks and hovering, multicoloured wheels that gave off enormous silver sparks.

Down below, the records office was still burning, and the fire had taken hold of several adjacent buildings.

'I had hoped this would be a moment to celebrate,' Karr told them. 'And we shouldn't lose sight of the fact that it is, whatever our own concerns and miseries.' He glanced over at Serrah. She sat by herself, staring out at the city. 'We struck a blow today. It might seem like only a gnat's bite on the thick hide of our oppressors, but it was a victory nevertheless.' His gaze moved from Serrah to take in Reeth and Kutch, Tanalvah and Kinsel. 'I have news for you.' He paused for effect, ever the theatrical politician. 'Our search is over. We've finally found the perfect location for the new state. We're taking the first step in a long journey. It's not going to be easy. Nor will it be without heartache. But I hope and pray it will lead to a healing.'

There was no great outburst of emotion at his words, no applause or congratulations. Just a quiet acceptance.

Kinsel and Tanalvah sought solace in each other's eyes. Kutch dwelt on visions of another place. Serrah silently confronted her own demons.

And Reeth Caldason looked to the North.

If you enjoyed reading
The Covenant Rising,
then read the following selection from

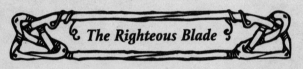

The Righteous Blade

available in trade paperback
from Eos in January 2006

There had been no reprieve for reality. It remained in abeyance.

The night-time city was smothered by a dense fog that choked sound but only dimmed the constant discharge of magic. The gleam of sorcery pulsed and sparkled. Phantasms were on the wing, apparitions walked abroad.

A young man shuffled through the damp streets. He was bundled against the autumnal chill, collar up, battered cap pulled well down, a few unruly wisps of blond hair poking from underneath the brim.

He couldn't see. His eyes were covered by a contrivance resembling a leather mask, with two round patches, tied fast. Behind each patch was a coin, wrapped in wadding.

In one hand he held a cane, and used it to tap his uncertain way. In the other he grasped a leash, tightly coiled. This was attached to a halter girdling the shiny black carapace of a millipede—a creature the size of a large hunting dog. It moved sinuously, huge insectoid eyes set in an unblinking gaze, its multitude of twiggy legs rippling in unison.

The youth was anxious. He reckoned he was in a less than salubrious quarter, and he'd lost track of the time. Rapping his stick left to right, he walked falteringly, as though newly sightless. The millipede strained at its leash, probing, snuffling, guiding its charge around obstructions. The young man tried to hurry.

Had he been able to see, he would have regarded the blizzard of magic on every side as of little account. It was too ordinary. But another sight might have given him pause. Ahead of him, a pair of lights bobbed in the murk, and they were getting closer.

He was aware of a sound. Tugging the millipede to a halt, he stopped and listened, head tilted to one side, his eye patches like dark hollows. He heard the steady crump of boots on cobblestones. A small group, marching in unison. Coming his way.

His sense of unease increased and he thought of hiding. Lifting a hand to his mask, he made to peel it off.

'You, there! Don't move!'

The rasp of blades being drawn underlined the warning.

Breath stilled, the youth froze. The millipede scuttled back to him, brushing his calves as a frightened cat might do, for solace.

From out of the swirling, yellowish mist came a band of men. Foremost was a three-strong watch patrol in grey uniforms. Beside them, his scarlet tunic contrasting with their drabness, strode a paladin clansman. The patrol's requisite sorcerer brought up the rear, dressed in tan robes and bearing an ornamented staff. Two of the watch held charmed lanterns, bathing the scene in a soft, magical glow.

'Drop the weapon!'

He realised they meant the cane, and let it slip from his fingers. The clatter it made was all the louder in the taut silence.

They approached him warily.

'Don't you know there's a curfew?'

The speaker was the watch captain, grizzle-faced and lanky. Despite the cold, his arms were bare. One was tattooed with a rampant, fire-spitting dragon, emblem of Gath Tampoor, the prevailing empire.

Still masked, the youth said nothing.

'Lost your tongue too, have you?'

'I'm sorry, I . . .'

'You're breaking the curfew,' the paladin barked. 'Why?'

The young man swung towards the new voice, swallowing hard. 'I . . . misjudged the hour. I thought—'

'That's no excuse,' the watchman snapped.

'Any more than being blind,' somebody added gruffly.

'But I'm—'

'Ignorance is no defence,' the paladin recited. 'The law's the law.'

Someone elbowed his ribs, making him wince. 'What're you doing here?'

'Where're you from?' asked another, breathing the fetid odour of cheap pipe tobacco.

'Who brought you?' rasped a third, his mouth unnervingly close to the youth's ear.

He reeled under the barrage of questions. Floundering, he tried to answer, tried to placate them. But they were as bent on harassment as interrogation.

The captain eyed the millipede. 'Where did you get a glamour this expensive?'

'It was a gift,' the young man lied.

'And who would *you* know with that kind of wealth?'

He didn't reply.

'Can you prove ownership?' the clansman pressed.

'As I said, it was—'

'Then we have the right.'

The clansman nodded at the sorcerer. Gravely, he produced a long-bladed silver knife, embellished and fortified with spells, and offered it hilt first. The watch captain took it.

'If you can't prove,' the watchman said, 'you can't keep.'

'Please, don't . . .' the youth implored.

The millipede looked up with doleful eyes.

Stooping, the captain raised the knife, then plunged it into the creature's back.

A myriad cracks appeared on the insect's husk. It bled light. Thin needles at first, piercing the gloom in all directions. A second later, shafts; intense as summer sun and just as dazzling. The millipede turned translucent, no more than a hollow outline, before melting into a silvery haze which flickered briefly, and went out.

The glamour died.

A little inrush of air filled the vacuum it left, and the leash the young man clutched hung slack, its collar vacant.

His persecutors mocked him with laugher.

'There was no need,' he protested weakly.

'You can't account for yourself and you're in violation of the curfew,' the paladin told him. 'We're taking you in.'

'C'mon.' The watch captain laid a rough hand on the youth.

'I won't!' the young man blurted, trying to shake himself loose.

'You *what*?'

'I mean . . . it was just a mistake. I didn't know I'd broken the law and—'

The watchman cuffed him, hard. It was enough to make the youth stagger.

'You speak when you're spoken to.'

A red welt coloured the youth's cheek, a trickle of blood snaked from the corner of his mouth. He braced himself for another blow.

'And you address us with the respect we're due,' the watchman added, raising his fist again.

'Take your filthy hands off him.'

A figure emerged from the fog. He was tall and dark. His flowing cloak made him look like some kind of giant winged beast.

The watchman swung to face him. 'Who the hell are *you*?'

Forgetting their captive, they all turned their attention to the newcomer.

'Stand aside,' he said. His tone was even. Calm.

'Who in damnation do you think you're giving orders to?' the paladin thundered.

'I said stand aside.'

'Who are you,' the watchman repeated, 'to be out in curfew and obstructing the watch?' Stupefaction tinged his building rage, unaccustomed as he was to having his authority defied.

'The boy's coming with me.'

'Is that so? Well, *we're* in charge here.' He sliced air with the sorcerer's knife to stress his words. 'If he's going anywhere, it's with us. And you with him.'

The stranger came closer. His movements were unhurried, almost leisurely. But now that he stood in the lantern's glow they saw that there was something disturbing about his eyes.

'No we're not,' he said.

The watch captain glared at him. He took in the man's brooding features. The somewhat angular structure of his face, the slight ruddiness of complexion, his long raven hair.

'Should have known,' the captain sneered, turning his head to spit contemptuously. 'We've got ourselves a real lowlife here, lads.'

His comrades laughed again, united in bigotry, if a little uneasily this time. The paladin stayed silent, and so did the sorcerer. Bewildered, the youth's head swung from side to side, trying to make out what was going on.

'Reckons he can insult his betters,' the watchman grandstanded. 'We'll show him the price of that.'

The stranger moved forward. He only stopped when the tip of the watchman's raised knife touched his chest. It didn't seem to bother him.

They locked gazes. The stranger didn't blink, or move a muscle. The captain's knuckles were white.

A flock of oversized butterflies fluttered past. They were

garishly coloured and appeared to be made of hammered tin. A faint squeaking emitted from their beating wings. Nobody paid them any mind.

'We can settle this peacefully,' the stranger said. 'Give me the boy and I'll let you go.'

'Let *us*—?' The captain seethed. He applied more pressure to the knife. 'It'll be a cold day in hell when we bow to your sort.'

'I can arrange for you to check the temperature personally,' the stranger offered, and smiled. There was nothing comforting about it.

Perhaps there was a glimmer of realisation in the captain's features, a suspicion of what he might be facing. The shadow of a doubt darkened his face. He half whispered, 'Who *are* you?'

'A man who doesn't like being on the business end of a blade.'

There was a blur of motion, an action so quick and fluid the others couldn't follow it.

Now the stranger had the knife. He held it by the blade, hilt up. Dazed, empty-handed, the captain gaped at him.

'I think this belongs to you,' the stranger said, and just as swiftly lobbed it. But his target wasn't the watch captain.

The knife winged to the sorcerer. It punctured his chest, driving deep. Whiskered mouth in an O of surprise, the wizard gawked, bewildered, at the blade quivering in his breast. He went down in a swirl of robes.

What had been a glacial scene instantly thawed.

Everyone bar the stranger seemed to be shouting. There was a confusion of movement. Weapons were deployed, lanterns discarded.

'What is it?' the youth pleaded, twisting in the chaos. 'What's happening?'

The stranger shoved him aside. The youth tottered, and fell.

From beneath his billowing cloak the stranger quickly drew a pair of swords. Then the patrol moved in to engage him.

On hands and knees, head low, the young man scurried away from the sound of ringing steel. Bumping into a wall, he huddled with his back against its coarse surface, making himself small.

A watchman circled the stranger to seize him from behind. He met the smartly delivered backward thrust of a granite-hard elbow. There was the audible crack of a breaking nose. Palms to face, the watchman reeled clear. The stranger resumed fencing with barely a pause.

He faced the captain and the third patrolman. His most dangerous opponent by far, the paladin, knelt beside the sorcerer. He was feeling the wizard's neck for a pulse, but his eyes were on the fight.

Anger rode the captain. It made him unruly. He fought with wild swings and a reckless stance. His companion was more sober. He came in with measured passes and well-aimed strokes. The stranger met both with equal vigour, his twin blades flashing smoothly from one to the other.

The alley was lit by an eerie gleam from the cast-off lanterns. It threw enormous shadows of the duellists onto the wall behind the cowering youth. The shades of frenzied giants, performing an eccentric ballet. Until one of them stopped.

An expression of consternation was etched on the captain's face. A blade jutted from his chest. The stranger tugged it free in a gush of crimson. Knees buckling, the captain dropped.

His cohort, momentarily stunned, battled on with renewed ferocity. The man with the broken nose, bloodied and ashen, recovered enough to join in. They tried to overcome their opponent with sheer force but he held them off with ease, dodging swipes, side-stepping thrusts with sure dexterity. Nothing they did slowed his attack. Then he took an opening.

The young man, cringing at the wall, had his hands covering his bowed head, fingers splayed. Half a dozen paces to his left was a sealed window. A grey-uniformed body hurtled into it, crashing through the wooden shutters. It came to rest half in, half out, legs dangling. The youth whimpered.

With Broken Nose out of the picture, the stranger turned to the remaining watchman and fell on him like a ravening wolf.

A slash of glistening arterial blood sprayed across the brickwork above the youth. Flecks splashed him, warm drops spattered his head, hands and shoulders. He quailed.

The stranger had no further interest in the downed watchman. His attention was on the paladin, still kneeling by the wizard. They stared at each other. The paladin was young, robust; his turn-out immaculate, with hair and beard neatly trimmed, in common with his kind. He slowly rose. With measured tread he advanced, drawing his sword as he came. For his part the stranger re-sheathed the flatter of his blades, leaving him with a rapier.

The paladin asked, 'Why do that?'

'So we can meet equally.'

'Gallantry from a savage?' he scoffed. 'Only a fool throws away an advantage.'

They'd begun to circle each other slowly.

'We'll see,' the stranger replied.

They moved simultaneously, and fast. Their blades met, pealing, and for a moment locked. Disengaging, both men pulled back and commenced their duel in earnest. Exchanging stinging passes, hacking and chopping, they set up a rhythmic beat of pounding steel. The paladin was a skilful fighter, and disciplined, but no match for his opponent.

The end came when the stranger parried a stroke and deflected his foe's blade. The follow-through ruptured a lung and brought the paladin down.

Rivulets of blood fed the lane's rain gully, colouring the sluggish flow.

The stranger looked around and saw the youth huddled at the wall. Ramming his sword into its scabbard, he swept to him, cloak flapping.

'Get up,' he said.

The young man didn't move, aside from trembling.

'On your feet!'

Still the youth didn't stir. The stranger took him by the scruff and roughly hoisted him.

'Now take that thing off.'

'No. I can't, I—'

He was slammed against the wall. 'Take it *off*!'

'I daren't.'

Brutally, the stranger ripped the mask from his face and flung it aside. The freed coins bounced across the cobbles.

The youth kept his eyes screwed shut.

'Open them,' the stranger demanded. *'Open them.'*

With some effort, and timorously, he did as he was told.

'How is it?'

The young man blinked and looked about sheepishly. 'It's . . . it's all right, I think.'

'There's no need for this. It's stupid and dangerous, and—'

'No need? You know what I've been seeing. How can you say—'

There was a groan close by. They turned and saw that the watch captain was feebly breathing. The stranger drew a knife.

'No,' the youth begged. 'Can't you just leave him?'

'We don't take prisoners. Any more than they do.'

He moved to the dying man and quickly finished him. The youth couldn't watch.

Wiping his blade on a scrap of cloth, the stranger said, 'You think I'm cruel. But this is a war. Maybe not in name, but that's what it amounts to.'

The youth nodded. 'I know.'

'Come on. It won't do to linger here.'

They set off together through the fog.

Something that looked like an eel swam past them. It was candy-striped and had a pair of wings far too tiny to fly with. As it made its serpentine way it left a trail of orange sparks.

In a voice much gentler, Caldason asked, 'How are you feeling?'

'I'm scared,' Kutch said.